D0425356

The Lightness of Hands

Also by Jeff Garvin

Symptoms of Being Human

The Lightness of Hands

JEFF GARVIN

Balzer + Bray
An Imprint of HarperCollins*Publishers*

Balzer + Bray is an imprint of HarperCollins Publishers.

The Lightness of Hands

www.epicreads.com

ISBN 978-0-06-238289-4

20 21 22 23 24 PC/LSCH 10 9 8 7 6 5 4 3 2 1

❖

First Edition

Please be aware that this novel
deals with issues of suicide and self-harm.

For Ami,

who always remembers to turn on the light

CHAPTER 1

THE TRICK WORKED LIKE THIS: I entered the gas station first, playing the part of the suspect teenager, the apparent shoplifter—misdirection incarnate. I prowled the chip aisle, fingering noisy snacks, and then, just as the clerk started to get suspicious, Dad would walk in. There was nothing flashy about the setup, no pyrotechnics or vanishing objects, just a story to obscure what was really happening. That's what magic is, after all: a lie that's more satisfying than the truth.

Outside, our rickety RV with its attached ten-foot trailer sat at the farthest pump, where it would suck diesel until the prepaid Visa ran dry. I hoped fifteen bucks would buy us enough time. Other than the two twenties in Dad's money clip, it was all we had left.

"Good afternoon, young man," Dad said to the clerk in his stage baritone. A wry smile turned up the corner of my mouth; even at a backroad gas station in the middle of nowhere, he couldn't help being the Uncanny Dante.

"How can I help you?" the clerk said. To judge by the mass of his neck muscles, he had probably played linebacker on his high school football team.

"Two packs of Chesterfield mediums, please."

Dad had quit smoking when he got his cardiomyopathy diagnosis. Also, Chesterfield didn't make mediums; Marlboro did. It was all part of the trick—and it worked. The clerk turned away to scan the cigarette display, and I made a beeline for the front door. On the way, I knocked a few cans of Hormel chili off the shelf.

Rule number one: *Magic is misdirection.*

The clerk spun at the sound. "Hey! Stop!"

I was halfway out the door when he grabbed my arm and yanked me back inside.

"What did you take?" he said.

"Nothing," I replied, basting my tone with indignation.

Over the clerk's shoulder, I saw that Dad had already completed his part of the grift; the old man was fast.

"Give it up," Linebacker said, "or I'm calling the cops."

"Go ahead." I glared, trying again to yank my arm from his grasp. "I'll tell them how you assaulted me!"

Now Dad approached, frowning. "Purcilla! What are you doing?"

Every time we pulled this bit, he gave me a fresh pseudonym, each more ridiculous than the last. We got a kick out of it.

"Forgive my daughter," he said, putting a hand on Linebacker's shoulder. "She's troubled."

He let go of me.

"Now do as he asked, Purcilla."

I rolled my eyes and unzipped my hoodie, revealing a can of BBQ Pringles and a package of Reese's peanut butter pumpkins. Dad was on me in a heartbeat, shaking me by the shoulders.

"You little thief! I didn't raise you like this!"

"Take it easy," Linebacker said, oozing with counterfeit chivalry. It was okay for *him* to manhandle me, but not my own father. What a hypocrite. "I just want to make sure she didn't take anything else." He glared at me. "What's in your pockets?"

I showed him they were empty. He seemed satisfied and was turning back toward my dad when I said:

"Oh, wait. I do have *these*." I reached into my back pockets, then presented both middle fingers.

Dad's eyes narrowed. "All right, Purcilla. Back to the bus with you."

I rolled my eyes again, pushed through the doors, and headed for the RV, leaving Dad to close the ruse.

The prepaid Visa had run out as expected, but when I squeezed the handle, the diesel started flowing again, this time free of charge. While I had been distracting the clerk, Dad had reset the pump.

As the tank filled, I took a few deep breaths, trying to slow my heart. The adrenaline rush from a grift was almost as strong as the high from performing—but it faded quickly, leaving me to worry how we were going to book the next job. Get the next meal. Survive.

I opened the secret pouch I had sewn in my hoodie and

took out what I had lifted: two unripe bananas, a bag of pork rinds, and Linebacker's wallet. He only had fourteen bucks, but I removed his driver's license anyway and jotted on the back in Sharpie: *$14—Dunlap, IN.* I stuffed our convenience-store lunch back into the pouch and leaned back on the RV. Dad was supposed to be on a low-fat, low-sodium diet for his heart. I couldn't keep feeding him this crap. We needed decent food. We needed money.

We needed a real gig.

Five minutes later, the RV was sputtering south on US 33.

"You're sure we're clear?"

"I'm sure."

Dad was paranoid about security cameras—but these old gas stations always had out-of-date technology. It had taken Dad only a fraction of a second to reach over the counter and reset the pump; if the move showed up on camera at all, it would be a momentary flash, and whoever was watching would be more focused on the girl stuffing chips down her shirt.

Still, Dad maintained his grim expression, his mustache turned down at the ends. I didn't ask why; I already knew. He hated stealing and insisted we keep track of every penny we took. Someday, he said, we'd "make restitution." I hated stealing, too, but unlike Dad, I didn't believe we'd ever pay it back doing birthday parties and bar gigs. And in the meantime, we had bills to pay.

"How are we on time?" Dad asked. The gold Breitling watch he'd inherited from his grandfather clung ever present on his right wrist, though it had stopped working years ago.

"It's ninety minutes to get back to Fort Wayne. We'll make it."

Right now, normal high school juniors were shouldering backpacks and piling into cars, heading off to football games or fast-food joints to hang with their friends. I was on my way to work a wedding with my sixty-four-year-old father.

As he drove, I opened the pork rinds. The aroma that rushed out of the bag triggered a flood of memories. Pork rinds had been our thing, Mom's and mine. We would polish off a whole bag while watching *Ratatouille* for the thousandth time, licking the red salt from our fingers and snorting with laughter. I popped one into my mouth, letting the familiar tang of vinegar overwhelm my senses. It was like I was six again, sprawled next to her on the couch.

I ate another one, but it turned bitter on my tongue and was hard to swallow. Outside, rows of dead corn zipped past, and I wished I were home. I missed the warm, dry breeze of Las Vegas. I missed the sun.

I missed my mom.

I had been a little kid during Dad's Vegas years; now I was living every sixteen-year-old's dream, residing in a forty-foot RV with my dad at the Cedarwood Mobile Estates in Fort Wayne. I'd spent more than half my life here, but it would never be home.

"What about closing with Sub Trunk tonight?" Dad said, eyeing me from the driver's seat. "Get you back on the boards? You haven't performed in weeks."

I shook my head, felt my jaw tighten.

"I'm behind, and I can't afford to let my grades slip any further." I kept my eyes on the barren cornfields outside, but I could feel Dad's gaze like a spotlight. We'd had this conversation a hundred times; I had to be the only teenager in Indiana whose father was urging her *not* to study.

"I'm sure you'd make a great nurse, Ellie. But performing is in your blood. You've got it on both—"

I cut him off before he could mention Mom. I didn't want to think about her right now.

"The party is half a mile from Eastside," I said. "There might be people I know."

It was a good excuse; Dad knew I didn't want to be recognized. Ellie Dante, the semihomeless chick who had dropped out halfway through sophomore year.

"I see how your eyes sparkle when you're onstage," he said.

When I'm onstage, sure. But what about afterward?

"Can I just stay in the RV? Please?"

Dad sighed and scrubbed a finger across his mustache. "All right, you don't have perform. But I need you to stage-manage."

Before I could argue, my ancient prepaid phone buzzed in the cup holder, and I snatched it up. The call was from an unfamiliar number with a Las Vegas area code. It might be a client, and we needed one—badly. I answered, but there was only a hiss of static before the call dropped. No service out here in the land of corn and soybeans. I unclicked my seat belt and stood up.

"I've got homework."

I made my way toward the back, holding on to bolted-down furniture as I went. Behind the captain's chairs, two couches faced each other. At night, one of them folded down to form a bed where Dad slept. Beyond them was the kitchenette: a tiny sink, a propane stove, and a mostly empty pantry, its door secured with bungees so they wouldn't fly open on a curve. A half-sized restaurant booth occupied the port side—that was where we ate and I did homework on my obsolete laptop. The bathroom was behind it, and at the very back of the RV was my luxurious eight-by-ten "suite."

I closed the flimsy accordion partition behind me and flopped down on the mattress, feeling the rumble of the diesel engine beneath me. I had tried to cover every inch of the faux-wood walls with posters, but it was still nothing like a normal teenager's room. Normal teenagers had closets instead of cubbyholes. Desks instead of fold-out tables. Beds that didn't vibrate at sixteen hundred RPMs.

Someday, I would live in a real house with a real shower and a back door and a foundation.

I sat up, trying to banish my spiraling thoughts. I needed to take my history test online before midnight, so I grabbed my phone and checked my usage stats: only two megs of data left, not nearly enough. I would just have to hope that tonight's gig site had Wi-Fi so I could take it while Dad was performing. In the meantime, I opened my dusty copy of *The Grapes of Wrath* and tried to focus. My phone dinged with a new text.

Ripley: Existential crisis pending. Assistance required. Are you alone?

Me: Out of minutes. Can you text?

Ripley: Ugh. Really need to talk. Where are you?

Me: On the road. Will try to get wifi and call after show

The three dots bounced for a moment, then disappeared. Maybe Ripley had been interrupted while composing his reply, or maybe he'd just given up. I couldn't blame him if he had; I was the most unreliable friend ever.

The adrenaline from the heist was wearing off, and I could almost taste the stress hormones turning sour in my bloodstream. In harmony with the low rumble of the engine beneath me, the chorus of an old Rihanna song began to play on a loop in my head: *Ella, ella, eh, eh, eh* . . . Over and over. I tried to shut out the song, to summon *any* other melody, but "Umbrella" only corkscrewed itself deeper into my mind. This happened off and on—some jagged shard of a song would get lodged in my mind and play itself back relentlessly. Once it was "Wrecking Ball," and another time it was "Believer" by Imagine Dragons. Those weren't so bad—but during the whole first semester of freshman year I'd had "It's a Small World" stuck in my head, and I'd nearly flunked out—and then for no apparent reason it had just stopped. The depression that followed had been long and deep and colorless. So I'd come to recognize these repeating song fragments as a warning that gray days were coming.

I reached into the drawer next to my bed and grabbed my prescription bottle. A single pill rattled inside the orange plastic cylinder, and I felt an invisible belt tighten around my chest. I wished I could save this last one for an emergency, but that wasn't how the medication worked. It had to build up in the bloodstream; if I stopped taking it, the effects would wear off quickly. How many days did I have left? Three? Five? A week?

I tapped the tablet into my palm and swallowed it dry. I had to be on tonight.

We needed the money.

CHAPTER 2

WHILE DAD PULLED PROPS OUT of the equipment trailer we towed behind the RV, I mounted the steps to the big Victorian house and rang the bell. A moment later, the door opened, and a boy stood on the threshold, shouting over his shoulder so that I didn't immediately see his face. He was slim but muscular, probably ROTC or crew team, maybe home from college for the weekend.

"I don't know anything about the centerpieces," he called back into the house. "I'm on bar duty." He turned and looked at me, and my skin turned to ice.

I knew him.

His name was Liam Miller, and we had worked together during Eastside's winter production of *Damn Yankees* when he was a senior and I was a sophomore. He joined the cast as a distraction between baseball seasons, and I designed the special effects for the show. We rehearsed together for a month, and I thought we had formed a sort of awkward, unlikely friendship. But when the play ended, he went back to being a sports god, and I was still a sophomore theater nerd.

Liam tilted his head. "Ellie Dante? What are you doing here?"

He remembered my name. For a moment I considered bolting back to the RV. Instead, I did my best not to scowl.

"My dad's the magician."

"Oh, right. *Dante.*" He shook his head. "I'm an idiot."

I agreed, but I didn't say so. How was I supposed to act around this guy?

"What are *you* doing here?" I asked.

"My sister is the bride."

"Oh." Now who was the idiot? I should have recognized the last name when his dad booked us.

Liam smiled, revealing a deep dimple on his left cheek. "Come on in."

I stepped inside—and tried not to gape. The foyer was opulent: marble floors, grand piano, massive crystal chandelier. His parents were obviously rich; I wondered why he had even gone to a public high school.

"We've got a dressing room for you," he said, gesturing at the wide marble staircase. "Upstairs, second door on the right."

"Okay. Thanks."

"I've got to go lift heavy things for Princess Becca. See you later?"

"Unless I disappear," I said. Liam gave me a quizzical look, and I wanted to break my own skull against the door frame.

I watched him retreat into the house, his back muscles moving against the fabric of his T-shirt. Was he strutting like that on purpose? It might have worked on the baseball groupies at Eastside, but it didn't work on me.

A moment later, Dad appeared on the doorstep carrying two heavy trap cases and a shoulder bag. Despite the cool air, his temples were already damp with perspiration.

"Let me," I said, taking one of the cases. He protested, but I shut him down. Carrying heavy things up stairs was on his doctor's no-no list.

The dressing room turned out to be Liam's bedroom. It was twice the size of our whole RV and impeccably clean, probably for the occasion. There were posters on the wall—the 2016 Chicago Cubs, Panic! at the Disco—but instead of being thumbtacked, they hung in expensive frames. A photo of the Manhattan skyline dominated one wall, and a Notre Dame baseball pennant in a shadow box was mounted above the hardwood dresser. I stared around in envy. My whole "suite" would have fit inside Liam Miller's closet.

I opened a set of French doors and stepped onto a stone balcony overlooking the backyard. Three tents draped with fairy lights stood on the perfect lawn, sheltering a wedding setup for at least a hundred guests. Round tables with red cloths; an explosion of roses; an archway of satin ribbon over a temporary stage where a band was setting up their amplifiers. I imagined myself standing on that stage, feeling a hundred pairs of eyes on me. Sensing the energy from the audience, controlling it, drawing their attention wherever I wanted it. I felt tingles crawling up the sides of my face—it was a rush, having that power.

I released the railing and took a step back, and the twitch of mania receded. I wouldn't be onstage tonight; I would be hiding up here, taking my history exam.

Ella, ella, eh, eh, eh . . .

"Do you see those thunderclouds?"

I turned and saw Dad leaning against the door frame.

"An outdoor wedding in northern Indiana in October." He shook his head. "I don't envy the groom. Come on," he said, beckoning me back inside. "Let's get cracking."

He had already unlatched one of his cases and was setting aside decks of cards and various props; I hadn't heard any of it. Spacing out was another symptom of impending gray. I needed to hold out for few more hours. Then I could crawl into my vibrating bed and curl up in the fetal position.

"What should I close with?" Dad asked, shutting his case. "Dove Production? Spoon Bender?"

I frowned. "Doves won't work if it rains."

"Good point," he said, rubbing at his mustache.

"And Spoon Bender is too small for that stage. I was thinking Card to Fruit."

The trick worked like this: The magician asked a volunteer to pick a card and sign it. Then, using sleight of hand—my favorite brand of magic—he vanished the card. Next, the magician selected a piece of fruit at random from a bowl, cut it open, and voilà: he pulled out the signed card, wet with fresh juice. I loved it because of the reaction it elicited from the audience: eyes widening, jaws dropping. The trick defied logic in the most visceral way, and Dad performed it as well as David Blaine had in his famous Harrison Ford YouTube video.

"Perfect," Dad said. He fished the necessary item out of his kit and tossed it to me.

As Dad took the stage, I watched from the balcony, just as I had watched him from the wings since I was a little girl. I'd been six when we relocated from Las Vegas to Indiana—and at the time, I thought we'd had to move because Mom died. Years later, I discovered the truth.

Dad had been grinding out a living at a small casino when he was offered the opportunity of a lifetime: a guest spot on *Late Night with Craig Rogan.* If it went well, he could finally move into a big theater on the Strip and see his name glowing alongside the greats': Lance Burton, Flynn & Kellar, Daniel Devereaux. He spent a month designing a brand-new illusion—but on the night of the live taping, it went horribly wrong.

My memories of the incident were like fragments of a bad dream. Probably I had manufactured them, cobbled them together from YouTube videos and overheard conversations. But they seemed real to me. Looking down at Dad onstage now, I wondered if he was wearing the same black tie he'd worn that night.

The lights came up, and the wedding guests began to applaud. I remembered the faint smell of burning dust in

Craig Rogan's studio, the heat of the overhead lights. I tried to repel the memories of that night, but they pushed against my mind relentlessly, like a song, until I closed my eyes and let them come.

I'm holding my mother's hand as the curtain ascends. When the lights come up on my father, standing center stage, she kisses my cheek, lets go of my hand, and crosses to him. As she turns to acknowledge the audience, her smile is luminous in the glare of the lights. She selects a volunteer, who binds Dad's wrists and ankles—and then a second curtain goes up, revealing an old red Chevy pickup truck and an enormous Plexiglas tank filled with water. My mother helps Dad into the truck, and a winch hauls it toward the rafters.

The hush of the crowd, the gleam of chrome—and the splash as the truck hits the surface and sinks until the water is over his head.

Laughter from below jarred me back into the moment. Dad was finishing his new opening bit: dropping a red toy truck into a half-filled fish tank. The audience responded with a bout of laughter; it had worked.

When our gigs had begun to dry up, we'd had to do something to address Dad's reputation problem. To point out the elephant in the room right at the top so everyone could move on and enjoy the show. But Dad was proud, and it had taken me a long time to persuade him to try the Toy Truck Drop. When he finally relented, it worked perfectly. Audiences laughed, relieved by his self-deprecating humor. They trusted him again, and he was able to perform with his old vigor and panache. For a year or so, the bookings picked up. But then they began to evaporate again, until we had only one gig on the calendar. This one.

I watched Dad step off the stage and circulate among the attendees, picking cards and finding coins to their delight. Most of the guests were older, probably friends of Princess Becca's parents. The bride herself sat at a high table next to her pasty, corn-fed husband, smiling for pictures and picking at her salad. Overhead, the clouds threatened to break open, but luckily for her, they hadn't yet.

I spotted Liam near the stage, holding court with a pair of girls. I recognized the pretty blonde; she'd been one of the baseball groupies at Eastside. She took his arm and started to lead him into the house, but then he glanced up to where I stood on the balcony.

Reflexively, I shrank away from the railing—but I was pretty sure he'd caught me watching him. God, I was embarrassing. What was I doing? Liam had been nice enough to me during *Damn Yankees* rehearsals, but once the show was over, he'd ignored me completely. Besides, that had been a year ago. It was ancient history now.

Liam and his girls had looked like they were making plans to escape the reception. I envied them; I had never had a group of friends, or any hope of escape. I had precisely *one* friend, who I knew only by his avatar and his voice.

I pulled out my phone and found the Millers' Wi-Fi, thinking I should call Ripley as promised—but the network was password protected. So I sent a text instead.

Me: No Wi-Fi. :(Can you text?

I stared at the screen for two solid minutes, but Ripley didn't reply. I imagined him lying back on his bed, texting with someone else instead, some new IRL bestie at his IRL high school who not only could afford reliable internet but could actually be present in his life. I pictured her as a pretty girl, taller and more elegant than me. His very own Princess Becca. It was a ridiculous thought—Ripley wasn't like that—but the idea ricocheted around in my head anyway.

Ella, ella, eh, eh, eh . . .

The chorus of "Umbrella" had resumed its loop. For the umpteenth time, I wondered: Why that song in particular? I'd been a toddler when it came out, and as far as I could remember, it didn't have any special meaning for me. Yet somehow it had burrowed itself into my brain like a Lyme-disease tick.

I was about to head back to the RV when I heard the sliding glass door open behind me. I turned. It was Liam.

He paused in the doorway, one hand in his front pocket, looking like a model from the J.Crew catalog.

"Mind if I join you?"

I pressed my lips together. Was he serious with that pose?

"It's your house," I said.

He closed the door behind him and crossed to the railing, leaving a respectful distance between us.

"It's my father's house, actually. He reminds me all the time."

"Probably beats living in an RV, though." *Shut up, Ellie. Shut up.*

Liam raised his eyebrows. "I don't know. You kind of live like a rock star."

"More like a senior citizen."

He laughed. It was a soft, deep sound, and it caused an unfamiliar warm sensation in my midsection.

"You look different," he said. "Your hair is longer."

"Yeah, that happens."

"Still a smart-ass, though." He laughed.

The truth was I couldn't afford to get it cut, but I wasn't going to tell him that.

Liam turned to face me, leaning his elbow against the railing. "It's good to see you again, Ellie."

I bristled when he used my name; it was such a bro technique. Use their name, make them feel special.

I turned away. "Your house is huge."

"Like I said, it's my father's. Well, technically, it belongs to his trucking company. It's a tax thing." He was quiet for a moment as he looked down at the wedding below. "He still treats her like she's five years old. Hence the backyard wedding in October." He gestured at the tents. "For favors, we're handing out umbrellas."

Great. Just when I'd almost gotten the song out of my head.

Liam leaned forward, about to say something else. *Please, not my name.*

He seemed to change his mind before saying, "Could I interest you in some vodka?"

I bit my lip. "Actually, do you have any food?"

Liam offered to take me out back for leftover canapés, but I didn't want to risk being seen by anyone else from Eastside. So while Dad set up for his finale, I sat on Liam Miller's front steps in the cool autumn evening, drinking apricot punch spiked with Smirnoff and eating the best goddamned peanut butter and jelly sandwich I'd ever tasted.

I *hated* PB&Js, probably because I'd lived on Wonder Bread and Jif for so long. But the sandwich Liam made me was of an entirely different paradigm. The bread was some kind of artisan multigrain ambrosia. The peanut butter was organic and had to be *stirred*. He just sat there while I ate, and I started to feel self-conscious. I must have looked like a starving orphan.

"You don't have to babysit me. Go be with your girlfriend."

Liam leaned back on the top step. "She's not my girlfriend. She's the maid of honor's little sister, and she's obnoxious."

"Oh. Okay." I was an idiot. I stuffed the last bite into my mouth.

Liam tugged at the zipper on his jacket. "Have I done something to piss you off?"

I frowned. "What do you mean?"

"It's just . . . you've been kind of cold to me since I answered the door."

I brushed bread crumbs from my lap. Did he really not know? Or was he just trying to pretend nothing had happened?

Finally, I said, "You basically ignored me at Eastside. Why should I be nice to you?"

His eyebrows shot up to his hairline. "That's not true."

"Yes, it is," I said. "Once the play was over, you barely said hi to me."

"I said hi to you in the halls."

"Once. When you were alone. When you were with your friends, you didn't even look at me."

He opened his mouth, closed it. "I don't remember it like that."

"I do." I held his gaze for a few seconds, and then he looked away, frowning as if reliving something unpleasant.

"Wow," he said. "Okay. Yeah. Maybe I was kind of an ass."

I watched him out of the corner of my eye. Was he being sincere?

I shrugged. "It is what it is. I was a theater nerd, and you were one of those guys on the baseball team."

"A dumb jock, right?"

"I didn't say that."

"But you thought it." I didn't want to argue, but he pressed the point. "I was the dumb jock, and you were the misunderstood girl. Like Laura and the Gentleman Caller."

Now it was my turn to raise my eyebrows.

"What?" Liam folded his arms. "Jocks can't like Tennessee Williams?"

I started to respond, but he cut me off.

"Don't worry about it," he said. "It's kind of refreshing to be underestimated for a change."

"What's that supposed to mean?"

"Everyone expects me to be perfect. My parents, my coach." His eyes drifted toward the woods across the road. "And then when I fuck up, I have to deal with their disappointment. It's kind of exhausting."

I gave him a searching look. I didn't know what I had expected when Liam Miller opened the door, but it wasn't this.

He blew out a breath. "I'm sorry I was a dick to you in

high school." He clasped his hands together and looked away; his discomfort seemed genuine. I didn't know how to react.

"Does this usually work?" I asked.

"Does what usually work?"

"Isolate the high school girl. Give her vodka."

He smiled. "Usually the peanut butter closes the deal. I must be losing my touch."

He expected me to laugh, but I didn't.

"I'm not like that," I said.

He looked right at me. "I know."

My face suddenly went hot. For a long time, I said nothing; we just looked at each other. The pause stretched until it became an uncomfortable silence. Literal crickets chirped. I felt a strange certainty that he was either going to get up and walk away or else lean in and kiss me. The air between us was delicate. Electric. I wanted more punch. I wanted to leave.

I could only keep his gaze for a few more moments, and then I turned away. "Why did you come find me?"

"You were on *my* balcony."

He was right, and I was making a total ass of myself.

"I'm kidding," he said. "I did come to find you. I just . . . I don't know. It's been a long time. I wanted to talk to you."

I felt that not-unpleasant warmth in my midsection again. "So talk."

He seemed about to say something, but my ringtone cut him off. I checked my phone: it was the same unfamiliar Las Vegas number. I forgot my embarrassment at once; this could be the gig we needed.

"I have to take this." I stood, walked up the steps to the Millers' porch, and accepted the call.

"Hello?" I said, leaning against one of the Victorian columns.

On the other end, a woman's voice said, "Is this the number for Elias Dante? The Uncanny Dante?"

"Yes, it is. How can I help you?"

"My name is Grace Wu. I'm calling on behalf of F—"

The phone beeped in my ear, cutting off the caller—and then a robot voice informed me I had less than a minute of prepaid time left.

"I lost you for a second," I said, panic rising in my throat. We needed this gig, whatever it was. "Could you say that again?"

"My name is Grace Wu," the woman repeated. "I'm calling on behalf of Flynn Bissette."

The name hit me like a slap. Flynn Bissette? As in Flynn & Kellar, the most successful duo in the history of magic?

"Hello?" the woman said. There was something overenthusiastic, maybe even insincere about her voice.

"Did you say you're calling on behalf of *Flynn Bissette*?"

"Yes!"

Irritation tightened my jaw. This was just one more in a long series of prank calls. They got our number off our Facebook page and thought they'd have fun taunting a has-been.

"It's Grace, right?" I said, unable to keep the contempt out of my voice.

"That's right. Grace Wu."

"Okay, Grace. What can I do for literally one of the most famous magicians ever?"

"Grace" was undeterred by my sarcasm. "Mr. Bissette is shooting a live magic special at the Dolby Theatre in Hollywood. He'd like Mr. Dante to—"

"Fuck off." I was surprised at the rage suddenly heating my face.

"Excuse me?" the woman said.

I was about to launch into a tirade, but the robot voice broke in once more and told me I was out of time.

CHAPTER 3

I POCKETED MY PHONE AND leaned against the column.

"What was that about?" Liam asked.

I looked away. "Can I use your bathroom?"

I sat on the toilet lid, one hand pressed against the wall, the other on my chest. My heart was pounding—which felt wrong, because depression was rolling toward me like a summer storm. Usually, that slowed everything down. But so much had happened in the last five minutes, thoughts were pinging around my skull like ricocheting bullets.

The prank call had been the trigger, but it was more than that. I was out of cell minutes, cut off from Ripley, cut off from clients—I couldn't even take my fucking US History test. We were almost broke, and we'd just stolen three hundred dollars' worth of diesel. This was our last gig on the books. We were running out of options.

Applause drifted in through the bathroom window; the show was over. I splashed some water on my face and headed upstairs to pack up. I didn't see Liam as we were loading the trailer, and I found that I was disappointed. Which was probably stupid: A year ago, he'd fooled me into thinking he liked me. Probably, he'd just done it again.

But as I stepped into the RV, he called my name.

"Ellie!"

I paused in the doorway.

"I'm sorry," Liam said, stopping at the bottom of the retractable steps. "Can I get a do-over?"

I cocked my head. "What are we, in third grade?"

The Millers' front door opened, and the blonde who had pulled Liam inside earlier came stumbling down the front steps with her tall friend.

"*Liiaaamm*," she called.

He ignored her and held my gaze. "I'm heading back to school in a couple days. But I thought, if you're not busy tomorrow night . . ."

I tried to look casual as I steadied myself against the door frame to counteract the dizziness that had suddenly come on. I'd been hit on a thousand times; I'd been asked out on a date precisely never.

"Are you asking me out?"

Cue the impossible dimple. "Yes, Ellie, I'm asking you out."

He kept saying my name—and I found that I didn't hate it.

"I don't really date," I said. "I'm never around."

"Are you around tomorrow night?"

"I don't know." It was the truth.

"Well, why don't you give me your phone number, and I can call you?"

I searched his face, trying to detect whether he was making fun of me, but my judgment was scrambled. I decided to play it safe.

"Your dad booked us," I said. "You can get the number from him."

Liam stood there with a stunned expression on his face—he was used to girls falling all over themselves for his attention. Case in point: the blond girl who was now slinking toward us, whispering and laughing with her friend. She was so pretty—professional tan, salon manicure, and an outfit worth more than my whole closet. How could I compete with that?

The two of them pulled Liam away. As they neared the girl's car, he looked back over his shoulder and gave me a quizzical look.

I turned and boarded the bus.

As the door closed, Dad looked over at me from the driver's seat.

"Say nothing," I warned. "Say absolutely nothing."

Dad mimed zipping his lips, then started the motor.

We pulled away, and I watched Liam Miller get smaller and smaller in the side-view mirror.

It started raining as soon as we pulled onto the highway, fat, angry drops striking the windshield like suicidal wasps.

I imagined Liam rushing around the Millers' backyard, rescuing centerpieces or carrying that cute blonde over a patch of mud. I closed my eyes and tried to picture anything else. The quickening that had struck me after my encounters with Liam and the prank caller slipped away fast, leaving my nerves raw and buzzing. Sometimes this happened after I performed; I felt as if I were standing at the top of a steep slope, waiting for something to run up from behind and push me over the edge. But tonight, I hadn't set foot onstage.

We got back to the glorious Cedarwood Mobile Estates just after ten p.m. I was looking forward to connecting to the Wi-Fi, cranking out my history exam, then hooking up the propane for a hot shower—but when Dad got out to enter his code at the entrance gate, something went wrong. I could see him through the rain-streaked driver's-side window, bent over the security keypad, coat stretched over his head in lieu of an umbrella. *Ella. Ella.* I moved over to his seat and cracked the window.

"What's wrong?" I yelled over the sound of the storm.

"It won't take my code," he replied, typing it in again. The LED indicator flashed red, and he grunted with frustration.

"Hang on," I said, trying to hide my irritation; the man was allergic to technology. I pulled up my hood, climbed out of the RV, and came around to the keypad. Dad stepped aside, clearly annoyed that I was doubting him. I punched in the numbers, my fingers trembling against the cold metal buttons, but the light still flashed red.

"You see?" Dad said.

I reached for my cell to call the manager, then remembered I didn't have any minutes left and pushed the Call button on the security gate's keypad instead. A low electronic burble issued from the crappy speaker. After four or five rings, Julius, the site supervisor, finally picked up.

"The office is closed." He sounded like I had woken him up.

"Julius, it's Ellie. The gate's not working."

I heard rustling as if he was moving the phone to his other ear. "Ellie who?"

"Elias Dante. Space Twenty-Two."

Long pause.

"Julius, can you please open the gate? It's raining cats and dogs out here."

"No, I can't open the gate."

I glanced at Dad, ready to share a look of annoyance—but his expression had frozen. He looked scared, or maybe guilty. I frowned at him and spoke into the talk box again.

"Well, the keypad's not working. Is there a manual override or something?"

"No," Julius said. "I can't open the gate because you aren't residents here anymore. You haven't paid in months."

My mouth suddenly felt dry. "What? No," I said. "We're on autopay."

"Your card got declined three months in a row. Look, talk to your dad about this. I'm going back to sleep."

There was a click, and the speaker went silent. I looked at Dad, but he wouldn't meet my gaze. I felt a rush of nausea; he had known this was going to happen.

We climbed into the RV soaking wet and toweled off in silence. He hadn't paid our fucking rent in three months. I was so angry, my whole body was trembling. Why hadn't he told me? I considered asking him, but what was the point?

When we were back in our seats, Dad put the bus in gear and pulled onto the highway.

"Walmart?" I asked, trying to keep the contempt out of my voice. He nodded. "Okay. But let's go to the one on Twenty-Seven."

"Coldwater is closer."

"Dad, please."

"We need to conserve fuel."

"It's Friday night. People from Eastside will be hanging out at the one on Coldwater."

"We don't need to go inside."

I tried to sound calm. "What if they recognize the RV?"

"Ellie, we—"

"I don't want to see anybody right now!" My voice was a squeak.

Dad fell silent, gripping the wheel with both hands. Finally, he said, "All right." It was almost a whisper.

When we reached State Route 27, Dad turned south, but it didn't ease the tension in my chest. I looked over at him. His grip on the wheel was white knuckled.

"How bad is it?" I asked.

"Well. The cards are maxed, obviously."

I blew out a breath.

"But we still have cash."

"How much?"

He hesitated. "About four hundred dollars."

"But that's—I thought the gig tonight was supposed to pay *eight*?"

Dad stiffened. "They called back after the initial booking, and I . . . I had to renegotiate."

"You can't just do that!" I said, my fists tight and white. "It lowers our quote for the next one!"

"No one will find out."

"Yes, they *will*!" I was shouting at him now. "People talk! On Facebook, on Yelp. Once you drop your price, it's impossible to raise it again. We've talked about this!" Dad said nothing, only adjusted his grip on the wheel and stared out into the storm. "I was going to use some of that eight hundred for Facebook ads! I haven't placed one in months. We're . . ." My voice had risen to a shriek. "How will we get gas? How will we buy groceries? You just—"

"We still have half a tank of diesel."

I wanted to cry. To scream. Instead, I closed my eyes and put my head back against the headrest. A heaviness threatened to settle in on me. I sank into the seat and let it.

"An opportunity will present itself," Dad said. "It always does."

I didn't respond, just turned to stare out at the flat Indiana darkness and tried to hope he was right.

After a long time, Dad cleared his throat. It was one of his tells; it meant he was about to broach a tender subject.

"Are you feeling all right, Ellie?"

"I'm fine."

"It's just . . . Your moods have been a bit darker lately. I wonder—"

"Forgive me if I'm having trouble adjusting to being homeless."

The words flew out like spit, and I couldn't take them back. Dad was silent for the rest of the ride.

By the time we parked in the far corner of the Walmart lot, the rain had stopped. Dad cut the engine and hit the switch to expand the RV's pop-outs. I watched as our narrow living room widened by two feet on each side. Once, the extra space had felt luxurious. Now it just felt like a bigger coffin. While I went in back to wash my face, Dad folded out the couch and closed his eyes.

I lay awake in bed, staring at the sagging fabric on the ceiling, the chorus of that goddamned Rihanna song playing over and over in my head. Sometimes it was like Dad was the child and I was the parent. Except I didn't get to make any decisions; I just had to bear the consequences. He danced through life, chasing his dream of performing, never realizing the cost to the people around him. The cost to me.

I turned over and buried my face in the pillow. He'd said my moods had been darker lately, and he was right. Was I being too hard on him? Maybe the encroaching gray was distorting my perceptions, making everything seem worse than it was. But we'd just been evicted; how could it get worse than that?

Still, my conscience nagged. I hated this feeling, hated never knowing if I was right or if I was just being crazy. Maybe I shouldn't have snapped at Dad. Maybe he had just been trying to protect me from bad news. And if he'd told me we were behind on rent, was there anything I could've done about it? I didn't know. But we only had each other now, and we couldn't afford to fight.

Reluctantly, I got up and opened the accordion door, thinking I might apologize, or at least try to make peace—but the old man was passed out, snoring like a lumberjack. I guessed I couldn't have hurt his feelings too badly.

The rain had stopped, so I pulled on a hoodie, snagged two hundred-dollar bills from the cash box under the driver's seat, and stepped out into the cool October air.

I had practically grown up at Walmart. Most locations allowed RV parking, and I'd spent the night in hundreds of them from San Diego to Hartford. At night, every Walmart parking lot looked the same—an asphalt sea illuminated by moth-riddled, flickering arc sodiums mounted high on corroding masts. And, as you neared the building, the windows glowed with an eerie fluorescence like something from a horror movie. On this particular occasion, the effect was amplified by the garish display of Halloween decorations in the window: fake spiderwebs, black and orange streamers, a toilet-paper mummy.

I grabbed a cart and headed for the canned-food aisle. Tuna. Peas. Fruit cocktail. I wanted to load up on fresh fruit and leafy greens for Dad's heart—but they wouldn't keep, and I wasn't sure how long this food would have to last. On the pet aisle, I threw in a bag of birdseed for the doves. I hit the dry-goods section and grabbed a box of spaghetti, two pounds of coffee, and a canister of generic instant oats. I found the magical bread Liam had used for the ultimate PB&J, but it cost six dollars a loaf, so I settled for the store brand instead. I did splurge on fancy peanut butter, though. I would probably regret it.

On my way toward the front of the store, I passed a guy wearing three sweatshirts and a filthy beanie. He reeked like old shoes and muttered to himself as he shuffled down the aisle. Walmart at two a.m. contains no moms with infants or dads towing toddlers; it's mostly the poor and the homeless, and I guessed I belonged with them. The realization weighed on me like a lead X-ray vest. Would I ever have a normal life? Shop at a normal store with a credit card and buy whatever I wanted?

I found the prepaid phone kiosk and reached for a ten-dollar card but hesitated with my hand halfway to the rack. My account was completely empty—the prank caller had burned up my last minute. Also, we had zero bookings on the horizon, so I didn't know when we'd get paid again. Should I spend the money now, or save it for food and diesel? I considered: recharge cards had to be activated at the register, so they couldn't be stolen, whereas gas and groceries could.

As I stood at the kiosk trying to decide, an overly cheerful man's voice came over the PA:

"Got the sniffles? Stop by our twenty-four-hour pharmacy today and pick up some homeopathic remedies, or get your prescription filled!"

I left the phone card hanging on its rack and headed toward the back of the store.

The graveyard-shift pharmacist blinked down at me. "Date of birth?"

"February twenty-second, 2004."

"Prescription number and insurance card?"

I slid my card across the counter. The Rx number was written on the back so I wouldn't forget it.

She typed at the register, frowned. "Just a moment." She went into the back and came out two minutes later with a bearded man whose name tag read: *Greg Fredericks, Assistant Manager.* He typed, glanced at the screen, looked up.

"I'm sorry, miss. It looks like your coverage has lapsed."

The weight that had settled on me seemed to multiply, hanging on me like a backpack full of gravel. Dad hadn't paid our insurance bill. Of course he hadn't. What would he have paid it with? And how long had it been since he got a refill on his heart pills?

The assistant manager gave me a patronizing smile. "Do you still want your prescription?"

I put my hand in my pocket and felt the two hundred-dollar bills. "How much is it?"

He pushed more keys. "Without insurance, it comes to . . . one hundred ninety-seven dollars and eighty-eight cents."

I closed my eyes and held in a scream. Food, gas, phone, meds: pick two.

"That's okay," I said, backing away from the counter.

"Would you like to apply for a Walmart Visa?" the assistant manager asked. The pharmacist shot him a look.

"No, that's okay. It's okay."

Stop saying okay. *Ella, ella, ella, eh, eh, eh . . .*

My face went numb as I pushed the cart toward the register.

There was another rack of prepaid phone cards at the checkout line. Fuck it. I grabbed a hundred-dollar card and tossed it onto the conveyor.

CHAPTER 4

I COULDN'T STAND THE THOUGHT of returning to my shoe-box bedroom in the RV, so I stepped out of Walmart and into the cool Indiana autumn. I punched the recharge code into my phone, and once the credits were activated, text messages started coming in.

The first was from the prankster in Vegas: *Disconnected. Call back.*

Sure, jerkoff. I'll get right on that. The next was from Ripley: *Sorry I missed you. Drama ensued. Call when you get this.*

Ripley and I had met on Bloglr sophomore year after a week of constantly reposting each other's *Firefly* GIFs. Our short DM exchange quickly morphed into daily texts. Ripley had become my best friend—but we'd never met face-to-face. We'd never even seen pictures of each other; we had made a sacred vow not to pollute the purity of our online friendship with anything tangible from the real world. All we had were words and voices—and I liked it that way.

Three and a half semesters of public high school had taught me just how bad I was at keeping friends in real life. During my sophomore year, I'd gotten close with a couple of girls, Hailey and Emma, when our biology teacher assigned us to the same group. They were nice to me at first, inviting me over for study groups, movie nights, and finally to a spring break pool party when Emma's parents went out of town.

It was the last high school party I ever attended.

I didn't black out; I remembered everything. But as I watched the videos that circulated the next day, the experience seemed distant. Hazy. As if I'd been drunk or high when it happened, even though I'd been stone-cold sober the whole night.

It's nighttime in Emma's parents' backyard. I'm sitting in some guy's lap on a pool chair, making out with him hard.

It's later. I'm standing by the pool, talking to a fully dressed Hailey—and then, unprovoked, I push her into the pool, sending her red Solo cup flying. I laugh wildly as she paddles to the far edge and gets out, her clothes dripping. She looks miserable and furious, but I'm doubled over like it's the most hilarious thing ever. I'm the only one laughing.

Now it's later and I'm with a different guy, straddling him on a white leather sofa. My shirt is off. A few people stand around, watching and whispering and taking pictures with their phones. I don't seem to care.

After the party, I went home and stayed up all night doing our bio project, start to finish, by myself. We got an A.

Hailey and Emma were cold to me at school that Monday.

People shot me sideways glances and whispered as they passed me in the hall. Some guy I didn't even know grabbed my ass and asked for my number. I gaped at him as he walked away, laughing with his friends. Over the span of one weekend, I had ceased to be an unknown theater nerd and become "that crazy chick" instead.

Two weeks later, I dropped out of Eastside and started looking for online programs.

It took months of therapy and reading before I understood that I'd had my first episode of hypomania. It was supposed to be the "upside" of the bipolar experience—but it was worse than any depression I'd ever suffered.

I was terrified that Liam had seen those videos. He'd been a senior on his way out—but he was popular, and the link had more or less gone viral at Eastside. If he had seen them, though, why had he bothered to talk to me tonight? Why had he asked me out?

I hated wondering, hated worrying who knew what about me. It was why I'd left Eastside, and it was why the idea of a phone-and-text-only friendship with Ripley appealed to me on a deep level. From a distance, I could filter out the worst parts of myself.

I tapped Ripley's number, and it only rang twice before he picked up.

"She lives!"

The sound of his voice sent a wave of relief through me; I hadn't realized how stressed out I had been. Or how lonely.

"Hello? Can you hear me?"

"Yeah," I said. "Sorry. It's been a long day."

"Tell me about it." He paused. "No, seriously. Actually tell me about it. Distract me from the napalm-and-raccoon-hair trash fire that is my life."

I laughed. "Well, to start with, we got evicted from our trailer park."

Ripley gasped. "Are you being serious right now? Or is this some weird Indiana country music reference I'm not getting?"

I snorted. "Serious. Apparently, we haven't paid rent for like three months."

"Holy shit. Where are you?"

"Walmart."

"At ten thirty at night?"

I looked at my phone. "It's one thirty-two a.m. where I . . . Oh, shit!"

"What is it?"

"I forgot my US History test. Fuck, fuck, fuck."

"I thought your school was flexible about tests. You can't just take it now?"

I slapped my hand against my forehead. "I can—it's just . . . I lose a full a letter grade. And I have to maintain a three point oh to get into Harrison."

"Right. Nursing school. Shit. What are you going to do?"

I wound a lock of hair around my finger and yanked. "I don't know."

I heard a scraping noise on the other end of the line, then some ominous thumps. Ripley liked to talk to me from the privacy of the little roof outside his window; I assumed he was crawling out there right now. I felt a sudden rush of envy that Ripley lived in an actual house.

"What about you?" I said, forcing myself to reengage. "What's your existential crisis?"

"Oh, that. Dad and Heather had an epic fight, but it's over now."

I closed my eyes and yanked on my hair again. I was the worst kind of friend: always needy but never available when it was my turn to listen.

"I'm sorry I wasn't there for you." My voice sounded small.

"Don't even. Your timing is perfect. The aftermath was worse than the fight; they made up loudly for like two hours. I think I'm permanently traumatized."

I laughed. "That's nasty."

"Oh, and I caught Jude vaping. Only twelve, and already a delinquent. So yeah, things are basically falling apart here. At least my mother hasn't turned up. That would fuck everything worse."

"Yeah." I tried to sound sympathetic, but a splinter of resentment stuck in my throat. If my mom were still alive, I'd want to see her, no matter what.

"But back to you. What are you going to do about money?"

I leaned back against the stucco exterior of the Walmart. "I don't know. We've never been this hard up before."

Immediately, I wanted to take it back. I didn't think I could look myself in the mirror if I heard a single note of pity in Ripley's voice. He was an optimist, a problem solver. That's what I loved about him.

"Are you going to resort to bump-and-grabs again, or . . . ?"

"I jacked eighty gallons of diesel and a wallet. Does that count?"

"Holy crap! I'd say so. Are you still keeping track?"

"Yeah."

"Let me know if you need me to hack in and delete any security-camera footage."

"You can do that?"

"Not yet, but I'm working on it."

"You're the best friend ever," I said.

"It is known," he replied, deadpan. I felt an impulse to laugh, but it died before it got out.

There was a coin-operated carousel in front of the shopping cart return. I threw my leg over a seahorse and sat down on the hard plastic saddle.

"I met a boy," I said.

"Ugh. Please don't make me listen to your romantic bullshit."

I laughed and told him anyway—the vodka, the asking me out, the sexual tension.

"I don't understand being attracted to someone for having a facial flaw and large arms."

"You don't understand being attracted to someone, period."

"Don't oppress me."

"Don't be a snowflake."

"I *can* feel attraction, you know. Pretty people are like art. I *like* art. But you don't see me racing into a museum to fuck a painting."

This time, the laugh did make it out. I apologized for being insensitive about his asexuality, and Ripley apologized for mocking my attraction to Liam. We moved on, blathering about random stuff, anything but our parents and the sad state of our lives. Part of me wanted to tell him about my decline, about being out of meds—but he was already down, and I didn't want to drag him deeper.

Besides my dad and my doctor, Ripley was the only person in the world who knew my diagnosis. According to my psychiatrist, I had bipolar II. Or *Bipolar 2: The Sequel!* as Ripley liked to call it. Lots of famous people had it: Carrie Fisher, Mariah Carey, Winston Churchill. But that was no comfort to me. Those people had *done* something with their lives, whereas I was standing outside a Walmart in Fort Wayne, Indiana, talking with my only friend on a four-year-old prepaid phone.

Like everything eventually did, my conversation with Ripley began to bottom out. A security guard came around and asked me to leave. I said goodbye to Ripley, trudged back to the RV, and fell dead asleep.

I was brushing my teeth when the irritating warble of my ringtone sounded. I rinsed my mouth and grabbed my phone: it was the prankster. I decided to answer.

"Stop. Calling. Me." I hadn't used my voice yet, and it came out like a croak.

"Don't hang up, Ms. Dante."

I frowned. This wasn't the caller from yesterday; it was a man with a deep, strangely familiar voice. I glanced down the aisle; Dad wasn't here. He'd probably gone into Walmart for something.

"Who is this?"

"Flynn Bissette."

I sat down hard and all the blood rushed to my head.

"I'm a busy guy, and I'm calling you personally. Don't screw this up." When I didn't reply, he continued. "Kellar and I are producing a magic retrospective for NBC. We're projecting ten million viewers. I just had somebody drop out—and we shoot live in Hollywood in ten days. I want Dante for the show."

A moment ago I'd been barely awake; now my heart was pounding so hard, I thought it might leap out of my mouth.

Before Dad's career imploded, he had been a consultant to some of the biggest names in magic. Siegfried & Roy. Ricky Jay. Lance Burton. Maybe one of those guys wanted Dad to help them behind the scenes.

I tried to sound calmer than I was. "Who needs the consult?"

"Consult? No. I want him on the show. I want him to re-create the Truck Drop."

My mouth went dry.

Dad hadn't escaped anything more complex than thumb cuffs since his appearance on *Late Night with Craig Rogan.* He had attempted the Truck Drop only once—the night he burned his career to the ground.

"Why?" I said. "I mean, why him?"

"Fair question," Flynn said. "Dante failed—but he failed *big.* I admire his chutzpah. I want to give him a second chance."

I frowned. Something Flynn had said tripped an alarm in my head, or maybe a memory. It put me on edge.

"Maybe you just want to make money off his humiliation," I said, not quite believing I was speaking this way to Flynn Effing Bissette. "People love to watch has-beens fall on their asses."

"That's true," Flynn said. "But they also love a comeback story."

I got up and walked to the accordion door. Dad was still gone, but he could walk in at any moment. I needed time to think. I needed to stall.

"I met you once," I blurted.

"Is that right?"

"I was ten. My dad took me to see your show at the Havana. I pulled a silk daisy out of your pocket, and you signed the nine of hearts for me and wrote '*fail big*' on the face."

He laughed. "I don't remember. I'm sorry." At least he was being honest. "Listen, Ms. Dante—how do I get a yes?"

"What do you mean?"

"What does he want? Alpacas in his dressing room? A bowl of green M&M's? What?"

I bit my lip. What we really needed was money.

As if reading my mind, Flynn said, "I'll pay him five thousand dollars to show up, and five thousand more if he pulls it off."

I sat down hard on the bed.

"Ms. Dante, you're killing me. All right, ten thousand more if he pulls it off. That's fifteen grand for a successful performance. Final offer."

Fifteen. Thousand. Dollars. That was more than we'd made in the last year. That was rent. That was meds. That was rescue.

"How long do I have to consider it?"

"Thirty seconds."

My pulse pounded in my wrists, my temples, my face. I thought about last night, about how Dad had commanded that yard full of rich wedding guests, drawing their focus away from one another and onto the stage. He still had it. He was wasted on weddings and corporate Christmas parties; he belonged on a national stage.

But another failure might kill him. The first one had probably killed my mother, and it had certainly torn our family apart. We couldn't afford to take that risk again.

But could we afford *not* to take it?

It didn't matter anyway, because there was no way Dad would say yes. Absolutely no way.

Flynn cleared his throat. "What's it going to be?"

I took a deep breath. "We're in."

CHAPTER 5

WHEN I HEARD THE CLICK of the RV's door opening, a fist seemed to squeeze my heart. What had I just agreed to? And how was I going to tell Dad? As he mounted the steps, I covered my face in a fake yawn, trying to hide the mixture of fear and excitement I felt. Dad was going to be on national TV again. He had a shot at a comeback.

He was going to be so pissed.

"Good morning," he said, setting two coffees in the cup holders. He held up a McDonald's bag, his face drawn tight in a forced smile—but when he saw me, his expression changed. "What's the matter?"

"I just . . . had a weird dream," I said, my heart pounding, my brain scrambling for some way to break the news. "I'm still waking up from it, I guess."

He squinted, and I couldn't tell if he looked concerned or suspicious.

We sat down in the captain's chairs and ate our Egg McMuffins in silence. Dad finished his first.

"We need to rest up and figure out our next plan of action," he said. "There's a KOA in Bluffton. We have enough. We'll spend the night there."

If Walmarts were my second home, KOAs were the motels I stayed in during business trips. They had washing machines, showers, and—most important—free Wi-Fi. Once we got there, I would figure out the right way to tell Dad about the Flynn & Kellar show. I would have to.

We arrived just after eleven a.m. Dad looked surprised when I offered him the first shower, but he grabbed his duffel bag and marched off all the same. I fired up my laptop, and as soon as it connected to the KOA_BLUFF Wi-Fi network, my whole body sagged with relief. It was good to be connected again.

While Dad was at the showers, I opened the email from Grace Wu and electronically signed the attached contract. As soon as I clicked Send, I felt a rush of anxiety. We were committed now; we had a direction. But I had no idea how we were going to pull it off.

I put it out of my mind for the moment, logged into my school site, and started cranking through my US History exam. When I finally clicked Submit forty-five minutes later, I figured I'd earned a B, which would count as a C since I had taken it a day late. I'd have to bust my ass to bring my average back up.

Dad came in once, saw me working, and announced he was going for a long walk. I brewed a pot of coffee and slogged through a chapter of the Joads crossing the Dust Bowl in a beat-up wagon. I found their plight disturbingly relatable.

As soon as I stopped reading, I could feel my internal machinery begin to grind to a halt. The coffee and the opportunity to work had triggered a brief high, but now I was sliding downward again. Schoolwork suddenly seemed a waste of time, like rearranging deck chairs on the *Titanic*. What good was a 3.0 GPA if I ended up homeless? I needed to focus on getting money while I still could. The taping was in ten days, two thousand miles away in Hollywood. The two hundred dollars we had left wouldn't even get us to St. Louis. And if we did somehow make it to LA, we'd need our props—the truck and the tank.

I opened a spreadsheet and did some rough calculations: all in, the trip and the props would cost us at least five thousand dollars. And even if we won the lottery, how would I persuade Dad to do the show?

The answer came back: You won't.

You can't.

The weight of hopelessness bore down on me, that lead X-ray vest heavy on my chest. For a moment I couldn't catch my breath.

Why had I said yes to Flynn? What had I been thinking?

I pictured how Dad would look when I told him. His eyes going dark. His face tightening like a fist.

I stood up and paced the aisle. In only a few more days, the effects of my medication would wear off completely. I had to set things in motion now, while I still had the capacity. I couldn't let the whirlpool pull me under. Not yet.

Desperate for distraction, I turned toward the pantry. I opened the bungeed door wide enough to grab the jar of fancy peanut butter, took a knife from the drawer, and sat down at the table again. I unscrewed the lid and began to stir, my mind spiraling like the peanut butter in the jar.

Food, diesel, props. Food, diesel, props. *Ella, Ella, eh, eh, eh . . .*

The song was back, signaling my further descent into the gray. *Ella, ella . . .*

I'd been an idiot to waste six dollars on fancy peanut butter. I should have gone for the cheap stuff. *Ella, Ella . . .* The cheap stuff. Peanut butter. *Eh, eh, eh . . .* The thoughts echoed in my mind, on a loop like the song lyrics. I looked down at the jar in my hand—and an idea struck me. A name.

A bubble of hope bloomed in my chest. The name. It was a long shot—*he* was a long shot—and Dad would absolutely lose his shit when he found out. But still, there was a chance. Maybe the only chance we had.

I texted Ripley and quickly filled him in on the last eight hours. His reaction was about what I expected.

Ripley: FLYNN AND FUCKING KELLAR?!

Me: I know. It's huge. 10 million viewers.

Ripley: WHAT?!? He's going to do it, right?

Me: I haven't told him yet.

Ripley: YOU HAVEN'T TOLD HIM?

Me: It's complicated.

Ripley: Where are they shooting?

I started to reply, then hesitated. Ripley lived only an hour away from LA, in a conservative town he had nicknamed

Dark Hills. At the moment, we lived two time zones apart, so it was easy to justify never meeting in person. But if I told him I was going to be practically in his backyard, he might want to break our pact.

And the truth was, I didn't want him to see me in person. Especially not when I was sliding toward a total meltdown. But what could I do, lie? All he'd have to do was Google the show. I had no choice. I typed out my reply.

Me: LA

The three dots bounced for a long time, and I chewed my lip vigorously. I guessed he was writing and then deleting responses. Finally:

Ripley: When?
Me: 10 days.
Ripley: COWBOY JESUS RIDING A DINOSAUR BITMOJI!

My prehistoric phone couldn't get Bitmoji, so Ripley had to describe them to me. It was pitiful.

Me: I know.
Ripley: Is any part of you excited? I mean, this is everything!

I closed my eyes and squeezed the phone in both hands. I couldn't think about that right now.

Me: I need to focus on getting us there.

Ripley: Right. Sorry.

Me: I need a favor.

Ripley: I would do anything for love, but I won't do that.

Me: Please be serious with me right now. Can you find someone for me? On the internet?

Ripley: Of course I can. Who?

I took a shower, hoping the warm water would ease my unquiet mind. But the water was cold, and as I stood there under the weak spray, I felt more pathetic than ever. I stepped out, dried off, and moved to the sink.

The warped steel plate that served as a mirror distorted my reflection, so I looked down instead and ran the faucet till the basin was full. Then I shut off the tap, emptied my lungs, and thrust my head under surface.

It was dark and cold and blessedly still.

When I got back to the RV, Dad was seated at the table, reading something in his ancient leather-bound journal. He'd had it as long as I could remember, but he never let me see inside.

Dad closed the journal and looked up at me. "While you were out, that young man from the party called."

I noticed my phone sitting in front of him on the table, and my stomach gave a wild lurch.

"When?"

Dad glanced down at the dead watch on his wrist. "I'm not sure. A few minutes ago."

"What did he say?"

"He asked for you, and I told him you'd return his call at your earliest convenience."

"You're sure it was him?"

Dad smiled. "Liam Miller, brother of the bride. Quite sure."

Holy shit. He'd actually called. My face felt freshly sunburned as I walked down the aisle to grab my phone. But before I could, Dad covered it with his hand.

"I think it's wonderful you're making friends."

"He's not a friend, Dad. He's just . . . I know him from Eastside."

"Well, I still think it's wonderful. Are you going to—"

"Thank you," I said, peeling his hand back and snatching the phone. I thought I saw him smile as I moved past him and shut the accordion door.

I lay down on the bed and stared at Liam's number on the screen. He had called, even after the way I'd called him out on his bullshit. Even after I had sort of burned him in front of those girls when he asked for my cell. It didn't make sense. Was he playing some kind of head game on me? Why?

And even if he was genuinely interested, I didn't have time to go on a date. I had props to acquire and gigs to book. I had to take care of my dad. Plus I was hopelessly awkward around people my own age—especially boys. Hadn't I proven that last night?

And yet the thought of escaping the RV and getting away from Dad, even if only for a few hours, was like the last ray of sunlight before an approaching storm. Liam had been earnest, even charming. And he had kept up with my "caustic wit," as Ripley put it. But more than that, he seemed genuinely interested in me. He didn't treat me like an alien. And if I was being totally honest, I was attracted to him. Stupidly attracted.

Plus, if everything went as planned—if Dad and I drove to LA and did the Truck Drop on national TV—I might never come back to Indiana. I might never see him again. So what did I have to lose?

I tapped his number and held my breath. The phone rang.

"Hello?" Liam answered. His voice was like warm syrup.

"Hi."

"Ellie. You called back."

"You didn't think I would?"

"No."

For a moment, each of us waited for the other to speak.

Then he said, "Panic! at the Disco is playing in Chicago tonight. Come with me."

My stomach lurched again. Liam Miller wanted to take me to a concert? In Chicago?

"That's three hours away," I said.

"I'll have you home by two a.m. Three at the latest."

I glanced toward the accordion door. "You realize I have a father, right?"

"I'm great with parents." He paused. "Do you not like Panic! at the Disco? Oh God, you're not a country fan, are you?"

"Not unless you count Mellencamp."

"Mellencamp, country? That's blasphemy."

I laughed. He laughed.

"So wait," he said. "Are you turning me down?"

I bit my lip. "No. I just . . . Could we do something . . . simpler?"

"What, like Culver's and a movie?"

I smiled. "Actually, that sounds great."

He laughed again. "Ladies and gentlemen, I've found myself a keeper! When can I pick you up? And where?"

CHAPTER 6

I OWNED ONE DRESS, a little black one, and a single pair of heels that had belonged to my mother and that increased my height to a respectable five five. Since Liam was at least six feet tall, I would probably only come up to his shoulder, but at least I wouldn't look like a hobbit.

I wanted to wait for him on a bench at the entrance to the KOA, but Dad insisted that Liam knock on the RV door and pick me up "like a proper gentleman." I was annoyed—but it was also weirdly nice to have him act like a regular father for once. In any case, it meant I had to spend the afternoon cleaning the RV top to bottom with all the windows open to air out it out. Then I took another shower and spent an embarrassing amount of time getting ready.

My hair was a tangled mess, so I took the bottle of baby oil from my bedside table, poured some into my hand, and began to work it in; I'd run out of conditioner weeks ago. The beauty blogs recommended avocado or olive oil as substitutes, but I couldn't afford them, either. A fresh crop of obsessive thoughts took root: Would I smell like a baby? Would he notice? I grabbed a brush and began to work out the tangles. I was rough with myself; each tug on my scalp brought a pang of satisfaction and comfort. Each was proof that I was still here, and that I could still feel. Self-harm for squeamish girls.

I had inherited my violent hair-brushing technique from my mother. She used to make me sit crisscross applesauce on the carpet while she perched on the sofa behind me, smoking and spasmodically yanking on my hair with a boar-bristle brush. We'd lived in an apartment on Paradise Road that smelled like smoke and Glade spray, with patchy brown carpet that made my legs itch.

"No crying," she'd said, ashing her cigarette into a ceramic turtle. "Beauty hurts. Might as well get used to it." She'd laughed and kissed my head. "The burdens of being a princess."

I realized my hand had stopped midstroke, the teeth of the brush still biting into the back of my scalp. I took in a shuddering breath.

I didn't want to think about her.

I started to make a braid, and then I remembered that Liam had noticed my long hair, so I let it hang free.

When the knock came, I felt far from ready—but I sprang to my feet, threw aside the partition, and rushed to beat Dad to the door. I was slightly breathless when I opened it to find Liam standing at the foot of the steps. He wore a blue-checked shirt and dark jeans, and when he looked up at me, his eyes widened slightly.

"You look . . . Wow."

I was helpless to contain my stupid grin. "Thanks."

He looked down at himself. "I'm underdressed."

He was, but it suited him. "It's not an unattractive look."

He smiled. I wondered how many girls he'd wrecked with that dimple.

"Now comes the part where you meet my father."

"I can't wait. Is he cleaning his gun?"

Dad was embarrassingly formal as usual, but five minutes later we were in Liam's vintage Mustang, the tires kicking up gravel as we drove out of the RV park.

"Where are we going?" I yelled over the roar of the oversized engine.

"You'll see."

We sped down the dark highway, heading east. The top was down, and my hair flew about in a wild tangle. But despite the cool air and the hot boy who smelled like sandalwood, my mind sank into dark thoughts. Maybe this date was a mistake. Liam was a rich college athlete; I was an awkward, emotionally unstable nomad. We had nothing in common. How long before I said something stupid and ruined the whole night? And even if the date went well, I'd be leaving soon. The relationship was doomed before it started. Relationship? Oh God, I was blowing it already.

In the void up ahead, I spotted a well-lit one-story building. A restaurant in the middle of nowhere. We pulled into the unpaved lot and parked under a red neon sign that read *Graziano's Italian Restaurant.*

Liam set the parking brake and killed the engine. "Do you like ravioli?"

"I like anything with cheese."

Liam opened my car door for me like it was 1970, and as we approached the restaurant, I definitely detected that varsity athlete strut. I found I didn't mind it so much.

When we walked in, the hostess gave Liam a big smile. She was pretty and tall and a couple years older than me.

"Hi, Liam," she said. Her tone was flirtatious, and I felt my spine stiffen slightly.

"Hey, Taylor," Liam replied.

Leaning forward on the hostess stand, Taylor said, "How's things in California?"

I tried to suppress my frown. California? What did this girl know that I didn't?

"Sunny and seventy-two degrees," Liam said.

"Taking care of that pitching arm, I hope?" She laughed as if he'd just told a hilarious joke, then looked at me. "Who's your friend?"

Liam seemed about to answer, so I cut him off. "Purcilla," I said. "College friend."

"Nice to meet you." She gave me a toothy smile and grabbed two menus. "Let me show you guys to your table."

To his credit, Liam kept his eyes on me as Taylor led us to our booth, swishing her hips for his benefit.

Graziano's was cozy—exposed wood beams, red-checked tablecloths, and shelves crammed with knickknacks. Our table was in front of a window looking out on dark farmland, where the almost-full moon shone on the stubs of harvested corn stalks. I could imagine the perfect blanket of snow that would cover this field in a few months, and wondered if I would be here to see it.

"Earth to *Purcilla*," Liam said. I blushed and hid my face in the menu. "What was that about back there?"

"I could ask you the same thing, Mr. California."

He leaned back in his chair and spun his butter knife on the tablecloth. "Yeah, well. I go to school out there. Cal State Fullerton."

"Cal State where now?"

He laughed. "Fullerton. It's like an hour from LA. Nothing fancy, but it's a big baseball school, and they gave me money to go."

"Oh," I said, hoping my face didn't reveal the storm of thoughts now gathering inside my skull. Liam lived near LA, too? What were the chances? I could almost hear Ripley saying, *Apparently, about a hundred percent.*

"What's wrong?" Liam said, frowning.

"Not a thing," I said, and gave him my best smile.

The food was rich and salty and amazing, and we ate and laughed and talked—mostly about nothing, bands and memes and the smothering omnipresence of fathers. Neither of us brought up *Damn Yankees*, or anything else about our time at Eastside. It was like we were starting over.

Time seemed to pass in fast-forward; one minute we were placing our order, and the next a busboy had cleared our plates. I had a moment of panic when the waitress set the check between us, but Liam put down his credit card without hesitation.

When we left the restaurant, the air was chilly, and Liam grabbed his lambskin jacket out of the back seat and draped it over my shoulders. It was warm and soft and smelled like sandalwood. I wanted to steal it.

"Do you have to go back?" he said. "It's still early. We could hit DQ."

The thought of running into more Taylors at the local Dairy Queen made me feel sick.

"If I eat any more, you'll have to tow me home."

"All right," he said, and reached for his keys, deflated.

I put my hand on his arm. "But let's go somewhere else, okay?"

We sat on the steps at Lakeside Park, watching the roses close up for the night. I still had Liam's jacket over my shoulders; I had tried to give it back, but he wouldn't take it.

After a particularly long stretch of quiet, Liam said, "I have a confession to make."

A chill ran up my spine; I wasn't sure I wanted to hear his confession. The night had been amazing so far, and I didn't want anything to spoil it. So I spoke up first.

"Why would a guy like you go to Eastside? Your family obviously has money. Why not Bishop? Or Concordia?"

He seemed annoyed by the change of subject, but he answered. "Eastside had the best baseball team."

"And you want to go pro?"

He sighed and stared out into the trees. "My dad almost got drafted by the Cubs in 1989."

"Wow."

"Yeah. But then, one weekend, he went waterskiing on Lake Wawasee and broke his collarbone." He made a gesture like snapping a twig. "Didn't heal right. He came back the next season, but it wasn't the same. Scouts stopped coming to the games."

"So baseball is his dream. But it's not yours."

He nodded. "I like playing, but . . . it's too much to live up to."

A surge of irritation ran through me. Poor, misunderstood Liam, forced to play sports at some prestigious school in California. I picked up a twig and tossed it onto the dying grass.

"Seems like you spend a lot of energy trying to be what everyone else wants you to be."

He sat up straighter. "What do you mean?"

"You ignored me after the play because that's what your friends expected. You say you don't like that girl from the reception, but you let her drag you off anyway. You even moved across the country to pursue a career you don't really want, just to avoid disappointing your dad." I shrugged. "I'd be exhausted if I were you."

He stared at me, his mouth hanging open. Suddenly, my irritation dissolved like salt in coffee.

"Sorry," I said. "I shouldn't have said that. I'm no different. I pretend all the time."

He still looked a little stunned, but he said, "I don't get that impression."

"No?"

He shook his head. "You're one of the realest people I've ever met."

I laughed. "You don't know me. You have no idea how real I am."

Liam raised his eyebrows. "Then educate me."

His blue eyes were too intense. I had to look away.

"Ellie isn't even my real name." The words sort of fell out of my mouth. "My mother thought I was going to be a boy. Something about how I kicked."

"So what did they name you?"

"Promise you won't say it out loud." I turned to look him in the eye, and he held my gaze.

"I promise."

I pressed my lips together, then said, "Elias Dante Jr."

Liam looked at me, and I couldn't tell if he was stifling a laugh.

Then he smiled. "It's different. I like it."

I felt a pleasant lifting in my chest—and then the quiet descended again, liquid and oppressive. I didn't know why I'd told him. I wanted to take it back.

Slowly, Liam moved closer until our arms touched. Mine broke out in goose bumps. I needed to say something to break the tension.

"What do you want to do when you grow up, Liam Miller?"

He let out an uncomfortable laugh and ran his hand over his short hair. It was a stupid question, but it had done the trick.

"I don't know. Travel, I guess."

"To New York?"

He looked at me. "How'd you know?"

"There's a giant framed photo in your bedroom."

"Oh. Duh." He smiled. I felt a twinge in my chest. "You've traveled a lot," he said.

"I guess."

"What's it like? You know, once you get past the soybean sea."

"Why are you asking me? You're the one who moved to California."

"Yeah, but that's moving, not traveling. There's a difference."

I looked at him, at his dark blue eyes and his slightly stubbled jaw. I felt an impulse to lean forward and kiss him; instead, I bit my lip and looked away.

"There's this saying," I said, "'Wherever you go, there you are.' Traveling is like that. New places are fun for a while, but then you start to miss where you were before. You find things not to like about the new place, and eventually you realize that the thing you don't like is *you*."

Liam stared at me. "You're like a ninety-year-old woman trapped in a sixteen-year-old's body."

It was a weird compliment—but it made me smile.

"What about you?" he asked. "Are you going to be a magician like your dad?"

My smile faltered. "No," I said. "Definitely not."

"Do you hate it?"

I leaned back and looked up. The clouds had cleared, and I could see Orion's shoulders hanging low in the western sky. "No," I said, "I *love* it."

I exhaled, and it was like I had shrugged off that X-ray vest. I'd been pushing back on Dad for so long, trying to stay focused on my future, that it was a relief to finally tell someone how I really felt. And now that I had started, the words spilled out.

"I love the way the lights blind you when you step onstage. That big black chasm full of people you can't see. The way they all gasp at once when you've really surprised them. It's . . ." I shook my head.

"I don't think I've ever felt that way about anything," Liam said. "Why don't you want to do it?"

I closed my eyes. What was I supposed to say? That I hated living in an RV and texting on a shitty phone from 2016? That I needed expensive pills to keep from drowning myself in a truck-stop bathroom? Here was a guy who had everything, who ate canapés and won scholarships and drove a vintage Mustang. How could he understand anything about me? I looked down at my mother's old shoes and hoped he hadn't noticed how scuffed they were.

"I'm going to be a psychiatric nurse," I said, glancing at him to see if he was going to laugh. He didn't.

"That sounds intense."

"I want to make a difference. Not just be a dancing monkey."

"I don't think you're a dancing monkey."

"Nurses are in demand. And they get paid really well." I was babbling now, and I couldn't stop. "I'm going to get my diploma and go for an associate's in nursing. I'll have a job and insurance before my dad turns seventy. And an apartment. With a balcony." Finally, I bit my lip to stop my blathering.

"Balconies are good," Liam said.

I shivered, and he reached over to turn up the collar of the coat he'd lent me. His warm finger brushed my cold cheek, and I shivered again.

He shifted closer. "Why did you leave Eastside?"

I felt a momentary rush of relief; he hadn't seen the videos. But even so, what should I tell him? That I'd gone crazy at a party? That I couldn't take the stares and the whispers anymore? I decided no—I would keep that to myself.

"I missed too many days traveling with my dad. Online school was easier."

"Oh," he said, but the word was weighted.

"*Oh?* What does *oh* mean?"

"I just . . . thought you left for other reasons."

My chest tightened. "Like what?"

"I'm sorry. Can we just forget it?"

"No, we can't." I folded my arms—why was I antagonizing him?—but I couldn't stop myself. "What did you mean?"

He looked away. "You were always, like . . . I don't know. One day you'd be chatty and smiley with your friends, and then it seemed like you wouldn't talk to anyone for a week. I'd see you sitting on the stairs, and I wanted to come say something to you, but you projected this, like, *fuck off* vibe, and I didn't want to bother you."

I gaped at him. Even after the play, he had paid attention to me. Enough to keep track of my moods.

"I shouldn't have said anything," he said.

"No, it's fine. I'm just surprised you noticed."

He looked at me with a bemused expression. "How could I not notice you?"

We were still for a moment. I could have sworn I felt our faces drifting closer, like two satellites drawing together, each caught in the other's microgravity. The tension was too much.

I said, "What's your confession?"

He pressed his lips together and looked straight into my eyes. "I had a crush on you during the play."

My lungs felt suddenly empty. "Liar," I whispered.

He smiled. "Your turn."

My mouth was dry. I licked my lips. "I've never been on a date before."

Liam didn't even flinch. He just leaned in and kissed me.

CHAPTER 7

HIS LIPS WERE FIRM BUT gentle, his hand warm on the back of my neck. My whole body began to heat up, and little red bursts of light bloomed on the backs of my eyelids. He drew me in tighter.

Suddenly, it was too much. I put a hand on his chest and pushed.

Liam pulled away immediately and took his hand off my neck, leaving a cold void where it had been.

"Was I too fast?" he asked.

I tried to say no but couldn't get the word out.

"Is it . . . Do you have a boyfriend?"

I shook my head. "It's my first date, remember?"

"Oh." His shoulders relaxed slightly. "What happened? You sort of . . . detached."

I hugged myself in his jacket and looked away. I couldn't

tell him the truth—that I was afraid of going manic and freaking out. That even just kissing was too intense. Who would want a girl like that?

"I'm sorry," I whispered. "I knew I was going to ruin this."

Liam looked at me as if I'd just spoken a foreign language.

"If you think this is ruined, I have bad news for you about dating."

I frowned.

"Tonight was awesome," he said.

My throat cinched up. "It was?"

"One of my best dates ever," he said. "Top fifty, easy."

I smiled and punched his arm. He smiled back. His attention was like a spotlight. I wanted to bask in it.

I wanted to flee.

He had made a move, and I had pushed him away. But he was still here, still engaged, being a total gentleman. I looked at his face, searching for a defect, something I could cling to when he finally saw the real me and ran away screaming.

I said, "Tell me something about you that I won't like."

He cocked his head. "What do you mean?"

"I showed you my baggage." I hadn't. "It's your turn."

He laughed. "I told you mine. Privilege with a side of daddy issues."

"That's not . . . I meant something actually bad."

He seemed to hold his breath for a moment. "Why would you want me to tell you something bad about me?"

I turned my head to stare into the trees. "Because I'm leaving soon, and I need this not to be perfect." It wasn't the whole truth, but it was the best I could do.

The lights in the parking lot flickered and went out. It was like a signal that our time together was almost up.

I could feel Liam's eyes on me.

"I want to kiss you again," he said.

Heat blossomed in my chest like a road flare.

"Okay."

Half an hour later, we cracked the windows, and Liam started the engine. We'd moved things to the car because I had started to shiver; now my cheeks were red from his stubble instead of the cold, but the shivers persisted. I wanted to bottle every sensation, capture it so I could replay it over and over. I desperately wanted to enjoy the present moment, but instead I was dreading the next one, when we said goodbye and I went back to my real life.

It was past midnight when we pulled up next to the RV. The lights were on inside.

"Can I walk you up?" Liam asked.

"No! I mean, I'm good, thanks."

I had to look away, or else we were going to start making out again. But he put his hand on my face, turned it toward him, and leaned in to kiss me. At the last minute I put my hand up to stop him, my fingers splaying awkwardly across his jaw.

He took my hand and kissed the tip of my index finger, sending an electrical storm through my nervous system. Then he folded my hand and sort of gave it back to me. Trembling, I reached for the door handle.

"Don't disappear," he said.

I didn't know how to reply.

I climbed the steps of the RV, closed the door behind me, and looked around. I had lived in this box half my life, but suddenly it was too small. The RV, my life, everything. I felt smothered. Claustrophobic. I had an impulse to rush back outside and tell Liam to stay. I could make coffee. We could sit at the picnic table and just talk. Stretch the night out a little longer.

I took a step toward the door, but then I heard the Mustang's engine revving and saw the taillights retreat as Liam drove away. I turned and started down the aisle.

Dad was waiting up for me, sitting at the table and pretending to read. He looked up and smiled as I approached, but his eyes were already inspecting me for signs of whatever dads feared they would find after a date.

"How did it go?" he asked.

"Good," I said. "I'm really tired."

Dad raised his eyebrows. "I promise not to interrogate you. But you've got to give me more than that."

I sighed. "He's really great, Dad. A total gentleman." A total gentleman I would probably never see again.

"That's wonderful."

Dad's smile was too bright somehow, like a flashlight in the eyes. I looked away, irritated.

"Did you see a movie?" he asked.

"Dad, I'm tired." I wanted to be alone. I tried to walk past him, but he took my arm gently in his hand.

"Ellie, what's the matter?"

To my surprise, my breath hitched, and the next moment, tears were leaking down my cheeks.

"Oh, Ellie." Dad stood and tried to hug me, but I backed away. "Sweetheart, what's wrong? Did he hurt you?"

"No," I said, though the word came out garbled. "He didn't. . . . I'm fine."

What was wrong was that I'd just had my first real kiss, and I had no one to tell. No sister, no girlfriend, no mother.

Something about that last thought shut off the tears. It was like someone had slammed a door, and now that way was blocked.

Dad held me at arm's length and frowned. He seemed even more concerned now that I had *stopped* crying. "You still have your pills? You're still taking them?"

I cocked my head. This was the first time he'd asked about my meds in weeks. Had he not been paying attention? Or did he need to see tears to understand that I was headed for a crash?

I didn't like lying to my father—but telling the truth now would only make things worse. So I said, "Yeah."

The tension drained from his face. "Are you sure there's nothing you want to tell me?"

"I'm fine."

"I know I'm your father, but—"

"Dad, please!" His face tightened again. I softened my voice. "I'm just exhausted."

"All right," he said, releasing his grip on my shoulders. "Get some sleep. I love you."

I felt a swell of regret as I closed the accordion door

behind me; I was shutting him out, and I knew it hurt him, but I couldn't bring myself to do anything else.

I lay in bed for a long time, remembering Liam's sandalwood scent, the feeling of his warm hand on the back of my cold neck. Thinking how I would never be the same. Thinking how it made no difference.

The blast of a big rig's air horn startled me awake, and it took me a moment to orient myself. I was in the RV—at Cedarwood? No, we'd been kicked out. We were at the KOA in Bluffton, where Liam had picked me up and taken me on my first date. I reached up and felt cheek where his stubble had rubbed it red last night. I expected a rush, a return of the shivers that had electrified my spine as I sat in the car with Liam's hands on me—but nothing came. Instead, a dull gray ache pressed against my temples, and my whole body felt twenty pounds heavier, as if gravity had increased while I'd slept. I checked my phone, but there were no messages, so I typed one to Liam: *Last night was amazing. Thank you.*

But I paused. Despite what he'd said, I knew the date had been awkward. What if I pursued him and he ghosted me? It was better to let it go. I deleted it.

I got to my feet, blinking and rubbing my eyes. I needed to splash water on my face, start the coffee, maybe go outside and feel the sun on my skin. But Dad was snoring on the other side of the partition, and I didn't want to wake him up. So I opened my tiny window to let in some fresh air, powered up my laptop, and got to work.

Flynn had promised us five grand just to show up, plus

ten more if Dad pulled off the Truck Drop—but first, we had to get to Hollywood. That meant buying fuel and food, and that meant we needed a gig between here and LA. I checked our email on the off chance someone had tried to book us, but the inbox was empty. No one had sent us a Facebook message, either. I was running out of options. It was time to call in a favor.

I picked up my phone, scrolled through my contacts, and placed a call. It rang and rang—and just when I thought I'd get funneled to voice mail, he picked up.

"Rrrrico Vega." He always sounded like this on the phone, a cross between Elvis Presley and Ryan Seacrest.

"Hey," I said. "It's Ellie."

"Elias Dante Jr.," Rico said, and I smiled despite the desperation tightening my jaw. "How are you and your pops?"

"We're fine. How about you? How's business?"

Rico was the son of the late Mariano Vega, Dad's best friend in Vegas. When Mariano had died four years earlier, Rico had taken over his dad's consulting business and grown it like crazy. Despite being only nineteen at the time, Rico flew everywhere and worked with the best magicians in the world, designing their illusions and honing their acts. He had it all—the thrill of magic and the stability of a steady income. I would have killed to trade places with him—but at least I still had my dad.

"I'm busier than a one-legged man in an ass-kicking contest," he said. "Are you in town?"

"Nope. Still in Indiana. I take it you're back in Vegas?"

"For the next couple of months, yeah. Hang on." Rico put his hand over the phone, and I heard him giving someone instructions. He came back on the line. "Sorry."

"Whose show are you working?"

"I can't tell you. I signed a nondisclosure agreement." He sounded serious. "So, Ms. Dante, what can I do for you?"

He'd cut right to the chase. I should have planned out what I was going to say. My brain felt like it was in low gear.

"Well . . . to be honest, we're kind of hard up."

"How hard up?"

I considered sugarcoating it but decided honesty would work better. "We have enough cash to last us three days, maybe a week if we do the Walmart thing."

"That's not good."

"Yeah."

"Can't you float on credit cards for a while until you book something?"

"They're maxed. And we got evicted."

"Jesus."

I swallowed. Here went nothing. "We need a gig. Badly."

I waited, but he didn't reply.

"Is there any way you could get us something in Vegas? I wouldn't ask if I didn't have to. You know that." Rico said nothing. My saliva had suddenly gone thick in my mouth. "I mean, a regular spot somewhere off the Strip would be great, but at this point, I'd take one night at the Four Jacks." Shut up, Ellie.

Rico blew out a breath. "Aw, man. You know how it is out here. Competitive as fuck. I couldn't get *me* a regular slot. I've got *America's Got Talent* finalists who can't get a whole weekend because they don't have the draw."

I felt myself deflate. "What about a consulting gig?"

There was a long, awkward pause. "I want to help, but . . .

God, I feel like a dick. You and your dad are like family to me. But reputation is really important in this business. And right now, your dad's is . . . I mean . . . Recommending him would be tricky for me. I'm sorry."

I took a fistful of my own hair and tugged. I'd been stupid to ask.

"Yeah, no, I get it."

Another long pause.

"Listen, I could probably get you a pay-to-play gig at the Tack & Saddle. The booker there owes me."

I cringed. Pay-to-play gigs were the lowest form of employment. Essentially, the venue made you buy tickets to your own show and then sell them yourself.

Rico must have read my reaction in the silence, because he said, "I know it's not ideal. But if he draws, maybe they'd hire him for some lounge shows, or an afternoon spot. You could probably capitalize on the whole *Craig Rogan*—"

"Even if we had the funds, he'd never go for it." I took a deep breath. I was out of options. "I don't suppose you could loan—"

But Rico cut in. "If you wanted to pick up some assistant work, I could definitely get you interviews. You've got the look. You've got more than adequate skills."

"No," I said, a little too quickly. "I mean, I can't. I've got school."

"Oh, right."

I considered asking again for a loan, but I couldn't bring myself to do it. Instead, I pivoted, asking about his sister and her career. The conversation rapidly devolved into awkward small talk; I knew Rico was just being polite, and he knew that I knew.

"I wish you'd reconsider the assistant stuff," he said. "You could work nonstop out here."

"Thanks," I said. I didn't want to talk anymore.

"If there's anything else I can do for you, just call, okay?"

We said goodbye. I dropped the phone onto the bed and squeezed my eyes shut tight.

What were we going to do?

I wanted to hide in my room—but then I heard Dad moving around in the kitchen and decided I couldn't stay in here any longer without making him worry. So I put on a fresh T-shirt and jeans and opened the door.

"There she is," he said. "I was just about to make some breakfast. Are you hungry?"

"Just coffee," I said. "I ate enough last night to choke a T. rex."

"Just coffee it is." He put on the electric kettle and nodded back toward my room. "Was that your young man on the phone?"

"No," I said. "It was Rico."

"And how is our young Master Vega?"

I poured some water into my coffee mug and took a drink, giving myself time to form an answer. Gig or no gig, I needed to persuade Dad to head west, and I had hoped my call to Rico would give us a legitimate reason. Since it hadn't, I was forced to lie.

"He booked us a gig in Las Vegas."

Dad turned to look at me now, his mouth slightly open. "Did he really?"

I shrugged. "It's only two nights at the Tack & Saddle, but . . ."

I'd picked the Tack & Saddle because I knew it wouldn't sound too good to be true. As expected, Dad's mouth twisted as if he'd bitten into a lemon. I knew what he was going to say: downtown was for third-rate acts and has-beens. I didn't want to remind him that's exactly what we were.

"Downtown? Ellie, no. That's—"

"I know," I said. I got up, put my hand on his arm. I was surprised how easy it was to roll with the story. "But we need the money."

His face went red. For a moment, I thought I'd made a mistake, that he would refuse to go, and we'd be back to square one. But then his shoulders sagged.

"You're right." The kettle whistled. Dad turned it off and reached for the canister of coffee. "Of course you're right."

The resignation in his voice made my chest ache, and all of a sudden I was desperate to take it back. To spill the truth, to tell him everything. But if I told him now, he would blow up. And then when his anger subsided, he would simply refuse to go. He would make me call Grace and cancel. But we couldn't afford to cancel. We couldn't afford Dad's pride. So I had to hold on to the lie, at least for a little longer.

"How are we going to get there?" I asked, thinking of our mostly empty fuel tank.

"This late in the year?" Dad opened the refrigerator and pulled out a carton of eggs. "South across Missouri to

Oklahoma City, then Interstate 40 all the way."

"That's not what I meant."

Dad raised his eyebrows.

"We need diesel and food, and we don't have much money."

"Oh, *that*," he said, waving it away like a fly. "I wouldn't worry about that."

"Why not?"

Dad smiled. "Because I booked us a gig, too."

"You did? Where? When?"

"Tonight, as a matter of fact," he said, smiling, the bristles of his mustache poking out like porcupine quills. "In Mishawaka. Our old stomping ground. And it's not too far out of the way."

"That's great!" I said.

Dad turned back to the stove and cracked an egg into the frying pan. My next question—How much?—was cut off when my phone let out a familiar electronic chirp from my bed six feet away.

Dad cocked an eyebrow at me. "I'll bet I know who that is."

"Dad," I said, turning, grateful that my bushy hair hid my ears, which were certainly turning red. "It's probably just Ripley."

"Uh-huh."

But it probably *was* Ripley, calling with an update on his online manhunt. Only when I snatched up the phone, I saw that it wasn't a phone call at all. It was a video-chat request. From Liam.

I put a hand to my beard-burned cheek; I hadn't showered

since before our date—hadn't even washed my face, let alone put on makeup. I couldn't let him see me like this. But I couldn't just *not* answer, either, so I slid the accordion door shut, turned the camera to face the wall, and tapped Accept.

"Hello?" I said.

"Good morning," Liam replied. "The playbook says to wait forty-eight hours before calling, but I couldn't do it." He paused, and I tried to think of a witty reply, but nothing came. "So I'm calling you now. Except all I see is a wall. Where are you?"

"I'm, um, still in my pajamas."

"Would you be more comfortable if I put mine on, too?"

"What? No."

"Well, I'm not going to strip nude, if that's what you think. I'm not that kind of guy."

I laughed. "Can't we just talk on the phone?"

"I want to see your face. Call you back in five?"

I squeezed my eyes shut. It was one thing to talk on the phone; I could hide any number of defects. But on video, I had to look right, fake smiles, conceal flaws.

"Ten," I said.

"Done." He hung up.

I splashed some water on my face and brushed out my tangles. I reached for my makeup, then decided against it; if Liam didn't like my real face, he should've just called instead. I rummaged through my drawers for the right thing to wear—something cute that didn't scream, Trying too hard. I settled on a blue cami that looked good with my skin tone.

When the phone chirped again, I was waiting, splayed

across my bed like a mermaid, trying to look totally casual.

"Hi," Liam said.

"Hi."

He was wearing a tight white V-neck that showed off his shoulders, and his face was slightly more stubbly than it had been last night. Behind him I could see the photo print of New York, as well as a stack of baseball caps perched on his bedpost and a pair of jeans flung across the bedspread.

"Housekeeper's day off?" I said.

"What?" He glanced over his shoulder, then turned the phone so all I could see was his face and the headboard. "There, Miss Nosy."

"You're the one who wanted to videoconference."

"Fair enough. Next time, I'll clean my room." He cleared his throat. "What are you doing tonight?"

"I can't," I said, and squeezed my toes into fists.

"I didn't even say what yet."

"I'm leaving. In like an hour."

His smile tightened. "Oh. Bad timing, I guess. It's a shame, too, because I had really good plans."

"Culver's and a movie?"

"What can I say? I like to sweep 'em off their feet." He ran a hand over his short hair. "Can I ask where you're going?"

I pressed my lips together. If I told him, he might want to come see me. I was headed for a crash, and I wasn't sure I could handle this video chat, let alone seeing him again in the flesh.

"If it's too personal, forget it. I didn't mean to pry."

"It's not, it's just . . . We have a gig, and then we're headed out west for a while."

Liam's eyebrows went up. "Out west like California?"

I swallowed hard. Now that we were both going to be in California, there was a possibility of an actual *thing* between us. Which sort of terrified me.

"I'm not sure."

He looked deflated but rebounded quickly. "What about your gig tonight? Is it local?"

"I don't have details yet," I lied.

"Oh. Okay." His voice had cooled.

There was a beep, and Liam looked at his phone. "It's my dad," he said. "I should probably take this."

"Okay." I felt simultaneously relieved and disappointed.

"Text me when you have details?"

I said I would—another lie—and then we said goodbye and disconnected.

For a while, I sat staring at the white Skype window where his face had been. Why did I have to make things so complicated? I could've just told him I was going to LA, and we could have set a time to meet. But the thing was, by the time we got to California, I'd be almost two weeks without meds. What if I was a total wreck? Up or down, I didn't want him to see those sides of me.

I didn't want anyone to see them.

CHAPTER 8

WHILE DAD PILOTED THE BUS northwest on US 33, I used my cellular connection to log into my school's website.

I'd gotten a D on the history exam.

I sat back and raked both hands through my hair. The onset of depression had decimated my focus over the past few weeks—and between that and spotty internet on the road, I just hadn't been able to keep up with my schoolwork. Not to mention all the time I had spent trying—and failing—to book us gigs. This was a huge setback—and history wasn't the only class I was at risk of failing.

I did a few quick calculations. Barring some miracle, I would finish the semester with a cumulative GPA of 2.5. That meant I had to get straight As for the rest of my high school career in order to get into nursing school. Dad's health was getting worse; our whole future—our lives—depended on me getting a good job, getting insurance.

Grades weren't my only problem. I needed to pull off any number of other miracles, including acquiring expensive props and persuading Dad to reprise his biggest failure on national TV. On top of all that, I had only a small window of time to fix this mess before the down made it impossible to work.

I squeezed my eyes shut and tried to focus. Our best chance was the Flynn & Kellar show. I had to get my hands on those props.

I texted Ripley:

Me: Any luck?

As soon as the message read "delivered," the phone rang in my hand.

"Good morrow, young Ellie."

"Hey, Ripley."

"Whoa. You sound terrible. What's going on? Is it the thing with the guy? Do I need to arrange a fatal accident?"

"I'm okay," I said.

"Like hell you are. You sound like a robot with dead batteries. Is it the guy? Or are you crashing?"

I blinked. Ripley knew me so well. He knew my tells.

"It's the guy," I said. It was only half a lie. "It got weird."

"Weird how?"

"Can we not talk about it right now?"

"Okay. But I'm officially registering my concern. Anyway, here's some good news: I found Jif Higgins."

My heart swelled. "Are you serious?"

Jif Higgins was a thirty-something multimillionaire who

owned a casino in Las Vegas—and he was a giant magic nerd. He was infamous for buying old props and set pieces and hoarding them in his storage complex. Supposedly, his collection of Houdini memorabilia was unrivaled, and rumor had it he'd bought the entire Siegfried & Roy catalog when they signed off. Nobody liked him; he was notoriously arrogant and abrasive. But when a magician retired or fell on hard times, Higgins would swoop in with bags full of cash, buy up their stuff, and retreat once more into obscurity. If anyone still had Dad's old Truck Drop props, it was him.

"The guy is almost a ghost online," Ripley said. "I had to dig, but I finally found a domain registered in his name. The Whois info was private, so I hacked like a bastard until I got his address and phone number. I'm a genius, Ellie. The NSA should headhunt me, but I'll refuse them, because I'm too rogue."

I closed my eyes and grabbed a fistful of hair. "Ripley, thank you *so* much."

"Sending it as we speak."

We chatted for a few minutes, and then Ripley had to take his little brother, Jude, to soccer practice, so he signed off.

I tapped the contact file he had sent me and stared at Higgins's name. I should have called him right away—there was no time to waste—but I couldn't bring myself to click the button. Ripley had said I sounded like a robot, which meant my voice was doing its flat-affect thing. It happened when I was low, and I usually didn't notice it. But Ripley had. What if Higgins did, too? What if it weirded it him out, and he just hung up?

I decided it was better to wait. It would take at least three days to get to Vegas; that was plenty of time. Besides, we needed to prepare for tonight's show.

I went up front and dropped into the passenger seat.

"Where are we?" I asked.

Dad didn't answer right away, so I looked over at him. He was completely zoned out. I felt a moment of panic.

"Dad? Did you hear me?"

To my relief, he seemed to come out of his trance at once. "What? Yes, I'm fine. Well, actually, I'm a bit tired. Maybe some coffee."

I frowned. How was he tired already? He'd only been driving for ninety minutes. Plus we'd just had an entire day off, which he'd spent relaxing. Whereas I'd been busting my ass all day trying to save my grades *and* make ends meet. Sometimes I wondered how he would survive without me.

"Pull over," I said. "I'll drive."

Sunny's Roadhouse squatted on the south side of I-20. It was a one-story brick rectangle with a detached, ramshackle smokehouse. I could smell the ribs before I killed the engine in the field behind the lot. Only a few Harleys and F-150s were parked in front; it was barely five o'clock.

Dad was passed out on the couch, looking pale and waxy. I sat down across from him and watched him sleep, his chest rising and falling, his lips puffing up and releasing air like a cartoon character's. It was a symptom of his apnea, which contributed to his heart problems. I felt guilty for being annoyed with him. Of course he was tired—he was sixty-four. Life on the road was getting harder for him, too.

I thought of the guys he'd come up with in the magic world: Mac Regent, Eric Starr, David Standard. They all had cushy gigs at casinos in Las Vegas or Atlantic City. It wasn't the high life, but it was a stable one, doing what they loved six nights a week for a steady paycheck. Dad's epic fuckup on live TV had killed that dream for him. For us.

Just then, a fire truck shot past on I-20, the siren so piercing that I had to cover my ears.

Dad opened his eyes. "What's wrong? Are we there already?"

"Yeah," I said. "Why don't you splash some water on your face before we go in?"

The owner of Sunny's, Caroline, was pulling pints behind the bar. She was big and redheaded, with thick glasses and a wide smile, and she looked up at Dad as we approached.

"Sumbitch! What's it been, five years? How you been?"

"Six," Dad said, and kissed her hand.

Caroline laughed. "And you," she said, turning to me. "You were a knobby-kneed little foal last time I saw you. Ain't you something now. Those brown eyes." She stroked my head like an old aunt, then looked at Dad. "Better get this one on the pill."

I tried to smile instead of vomiting on the bar. Dad turned pink.

Caroline's smile widened. "Are you hungry?"

I ate a pulled-pork sandwich the size of a car battery and drank a root beer in a frosty pint glass. I barely tasted either as I glanced around the roadhouse. It was a converted barn with a horseshoe-shaped bar at one end and an elevated stage at the other. The stage was big, and a cluster of lights clung to a truss overhead. I felt the first few butterflies begin to spread their wings in my stomach. I wouldn't be performing tonight—but for a moment, I pictured myself up there, and my nerves began to hum.

The song on the jukebox ended, and in the momentary silence, "Umbrella" started up again in my head. *Ella, ella, eh, eh, eh . . .* It was for the best that I wouldn't be performing. Maybe I would just curl up in the RV and try to sleep.

Caroline grabbed a remote from behind the bar and clicked it, and the lights on the truss came on, bathing the stage in a deep blue. I saw a drum set and two amplifiers sitting upstage.

"Looks like this place is more of a rock bar now," I said. "Are people really going to be into a magic show?"

Caroline smiled. "So long as *you're* onstage, pretty thing, I don't think there'll be any complaints."

I shot Dad a look—but he didn't meet my eye.

"Of course she will be," Dad said.

The root beer turned to acid in my stomach.

I strode across the field to the RV, making Dad jog after me. I went straight into my shoebox of a bedroom and slammed the accordion door. A moment later, I heard Dad enter and move down the aisle. But when he got to the partition, he stopped and knocked gently on the wall. The only thing keeping him out was a flimsy plastic barrier, but he respected it. Somehow, that made me even angrier.

"Can we talk?"

I glared at his silhouette through the yellowing plastic panels. "About what?"

"About the show. About how you'd like it go." His voice was infuriatingly calm.

"I'm not doing it. That's how I'd like it to go."

He cleared his throat—a tell that indicated he was about to try to sell me.

"But you've gotten so good!" His stage baritone grated like nails on a chalkboard. "Caroline asked for you specifically. She said—"

I tore open the partition. "She what?"

Dad blinked. "She . . . asked for you when she booked the gig. She had seen the video of you doing close-up in Columbus, and wanted—"

"Did you tell her I would perform?"

Dad opened his mouth, closed it again.

"Did you?"

"I . . . Yes. I did." He straightened. "It's the only way she would book us."

I thought the veins in my neck might explode.

"You're in demand!" Dad said. "Think of it! Most performers would kill for that."

"I'm not a performer," I said, and this time I could hear the flatness in my voice. "Not anymore."

"Not a performer? That's absurd. I've seen the way your eyes light up before you step onstage."

And had he seen the way they darkened when I stepped off?

"I can't do it, Dad. I need something normal. A normal life."

"Your talent is a gift!" Dad shook his head, incredulous. "For Christ's sake, Ellie, it's in your *blood*."

I slammed my hand into the bunched-up accordion door, splitting one of the brittle plastic panels with a *crack*.

"And what else is in my blood, Dad? Heart attacks? Suicide? Are those gifts, too?"

He flinched, took a step backward, and sank into the booth seat.

"Ellie?" His voice was softer now, concern showing through the cracks in his bravado, but I didn't respond. Was it possible he didn't know how hard this was on me? After all my protests?

Outside, the generator hummed. Traffic rushed by on the interstate.

Yes, it was possible. It was the only explanation, really; whatever his faults, Dad loved me. He wanted what was best for me, even as he pushed me toward what was worst. And I had never told him, not in clear terms. So of course he didn't know.

I could fix that right now. I could say the words: *I'm not well enough to perform. I can't face the aftermath.*

I'm afraid it might kill me.

But we needed this money. This show was our only lifeline.

I looked at his face. He seemed smaller now, deflated. His mustache was wilted, not at all the bristle brush it had been when I was a little girl. Suddenly, I wished I were that little girl again. That I didn't face these impossible decisions. I wished someone else would step up and take charge. I wished someone else were here to take care of Dad, to take care of us both.

"I'm not her," I said. "I'll never be her."

Then, out of the quiet, he whispered, "I know it."

The words were like a cold blade in my chest. I moved forward and dropped onto the couch across from him.

"But what if I am?" I tried to swallow, but my throat was too swollen. "What if I'm *exactly* like her?"

He looked up, his eyes swimming. "That's not what I meant. She was . . ." He shook his head as if he couldn't bear to talk about her. "You're strong. And resilient. She . . ."

"She what?"

Dad pressed his lips together, as if he wanted to hold back what he was about to say. "She had a darkness about her, Ellie. A darkness you could never be capable of. Not in a hundred years."

But I *was* capable. I knew it, and I wondered what it meant that he didn't.

He leaned forward and looked me in the eye. "She was never a magician, Ellie. But you are."

My whole body seemed to contract. "What if I don't want to be?"

What if I can't?

Dad scrubbed a finger across his mustache, then let his hands drop into his lap. "I don't think any of us gets to choose what we are. For better or for worse." He looked at me. "But if you don't want to do magic, I won't force you to."

I stared out the small window over the booth. The sun was just going down, and the roadhouse's big neon sign flickered to life, its red and blue piping reflecting off the hoods of the pickup trucks like an electric flag.

Dad got to his feet. "I'll go explain things to Caroline.

Call it off. Don't worry, we'll find another—"

"No," I said. "No. I'll do it."

As soon as the words were out, I'd known I was going to say them all along. I was already headed for a crash—there was no preventing it now—and that stage was calling to me. I *wanted* to do it. I needed to feel alive.

He turned to me, his eyes cautious but sparkling. "Are you sure?"

"Yes."

"That's wonderful, Ellie."

"But this . . ." I licked my lips, already feeling my heart rate start to climb in anticipation of the performance. And of the descent that would follow. The rest of the sentence came out almost a whisper. "This is the last time, okay?"

His smile dimmed slightly, but he nodded. "Deal."

The disappointment on his face pushed the cold blade in deeper, but I ignored the pain and stood.

"We'd better get to work."

The windows darkened, and the lights in the parking lot flickered on. Dad and I spent the hour after dusk reworking the set list, adding more close-up bits to leverage my talents.

When it came to performing, my gift was legerdemain. Sleight of hand. Anyone could be the girl in the box, but when you could vanish an object right in front of someone's eyes? That was real magic. Dad was good with coins and cards, too—but I was better. It's what made me a good thief when I had to be.

As I practiced, visualizing the audience's reactions, I felt my heart rate climb even further. My vision grew sharp around the edges. Dad was right. Performing did light me up, just a little too brightly. I forced myself to take slow, deep breaths. The higher I got during the performance, the farther I had to fall.

With an hour left till curtain, I retreated into my room to get ready. I closed the cracked accordion partition, sat down on my bed, and faced the small mirror Dad had mounted on the opposite wall.

The thing I hated most about my appearance was my nose. It was long and masculine and belonged on the face of a French waiter. Apart from that, I resembled old photos of my mother: high cheekbones, mahogany eyes, almost-black hair. Suddenly, I couldn't stand to see her face in my mirror. I opened the cheap plastic toolbox I used for a makeup kit and went to work, eyebrows first, then eyes, then lips. I brushed my hair out long, smoothed it out with baby oil, and let it hang free, a dark brown curtain.

I took a last look in the mirror, and then it was showtime.

CHAPTER 9

I COULD HEAR THE AUDIENCE laughing from where I lay folded inside the trunk. Dad had finished his opening bit, dropping the toy truck into the fish tank. And by the sounds the audience was making, it had worked; they were on his side now.

The lights came up, their red glare shining through the seams in the trunk. My pulse accelerated. Sparks seemed to pop inside the darkness of the box. My mind's eye pulled back like a camera, and I visualized the show as if watching it from high above the stage.

Music blares through the speakers—Ella Fitzgerald's "That Old Black Magic." Dad moves downstage and snatches a playing card out of thin air, then another. He squares up the pair, then fans them out, revealing a dozen. The audience applauds. With the strike of a match he sets the fanned-out cards ablaze, then smashes his hands together.

When he separates them again, he's suddenly holding an oversized deck—custom Rider Backs twelve inches high. The applause swells, then fades, and his patter begins.

Dad's stage baritone rumbled through the subwoofer, and I felt its vibration against my rib cage. It brought me back to myself.

Dad selected a volunteer, and the audience laughed as a pair of what sounded like work boots tromped up the stairs and onto the stage. I listened as the volunteer picked a card, then returned to his seat.

Next came the false reveal, where Dad would draw the ace of spades from the deck.

"Is this your card?" he asked.

"Nope!" replied Work Boots. The audience laughed uncomfortably.

"Oh, dear. Let me see . . ." I pictured Dad's well-rehearsed frown as he thumbed through the deck again, this time plucking out the queen of diamonds.

"Voilà!" he said.

"That's not it, either." A titter in the crowd. A few boos.

"Wait, wait. I have it." Now Dad's footsteps approached the box I was hiding inside. He produced a big brass key, unlocked the padlock, and flipped open the lid. I couldn't make out his features against the glare of the lights, but I knew he was smiling down at me.

He backed away as I rose, unfolding myself from the box and raising my arms in a victorious V. On the front of my bodysuit was emblazoned the volunteer's card: the nine of hearts.

The lights were blinding, and in the black void beyond their glare the audience exploded in cheers and applause. My face split in a wide smile, and I felt the hairs on the back of my neck stand on end. The adrenaline was pumping now, coming on too fast. I gritted my teeth and tried to hold steady.

Dad's voice drew reality back into focus as he launched into the patter that introduced Linking Rings.

We had switched our usual roles; tonight Dad was the foil, yanking at his solid steel rings in a vain effort to separate them, while I slipped mine apart with ease to whistling and cheers. My pulse climbed higher. I felt light inside, as if a helium balloon were inflating in my chest. When Linking Rings ended, I moved downstage to interact with the audience; now it was time for my kind of magic.

I started small, approaching the bartender to order a shot, which I had him drink before I vanished the glass by slapping it flat into the bar top. Then I moved into the audience and found the bartender's watch on the wrist of a woman in the front row. I returned it to the barman, only to find the woman's iPhone in his back pocket.

Next came my take on Card to Fruit, barroom style. I had a biker pick a playing card, sign it, and place it securely in his girlfriend's purse. Then I crossed back to the bar and grabbed a lemon from a bin on the counter. Borrowing a paring knife, I sliced it open and pulled out the biker's card. I held it up so the audience could see his signature on the back, now wet with lemon juice. There was even a seed stuck to it.

The cheers were deafening; the audience was with me

now, eating out of my hand. My heart beat in my throat as if I'd just sprinted four city blocks. I was high, racing at the speed of light.

Next, I found a man wearing a Chicago Bears cap. I pulled it off his balding head, reached inside, and extracted the shot glass I had slapped into the bar. Then I took a silk from my pocket and draped it over the glass. I reached down for the fifth of Wild Turkey bourbon I was supposed to produce from under the silk—but as I was bringing it up, it slipped out of my hand and shattered on the tabletop, soaking the guy's lap in whiskey.

My face went cold—but Bears Cap was so hammered that he just laughed it off. I laughed along with him; I'd gotten lucky. I shrugged, playing it off like the spill was intentional, and mopped his shirt with the silk handkerchief before making it disappear into my fist.

It was a huge gaffe—and even though the audience had laughed, I could tell they were uncomfortable now. Embarrassed. I was losing them. The balloon in my chest had become overinflated, and my breath came in short gasps as I made my way back to the stage.

The lights dimmed, and the slow-motion ricochet beat of Tori Amos's "Hey Jupiter" began to thump through the speakers. I locked my thumbs together and raised my hands over my head, making the shadow of a bird on the back curtain. When I separated my fingers, a live white dove burst forth and flew in an arc around the audience. They applauded as the bird returned to alight on a perch upstage.

I remember that first dove; after that, I lost myself in the movement of my arms and the breeze of white wings as I produced dove after dove, until a dozen perched upstage. When the song ended, the applause broke over me like sunshine, like a cold ocean wave. I was trembling, my limbs tingled, and my vision twitched at the edges like the picture on an old TV. I couldn't remember the last time I had felt this way—and yet the sensations were familiar, as if they'd been hiding just beneath my skin, waiting to erupt and take me over. I wanted to feel this way forever.

The lights dimmed, and distorted guitars grated against a throbbing beat as Dad walked onstage. He approached the trunk I had appeared in at the top of the show and spun it, showing all four sides to the audience. Again he produced the large brass key, this time using it to lock the trunk.

I invited Work Boots back onstage to inspect the setup. When he was satisfied, he returned to his seat.

Dad climbed onto the lid holding the top edge of a white Kabuki cloth. He smiled, then raised the cloth over his head, hiding himself from view.

A moment later, the curtain dropped. The music stopped. Dad was gone.

Silence fell. And then a pounding came from inside the trunk, so hard it rattled the padlock; Dad had disappeared, then reappeared *inside the box*.

I spun the trunk to show it was still closed on all sides. Cheers and applause followed—but this was only the setup. Now I climbed onto the lid and lifted the curtain over my own head. I took a deep breath. I closed my eyes.

When the curtain dropped a second later, I had vanished,

and it was Dad standing on top of the trunk. The crowd in the barroom lost their minds as he stepped down, brandishing the big brass key. He released the padlock and flung open the lid. I emerged once more, arms raised in a triumphant V.

In that moment, I felt something shift inside me. Was it just the manic side of the bipolar coin taking its turn to face up? It made sense; cycles had been triggered by far less than applause and lights and the smell of bodies and beer. But what if it was something else? Something deeper? It was impossible to separate sense from sickness—and why bother when it felt so good?

My heart beat at a glorious gallop, like a filly's hooves pounding down the dandelions in an open field. For a fraction of a second, it seemed to me that everyone in the bar was synchronized. Like migratory birds banking in unison. Like wildflowers turning toward the sun.

I had done that.

I glanced at Dad, already feeling the smile that stretched my lips until I felt they might crack open.

The look on his face. Surprise. Pride.

We held hands and bowed, and a hundred people sounded like a thousand. I only made it halfway to the door before someone stopped me for a selfie. Then an autograph. Then a circle of people formed around me.

Dad insisted on loading out the small stuff by himself while I signed half a dozen cocktail napkins, a cell phone case, and some trucker's biceps. There were wolf whistles, too, and the drunk guy in the Bears cap tried to grab my ass, but his friends pulled him away. I was immune, invincible, thrumming like a tuning fork.

And then I spotted Liam.

He was leaning against a high table, smiling that smile of his and shaking his head. As I crossed the room toward him, I thought my heart might crack through my sternum.

"Ms. Dante," he said, tipping the brim of an imaginary hat. My knees gave a warning twinge, and I casually reached out to steady myself on a bar stool. Probably it was the heat of the lights and the rush of the performance. Probably.

"What are you doing here?" I asked.

He shrugged. "Our call was weird. I didn't want to leave things like that. So I Googled and saw that the Uncanny Dante was playing at Sunny's." His smiled faded a little. "I almost didn't come. I figured if you wanted me here, you'd have texted."

I bit my lip, trying to form a response.

"But then I figured what the hell, and I came anyway."

I gripped the back of the bar stool a little tighter. "I'm glad you did."

Just then, the jackass in the Bears cap staggered toward me yet again. Liam took a step forward and put a hand on the guy's shoulder. "Easy, bro. You look a little pukey."

The guy glared at Liam, sized him up, then stumbled out the door.

My eyes met Liam's. "My hero."

He shrugged. "I'm old-fashioned. It's a vice."

I laughed and held out my trap case. "Carry this for me?"

He took my case, and then he took my hand. As our palms pressed together, the tingling in my fingertips that had started during the show now spread up my arm.

Outside, the crowd had thinned, and most of the Harleys and pickups were clearing out. Liam and I set off across the parking lot, bathed in orange light. When we reached the relative darkness of the field where we had parked, my eyes took a moment to adjust—and then I noticed a misshapen shadow lying below the RV's front door, which stood open. I picked up my pace, and the shadow resolved.

It was Dad.

CHAPTER 10

I DROPPED LIAM'S HAND AND sprinted toward my father.

He lay on his side, eyes closed.

"Oh my God!" I fell to my knees and tapped his shoulder hard. "Dad? Are you okay?"

Nothing.

Liam caught up and knelt next to me, but I paid him no attention. I placed my hands on Dad's head and tilted it back to open the airway. I put my ear to his mouth. He was breathing.

"Dad!" I pressed down on his shoulder even harder. "Dad, wake up!"

Finally, he moaned, and my heart leaped into my throat.

"Oh my God, Dad. What happened? Are you okay?"

He blinked rapidly. "How embarrassing," he said. "I got a little light-headed, and then . . ."

Liam put a hand on my shoulder. "We should call an ambulance."

"No," Dad said. "That's not necessary. I only fainted. Probably just dehydrated." He propped himself up on his elbows as if that proved he was perfectly healthy.

"He's right, Dad. We ought to call 911. Your heart."

"My heart is fine. See for yourself." I put two fingers to his neck. He was right; his pulse was strong and regular.

"Okay," I said. "But I still think someone should take a look."

Liam got to his feet. "There was a guy inside earlier wearing an EMT uniform. Maybe he's still here. Hang tight for a minute." He turned and trotted back toward the roadhouse.

Dad watched him, smiling. "That's quite a young man you've got there," he said.

"I haven't 'got' him, Dad."

I helped him up and guided him into the RV, my hands shaking. He practically collapsed on the couch, and I struggled to stay calm; he was so pale. I rummaged through the cabinet over the sink and found his prescription bottle. There were only five pills left.

He swallowed one with a gulp of water from a plastic cup, and then a knock came at the door. Liam entered with a compact man toting a red backpack.

"This is Kyle," Liam said. "Will you at least let him take a look?"

The EMT told us what we expected: that Dad's pulse and BP were normal. That there was no immediate danger, but we should get him to an ER all the same.

While Kyle packed up his blood-pressure cuff, Dad gave me a look. I knew what it meant; we'd been to the ER before. They would charge us five grand to run a battery of worthless tests. Then they'd tell us he was all right, but that he ought to see a cardiologist. The cardiologist would charge us another grand to tell us Dad needed to reduce stress, eat better, and take his meds.

We thanked Kyle, and Liam said he'd wait for me outside. When I turned back to Dad, his eyes were glistening.

"How are you feeling?" I asked.

"I'm fine," he said in a choked voice. "I'm more than fine."

I sat down, took his hand. "What is it?"

He smiled. "There are moments as a father when your child . . ." He blinked rapidly. "When your child reveals to you how very extraordinary she has become."

My heart seemed to inflate. "I shanked the bottle production. I'm lucky the guy was drunk."

Dad waved a hand. "That happens to everyone. You recovered. That's the thing. Besides . . . the watch, the phone. Brilliant! And the doves, Ellie. The doves . . ." He shook his head. "You were elegant." He laughed. The sound lit me up from the inside. "Your mother would have been proud."

We sat in silence for a minute. Dad's eyes got wet. Mine did, too. In that moment, I felt more connected than I ever had—to him, to her, to everything. I felt *alive*.

Did I feel this way because the meds had finally worn off? Was I, for the first time in a year, experiencing life, pure and unfiltered?

Was this how *she* had felt on her good days?

I wanted to sustain that feeling, to grab it and pull it toward me. I closed my eyes and took a deep breath, as if I could hold it in my lungs.

Dad coughed. I opened my eyes and looked down at him.

"They're right, you know," I said. "About seeing a doctor."

He patted my hand. "When we get to Las Vegas, I'll go and see Dr. Shah. She knows me. She'll give us a break on the fee."

"Promise?"

"I promise."

Half an hour later, I was sitting with Liam on an old railroad tie a few yards from the RV. Dad was sleeping, the parking lot had cleared out, and we were alone.

It was freezing outside, but under my thin hoodie my skin was burning. I moved closer to him until our arms touched and wondered if he could feel the heat. The big neon *SUNNY'S ROADHOUSE* sign buzzed, then went out, and my body thrummed as if it had absorbed the electricity.

"Now that it's over, are you freaking out?" he asked.

I shook my head. "I feel really good, actually."

"Well, you deserve to," Liam said. "You were incredible up there."

I didn't think I could smile any wider. It was like he knew exactly what to say to me.

"I couldn't keep my eyes off you," he went on. "It was like you were—"

I leaned in and pressed my lips against his.

He froze for a moment—and then he kissed me back. The warmth in my skin seemed to spread inward, heating me to the core. I put my hands on the sides of his face; his skin was cold by comparison. I inched forward, pressing against him, trying to get closer.

A second later, he pushed me away.

"What's wrong?" I asked.

"I just . . . I need a minute." Liam bowed his head and took a few deep breaths.

My own breath was coming fast and heavy. I wanted to kiss him again. His Mustang was the last car left in the lot; I had an impulse to lead him across the field and push him into the back seat. I looked at his face. His cheeks were flushed from the cold and the kissing, and his expression was a mixture of want and confusion.

"Why did you stop?" I asked. "Did I do something wrong?"

"Not at all. It's just . . . I feel sort of weird. I mean, your dad *just* passed out."

My insides seemed to shrink; he was right. Less than an hour ago, I thought my dad might be dead—and now all I wanted to do was make out with Liam. Hard. Embarrassment climbed up my throat. What was wrong with me?

And then it hit me: Of course I felt good. I felt *too* good. I hadn't been brilliant onstage, I hadn't tapped some vein of hidden talent, and this wasn't a normal postperformance adrenaline high. I was just *up*.

"You want to tell me what's going on?" Liam said.

I stared out at the dark field. This good feeling I had—it was an illusion. A lie. A symptom.

"Ellie?"

"I'm . . ." I swallowed the word. I didn't want to hear it in my own voice. "When I'm up, like I am now, everything feels great. Better than great. It's like being on a lucky streak. Only I can't leave the casino with my winnings; I have to keep playing until I lose it all. It's part of my . . ." Senselessly, I gestured at my head. "Performing triggers it, like taking a drug. But then I crash, and it's . . ." I pressed my lips together and looked away. I didn't want him to see my face. "It's what killed my mom."

I still hadn't said the words. *Bipolar. Suicide.* I expected Liam to ask for an explanation. But he just said, "I'm sorry," and put his arm around me.

He was too perfect. Something had to be wrong with him.

"It's okay," I said. "I was a kid when it happened."

Liam nodded, then just sat there with me for a minute, silent, maybe waiting for me to go on, maybe waiting for the right moment to disentangle himself from the crazy girl and escape.

I blurted, "I'm going to California."

Liam raised his eyebrows. "Why didn't you say so before?"

I stared down at my stage shoes, now covered in dust from the dirt lot. "I guess I thought it would put weird pressure on . . . whatever this . . . on us."

"Oh," he said. In the silence that followed, every doubt I'd ever had about myself seemed to reverberate.

Then Liam laughed, and I flinched.

"You are full of surprises," he said. "On our video call it seemed like you were sort of done with me."

"Then why did you come tonight?"

He shrugged. "In case you weren't."

I shook my head. He was so fucking charming; it threw me off balance. What did he see in me? What did I have to offer that he couldn't get from a university full of California girls?

"How about this," he said. "Let's just talk on the phone. Text. Maybe, if you feel like it, we Skype. Then, when you get to California—totally up to you—maybe you ghost me, or maybe we go get In-N-Out." He made a gesture like balancing a set of scales.

I stared at him.

"Because they don't have Culver's in LA," he said.

"I'm . . ." The rest of my sentence evaporated off the tip of my tongue. "That sounds nice."

"Nice," he agreed.

And then he leaned forward and kissed me. This time, the tingles spread way farther than just my arms.

When we broke off, I asked, "Can I walk you to your car?"

"Better not," he replied.

"Yeah. You're probably right."

From the steps of the RV, I watched him cross the parking lot. Just before he got into his Mustang, he looked back and smiled. Then he got in, started the engine, and drove off.

I wanted to freeze the moment and put it in a snow globe, preserve it, keep it as an amulet against darker times, something to remind me how good life could be. I wanted so hard to enjoy the feeling of having been kissed, of having a maybe boyfriend, of this normal teenage moment—but I couldn't. Already I could feel the low rumble of the down approaching like a thunderhead. There would be no normal for me, not really, only a series of low hills and valleys punctuated by an occasional peak like tonight. Was that worth living for?

Right now, it was.

My heart was pounding when I got back into the RV, the scent of sandalwood still sharp in my nostrils. I tasted adrenaline like pennies against my back teeth. I needed to do something. Run a marathon. Burn down a cornfield.

The props. I could secure the props.

My mind was cranking now, already going to work on the problem. It was only nine p.m. in Las Vegas; Higgins would be up. I pulled on a beanie, went back outside, and tapped the number Ripley had sent me. Higgins answered on the first ring.

"Who the hell is this?" There was a rustling of plastic and the sound of openmouthed chewing.

"Hi, Mr. Higgins," I said, trying to sound casual. "My name is—"

"How did you get this number?"

"I, um . . ." I decided on impulse that the truth would be best. "I used an investigator."

He barked with laughter. "All right, well, now I have to get a new number. Kindly piss off."

"Wait! Mr. Higgins, I have an offer for you."

More rustling of plastic, then: "What do you have?"

"Actually, it's something *you* have."

Higgins made a hacking sound as if something had gone down the wrong pipe. "I don't sell. I'm a collector. I collect."

"I'm not looking to buy."

"What are you, a movie person? Try Cineprops on Maryland Parkway. I don't work with movie people."

"It's the truck."

Higgins paused. "What truck?"

"The 1947 Chevrolet. Cape Maroon. You acquired it after its final appearance on *Late Night with Craig Rogan*."

He was silent; I had his attention.

"I need to borrow it. And the Plexiglas tank."

He laughed. "You're funny. Who did you say this was?"

I hesitated. The truth might elicit questions I didn't want to answer. But he would find out sooner or later.

"My name is Elias Dante Jr."

"Dante." Another pause. "Oh. I get it. Looking to buy up Daddy's legacy before the old man kicks it and drives up the price?"

Wow. He really was an asshole.

"I don't want to *buy* them; I just . . ." I took a deep breath. "What if I told you the Uncanny Dante was going to do that trick again on live TV in nine days?"

"I'd say you're full of shit." Chewing noises.

"What if I could prove it?"

Slurping through a straw. "I guess I'd set my DVR."

I closed my eyes and clutched the phone tight in my hand.

"Mr. Higgins, I know you must get strange opportunities all the time. But the one I'm about to present will double the value of your property. Maybe triple it."

There was a long silence. And then Higgins said, "I'm listening."

CHAPTER 11

I WOKE TO UNWELCOME SUNLIGHT on my face. The tang of diesel. A heaviness in my chest.

I rolled over on my vibrating bed and reached for my phone. It was almost one p.m.; we'd been on the road a day and a half since leaving Mishawaka. A day and a half, and not a single message from Liam. He'd sent the most recent one the morning after we'd made out on that railroad tie:

Last night was better than great.

He'd used my own words, and that had made me feel light, somehow, as if my heart were impervious to gravity. Now it was a bowling ball. I was an idiot to think he'd actually wanted to see me when I got to California. He had felt sorry for me, that was all—but it had worn off, and he had moved on.

I sat up. My head felt full of cotton, my legs lead. I

crawled out of bed and looked out the window: barren farmland rushed past, punctuated by rotting barns and corroding aluminum lean-tos. Google Maps put us just outside Elk City, Oklahoma. Dad had stopped for diesel twice since leaving Indiana, which meant our bankroll was almost gone. We were bound for Las Vegas, but we would run out of gas long before we got there.

We had no money, no props, and Higgins's price was impossible.

When he'd finally understood that I really did want to borrow Dad's old props, he had begrudgingly agreed to rent them to us—for the outrageous price of five thousand dollars. I accepted—what choice did I have? But now I was back where I'd started: five grand short.

I stumbled to the bathroom, stopped up the sink, and filled it with water. I plunged my face under the surface and counted until my lungs began to burn.

When I emerged a few minutes later, I could hear Dad whistling something old and jazzy. It was piercing to my ears.

"There she is," he called from the driver's seat. "I've got coffee up here." He resumed whistling.

I made my way to the passenger seat, dropped into it, and took a sip of tepid coffee. My neurons twitched and slowly came to life.

"You were out for fourteen hours." He looked over at me with that Concerned Father expression. "Are you all right?"

I got the feeling Dad had been mostly blind to my mother's mood swings, just as he seemed mostly blind to mine. Even when he managed to detect that something was wrong, he handled me clumsily. *Are you all right?* he asked, as if my mental health had a check-engine light. *Are you all right?* asked in a hopeful tone, putting the impetus on me to reassure him.

"I'm fine." My voice was worn gravel.

I had heard that other parents lamented their teenagers' defiance. My defiance was a relief to Dad. It excused him from having to worry.

He nodded half-heartedly, accepting my response without appearing to believe it. He was subdued for a moment, maybe out of respect for my dark mood, but after a few minutes he started whistling again. I considered dumping my hot coffee into his lap. That would shut him up. I noticed he was bouncing his knee and realized: he was giddy, probably at the thought of returning to Las Vegas for a two-night engagement. An engagement, I reminded myself, that didn't exist. There was a real gig coming, of course—but between here and there were five thousand dollars, twelve hundred miles, and one big lie.

I checked my phone; no notifications. Not from Liam, not even from Ripley. I thought of the sink full of water. I fished a pair of gas-station sunglasses from the glove compartment, put them on, and closed my eyes.

We pulled into the Amarillo KOA an hour before dusk, gravel crunching under the tires. There was a cluster of faux log cabins, a sandbox for kids, a pond that would've been infested with mosquitoes a month prior. I checked in at the lodge and paid for one night in cash. Got the Wi-Fi password and a key to the restrooms.

I stood in the shower in my faded flip-flops, watching the water circle the mildewed drain. Thirty seconds in, the hot water ran out and ice-cold pins and needles rained down on me. We had run out of shampoo, so I was using a bar of Irish Spring I'd found in the stall—but my hair was too greasy from the baby oil. I needed real shampoo. I needed hot water. I needed a shower that didn't require shoes.

The soap slipped from my hand and landed on the filthy tile with a *clack*. I bent over to retrieve it, only to see that it had collected a nest of black hair. I gagged, stood up, covered my mouth. It was disgusting, living like this. I couldn't take it.

I couldn't take it.

My shoulders began to tremble, and I stuffed my washcloth in my mouth to muffle the oncoming sobs. I leaned against the stall door to brace myself for the fit, but it didn't come. Instead, I had only a shallow, ragged cry; the kind that brought no relief and only mattered because it couldn't be contained. When it had passed, I rinsed my face in the spray and turned off the water. I walked back to the RV, heavy and hollow and raw.

Dad closed his journal and looked up. "Ellie?"

Ella, ella, eh, eh, eh . . .

"You look awful. What's the matter, really?"

Are you all right?

"I'm just tired." My voice sounded flat.

"But you slept all day."

"Teenagers need more sleep. It's a medical fact." I had tried to add some inflection, but it came out sounding dull.

"I don't buy it," Dad said. "And I'm concerned. You're still taking your medication, aren't you?"

Wow, I wanted to say. *Do you really not know? Or are you just in denial?* I supposed it didn't matter. Either way, there was nothing he could do about it.

"Nope," I said, giving him a flat look. "The doves looked manic. I've been feeding it to them."

His frown wilted, and now he looked confused. A lost, sad old man. "I'm only trying to help. Please, tell me what's really bothering you."

"Really?" I said, raising my eyebrows. "What's *really* bothering me?" I held up my threadbare towel. "I just took a cold shower in a filthy stall with a bar of soap I found on the floor."

Dad opened his mouth, but I cut him off with a gesture toward the accordion door.

"The only privacy I get is a plastic screen." My voice was rising, thinning out like a high note through a reed. "I'm flunking school because I only get internet every third day, and I haven't bought new clothes since I was fifteen. Oh, and I live in a *FUCKING RV*!"

Dad bolted to his feet. "Watch your tongue, young lady." His voice was acid. "I'm sorry you weren't born to a family of accountants with a trust fund. But in *this* family, we are artists. And artists don't always have the luxury of—"

"Artists?" I said, barely containing a laugh. "You think we're *artists*? We make more money robbing gas stations than we do performing 'art.'"

Dad's face blanched.

I should have stopped. Apologized. I should have told him

the truth, that I was out and low and standing on the edge.

Instead, I goaded him.

"What are you going to do now, send me to my room?" I gestured again at the flimsy partition. "Don't bother. I'm already going."

I took two short, exaggerated steps and slammed the plastic door with a weak *click*.

Dad made no further effort to talk to me that night; he must have been truly furious. Around eleven, I slid open the door to find him asleep on his couch. I tried to sleep, too, but my mind was still spinning from the fight, replaying every terrible thing I had said. We had never fought like that before—not ever—and a low, heavy dread settled on my heart. He'd been trying to help, and I had not only pushed him away, I had hurt him, deeply. I'd made him feel like a failure as a parent, and then I'd struck the death blow, belittling the thing he cared about most: being a magician. It was all he had left. What if he never forgave me? My eyes ached. My limbs were leaden. I felt like downed power lines.

I rolled over, opened my bedside drawer, and stared at the empty orange cylinder inside. I had taken my last pill four days ago—how long before the drug was completely out of my system? I retrieved my phone from the floor and Googled it. WebMD said three to five days.

Maybe that's why everything seemed so impossible.

With Dad snoring on the couch, I slipped outside and walked across the gravel lot to the picnic area. It wasn't as cold here as it had been in northern Indiana, and I lay down on one of the tables to stare up at the low charcoal clouds. A warm Texas breeze picked up, and for a moment, it was like being back in Las Vegas.

Mom had loved the desert. Sometimes in the summer she would wake me up and take me for a midnight drive. After buying two cups of hot cocoa from the 7-Eleven, she would head west on Flamingo, past the Strip, and into the darkness. We would pull off the road and lie side by side in the bed of her old Toyota pickup, staring up at the stars. She would point out constellations: Ursa Major, Cassiopeia, Orion. Usually, I fell asleep.

I don't think she ever did.

I sat up suddenly, blood rushing to my head. Those little drives—our "insomniac adventures," she had called them—must have happened when she was manic. Why had it taken me so long to realize? I lay back down, searching the sky for Orion, but all I saw were clouds.

If her mania was responsible for all those good times, did it make them less real? Less special? If I dismissed all the valleys as flukes of neurochemistry, didn't that make the peaks just as meaningless?

Mom would have known the answer. She had known all the answers, until she threw them away. I twisted a lock of hair in my fist and pulled until my eyes stung. *No crying,* she would've said. *Beauty hurts. Might as well get used to it.* I'd always thought she was talking about brushing hair, wearing tight clothes and uncomfortable shoes—all the inconveniences you had to bear and the sacrifices you had to make when you were a girl in the world of performing. But lying there, staring up at the west Texas sky, inhaling the warm breeze, I thought I knew better now. I felt connected to her words somehow, a thousand miles away and ten years dead. Beauty *did* hurt. Just noticing how things were, experiencing them fully, was painful for people like her and me, and probably always would be.

My phone buzzed. Probably it was just Ripley wanting to chat, and I didn't feel like talking. It buzzed again, and I reluctantly pulled it from my pocket. My heart seized. It was a text from Liam.

> Really sorry. Crazy couple of days. Will try to call tomorrow.

Dumbstruck, I stared at the glowing screen. What the fuck. *Crazy couple of days?* What did that even mean? *Will try to call?*

I clutched the phone to my chest and squeezed my eyes shut. I was an idiot. If Liam were really interested in me, he would have texted before now. I should have trusted my instincts. All that flattery, all that making me feel special—it had been nothing more than misdirection. A lie that was more satisfying than the truth.

And what did it matter? What did Liam matter, after what had just happened with Dad?

All at once, loneliness descended on me like a shroud. I started to type out a reply but deleted it. Composed another, and deleted that, too. I felt my mind slowing down, my thoughts beginning to corkscrew. I turned my head to look at the man-made pond. The water was black, and I couldn't see the bottom. How deep was it? A foot? Eighteen inches? Deeper than a sink, anyway. Deep enough.

I closed my eyes and imagined how it would feel as the surface crept over my lips, my nose, my eyes, sealing me off from the air above. I had held my head under the surface a hundred times but never had the courage to inhale. Would it burn when the cold water hit my lungs? Would I let it take me, or would I cough and sputter and fight to survive?

My doctor in Indianapolis had given a name to this particular loop of thought. He called it suicidal ideation, and I was supposed to consider it an alarm bell. I was supposed to reach out. Only I didn't feel like reaching out. I wasn't even sure I had the energy to type the pass code into my shitty phone and place a call. I felt myself tipping downward, as if I'd reached a steep slope and tapped the brakes, only to find they didn't work.

I rolled over, got to my feet, and walked toward the pond. I had the National Suicide Prevention Lifeline in my contacts, but I had never used it. I told myself that if I did, I would be one step closer. I'd be a statistic.

I took another step toward the edge of the water and held out my phone, daring myself to drop it in, to sever my connection with the outside world.

Then I pulled it back, unlocked the screen, and called Ripley.

It rang four times and went to voice mail. I smacked the phone against my forehead.

It was midnight. He hadn't answered. I was alone. The

water drew my eyes again—and the phone rang in my hand.

"Ellie? Are you all right?"

I managed only a croaking whisper. "No."

"Okay. I'm here. Hold on."

I heard the scrape of his window opening and a faint chorus of crickets.

"I'm back," he said. "Talk to me."

I could hear how toneless my voice was as I told him about my fight with Dad and Liam's withdrawal. I felt the pain, but it was dull and distant. I didn't feel sad, just tired.

Ripley had experienced many parental blowouts and assured me the thing with my dad would work itself out. But then he fell silent. After a long pause, he said, "I'm not sure it's fair to blame Liam for backing off."

I gaped. "Wait, you're siding with him?"

"No. Of course I'm on your side. I'm always on your side. And if you want me to hate this guy, I will hate him with all the fury in my soul. But think about how this went down. You wouldn't give him your phone number, but he called you anyway. And when you left Fort Wayne, you refused to tell him where you were going—but he drove across the state to show up at your gig. Then he basically asked you to be his girlfriend, and you were sort of *well, okay* about it. I'm not saying I know anything about relationships, but it seems like you kind of set the tone here."

My jaw tightened; he was right. I had sent Liam a barrage of mixed signals, advances and retreats. Of course he'd backed off. I'd been acting like the crazy person I so desperately wanted not to be.

I couldn't think of what to say to Ripley, couldn't separate the tangled strands of thought in my head. I closed my eyes and grasped one single thread, one thought that explained everything.

"I'm out of meds."

"Oh, no," Ripley said. "Shit, Ellie. I didn't . . . Don't listen to me. I don't know what I'm talking about."

I should have reassured him, let him off the hook, but I couldn't.

"I take everything back. He's a douche canoe, Ellie. A leaky, sinking douche canoe."

"He's not a douche canoe." I spoke in a monotone.

"An ass raft, then."

This time, a flat laugh escaped me. "Okay. He's an ass raft."

Ripley let out a dramatic sigh. "Thank God. I wanted to stay on theme, but I was running out of boat-related insults."

I laughed again, and this time I sounded more human. I sat down, not caring that the moist earth was soaking into my jeans. The clouds must have parted, because now the moonlight made the surface of the pond look like a silver blanket spread out among the weeds.

"I'm not going to vomit advice on you, okay? I mean, you definitely shouldn't search guided meditation on YouTube or treat yourself to a candy bar or walk in the sun. Do none of those things."

I managed to smile.

"Wallow, Ellie. Wallow and sulk like a Morrissey fan at a steakhouse."

I expected to laugh again, but it came out choked. "Thanks, Ripley."

"I'm kidding, you know. You should do all those things. And you should tell your dad, and get back on your meds ASAP."

"I know," I said, knowing I would do none of it.

"If you get caught in one of your spirals—promise you'll call me."

Half-heartedly, I promised. But my mind had already moved on.

It was ridiculous to be worried about some boy and whether he liked me; I had real problems. Problems that couldn't be solved by a walk or a candy bar.

"We're fucked, Ripley. We're so fucked."

"What? You're the opposite of fucked. You just booked a five-figure gig on TV."

I covered my face with my free hand. "We'll never get there. We have less than three hundred dollars left."

"We can work with that. You're just going to have to run another diesel grift."

"It won't matter. Even if we had the gas, Higgins wants five grand for the props. We don't have it. We can't get it. It's impossible."

Ripley blew out a breath. "Five *grand*?"

"Yes."

"Mother effer."

I could almost hear the gears cranking in his head.

"Ellie, are you sitting down right now?"

"Yeah, why?"

"Get up and move your body. Do it."

With a great effort, I hauled myself to my feet and started making a lap around the pond. Almost immediately, I felt a little better. "Thank you."

"Right. We need to focus. Priority one is getting to Las Vegas. That means a gig or a diesel grift."

I sighed. "A diesel grift is risky. And now that we have a chance at a real payday, we have more to lose if we get caught."

"Then a gig it is. Where have you played between Amarillo and Vegas?"

I tried to think, but my brain seemed to be suspended in molasses.

Ripley didn't wait for my reply. "I'm going to start calling out towns. Albuquerque."

I blinked. There was a good theater in town, but no way we could fill it. "No."

"Roswell? Las Cruces? Flagstaff?"

"We played Flagstaff once. But it was years ago."

"Where?"

"Some casino. Big Arrow? Long Arrow? I can't remember."

"Lone Arrow. Pulling up their calendar now." I heard furious typing in the background. Naturally, Ripley had taken his laptop out on the roof. "Okay, the main auditorium is booked through Christmas. But both lounges have openings during the next three days. I'm sending you the booking contact now."

I put him on speaker and checked my email. "It's Sharon.

I know her. I'll call her first thing tomorrow."

"Nope. You're emailing her now, before you lose steam."

I took a deep breath. My chest was impossibly heavy. "Ripley . . . even if we get a gig, it won't be enough. We need *five thousand dollars.* There's no way—"

"One thing a time, Ellie. Book that gig."

I scrubbed at my eyes with the back of my hand. "Thank you, Ripley. I don't know what I'd do without you."

"I know. I'm your personal ginger Jesus."

He stayed on with me until I sent the email. Then he made me swear I would call him at the first hint of "baddish feelings." I promised—but I knew that if things got *really* bad, I wouldn't want to call anyone. That's just how it went.

Immediately after I hung up, the loneliness descended again. My head buzzed, my hands tingled, and my limbs felt waterlogged and heavy. The conversation with Ripley hadn't been a cure; it had been a Band-Aid—just enough to keep me from bleeding out. I needed more. I needed help. So I unlocked my phone again and called the Suicide Prevention Lifeline. They stayed on with me until almost two a.m.

CHAPTER 12

OVER OATMEAL AND COFFEE THE next morning, I told Dad about the potential gig in Flagstaff. I expected him to celebrate, or at least to show relief—but instead he acknowledged the news with only a grim nod. Probably he was still stung from our fight.

We filled up at a TA truck stop, and then Dad piloted the RV west on US 40. I felt an impulse to apologize for what I'd said yesterday, but it was shunted aside by a swell of resentment. What would he have done if I hadn't booked yet another gig? Just driven west until we ran out of gas? He had no plan; he'd just woken up and waited for me to fix our problems.

I felt a sudden pressure squeezing my lungs. Was I in charge now? Was it was up to me to handle everything? What if Dad got sick or had another heart attack and couldn't work—how would we get by then? He had to have realized what we were facing—yet he just drove on cluelessly westward, assuming the way would unfold before him. I wondered if he had been so ridiculously optimistic with Mom. I wondered if she'd ever wanted to strangle him like I did now.

I forced myself to take a deep breath. We had six days to raise five grand, acquire one-of-a-kind props from a stingy recluse, and transport it all to LA. I needed to get to work.

I couldn't count on the Lone Arrow gig because I hadn't heard back from Sharon yet. So with the help of strong coffee and constant text-message encouragement from Ripley, I managed to call a handful of other venues en route. Two were already booked. A third made me an offer, but the money wasn't enough to justify the detour. The rest refused to hire Dad because of his reputation. We were out of luck and out of options; everything now hinged on this one casino gig.

I put down the phone, tugged at my hair, and stared out the window at the desert. Maybe it was time to tell him—about Flynn & Kellar, about being out of meds, about everything. Sooner or later we needed to rehearse the Truck Drop, and we could've been spending our time on the road talking through it instead of giving each other the silent treatment. I bit my lip and glanced toward the front of the RV. I detected anger in the stiffness of Dad's neck and the tilt of his head. I couldn't tell him. Not yet. I would wait until the props were secure. Until I had the money figured out.

Three hours into the drive, Grace Wu called, and I had to pretend it was a friend from school while I retreated into my shoebox to go over the paperwork for *Flynn & Kellar's*

Live Magic Retrospective. It was all boilerplate stuff, but seeing the dates and the amounts in print suddenly made everything real.

PERFORMANCE DATE: OCTOBER 30,
4 P.M. CALL, 7 P.M. SHOW
LOAD-IN, TECH REHEARSAL:
OCTOBER 28, 2 P.M.–8 P.M.

Jesus. We had to be in LA in *four days.* Time was moving impossibly fast.

APPEARANCE FEE: $5,000
BONUS UPON SUCCESSFUL
PERFORMANCE: $10,000
MAXIMUM PAYOUT: $15,000

As I stared at the numbers, it occurred to me that if Higgins didn't drop his price, the five-thousand-dollar appearance fee would be a wash. The publicity from another epic failure might generate some gigs, but not for long. Six months from now, we'd be back where we'd started.

Which meant we actually had to pull off the Truck Drop.

My brain couldn't process the added stress of this realization. I wanted to sleep, but instead I finished the paperwork, sent it back, then logged into my school website, dreading what I was about to see.

I had *three* new messages from teachers.

The deadline for my *King Lear* essay had passed; I could

submit it tomorrow for partial credit. Where was my Steinbeck report? Wouldn't it be a shame to let my grade slip further? If I didn't turn in my earth science summaries by midnight, I would receive a zero. Did I know I was in danger of failing?

I put my head down on the table. In danger of failing. That's precisely what I was.

In search of distraction, I picked up my phone—and then, stupidly, opened my text messages. I thumbed through my conversation with Ripley first, smiling at his clever wordplay, but eventually the temptation grew too strong and I opened my text chain with Liam. I reread his last message over and over, obsessively trying to extract some deeper meaning from his vague comments:

Really sorry. Crazy couple of days. Will try to call tomorrow.

Well, tomorrow was here, and he hadn't called. I told myself I should wait, that text messages couldn't convey tone, that I was overreacting. If I pinged him now, I would seem desperate. I just had to be patient. Wait for him to call.

I ignored my advice and started typing.

Hey. Sorry you've had crazy days. I know what that's like lol!

Ugh. I deleted the *lol.* It made me sound like a twelve-year-old.

I enjoyed our second "date." I've always wanted to make out on a railroad tie.

Was I really going to send this? Yes, I was. But first, I added:

If everything works out, I'll be in LA in four days. Are you still down for In-N-Out?

Then, before I could chicken out, I clicked Send.

I headed into the back to take a nap. If we booked the gig, I was going to be up late.

I had just closed my eyes when my phone rang. The call was from a northern Arizona area code.

"This is Ellie."

"Hi, it's Sharon at Lone Arrow Casino. How are you?"

My heart crawled into my throat.

Six years ago on our way to Las Vegas we'd played one night at Lone Arrow. I had looked it up in Dad's old gig log: They had paid us fifteen hundred dollars, *and* they'd comped a hotel room.

"I'm good," I said. "How are things up the mountain?"

"Getting colder," she said. "I got your message. It's not exactly high season here, but I'm sure we can do something. When are you coming through?"

I bit my lip. "Tonight, actually."

"Oh, jeez. I didn't realize."

I heard her flipping pages. My stomach turned over.

"I could bump the DJ and put you in the lounge. But it's

a Wednesday, and it'll be mostly kids from NAU. I'm not sure if that's your crowd."

A Wednesday wouldn't pay for the props, but it might get us to Vegas. Plus I could get back on Wi-Fi and try to catch up on school. Take a real shower. Raid the maid's cart for soap and conditioner.

"That's perfect," I said. "We've done colleges." One college, actually: a private school in northern Ohio, and it had been a disaster.

"Okay, great."

I closed my eyes and pumped my fist. "So, fifteen hundred plus a room. I'll email you the contract."

"Oh," she said, and my stomach flipped again. "I could do maybe a thousand on a Friday. But on a Wednesday same-day booking, the best I can do is a room and five hundred."

I felt myself deflate.

Sharon seemed to sense what was happening on my end. "I can comp dinner and breakfast. That's my best offer."

At the Flying J in Albuquerque, I bought coffee and two turkey-on-wheats. When we pulled back onto I-40 west, I texted Ripley: *Gig booked. NOW WHAT?*

He didn't reply, and I was left to thrash around in my own thoughts. We were still forty-five hundred dollars short. There were no more gigs to be had this close to Vegas—and unless we upgraded to grand larceny and actually raided a cash register, a grift wasn't going to cut it.

Earn and *steal* were out. That left *borrow* and *beg.*

The problem was, Dad's friends had evaporated after the

incident, and none of mine were rich. Except Liam—but I didn't think I could ask him, even if he did call me back. So it was down to *beg.* I would have to wait until we got to Las Vegas, and then I would throw myself on the mercy of Jif Higgins.

Maybe in a few hours, Dad and I would start speaking to each other again, even if only about the gig. Maybe when I told him about Flynn & Kellar, he wouldn't be angry but relieved that money was coming. I decided I would do it tonight, while he was still in the afterglow of performance.

I turned on my laptop, opened my earth science book, and started typing summaries. My focus was so erratic, the text might as well have been in Cyrillic. It was becoming clear: I was going to fail this semester. I stared at the screen until my eyes slipped out of focus. I tried to tell myself it was only a setback, but the math said different. A 3.0 was out of reach. I would have to go for my GED, then community college, *then* nursing school—but it would add two years to the timeline. Two years I didn't have.

Feeling powerless and lost, I slammed my laptop shut and moved to the front to stare at the road. Dad barely acknowledged my arrival. I looked over and noticed he was blinking rapidly.

"Dad. You're exhausted."

"The coffee will kick in." They were the first words he'd said to me all day, and I felt a rush of relief when he spoke them.

"Come on, Dad. You drank the dregs an hour ago. If you don't get some rest, you'll be no good for the show tonight. Go in the back. Put on some Brahms. Take a damn nap."

He sighed. "You're right. Of course."

We pulled over at the Route 66 Rest Stop. Dad went into the back, and I took the wheel.

Operating a forty-foot RV with a trailer is less like driving a car and more like piloting a sailboat. When the wind hits the side, it's like the sails are up, and every bump in the road is a ten-foot swell. It is not relaxing. You cannot put on a playlist and zone out. You white-knuckle the wheel and grit your teeth and swear at every pothole.

It was four forty-five p.m., and the sun was a blinding orange torch in the western sky when a shrill bleat issued from the front of the RV, making me jump in my seat. I shielded my eyes and glanced down at the dashboard. A warning light there burned red with the words:

WATER IN DIESEL
CLEAR FILTER AT ONCE

There was a button marked "RESET" on the dash. I pressed it, and the bleating stopped. I let out a heavy breath. It had to have been a false alarm; we'd filled up hundreds of miles ago at a reputable station, and Dad was always careful.

Then the bleating cut the air again, and I flinched, jerking the wheel. The right front tire made contact with the rumble strip on the edge of the pavement, and an angry, low-pitched buzz harmonized with the squealing dashboard alarm. I nudged the RV back into the lane, then reached up to reset the indicator a second time.

That's when the engine went dead.

The RV drifted right, picking up the rumble strip again,

vibrating the chassis like a jaw under a dental saw. I tightened my grip to correct course, but the power steering didn't respond. The front tire went off the edge of the asphalt and onto the soft shoulder. I stomped on the brake pedal—but the power brakes had failed, too. The wheel tugged at my grip; I resisted. The front bumper clipped a creosote bush. Then another. I was driving on dirt now, parallel to the highway but breaking away fast. We were headed straight for a third bush, and I couldn't turn the wheel. The bush went under the RV with a horrendous scraping sound.

I needed to get the power steering back online. I reached beneath the column and turned the ignition key. Nothing.

Shit.

The RV ran over more low scrub. The squeal of wood on metal was earsplitting. I turned the key again; nothing. I bounced in my seat as the left front tire ran over a skull-sized rock. The trailer tugged at the back end.

I tried the key a third time, and now the engine roared to life. I cranked the wheel, applied the brake. There was a sound of buckling metal, and then a tremendous *SNAP*, and my breath caught. The RV ground to a stop.

I sat there shaking, my heart thudding in my throat. Then I set the parking brake, unfastened my seat belt, and started toward the back.

"Dad?" I called out. "Dad!"

"Ellie!"

The accordion door opened, and Dad stood on the threshold looking pale and disoriented.

"Oh God. Dad, are you okay?"

"I'm fine," he said, leaning against the door frame. "What about you? Are you hurt?"

"I'm all right," I said, and saw a thin stream of blood trickle down from his scalp. "You're bleeding!"

He reached up to touch the spot. "That damn cabinet came open, and I hit my head on the corner of the door." He produced a handkerchief from his pocket and held it to the spot.

"You should sit," I said.

He waved a hand, dismissing my concern. "What happened?"

My calm seemed to crack all at once, and I collapsed into him, shaking. "There was an alarm—water in the fuel or something. The engine died, the steering locked up, and I couldn't turn. I tried, but . . . it just ran off the road!"

"It's all right," he said, kissing the top of my head. "It's all right. You're alive, I'm alive."

I pushed away, took a deep breath, looked around. My laptop was on the floor, along with Dad's journal and my empty thermos. The pantry door had slipped its bungee cord, spilling cans and boxes everywhere. A package of pasta had burst, scattering spirals across the aisle.

"We can clean up later," Dad said. "Let's go check out the damage while it's still light."

CHAPTER 13

THE TRAILER LAY ON ITS side in the dirt. The struts that had connected it to the hitch were twisted as if they had been wrung out by a giant. Dad retrieved his key ring and opened the padlock. We had to pry the door open.

The sub trunk lay in splinters on the trailer's side, which was now its floor, and Dad's trap case had come apart at the hinges. Coins and playing cards were strewn about like shrapnel. Miraculously, the dove cage had survived, and the twelve birds inside cooed indignantly.

I looked at Dad. His eyes didn't seem to be calculating damage, but rather, counting the dead.

"Dad," I said. "I'm so sorry."

I wanted his arm around me. I wanted him to tell me it was all right.

"See what you can you salvage," he said. "I need to check the bus."

My hands shook as I dug through the detritus, sorting out what could be saved and what was lost. I replayed the crash over and over. The dash lights going dead. The steering locking up. I should have braked sooner. I should have tried the ignition first.

Ella, ella, eh, eh, eh . . .

I began to pile the usable props on a tarp next to the bus; the hopeless remains I left in a heap inside the broken trailer. All the big stuff was wrecked: the guillotine, the sub trunk, the spike box. Thousands of dollars, hundreds of shows, all gone in a moment. The fishbowl Dad used for his mock truck drop had shattered. I grabbed the red toy truck, looked down at it in revulsion, and hurled it out into the desert, where it cracked and rolled to a stop in the dust. Then I turned back to the trailer. The close-up props and some of the smaller items—the lockbox, the collapsing chest—had survived the crash intact. Grand illusion wouldn't be in the program anymore, but we would still be able to put on a show.

The show. Lone Arrow. Shit.

I reached into my back pocket, but my phone wasn't there. It must still be on the bus, probably knocked to the floor when we went off the road. As I jogged toward the RV, I noticed that the engine hatch and the fuel filter compartment were open, but Dad was nowhere in sight.

I opened the door and then froze. Dad was standing on the top step with my phone pressed to his ear. He stared straight ahead and didn't acknowledge my presence.

"I see," he said into the phone. "No. That won't be necessary."

Finally, he looked down at me. I couldn't read his

expression, but he was paler now than he had been moments after the accident. I grasped the handrail and waited.

"Thank you." He ended the call and leaned heavily on the dash.

"Sharon from Lone Arrow called," he said.

My heart slowed: it hadn't been Flynn or Grace. Thank God.

"I explained about the accident. She understands. She'll book us some other night."

"That's good," I said.

Dad looked down at the phone. "Then another call came in. Las Vegas area code."

I stiffened.

"I thought it must be the Tack & Saddle." He inhaled sharply through his nose. "It was Jif Higgins."

The breath rushed out of my lungs like air from a breached spacecraft.

"He said—he said you tried to rent my old . . . that vehicle." Dad looked at me, his jaw tight.

This wasn't how he was supposed to find out. Not like this. Not now. He wasn't ready. *I* wasn't ready.

"He said you told him we'd booked a live television appearance. Flynn and . . . He . . ." A laugh burst out of him, a dry, ugly sound like an old car backfiring. "Ellie," he said, his lips drawn back in a grimace. "Tell me he's a liar."

I tightened my grip on the handrail, tried to moisten my tongue, tried to speak. But all I could do was shake my head.

Dad's eyes went unfocused. When he spoke, his voice was gravel and ash. "You want to make a fool of me. Is that it?"

I shook my head again.

"You want to humiliate me. Show everyone what a miserable failure I am."

"No, Dad. That's not—"

"Goddamn it, Ellie!" He pounded the dashboard.

I flinched.

"You had no right. You had *no fucking right*!" He raised the phone high in one hand and hurled it at floor. It hit with a *crack* and tumbled down the steps to rest at my feet. Dad moved toward me, and I backed away like a frightened dog, my body moving of its own accord.

I had never seen him so furious.

He blew past me and strode toward the back of the RV, feet crunching on the gravel. I watched him for a moment, then leaned over and picked up the phone. The screen had spiderwebbed, but I could still read most of the display.

Clutching the phone in shaking hands, I sat down on the steps. I had to make this right. I had to fix it. I collected myself and got to my feet.

I found Dad squatting near the back tire, shining his small Maglite under the carriage. He sensed my presence, turned off the flashlight, stood.

"Does the phone still work?" he asked without looking at me.

"I think so," I said, offering it up.

He took it gently and began to walk to the front of the RV.

"The axle is broken," he said. "We're going to need a ride."

Dad rode shotgun in the big rig that picked us up, while I curled up in the bunk behind the trucker. He was a big man with a marine corps tattoo who chain-smoked Marlboros and blared old-school metal. The smoke masked the body odor that seemed to permeate the cab, and the music drowned out any possibility of conversation. I was grateful for both.

I had crashed the RV just east of Sun Valley, Arizona. We didn't have enough money for a cab, let alone a flatbed tow truck, and we couldn't afford impound fees; so Dad removed the license plates from the RV and the trailer, then walked to the side of the highway and stuck out his thumb. When dusk came, not a single car had pulled over, so Dad reluctantly let me take a turn.

The first truck stopped.

Since I turned fifteen, I'd gotten used to being ogled, teased, and harassed by men at parties and bars and corporate events. Being objectified was part of the performer's life, I told myself. But when that trucker pulled over, it was different. The way he looked me up and down, evaluating me like I was something on a menu. I felt gross. Frightened.

And then his manner changed entirely when he saw that I wasn't alone.

Dad didn't say a word to me, didn't even look at me—but with the driver, he was quick and charismatic. He spotted his tattoo and engaged the guy in conversation about the Gulf War. The trucker went from potential rapist to harmless uncle in an instant.

One thing I've learned: Men are capable of far more shocking transformations than magic could ever account for.

"I'm not going to Flagstaff," the guy had said, scratching his graying beard. "But I can drop you near Phoenix. How does two hundred bucks sound?"

As if we had a choice.

Thirty minutes into the ride, the war stories ran dry, and the driver cranked up his radio. I wanted to sleep, but my mind was whirling, counting and recounting everything we'd left behind.

Some of the big props had looked fixable—but with the RV's axle broken and the trailer hitch beyond repair, we had no way to take them with us. I'd crammed all our close-up stuff—cards, coins, cups—into my backpack and duffel bag, along with toiletries and a few changes of clothes. We had padlocked the overturned trailer in case we ever came back for it, but I had little hope. It lay in plain sight of the road, where anyone with a pair of bolt cutters could get in. Our props were gone, our RV was wrecked, and all prospects of financial rescue had evaporated. All my rage at Dad had been wasted; I was the one who had made us hit bottom.

At sunset, I had walked a quarter mile north, opened the door to the bird cage, and watched the doves flap away into the spreading desert darkness.

Now I lay in the back of the cab, staring up at the cracked screen of my phone. Some of the shards looked jagged enough to open a vein.

But no. I couldn't afford to think like that, couldn't afford to start down that slope.

I considered calling Grace to beg for help. If Flynn & Kellar were going to pay us five grand just to appear, maybe they could offer some kind of advance to help us get there. On the other hand, if Grace found out we didn't even have props yet, she might take us off the bill. I couldn't risk it.

And then it occurred to me that none of it mattered anyway, because Dad wasn't going to do the show.

The trucker dropped us off at a motel half a block from a big mall. I thanked him and smiled and tried not to vomit as he looked me up and down one last time before I shut the door and walked away.

The water pressure was low, the mattress was hard, and Dad maintained his silence. I could feel him ignoring me as he moved around the room, unpacking what little there was to unpack. He put a few shirts in a drawer, hung his coat in the closet, set his nearly empty prescription bottle on the nightstand with a rattle. He hated living out of a suitcase, he said, so he preferred to make himself at home wherever he was. I didn't see the point.

I lay on one of the beds, which smelled like chlorine and cigarettes, staring at the water-stained cottage-cheese ceiling and trying to fight off spiraling thoughts. I picked up my phone and thumbed the cracks in the screen, thinking about that open vein. A quick step into fast traffic. A bedsheet and the closet pole. A razor and a red bath. The images were sharp and incessant and impossible to banish.

My eyes felt dry and too big for their sockets, and my pulse beat low and slow in my wrists and neck. All that blood, like a river. In the back of my mind somewhere, a thought swam. Ripley would want me to call him. Molly, the nice woman at the Suicide Prevention Lifeline, would want me to call her. But I didn't want a pep talk. I wanted to sleep and maybe not wake up.

I glanced up as Dad closed his suitcase and moved toward the door.

"I'll be back in an hour," he said. "Lock the door behind me, and don't leave the room."

Before I could remind him that I wasn't six years old, he was out the door.

I got up and paced, thrashing around for something else—anything else—to think about. I spotted my laptop bag, then glanced at the clock on my phone. I still had two hours before my earth science summaries were due. I could sit down and start working.

But as soon as the thought of homework occurred to me, it seemed ridiculous—rearranging those deck chairs on the *Titanic*. I glanced down at the comforting glow of my phone. The icon for my messaging app sat there in the corner. Against my better judgment, I tapped it and reread my last text to Liam:

> If everything works out, I'll be in LA in four days. Are you still down for In-N-Out?

It had been over twelve hours, and he still hadn't replied. Even if his battery had died, or he'd left his phone at home, he should have texted back by now. I should tell him exactly what I thought of him. I should make him feel as small as I felt. I typed out a new message:

> What the fuck, Liam? Do you even care? Or were you just trying to get in my pants?

But I knew the answers. Liam was a good guy. He'd had several opportunities to get more physical with me in his Mustang—and I probably would have let him—but he hadn't. Which meant he wasn't using me. He probably had wanted me on some level, but my behavior had pushed him away. What kind of girl gets horny when her dad collapses? Probably, he had been disgusted by me. *I* was disgusted.

I deleted the fuck-you text and typed:

I miss you.

I clicked Send and immediately wished I could take it back—but a second later, the phone rang. I stared at it stupidly, as if it were a rock that had suddenly come to life in my hand. It rang again. The name on the display was *Liam Miller.* I snapped out of it and answered.

"Liam?" There was a long pause on the other end, then:

"Who are you?" It was a girl's voice. Low-pitched and husky.

My body stiffened. "Who is this?"

"I'm Liam's girlfriend."

Heat spread up the sides of my face.

"You need to stop texting him," the girl said, her voice shaking. "Delete his number. Now."

The line went dead. I sat there with the phone pressed to my ear, and then I let it drop to the mattress.

I should have known. I should have known. I should have known.

Sobs overtook me. I fell facedown on the bed and buried my face in the pillow. Of course he had someone else. I was so stupid. My shoulders shook. My stomach muscles spasmed.

From the corridor outside, I could hear footsteps and laughter passing my door—

And then the tears just stopped, like someone had shut off the faucet. The heat drained from my face, and the fist around my midsection let go. I felt flat. Hollow. Like a sleepwalker, I stood up, not knowing where I was going, my legs moving on their own.

I stood in front of the sink. The counter was stained with rust. The cold tap squeaked as I turned it, and I listened to the pipes moan as the basin filled. Then I turned off the water and plunged my face under the surface.

As the water rose over my ears, sound faded to silence. The red circles of my eyelids grew dimmer, taking on a sickly green tint. Slowly, I expelled the air from my lungs. Gently. Calmly. The last of the bubbles tickled my face as they floated to the surface.

Underwater, I could hear my own pulse, hear the *shoosh-HOOSH, shoosh-HOOSH* of blood squirting through the small vessels in my ears. Somehow, the quiet and the dark made everything louder. Brighter. Clearer.

Green bled into black at the corners of my vision. Stars burst across my field of view. I felt my head go light and my knees get weak. I counted to ten, then twenty, then thirty.

At forty, I gave up.

I pulled my face slowly out of the water, feeling the surface tension break, one pore at a time. Then I gasped, sat down on the toilet lid, and reached for a towel.

CHAPTER 14

I WAS IN BED WHEN I heard Dad's footsteps approaching the door to our motel room. I didn't want to talk to him. I didn't want him to see my face and know everything. I shut my eyes and pretended to sleep.

He entered, locked the door behind him, and approached the bed. I felt his weight warp the mattress as he sat.

"I'm sorry for being so angry," he said. "None of this is your fault." He put the back of his hand on my cheek, his fingers warm and thick and strong. He hadn't done it since I was a little girl. It took all my control not to stir. I wasn't ready to face him.

"Forgive me," he said, and I felt his weight come off the mattress. I heard a drawer open, the rattle of his heart pills in their orange bottle, the squeak of springs as he got into bed.

Ten minutes later, he was snoring.

I lay in bed exhausted but awake, mind spinning, thoughts blurring. Pieces of the crash: the hum of the rumble strip and the bleating dashboard alarm; splintered wood in the blinding red sunlight; twisted steel and the jagged feel of spiderwebbed glass under my thumb. Liam's girlfriend, tall and pretty next to him in bed as they laughed. Dad hurling my phone down the steps, collapsing in the field behind the roadhouse, standing over me weeping in the dark as I drowned.

For a moment I thought I really was hearing the rumble strip—but it was my phone, vibrating on the particleboard nightstand. I lurched for it, thinking it might be Liam calling to apologize, to tell me that the girl had been just a friend playing a prank, calling to tell me *anything.*

But it wasn't Liam; it was Ripley. I frowned, rubbed my eyes. He had never called without texting me first.

Something was wrong.

I held my thumb over the green button but couldn't bring myself to tap it. I was drained, exhausted, unable to comfort myself, let alone another person. I was using every watt of energy I had just to stay alive, to keep from going under. There was nothing left for anybody else.

But then I thought about how Ripley had been there for me when I needed him most, despite the shit going on in his own life. And now, for once, he might need me. So I took a deep breath, squeezed my eyes shut, and answered the phone.

"Ripley?"

There was no response at first, only sounds of rustling

fabric and something hard dropping to the floor.

"Ripley, are you there?"

I heard arguing voices somewhere at the outer range of the phone. Then Ripley's voice, nasal and high-pitched:

"You're high. Go home!" More rustling as if the phone was in his pocket instead of his hand. "Why did you even let her in?" Something else incomprehensible.

I got up, glanced at my dad to make sure he was still asleep, and left the motel room as quietly as I could. The night air was a cold slap in the face; it tethered me back to reality.

On the phone, I heard a kid crying.

"Ripley, are you okay?"

"Jude, come back!" A door slammed. Then, for the first time since the phone had rung, Ripley spoke directly to me. "Hang on." Another door slammed. When he spoke again, his voice was thick and shaky. "Are you still there?"

"Yes, I'm here. What's going on? Are you all right?"

"My mom came back."

"Oh, no." I moved down the walkway, out of earshot of the room, and leaned against the railing for support.

"Nothing for three months, and then she shows up and rings the fucking doorbell. Wakes up Jude."

I tried to focus on what Ripley was saying, but the sound of every car on the road made me flinch with memories of the crash. I went down the steps and into the alcove where the ice machine was. Its hum insulated me from the sounds of the street.

Ripley was saying, ". . . and then Dad let her in like an idiot."

"What happened?"

"He started talking to her. Being nice to her, as if she hadn't wrecked our whole fucking family."

I made a sighing noise that I hoped sounded sympathetic. I pictured my own mom showing up on the doorstep. Even if she was drunk or high or half-dead, I couldn't imagine doing anything but throwing my arms around her.

I swallowed. "She was high?"

"Fuckin' A. Eyes popping. Talking a million miles a minute. And Dad had Heather over!"

I blinked, trying to remember who Heather was.

"She had cooked us dinner and everything. She was literally in the kitchen washing the dishes. And then *she* showed up." Ripley's voice caught. "So what does Dad do? He ignores his girlfriend of eight months and runs to comfort his deserting addict wife. He's so pathetic. They both are." Ripley sniffled.

My throat was tight and my head buzzing; it was a huge effort to stay in the moment, to listen. "Ripley, I'm so sorry."

"I know." Ripley, usually sensitive to my feelings, clearly couldn't detect my distress through the storm of his own. I couldn't blame him. I knew how that went.

From my position in the alcove, I could see across the road to the mall. The lights in the parking lot were still on. I heard a car honk, but not from the street. From the phone.

"Where are you?" I asked.

"Walking down Imperial Highway," he said. "I had to get out of there."

"It's past midnight."

"I'm in Park Hills, Ellie. The worst that could happen is that I get busted for curfew."

Across the street, faceless white mannequins stared at me from the Neiman Marcus window.

"Is there any way I can help?"

"Teleport here and take me to IHOP?" He gave a humorless laugh.

"It's bad, huh?"

Ripley sniffled again. "Jude's taking it harder than I am."

I tugged at my hair, hoping the pain would keep me focused on Ripley instead of myself.

"Have you ever thought of taking him to Alateen?" I realized this was my version of pawning him off on the Suicide Prevention Lifeline, but it was all I could think to say. "It's like AA, but for the kids of addicts."

"I've heard of it. It sounds awful."

"Yeah," I said. "Probably is." I felt like an idiot for bringing it up, as if I knew more about this stuff than he did. "What are you going to do?"

"I think I'm going to leave."

"Like *leave*?"

"For a while, anyway. I hate to abandon Jude, but if I stay, I'm afraid I might . . . I don't know. Melt down or something."

A siren squealed, and I looked up. An ambulance was blowing through the intersection at Camelback Road.

"Is that a siren? Where are you?"

"Across from some mall."

"You're sleeping outside?"

"No, at a motel."

"You guys splurged on a motel? Must be doing okay."

"Not exactly."

"What does that mean?"

"Nothing. You didn't call to hear me complain. What about you? Where are you going to go?"

"My aunt's, maybe. I'll figure something out. But seriously, enough about my cliché family drama. Distract me with your woes."

It was a relief to hear him say that, but I felt guilty anyway, filling him in on everything: The broken axle. The smashed props. Our dwindling cash supply.

Dad's fury on discovering I'd agreed to do Flynn & Kellar's show.

"Oh my God," he said. His sniffles were gone; my misery really had distracted him. If that was my superpower, it was a shitty one. "If I had any money, I'd Venmo you."

"I know."

"And you're sure he won't do the show?"

"Completely."

I walked to the corner, then crossed the street toward the mall's main entrance.

Ripley asked, "What's your plan?"

"I don't have one," I said, mounting the steps to Neiman Marcus. "The RV is dead. Our gear is gone. Even if I could book us a close-up gig, how would we get there? And we can't afford to keep sleeping in motels. We'll have to find a hostel, or a shelter, or . . ." My throat closed up.

"You're crashing," Ripley said.

I stopped on the top step. "How do you know?" *Ella, ella, eh, eh, eh . . .*

"Because Ellie Dante doesn't give up. You're relentless. This isn't you talking. This is your illness. Did you get your meds?"

I felt tears welling up in my eyes and glanced around, as if anyone would be watching me on the steps of a closed mall at twelve thirty in the morning.

"Our insurance ran out."

"And you're out of pills? Totally out?"

"Yeah."

"Since when?"

"A week? I don't know."

"How much are they without insurance?"

"Two hundred bucks."

"Jesus."

"I know."

"Hey, wait. You said you're at a mall in Phoenix? Which one?"

I looked up at the sign. "Fashion Square. Why?"

I heard rustling and clicking—Ripley was looking something up on his phone. When he spoke again, I could tell I was on speaker. "Okay, technically that's in Scottsdale, which is part of the Phoenix metropolitan area but is in fact its own city."

I squeezed my eyes shut; Ripley could be like this sometimes. "And this is important why?"

"Because that part of Phoenix is rich."

I turned to glance through the glass doors. Ripley was

right; it was a rich mall. I saw signs for Tiffany & Co. Burberry. Prada.

"So?" I said.

"So? You've swiped Rolexes in front of a live audience. You can't think of any practical applications for that skill?"

CHAPTER 15

THE NEXT MORNING, DAD WAS still asleep as I dug through my duffel for the items I would need and stuffed them into a knockoff Louis Vuitton bag I'd picked up at a thrift store on impulse. It would help me get into character. I jotted a note on the motel stationery—if Dad woke to find me gone without a trace, he would either have a heart attack or call the cops—and then I slipped out the door.

I killed an hour wandering the aisles of a Sprouts, which were exploding with Halloween candy and orange and black streamers. I bought a Rockstar and two 5-hour Energies, then walked to a diner, ordered a coffee, and settled in to wait. At ten, my cell rang. The number had a Phoenix area code; probably Dad calling from the motel. My shoulders tensed. If I didn't answer, he would give me hell when I got back. But if I did, he'd demand to know where I was and what I was doing, and I might lose my nerve. Before I could decide, the call went to voice mail. I stuffed the phone back into my bag, knocked back the dregs of my coffee, and paid the bill.

By ten thirty, the mall parking lot was filling up, so I crossed the street and went in the front entrance. I made my way to the restrooms near the food court, locked myself in a stall, and rummaged through my bag. I'd barely been up two hours, but already I could feel the lack of sleep in the dryness of my eyes and the heaviness of my limbs. I cracked open the Rockstar and pounded it right there in the stall. Then I put on my little black dress. It was wrong for the time of day, but I couldn't walk into Neiman Marcus looking like I lived in a trailer. I stuffed my jeans into my bag, left the stall, and stood in front of the mirror.

I barely recognized the girl I saw. She was hollow eyed, frizzy-haired, and thin. She looked like the poster child for a teen rehab clinic. The chorus of "Umbrella" started to creep into my mind, but I shut it out; I couldn't afford to lose focus. I needed to hold on for a few more hours. If I could just get my hands on enough money for another two nights in a motel, maybe Dad could figure out the rest.

I drank my last 5-hour Energy, then brushed out my hair and tamed the frizz with motel conditioner. After applying some makeup, I inspected myself. My marks would mostly be men, and they would see a teen girl from the wrong side of town trying to blend in with the rich girls—which could work to my advantage. I shouldered my bag and left the restroom.

I spent ten minutes wandering the mall, lifting wallets from gawky teenage boys before retreating to a restroom to count my take. I'd collected forty-five dollars in cash and a pile of credit cards I couldn't use. I closed my eyes and tugged at a lock of hair in frustration. If I kept doing clunky bump-and-grabs, I would get caught. I needed fewer marks and bigger payoffs. After checking my makeup in the mirror, I headed for Neiman Marcus.

When you select a volunteer from an audience, you look for someone who's not too shy, but not too charismatic, either. Someone approachable but easily influenced. A follower, not a leader. The same principle applies to grifts: you choose marks you can control.

I wandered into the men's department and stopped at a table covered with neckties. While pretending to look through them, I scoped out the store.

There was a good-looking blond guy in his late twenties shopping for a belt, but I dismissed him out of hand; he was too self-confident. Next I considered an older balding guy who was standing at the watch counter. He might have been a good choice, but he was already engaged with a salesperson in a highly visible part of the store.

I moved toward the sportswear section and promptly spotted my first mark. He was short, maybe five five, and his hair was just starting to go gray at the temples. He wore an expensive watch and no wedding ring; he was rich, and probably divorced. More than once I saw him eye the petite blonde behind the counter as he scraped through a rack of overpriced golf shirts.

I approached the adjacent rack and pretended to browse for a few minutes. Twice I felt his eyes on me, so I looked up and met his gaze. He turned red and became suddenly fascinated by a neon-green polo. When he started to move away, I stepped back and bumped into him, dropping my bag.

"Oh, sorry," he said, looking scandalized.

"No, it was totally my fault."

He stooped to pick up my bag.

"Thanks," I said, giving him a shy smile.

Five minutes later in another restroom stall, I opened his wallet: there were five crisp hundred-dollar bills inside. I let out a sigh of relief, stuffed the cash and his driver's license into my bag, then dropped his wallet and credit cards into the trash on my way out.

It had been less than an hour, and I was already up more than five hundred dollars. It was more than I could have hoped for. I should have left right then. But the caffeine and the adrenaline had me feeling better than I had in days. I couldn't bring myself to go back to the motel. Not yet.

Tiffany tempted me, but there were cameras everywhere and a security guard at the door. I considered casing Burberry or Prada, but both were full of women, who were mostly immune to my best tactics. Then I spotted the Apple Store. Perfect.

I'd hit six marks in this outfit; it was time for a change. Besides, my instincts told me that the MacBook set would respond better to a low-key girl. So I revisited the restroom by the food court and changed back into my jeans and V-neck.

I entered the already crowded Apple Store and found my next mark standing at a laptop display. I sidled up next to him: a chubby, bearded guy in his late teens or early twenties wearing an outdated jean jacket. After I played with a demo computer for a few minutes, I put on my best confused frown and started looking around as if I were trying to attract the attention of a salesperson.

Right on cue, Beard Boy said, "Can I help you with something?"

I made an effort to look relieved. "You're going to think I'm stupid," I said.

"I promise to hide it if I do." He smiled. He was actually kind of cute. Not in a college-athlete kind of way; more like a lovable geek. It was refreshing.

"I can't find the start menu."

"Yeah, well. That's a Windows thing. This is a Mac."

"Ugh. I told you."

"Don't worry about it. You're leaving the Dark Side, that's what's important."

I laughed, and his smile widened.

"I want to try out the speakers," I said. "The ones on my laptop suck."

"No problem. Here."

As he approached, I scooted over—but not by much. He clicked an icon and started typing. I leaned in, brushing my arm against his. He moved over a few inches, as if the contact had been his fault. Was it possible I was about to rob an actual real-life gentleman? I felt an anticipatory pang of guilt.

"What do you want to hear?" he asked, scrolling through a page of playlists.

I noted the Seven Seize logo on his T-shirt. "Something heavy?"

"My kind of girl."

While he searched for the perfect song, I checked him out more closely. He wore an Apple Watch, designer jeans, and custom-colored Doc Martens; the guy had money. I leaned back slightly and located his wallet. It was tethered to one belt loop with a long chain—that would be a speed bump, but not a roadblock.

"Here," he said. "Check these guys out."

He clicked on a track by a band called DragonForce, and my ears were assaulted by dueling guitars and a machine-gun double-kick drum. Beard Boy nodded his head to the music, glancing over to see if I was into it. I pretended I was.

"Do they have videos?"

"Hell yeah, they have videos."

When he started searching YouTube, I saw my chance. I leaned into him, pointing at the screen.

"Play that one," I said, pressing myself against his arm as I undid the snap on his wallet chain. He didn't notice, and he didn't move away.

By the time the video started, the guy's wallet was in my bag. I pulled out my phone and pretended an important text had just come in.

"Crap," I said. "I have to go." I stuffed my phone back into my purse and gave the guy a more or less genuine smile. "Thanks for your help."

"Hey," he said, reaching out as if to grab my wrist, then withdrawing it suddenly as though he'd touched something hot.

"Sorry," he said. "Do you . . . I'm Mike."

"Purcilla." It was the first name that came to mind.

"Purcilla." He frowned slightly but was too polite to crack a joke. "Do you maybe want to get a coffee?"

"Sure," I said, glancing at the door. "Bu later, okay? I kind of have to go."

"Let me give you my card," he said.

And then he reached for his wallet.

I hesitated only a moment—then broke for the exit. The door was only paces away when I heard him yell:

"Hey! Come back!"

I took off, running as fast as I could for the food court. I would lose him in the crowd.

"Wait!"

His voice trailed off as I slalomed between lines of people queued up at Wolfgang Puck and Panda Express. The restroom was dead ahead. I could go in and change clothes. Put up my hair. Do some dramatic makeup. But when I glanced over my shoulder, he was only twenty yards away and looking right at me. If he saw me going into the restroom, no disguise would help. I bolted back into the dining area and headed for the exit.

Once I made it outside, I paused to get my bearings. The entrance to Neiman Marcus was only a hundred yards away. I took off again—but just as I reached the doors, I heard him yell.

"Purcilla!"

Something in his voice tugged at me. He didn't sound angry; he sounded concerned. Against my better judgment, I looked back. He was bent over, panting, hands on his thighs.

When he saw me turn, he straightened up.

"You dropped this," he said, and held up a small black object.

I thrust my hand into my bag. My phone wasn't there. It must have bounced out of my bag while I was I running.

He started toward me, smiling as if finding it had been a lucky break. Was he trying to trick me? Or had he really not realized I'd stolen his wallet?

He stopped in front of me, held out my phone.

"Thanks," I said, cautiously taking it and dropping it back into my bag.

"Why did you run?" he asked, frowning. "What's wrong?"

I scrambled for a response. "I got a text from my dad. He needs me."

Beard boy nodded, looking slightly crestfallen. "Okay. I won't keep you, then."

Trying to hide my relief, I turned to go, but he reached out and took my upper arm in his hand. Shit, I thought. This was it.

"Can I give you my number? I don't want to be weird. It's just I never meet beautiful girls. And when I do, I can't talk to them. Only this time I did. And I'll kick myself later if I don't ask."

I smiled, but inside, a hot sludge of guilt and self-loathing swelled in my gut.

"You don't have to give me yours," he said. "Just . . . here." He held out his hand, and I reluctantly handed him my phone. He typed his number, looking up at me once, maybe to check that I was still there, then gave it back. "There," he said, clapping his hands and holding them up like a blackjack dealer ending his shift. "I did it." He smiled again, and a row of straight, white teeth peeked out from his beard. "I hope you call."

As I put my phone back into my bag, I felt his wallet poking up from between my rolled-up little black dress and my dwindling make-up bag. I felt an almost irresistible urge to take it out and hand it back.

Instead, I turned and headed out across the parking lot.

CHAPTER 16

WHEN I OPENED THE DOOR to the motel room, I found Dad sitting at the desk, writing in his battered leather journal. He didn't look up as I entered.

"Did you get my note?" I asked in my most contrite voice.

He set down his pen with a sharp *clack*. "You didn't answer the phone."

"I must have missed your call."

"Where were you?"

I considered lying—but he was going to find out about the money sooner or later.

"I was at the mall." I crossed to the bed, opened my bag, and pulled out Beard Boy's wallet. It contained a twenty and three ones. After all that—what a waste. With Dad looking on in surprise, I counted out the rest of my take: five hundreds from the polo-shirt guy and forty-five bucks from everybody else.

Dad let out an angry breath and got to his feet. "Where did you get all that?"

There was an edge of contempt in his voice, and I felt my face heat up. This was our only option, and he knew it.

"Where do you think?"

"You—at the *shopping mall*?" Dad's eyes burned.

"Is there some other kind of mall I should know about?"

"That was a stupid risk," he spat. "You could've been caught."

"Somebody had to do *something*."

"Not this way."

"What way, then?" I said, my voice rising. "I booked a fifteen-thousand-dollar show—fifteen *thousand* dollars!—but you won't do it. What way, then?" My chest rose and fell, my breath shallow and furious. I grabbed a fistful of cash and hurled it at him. The bills fanned out like dead leaves, dropping pointlessly to the bedspread. Dad watched them fall, and his face fell with them.

"I . . ." He didn't finish the sentence, just closed his eyes and put his face in his hands. He seemed to shrink as I watched, shoulders sagging, hand on the desk to steady himself.

Guilt dissolved my anger like acid. *I* had done this to him, reduced him to a powerless old man. After all, I had led us here, not him. I was the one who had wasted time going on dates, and squandered our money on cell minutes instead of food. I had crashed the RV and destroyed our livelihood.

This was my fault. All of it.

I sank onto the bed. For lack of something meaningful to do, I gathered the bills into a stack and put them back in my bag. I retrieved the drivers' licenses and began to write the date and the amounts on each. I wanted to apologize to Dad, to tell him I knew this was all on me, but I couldn't seem to make my voice work.

Dad moved, and at first, I thought he was headed for the door. Instead, he sat down at the desk and opened his journal.

"Did you know the Truck Drop was your mother's idea?"

I sat up. Dad *never* brought up the Truck Drop on his own—and I could count on my fingers the number of times he had mentioned my mother. I was the one who carried her memory; he seemed capable only of enduring it.

"No," I said.

He nodded. "We found the truck at an estate sale in Las Vegas. She fell in love at first sight. She said it reminded her of her father's truck, and of how he used to take her for midnight rides to the beach."

I stared. "She used to take me on drives, too. To the desert instead of the beach, but . . ."

Dad cocked his head. "I never knew."

"You remember how sometimes she couldn't sleep?"

Recognition passed over his face like a shadow. "I remember."

I pressed my lips together. I wanted to say more, to ask a thousand questions about my mother, but I didn't want to rekindle his anger.

He ran a hand across the scuffed cover of his journal. "She designed the whole illusion. The narrative, the mechanics." He swallowed. "When I failed on that show . . ." His voice faded to a whisper. "I think she blamed herself. I think that's why she . . ."

Dad had never talked about her death. Never. My heart felt pinched. Slowly, I moved toward him and sat down on the edge of the bed. I was still afraid of making him angry—but my longing to know more about my mother was stronger than my fear.

"Tell me about her. Please."

He let out a long breath and turned his face toward the window. "She was funny," he said. "Talented, beautiful. Tempestuous." Now his eyes met mine, and I understood at once that this last part was about me, too. "She came to Las Vegas to get away from her family. She prized her freedom over everything else. You couldn't tell Cora Prince what to do. And if you tried, she'd do the opposite just to spite you." He smiled, shook his head; and the smile faded. "Sometimes I think, if I hadn't . . . I wonder if she might still be here." He looked at me, his eyes wide and wet and seeming to beg my forgiveness.

"It doesn't work like that, Dad."

He tilted his head as if he wanted desperately to believe me. The weight of his gaze compressed my rib cage.

"Anything can trigger it," I said. "Anything and nothing. And when it's bad . . ." I shook my head. "It's a sickness, Dad, and sometimes people die from it. You can't . . ." I shrugged, helpless to explain it any better than that.

Dad looked away, his jaw tight. "I miss her. So much."

"You never talk about her."

"No."

"But you still think of her?"

"Every day. Every moment." He faced me again. "You look so much like her."

I bit my lip. I wanted to hide my face. I wanted to look in a mirror.

"Dad, I'm sorry."

His eyes drifted out of focus. I tensed, anticipating the return of his anger. I didn't think I could handle it now.

"I'm sorry I lied. I'm sorry I went behind your back." My eyes flooded with heat. "I'm sorry I wrecked the bus." My breath hitched. I put my face in my hands and felt the sobs take me over, wracking my body.

He sat next to me on the bed, put his arm around me.

"Hush, now," he said, stroking my hair, but it only made me cry harder. "You were right," he said. "You did everything right. None of this is your fault."

His forgiveness punctured some invisible membrane inside me, and I dissolved into hysterical crying, pressing the heels of my hands into my eyes, gasping for air. Dad held me until I became still.

After a long silence, he released me, reached into his pocket, and pulled out his prescription bottle.

I frowned. The last time I'd checked, he had only a few pills left—but the bottle he held now contained at least ten tablets. Also, they were the wrong color; it was apparent, even through the orange plastic vial. I read the label, and my mouth fell open.

"How—"

"You need them, Ellie," he said, pressing the bottle into my hands, "and I need you."

My throat tightened. "But what about yours? Your heart!"

He pulled another bottle from his coat pocket, smiled, and rattled the pills inside. "Got it covered."

"But we were broke. How did you get these? Did you—"

"I didn't steal. I never had your light hands."

I shook my head and felt the ghost of a smile on my lips. Dad returned a more substantial one. Then he held up his wrist, showing a band of pale skin where his watch had been. "Nothing up my sleeve."

"You sold your grandfather's watch?" My smile vanished. That watch had been in our family for almost a century.

"Pawned it," he said, smiling more broadly. "But you can buy it back for me, once we've received that big fat check from Flynn & Kellar."

I gaped at him, and a tornado inside me seemed to suck away my breath.

"You're going to do it?"

He nodded.

I threw my arms around him, and he squeezed me tightly.

"I've been a fool," he said. "Trying to protect my reputation, my pride. What I should have been protecting is you." He put his hands on my shoulders. "I can't afford to lose you, Ellie. So we'll do the show. I won't pretend to be happy about it. But yes, of course, we'll do the show."

I opened my mouth to reply, but he shushed me.

"I have conditions," he said.

I nodded, ready to accept any conditions he laid out.

"First, you will take your medication every day, and you'll tell me when you're running low. Agreed?"

"Agreed."

"Then start now."

I opened the bottle and tapped one of the little blue tablets into my palm. I stared at it for a moment, feeling relieved but also terrified. It would be good to feel even again, to level out, to have that chemical safety net. The drug would protect me from the lows—but what if it blocked out the highs as well? What if it dimmed the stage lights, numbed the rush of performing, tamed the impulses I'd give in to so freely with Liam? Would all those precious highs dissolve as the medication took hold? I didn't know. Somehow, I couldn't remember how it had been before.

"Take it, Ellie," Dad said.

I closed my eyes, placed it on my tongue, and swallowed it dry.

"Good." Dad smiled. "Second, you will take the rest of this semester off."

My shoulders stiffened. Taking a semester off would push everything back half a year: graduation, job, insurance. Dad was looking older by the day, and I wasn't sure we could afford the delay.

He put a hand on my arm. "You're not dropping out—you're just taking a health leave. I've already called your doctor, and he's writing your principal a letter. You can take double courses in the summer if you must." I opened my mouth to protest, but he cut me off. "I won't budge on this, Ellie."

I closed my eyes. He was right. I couldn't handle school right now; my grades proved that. I had to start taking care of my own health, too.

"Okay," I said. "But when this is over, I want to land somewhere and stay. I don't care if it's LA or Vegas or Fort Wayne. But one of us needs to get a real job, with a steady paycheck and medical insurance."

Dad's eyes lost a little of their sparkle, but he nodded his agreement.

"Now," he said, "there's something I want to show you."

He retrieved his leather journal and sat back down on the bed. My breath quickened. Dad had never showed me anything in his journal; he'd guarded it fiercely for as long as I could remember. Now he ran his thumb over the cover, which was embossed with an owl, wings spread, clutching a ribbon in its beak that read: *The Academy of Magical Arts.*

Other kids grew up dreaming of Hogwarts: the moving staircases, the talking portraits. But I had spent my Sundays witnessing real magic in a real castle, one you entered by speaking an incantation to an owl with ruby eyes and walking through a secret door concealed in a bookcase. They were tricks, of course—but they had been real to me. They had had physical form, and they had made promises to my young mind. Promises that magic was real, and that I could learn to perform it.

I hadn't been back to the Magic Castle since I was a child. Dad's membership had lapsed, and anyway, he couldn't have shown his face in the bar or the close-up room. There would have been whispers and the intolerable hum of pity.

My heart pounded as he opened the journal to a page near the middle. The date stared at me from the corner of a dog-eared page. It was *the* date. The day that had wrecked his career and our lives.

"Ten years ago," he said. "Almost to the day."

I took the journal from him, ran my thumb over the rough paper, stared at the drawing within. The page showed an intricate ink diagram of the Truck Drop as seen from backstage. It was rendered so perfectly that I wondered if I had seen the drawing before, or if I was simply remembering that night. I closed my eyes.

I watch from the wings, clutching my mother's hand as the curtain goes up. My father stands center stage. Half a dozen cameras train their lenses on him.

My mother kisses my cheek, then strides away. I try to follow, but a man wearing a headset holds me back.

Gracefully, my mother crosses the stage, her hair falling black and straight to her waist. When she reaches my father, she stops and raises her arms in a V, showing the audience a length of rope. She selects a female volunteer, who binds Dad's wrists and ankles with the rope before returning to her seat.

Upstage, a second curtain ascends, revealing a gleaming vintage pickup truck, its waxed hood shining in the stage lights: a 1947 Chevrolet in Cape Maroon. Mom helps Dad into the driver's seat and closes the door. A spotlight follows the truck as a winch hauls it toward the rafters with Dad inside.

Six stagehands push a massive Plexiglas tank downstage into a pool of light beneath the truck. The water inside laps against its transparent walls as it comes to a halt.

My mother smiles. Her skin is clear and smooth even in the harsh white spotlight.

The sudden silence of the crowd, the glare on the chrome hubcaps—and the splash as the truck strikes the surface of the water and begins to sink. As Dad makes a show of struggling with the ropes around his wrists, water gushes into the truck through the open windows.

By the time the tires touch the bottom of the tank, Dad is supposed to be free of his bonds—but he's still struggling. The water level rises, and now it's over his head.

He should be climbing out of the truck already—but instead, he's thrashing, straining desperately at the ropes.

Something is wrong.

Fifteen seconds pass. Thirty.

A fist stops my heart.

My mother runs into the wings. I reach for her, terrified—but she moves right past me. She's whispering hoarsely to the stagehands, gesturing at the tank. I don't understand what's happening.

Forty-five seconds. Sixty.

Dad's face is turning dark. He kicks desperately against the driver's side door.

My mother puts her hands on the sides of her face and screams.

Ninety seconds.

Finally, the stage manager gives a signal, and the main curtain drops, cutting off the audience's view. I can hear them murmuring anxiously on the other side of the curtain.

Onstage, the crew rush in, grab the emergency release levers, and open the dump hatches. Water gushes out of the tank, onto the stage, and into the audience. It's a tidal wave. It's a nightmare. The soundstage is flooding.

My mother screams again as my father floats motionless inside the truck.

"Ellie."

I flinch and look up at Dad.

The memory was almost tangible. I smelled the chlorine, tasted the stage fog.

"Are you all right?"

"Yes." I was afraid to look him in in the eye, so I flipped through the journal instead. Most of the writing was old and faded—but on the later pages, the ink was fresh.

"I've replayed it over and over in my mind," he said. "Trying to figure out where it went wrong. But I always come to the same conclusion." He looked at me. "I let myself become distracted. I failed the escape. That was all. I just . . . failed."

He took back the book, closed it with a decisive snap, and sat up straight.

"You've located the props," he said.

I nodded, trying to keep up with the abrupt change of subject. "Ripley helped. But yeah. Higgins agreed to rent them to us."

Dad raised his eyebrows. "How did you persuade him to do that?"

"I told him the value would double, even if everything went wrong."

Dad laughed out loud, and my heart swelled. But then his smile faded.

"How much does want?" he asked.

I braced myself for his reaction. "Five grand."

Dad's face reddened. "Five thousand—that bastard!" He flexed his fists. "There's got to be another way."

"Even if we could rent a tank and tear the engine out of a different truck, it would cost at least that much. And we don't have time."

Dad nodded, but I could see the wheels turning.

"Besides, we want the original truck. The one you used

that night. They're going to show the old video—you know they will. And if we use the same truck . . . Think of it. The resonance of the thing."

He nodded again, stroking his mustache as he always did when he was problem solving. We sat side by side in silence. My heart fluttered in my rib cage like our lost doves.

"If we do this," he said, "we have to make it better than before."

"Yes."

"Bigger," he said. "More spectacular."

"We have to play on the failure," I said. "Give them something they won't expect."

Dad pointed at me. "Precisely! A twist. So," he said, folding his arms, "how do we do this?"

"Why are you asking me?"

He raised his eyebrows. "You masterminded this operation. Signed the contract. Lined up the props. Steered us west. You must have something in mind."

I shook my head, backing away slightly. "I do close-up. Not the big stuff."

"You've been around grand illusion your whole life. You know what there is to know."

I threw up my hands. "I was six years old when you did the Truck Drop!"

He gave me an infuriating smile. "Yes, but I'm sure someone has made a YouTube out of it. And I imagine you've watched it more than once."

I tightened my jaw and looked away. After all this—booking the show, finding the props, getting us here—he expected me to fix the illusion, too?

He was right, though. I had watched the video—hundreds of times.

Dad smiled again, as if he could hear my thoughts. "I'm only asking for your ideas."

I glared at him.

I'd started bugging Dad to teach me magic when I was seven years old, but he had refused. Ten years old, he'd claimed, was the youngest a person could be and still keep a secret—which was important because of rule number two: *Never tell them how it's done.*

Then, shortly after my eighth birthday, he caught me lighting one of his playing cards on fire while I was trying to re-create his large-deck production, and he agreed to teach me just to keep me from burning down the house.

Dad had taught me magic in this way: he would perform a trick, and I would have to guess the method. I learned quickly to think before I spoke, because once I posed a theory out loud, he would make me demonstrate it. If I got close, he would nudge me this way or that. If not, he would let me fail and make me tell him why. At the time, I found his method maddening. But it taught me how to think like a magician. How to follow the truth instead of the lie.

I reached for the journal, and Dad yielded his grip. I flipped to an early drawing, examined it, and looked up into my father's expectant face.

"What if we—"

I was interrupted by a knock on the door. Dad put his hand on my shoulder.

"I'll get it."

There was another knock—and then a voice, muffled and vaguely familiar, called out from the other side.

"Ellie? Are you in there?"

I gripped the bedspread. It had to be Beard Boy. He'd discovered that I'd ripped him off and had somehow tracked me here.

"Who's there?" Dad said.

"I'm a friend of Ellie's. Is she there?"

I frowned. It couldn't be Beard Boy; I had told him my name was Purcilla. And besides, this voice was younger. Higher-pitched.

My jaw went slack. No way.

Dad turned to me, eyebrows drawn together. I nodded. Cautiously, he opened the door.

A teenager stood on the peeling threshold: a slender boy at least six feet tall with red hair; round, handsome features; and amber-brown eyes. He wore skinny jeans and a rust-colored hoodie with the Atari logo screen-printed across the chest.

I had never seen him before in my life.

Slowly, I got to my feet. "Ripley?"

CHAPTER 17

"IT'S YOU, RIGHT?" THE WORDS tumbled stupidly out of my mouth.

"Yeah," he said, with an awkward under-the-breath laugh. "It's me."

"What are you doing here?"

"I just . . ." Ripley swallowed nervously, his Adam's apple bobbing like a cork in a wave.

Dad eyed me and cleared his throat.

"Sorry. Dad, this is Ripley. Ripley, Dad."

Dad's face lit up with recognition. And, I thought, a little relief.

"Of course. I've heard so much about you." He put out his hand. Ripley seized it and pumped a little too hard.

"Nice to meet you, Mr. Dante."

Dad took a step back. "Why don't you come in?"

I took one glance around our disgusting motel room and quickly intervened.

"Actually, is it all right if I step out for a few minutes? Ripley and I need to talk." I grabbed my hoodie.

Dad frowned, tugged the end of his mustache. "All right. But take your phone. And this time, answer it."

Ripley and I moved down the walkway. His gait was long and loping and didn't seem to match the voice I'd heard on the phone for the last two years. He felt alien to me, as if the role of my best friend had suddenly been recast with a new actor.

We turned the corner and came into a deserted smokers' grotto. I turned and looked at Ripley.

"How did you get here?"

"Carjacked a soccer mom," he said. "I'm an interstate fugitive."

I laughed, but the laugh broke in the middle and I had to choke back tears. God, I was a mess. I needed to get control of myself or I was going to scare him away, too.

But instead of withdrawing, Ripley stepped forward and put his arms around me. They were stronger than I had imagined. He smelled like new-car-scent air freshener and spearmint gum—not bad smells, but again, not what I expected.

I broke off the hug. "I can't believe you came."

"I needed to get away." He looked down at his feet, traced a line in the small pile of cigarette ashes on the concrete. "After we got off the phone last night, I went back for Jude, and we walked to Heather's."

"Is he okay?"

"He's a tough little fucker; he'll be fine. Heather's going to watch him till I get back. Anyway, she let me borrow her car, and I got on the road."

"You drove straight here?"

"I mean, I stopped at the DQ in Blythe for a pee and a Blizzard."

I laughed, and it felt like a hot water balloon had burst in my chest. "It's really great to see you, Ripley. I mean, I guess, it's really great to *meet* you."

"The pleasure is all mine, milady." He did a sort of awkward Elizabethan bow, and I laughed. It was 100 percent Ripley, and I was relieved that some part of him matched my expectations.

There was an awkward pause. Ripley stuffed his hands into the pockets of his jeans. "You don't look like your avatar," he said.

Neither of us used our real photos online. Ripley's avi was a pixelated emoji with Xed-out eyes, and mine was Death from the Sandman comics.

I flipped my hair. "Cuter than you thought, huh?"

"Yeah," he said, clearly uncomfortable. "I mean, no, but . . ."

A laugh escaped me. Of course he didn't find me cute. I was a red-eyed, insomniac mess.

He cocked his head. "Are you fucking laughing at me right now, Elias?"

"Absolutely. You should have seen your face!"

"Okay," he said. "It's fine, go ahead. Make fun of the skinny ace Jew."

I suppressed a manic giggle. "You're Jewish?"

"Well, my dad's about as Jewish as a ham-and-cheese sandwich." He smirked. "But it comes down on your mom's side, and her maiden name was Adelstein."

"And she named you *Ripley*?"

"Believe it or not." His smiled faded, and an instant later he wasn't the best friend I'd known for years; he was the alien who had loped down the walkway next to me. He fidgeted with a small black ring he was wearing on the middle finger of his right hand. I needed to say something to puncture the uncomfortable silence.

"Joking aside, what *did* you expect?"

"I don't know," he said. "Someone more gothy, I guess? Pixie cut, winged eyeliner. Maybe those vampire contacts."

I crossed my arms. "So basically, you saw me as a character on a CW show about high school Wiccans."

"I would totally watch that show!"

"I would, too."

He smiled. "How about me? Am I what you expected?"

The truth was I had expected someone geekier, less put together. But I was ashamed to admit it, so I said, "Almost exactly."

"Suuure," Ripley said, rolling his eyes. "Well, anyway, my look has its perks. I'm going as Mark Zuckerberg for Halloween."

We both smiled.

"Epic hair," he said. "You could play guitar for Seven Seize."

"At public school they used to call me Homeless Hermione."

He grimaced. "That's fucked up."

"Yeah."

My gut felt full of hot rocks; we weren't supposed to meet like this. We weren't supposed to meet at all. And now Ripley had showed up at my lowest point ever. I didn't want him to see me like this, when I couldn't hide what a mess I was.

He must have noticed a change in my expression, because he asked, "What's wrong?"

When I answered, it was almost a whisper. "I thought we promised we'd never meet in person."

He looked suddenly miserable. "I know," he said. "I'm sorry."

I shrugged. "It was a stupid promise."

Ripley smiled and let out a relieved laugh. "Yeah, it was."

My phone buzzed. I assumed it was Dad wanting to know why I was taking so long—but the name on the screen was *Liam Miller.*

I felt suddenly dizzy. Too many emotions were rushing through me at once, and I couldn't track them all. I couldn't take the call, not with Ripley standing right here. What would I say? In a slight panic, I sent it to voice mail.

"Who was that?" Ripley asked as I stuffed the phone into my pocket.

"One of those stupid robocalls."

Ripley seemed skeptical but didn't press it. "Now that I'm here, how can I help?"

"We have to get to Las Vegas." I tugged on my hair. "There's a bus every eight hours. We should have enough to get there."

Ripley shook his head. "I have a better idea."

He grinned and held up a set of car keys.

Once I explained that we were due in LA for a tech rehearsal in three days, Dad reluctantly accepted Ripley's offer of a ride—though he insisted on driving, since Ripley had been awake for twenty-four hours and I was still shaken from the accident. We bought road food and filled up Heather's Hyundai, and it was a little after five p.m. when Ripley curled up in the back seat, Dad took the wheel, and we set out northwest on US 60.

While Dad drove, I paged through his journal, reading every entry, examining every diagram, absorbing every detail of the theory and technique behind the Truck Drop. I went through the execution step-by-step, looking for ways to expand it, to make it more surprising. After three hours, I was carsick, my eyes stung, and I had zero ideas.

I closed the journal and looked up. We were crawling along the highway, pursuing an endless snake of red lights.

"Where are we?" I asked Dad.

"About two miles south of Kingman. There's some kind of pileup ahead."

I glanced into the back seat and saw that Ripley was still asleep.

"Pull over," I said. "I'm going to drive for a while."

"Are you sure you're up to it?"

"Yeah," I said. "I think I might be coming out of it."

And despite the carsickness and my burning eyes, I thought I *was* coming out of it. A lightness had stolen over me during the ride, and I felt my mind clearing, shifting into a higher gear.

Dad glanced in the rearview mirror, possibly to check that Ripley wasn't eavesdropping.

"It's okay, Dad. He knows."

Dad nodded. "You know, Ellie, it'll be a few days before the pills take effect."

I rolled my eyes. "Why, yes, Father, I'm quite familiar with the chemistry."

He gave me an exasperated look.

I expected Ripley to stir when Dad pulled over to swap seats, but he was out cold. His family drama and the overnight drive must have drained his tank to E.

As I pulled back onto the highway, Dad reclined his seat, put an arm over his eyes, and fell asleep.

But I wasn't tired at all. Traffic had evened out, and it was only a few more hours to Vegas, so I gripped the wheel at ten and two, activated cruise control, and let my mind go to work, visualizing the Truck Drop over and over on a loop.

A little before midnight, we came around a low hill and the darkness seemed to peel away, revealing the full nocturnal radiance of the Strip. Casino lights blazed like tiny suns, their colors too sharp, too vibrant. I felt a swell of heat behind my eyes: This was home, and I wanted to take in everything about this moment. The thrum of the motor. The hiss of tires on old blacktop. The perfume of desert flowers and gasoline. It was an orchestra of sensations all vibrating at my frequency. It seemed impossible that twenty-four hours ago I'd been ready to give up. We needed to raise five grand, acquire the props, and get to LA—and suddenly I was certain we could pull it off.

I exited I-15 at Sunset Road so I could drive up the Strip. I needed a little dose of home. Since it was so late, I was surprised to see a cluster of tourists standing under the *WELCOME TO FABULOUS LAS VEGAS NEVADA* sign, but it didn't dampen the rush of nostalgia. The last time I'd seen this particular landmark, we'd been on our way to visit Mariano and Rico Vega and see Flynn & Kellar. I'd been ten years old.

Things looked mostly the same as I drove north on Las Vegas Boulevard. The Luxor's bright white beam still shot up from the top of its black pyramid to light the bottom of the clouds. The campy facade of the Excalibur castle looked just as faded and peeling as ever. And, in the distance, Trump Tower jutted up into the sky like a gaudy golden dildo.

But there were differences, too. The Tropicana had been totally revamped, the Statue of Liberty at New York New York was wearing a Golden Knights jersey, and the windows of the Tangiers Hotel & Casino were plastered over with a huge vinyl decal reading:

DANIEL DEVEREAUX: SKY'S THE LIMIT
COMING THIS CHRISTMAS

Devereaux had been performing on the Strip for over a decade—how long had it been since he'd taken time off to revamp his show? Casinos paid their marquee performers tens of millions of dollars and depended on them to draw big crowds; going dark for a month was an expensive proposition. I wondered what he was going to do next.

The dash clock read 12:22 a.m. when I passed Gold & Silver Pawn Shop and entered the Downtown district. Ripley sat up and looked around.

"Morning, sunshine," I said.

"Where are we?"

"Viva . . . viva . . . Las Vegas!" I snorted at my own terrible Elvis Presley impression, but Ripley seemed unamused.

He ran a hand through his tangle of red hair and gaped out the window. "Holy shit."

"This is where I grew up. Home sweet home. Sin City." I rolled down the windows and savored the dry breeze as we turned right and approached the blinding canopy over Fremont Street. This was old Vegas, and I could feel the legacy of a thousand magicians tickling like champagne in my veins. We passed the Tack & Saddle, the site of our fictional two-night engagement. We passed the Golden Nugget. The Four Jacks. The El Cortez. I drove farther east, away from the lights and toward crumbling concrete and graffiti in search of our motel.

Dad sat up, checked the clock, rubbed his eyes. "Goodness. Traffic must have been bad."

"It was hideous," I said, laughing. "We were gridlocked for two hours after we drove through Kingman. Didn't break up till Boulder City. Jackknifed big rig. Huge pileup." I realized I was babbling but couldn't stop myself.

Finally, we pulled into the motel that would be our home base for the next day or two. Despite its charming art deco facade, the ironically named Uptowner looked like the kind of place you'd score an eight-ball—so it was perfect for our budget. Ripley said he'd pay for his own, separate room, and Dad was about to let him, but I shut that down. He'd driven all this way to rescue us; paying for his bedbug bites was the least we could do.

Finally, we pulled into the motel that would be our home base for the next day or two. Despite its charming art deco facade, the ironically named Uptowner looked like the kind of place you'd score an eight ball—so it was perfect for our budget. Ripley said he'd pay for his own separate room, and Dad was about to let him, but I shut that down. He'd driven all this way to rescue us; paying for his bedbug bites was the least we could do.

We got a room on the second floor facing a concrete outdoor walkway. The view wasn't bad; I could see part of the Las Vegas skyline. But when I stood at the railing and looked down, I saw only an underfilled swimming pool and the cracked parking lot beyond.

In comparison to the motel's rundown exterior, the room itself wasn't as gross as I had feared; the carpet was stained, but the sheets were fresh. Dad immediately crashed on one of the two beds while Ripley collapsed into a sketchy-looking armchair. I took a long, tepid shower with my flip-flops on, just in case. Then I changed into jeans and a T-shirt, grabbed Dad's journal, and sat down at the scratched-up motel desk to work.

"What's up?" Ripley asked, moving to sit on the edge of the desk.

I replied in a whisper so as not to disturb my dad. "We're retooling the Truck Drop."

Ripley raised his eyebrows. "Do you really have time for that?"

"We can't just do what we did before," I said, flipping to a fresh page. "We need to top it."

For the next hour, Ripley and I spitballed new ideas. We got more comfortable with each other, and eventually we were talking in person just like we had on the phone. Bouncing ideas off each other just like we had online—only now were sitting two feet apart.

Ripley suggested adding pyro to the act, setting the truck on fire with Dad inside it. It was a flashy concept, but we didn't have the time or the money to pull it off. I came up with a Sub Trunk variation in which Dad would put me in the truck, and we'd suddenly switch places before the drop—but it didn't feel big enough, and I rejected the idea myself before Ripley could comment. We went round and round like that, and even though our ideas only got more grandiose and impractical, I was having a blast. This was the part of grand illusion that I loved: The design. The creativity. Weaving a story, then constructing a frame of deception to support it. After an hour or so, Ripley yawned, apologized, and passed out on the second bed.

I kept working until, sometime later, my phone buzzed. I had come to dread the sound; it only seemed to bring bad news. This buzz was a text from Liam.

I'm sorry. I can explain. Please call me back.

My heart seemed to contract. What was he sorry for, exactly? Lying? Cheating? With great effort, I pushed the anger and the sadness away. I didn't have time to cry; I had work to do. The Truck Drop already had a great narrative: the impossible escape. What we needed was a new effect, something that would blow everyone's expectations out of the water. I flipped to a later page in Dad's journal and found a diagram of the Truck Drop as imagined from upstage looking out at the audience. Until now I had been picturing the illusion as the audience would see it. Maybe I needed to work on it from behind the curtain—from the magician's point of view—until I could see something new.

From the perspective of Dad's drawing, the trick's infrastructure was apparent: the truss above from which the truck would be suspended, the dump hatches on the back of the tank—all the bits and pieces that would be hidden by the curtain. I focused on one element at a time, imagining how we might exploit each one to greater effect. When my eyes came to rest on the motorized winch mounted in the rafters, I paused—and something clicked.

I sketched and made notes for I don't know how long, my mind whirring, my fingers cramping around the cheap motel ballpoint. At some point I looked up and realized the room had grown brighter. I glanced at the clock. It was 6:38 a.m.; I'd been working for almost five hours straight.

I stood, stretched my cramped muscles, and started up the in-room coffee maker. After brushing my teeth, I wandered out to the walkway to raid the vending machines for breakfast. There was a decent view from the second story, and dawn was breaking over the Strip. To the south, the sun reflected off the windows of the Del Oro hotel in a cascade of molten gold. The air smelled like dust and cigarettes. It felt incredible to be here, to be home.

When I returned to the room bearing three individually wrapped strawberry Pop-Tarts, Dad was sitting on the edge of the bed, looking exhausted.

"Morning," I said, tossing his breakfast onto the comforter.

He glanced at it, then at Ripley, still passed out on top of the undisturbed bedspread.

"You didn't sleep?"

"Just woke up early," I lied, biting into my first Pop-Tart and savoring the sweet rush of high-fructose corn syrup. "I want to show you something."

I poured us each a paper cup of hot brown water and sat down on the desk chair facing him. I flipped a few pages in his journal and handed it over. He frowned, took a sip of coffee, turned the page. After a minute, he looked up at me, blinking.

"This is . . . How . . . ?" He flipped back a page, reread what I had written, then stood up and began to pace. "Vanish the truck," he said, and stopped in his tracks.

"There you are, struggling to free yourself from the ropes." I stood and gestured for effect. "The curtain drops. When it comes back up, you're still in the tank—but the truck is gone."

"It could work," he said.

"I know. All we need is a fast winch, and the Dolby Theatre has one."

"This could really work."

"I *know.*"

He sat on the edge of the bed. "You did all this last night?"

I nodded.

Dad looked at my sketches again, shook his head, and laughed. "Ellie, this is brilliant."

I smiled. Then he frowned slightly and closed the journal.

"What?" I said.

"It's an ingenious design," he said. "But without the props . . ."

"We'll get them."

"How?" he asked, raising his voice. Ripley stirred on his bed, and Dad continued more softly. "We don't have anything to offer Higgins that he can't already buy."

I shrugged. "'An opportunity will present itself.' Isn't that what you always say?"

CHAPTER 18

JIF HIGGINS LIVED WAY THE hell out west on Lake Mead Boulevard in an affluent suburb of Las Vegas called Summerlin. It was basically a giant golf course dotted with Costcos and McMansions—but Higgins's house looked more like a cult compound. Slump-stone walls obscured most of the property, and the barrier on the street-facing side was an elaborate wrought-iron fence with a topiary that must have cost the GDP of a small nation to irrigate.

As the three of us approached the house, Ripley turned to me and said in a half whisper, "Are you sure you want me here? Maybe I should've stayed back at the motel."

"You're great with words," I said. "You might come in handy." Ripley seemed pleased; Dad did not.

When we reached the gate, I pressed the buzzer, and a voice came over the talk box.

"Who is it?"

I was surprised to recognize Higgins's low, nasal voice; I had expected a butler or a housekeeper or something.

"It's Ellie Dante," I replied.

"Oh, yeah. That's today," Higgins said. "How do I know you're really Dante's daughter?"

There was a camera mounted above the talk box. I looked directly into it.

"Don't take my word for it." I stepped aside and motioned for Dad to come forward.

"That old guy is the Uncanny Dante? No fucking way."

Dad stiffened.

"Who's the other kid?" Higgins asked.

"He's our consultant," I replied.

For ten seconds, he said nothing. Then the talk box buzzed and the gate rolled open.

Ripley let out a low whistle as we walked side by side up the cobblestone driveway.

"This place looks like the lair of a millennial James Bond villain."

I snorted. Dad shot us a warning look. We ascended three steps, and I smashed a lion's head knocker against a thick oak door. It opened almost at once.

Higgins stood on the threshold, spindly limbs hanging from a six-foot frame. He was dressed like a teenage boy: gray skull T-shirt covering his beer belly, black skinny jeans. I had expected an older guy, but there wasn't a hint of gray in his sandy hair, and the corners of his eyes were free of wrinkles.

"Come on in," he said, then turned and walked farther into the house, his flip-flops slapping the marble floor.

You could have parked three pickup trucks in the foyer if it hadn't been crammed with wall-to-wall boxes. There were hundreds of them: cardboard cartons, milk crates, and plastic bins haphazardly stacked and spilling over with random junk. I saw hole-punched decks of cards from the long-gone Stardust casino. A cups-and-balls set still in its clamshell packaging. An ancient VHS player. Higgins wasn't just a collector; he was a hoarder. I glanced at Ripley, and the look on his face told me he felt as claustrophobic as I did.

Higgins led the three of us into a big, modern kitchen, where every square inch of countertop was covered with plastic grocery bags filled with chips, cereal, canned goods, and bottles of rubbing alcohol and bleach. He moved two of the bags aside, revealing a coffee maker.

"Caffeine, anyone?"

"No, thanks," I said. My mind was already buzzing.

Dad and Ripley took him up on his offer, and he poured them each a cup.

Dad accepted his with a nod. "May I ask you a question, Mr. Higgins?"

Higgins took a long slurp from his *ORIGINAL AF* mug and seemed to size him up. "All right."

"How did you get your hands on our gear?"

Higgins's face broke into a grin. "At the bankruptcy auction," he said. "I prefer buying direct, but . . ." He shrugged.

Dad gave him a tight, aggressive smile.

Higgins seemed to enjoy his reaction. "Now I'll ask you one."

"Fair's fair."

"Are you sure you're up to this?" Higgins leaned back

against the counter. "According to the internet, the first time kind of wrecked you."

Dad shot me a glance, and I saw some of the old fire in his eyes. Good.

But then he jabbed a thumb in my direction. "This was her idea. I'm not even sure I want to try."

I wondered whether the second part was tactical or true.

Higgins cocked an eyebrow at me. Naturally, he'd assumed Dad was running the show. That I had called on his orders. Of course, that's how it *had* been for a long time. But over the last year, things had shifted, and now I had taken the lead. I felt an unexpected rush of pride at the thought. I might have wrecked the RV—but I had also saved us.

Higgins shot each of us a searching look, then crossed his arms. "You want to see it?"

He led us out through a sliding glass door, around a huge swimming pool, and toward a building the size of a small airplane hangar. When we got close, he pulled out his phone and tapped the screen. The door of the hangar rolled up.

In keeping with his pathologically cluttered house, the hangar was packed with piles of miscellaneous junk: old framed posters, dusty props, antique furniture. Spaced evenly among the piles and running all the way to the back wall were four steel warehouse racks, all crammed with cardboard boxes and plastic bins. Higgins moved down the center aisle, taking us deeper into the hangar. He stopped at a large black guillotine with an old rope handle—a stage prop that looked older than me. He smiled at us, stuck his leg through the hole, and yanked the rope. The blade dropped hard and fast.

Ripley gasped—but, of course, Higgins's leg was fine.

He smirked at Ripley. "Consultant, my ass."

Ripley went red.

I thought Higgins was going to interrogate us further about Ripley, but he only laughed, withdrew his foot, and hoisted the blade to eye level. "Got this when Eric Starr quit doing it," he said, running his thumb along the edge. "Not even sharp." He motioned for Ripley to try it himself—maybe in an attempt to make up for his snide remark? It was hard to tell. Ripley humored him, Higgins reset the blade, and we moved on.

"Oh, yeah," Higgins said, stopping in front of a refrigerator-sized object hiding beneath a black Duvetyne cover. "This might interest you." His tone was falsely casual, as if he expected a big reaction. He grabbed one corner of the black cloth and yanked.

Standing before us was a wood-framed tank with brass fittings and a thick pane of antique glass. Dad and I both gasped.

"Is that what I think it is?" Dad asked.

Higgins leaned against it like it was an old car. "Yup," he said, patting the side. "Houdini's Chinese Water Torture Cell. The genuine article."

Dad approached, hands folded as if he were walking toward the Venus de Milo. This was probably the most sought-after piece of magic paraphernalia in the world. "It has to be—"

"A hundred and eight years old." Higgins glanced up at it. "Pretty neat, huh?"

Higgins seemed pleased at Dad's reaction. Clearly, he

was proud of his collection, and eager for actual magicians to admire it.

"I can't believe you've got all this stuff," I said, figuring it couldn't hurt to butter him up a little. "You could start a museum."

Higgins grinned. "But you didn't come here to admire ancient relics," he said. "You came to rent some." He turned to walk farther down the aisle. Ripley shot me a look that said *don't overdo it.*

We turned right at the end of the row, and that's when I saw it, parked at a perfect angle in the center of the concrete floor:

The 1947 Chevrolet pickup.

Higgins must have had it polished, because the bloodred hood and chrome grille shone under the fluorescent lights. It was bigger than I remembered, and somehow more aggressive, as if it might roar to life at any moment and run us down. I glanced at Dad and saw an expression on his face I'd never seen before—a mixture of revulsion and longing. I touched his arm, and he flinched.

"Step right up," Higgins said in a corny carnival-barker voice. "Don't be shy."

Ripley and I stood back as Dad slowly approached the truck. He circled it once, then placed a palm on the hood and closed his eyes. Whatever memory he was reliving in that moment was a painful one.

"Looks good, right?" Higgins said. "Check these out." We followed Higgins down the aisle. He yanked aside a blue tarp, and there stood the massive Plexiglas tank.

Dad looked at it like he was sizing up a hostile bear. Then

he spotted the steampunk prop lever, an old tractor brake that he had spray-painted antique bronze and topped with a fiberglass handle, and his eyes lit up. He grasped the lever and pulled it. Nothing happened, of course—it was just a prop—but a faint smile played on Dad's lips nonetheless. "Still works," he muttered.

I approached and reached for the handle—then shrank back.

My mother had pulled this lever. Her hand had been right there. I felt a stab of sadness and turned away. Higgins was watching, enjoying our reactions. I couldn't tell if he was just proud, or if there was something darker at play, some kind of emotional vampirism.

He looked from Dad to me, and then said, "About that rental fee."

My stomach tightened. This was the make-or-break moment.

I cleared my throat and turned to Higgins—but before I could say anything, Ripley cut in.

"I read on Forbes.com that you're worth forty million."

I sucked in my breath. What was Ripley doing? Dad looked about to intervene, but then Higgins eyed Ripley and snorted.

"Forty. As if."

"Oh," Ripley said, crossing his arms. "So it's less."

"What are you, an idiot? Forbes only reports *public* information." He gestured around the warehouse. "As you can see, I keep my assets well sheltered."

Ripley pretended to be taken aback. "You bought all this with cash? Under the table?"

Higgins grinned.

"But you must have the biggest collection in Vegas," Ripley said.

"In the *world*, actually. There's a guy in Japan who thinks he's got me beat, but I've been to his place. His whole collection would fit on one of my racks." He shrugged, then clapped his hands and rubbed them together. "Back to business. I believe we agreed on a fee of five thousand dollars?"

I looked at Dad; his face was stone. My heartbeat accelerated. That invincible feeling was gone. Then Ripley cut in again.

"It's probably none of my business—but how does five grand make a difference to a guy worth more than forty million?"

Now I understood his strategy, and I had to hide a smile. This was the Ripley I knew: clever, resourceful, and unafraid to speak up when it mattered.

I played along, shooting Ripley a *shut up* look. Higgins grinned as if we were all behaving exactly as he had expected us to. When he spoke again, he looked directly at me.

"When I turned sixteen, my father refused to buy me a car. The jackass was worth twice what I am now, and he wouldn't drop five grand on a used Corolla. Said I wouldn't take care of it unless I bought it with my own money." There was no trace of the cocky teenager now; he was confident and in control. "So my mom stepped in and bought me an eighty-thousand-dollar Range Rover with his alimony. Did it just to piss him off, probably." He placed a hand against the Plexiglas tank and looked up at it. "A month later I wrapped it around a telephone pole on Pecos; Dad was right. I ended up riding the bus to school for a year while I saved up for another car." He let out a frustratingly parental sigh. "I can't rent you the props for nothing. You wouldn't respect them, and you wouldn't respect me."

Dad's expression was blank; he appeared to have surrendered. Ripley looked equally defeated.

It was up to me.

"What if we pay you nine hundred now and six grand more when we get to LA?"

Higgins laughed. "What am I, Han Solo?"

He was acting more like Jabba the Hutt, but I didn't say so. I gestured at the truck. "Until we use that thing on TV again, it's worthless."

"It's not worthless to you."

I grunted in frustration. This seemed to amuse Higgins.

"I can't think of anything you've got that I want," he said, rocking back slightly on his heels. "Can you?"

When none of us spoke up, Higgins dropped his grin.

"Let me show you something."

CHAPTER 19

HIGGINS'S LIVING ROOM LOOKED LIKE something from an Arthur Conan Doyle story: leather furniture with brass buttons, stone fireplace, old books lining the walls—and for once, there were no boxes or bags in sight. He stepped up to one of the bookshelves, grasped a particularly hefty cloth-bound volume, and tipped it backward. With a soft *whoosh*, the bookshelf slid to one side, revealing a dark opening. It reminded me of the secret door that let guests into the Magic Castle, and I figured that was where Higgins had gotten the idea.

"After you," he said, that self-satisfied grin pulling back his pudgy cheeks.

We descended a spiral staircase into a lushly furnished home theater. Velvet-covered reclining seats. A wall that was all screen. We sat in the front row as Higgins moved to a media cabinet crammed with every conceivable type of player: a Blu-ray, an old LaserDisc machine, and several antiquated tape decks. He pulled a video cassette from a drawer and held it up.

"You want to see some real magic?"

He inserted the cassette into one of the players. Jagged horizontal lines popped onto the screen, and then a pixelated time stamp appeared in the bottom corner: *JUN 8 1992*.

A spotlight came up on a tall man dressed all in black. He crossed downstage and sat on the apron, looking out at the audience as if he were about to read them a bedtime story. The image cut to a closer angle, and I recognized the man. It was the most famous illusionist alive: Daniel Devereaux.

But this wasn't current, sixty-something Daniel Devereaux; this was Devereaux in his prime. Midthirties, trim, athletic, with those sparkling brown eyes that seemed both wise and full of wonder. The spotlight dimmed, the house lights came up, and Devereaux began to speak.

"When I was young," he began, "I didn't fit in. The kids in my neighborhood didn't want to play with me, so I retreated into an inner world of fantasy and daydreams." Devereaux stood, and the spotlight followed him upstage. "As I grew up, those daydreams faded. All except one." He glanced back at the audience. "The dream that I could fly." He lifted his arm, and the curtain rose.

Like every magician, I had watched Devereaux's flying illusion—but only online. He had stopped performing it before I was born, so I'd never had a chance to see it live.

The trick worked liked this:

Devereaux selects a woman from the audience and invites her to explore the stage. Once she's satisfied that there are no ropes or trap doors, stagehands appear and present her with a square metallic vertical frame six feet across. The volunteer inspects it. It's solid.

Next, the stagehands roll out a huge Plexiglas box. The woman knocks on each side, demonstrating that the box is solid. Devereaux dismisses the volunteer amid underwhelming applause. The audience is getting antsy.

The music swells, and Devereaux is swallowed by a billow of fog. When it clears, he's sitting upstage with a single white dove perched on his hand. He releases the bird, and it flaps out over the audience as Devereaux lies down on his back.

And then, with no visible means of support, he rises into the air.

The audience applauds, but with little enthusiasm. This levitation routine dates back to the nineteenth century. They expect more.

Suddenly, Devereaux rolls over, assumes the Superman pose, and takes to the sky.

In Las Vegas almost thirty years later, my heart swelled as the music reached a crescendo and Devereaux soared around the stage. He wasn't just doing a trick, he was delivering a dream. He was flying, and for the moment, so was I. Even with the fake clouds and the artificial smoke and his terrible mullet, it was beautiful.

I turned my head to steal a glance at Higgins. His face was contorted in a frown, his jaw twitching. He was caught up, but not in the ecstasy of flight. It looked more like he was trying to solve an impossible puzzle. I turned back to the screen.

Devereaux pivots in midair. He swoops, turns, and dives, impossibly graceful.

If there were wires, I couldn't see them.

If there were wires, I didn't *want* to see them.

Finally, he swoops low and turns over to face the sky, hovering six feet off the planks. His stagehands approach, bearing the metal frame the volunteer inspected earlier. Devereaux floats through the frame, demonstrating that he can't possibly be suspended from above.

Next, the Plexiglas box is rolled center stage and, nimble as Peter Pan flying through Wendy's window, Devereaux lowers himself into it. A stagehand affixes the lid, then walks across it, proving that it is indisputably solid. Clearly he can't be suspended from the sides, either.

The box opens and Devereaux flies a final loop around the stage, finally touching down on the apron like an Olympic figure skater landing an impossible jump.

The audience erupts; it's a standing ovation.

Back in Higgins's home theater, tears left tracks on my cheeks. I wiped them away. The beauty of Devereaux's work hurt my chest. This was what magic was for. This was the highest form of the art.

As I sat there in the dark, watching Devereaux bow, I realized how much I was going to miss performing. How much I was going to miss making other people feel the way I felt when I watched Devereaux fly. I wanted to fly, too—but I couldn't handle the landings, and probably never would. And even if we had the right doctors and the right medicine, Dad and I just couldn't do it anymore. Even if we nailed the Truck Drop and walked away with the full fifteen grand, that would only buy rent and insurance for a few months. Then what? I was too fragile to tour, and Dad was too old—and I needed to be healthy enough to take care of him as he got even older. Magic would never provide that. We both knew we would have to find something else.

But first, we had to do one last show.

Higgins stopped the tape. The screen went blank, and the lights in his home theater faded up.

Dad got to his feet. "What's the point of all this?"

Higgins sighed. "I bought your props because I was bored. Escapes like the Truck Drop don't impress me; Houdini did it all a hundred years ago. But that . . ." He pointed at the screen. "That's real magic."

Dad's face turned red, and he started toward the door; I stayed put.

"That's what you want, isn't it?" I asked Higgins, nodding toward the screen. His jaw tightened; I'd struck the right nerve. "You want Devereaux's flying rig."

Higgins snorted. "I want all of it," he said. "The props. The rigs. The tricks. The secrets." He licked his lips. "I want to know how it's done."

I sat back in my seat; it all made sense now. There were two kinds of magic fans: those who loved being carried away by the illusion, and those who couldn't stand not knowing the secret. Higgins was one of the latter.

Dad turned to glare at him. "You've got the means. Why don't you make him an offer?"

Higgins expelled a bitter laugh. "You think I haven't tried? His people don't return my calls. Total cock block. I even tried using proxies. Other collectors. One of his old employees."

He shook his head. "They hate me. Everybody hates me until they're ready to retire and desperate for cash. Unfortunately for me—but lucky for you—Devereaux is neither."

I wanted to chime in, but I bit my tongue. Devereaux's flying illusion was, like Higgins had said, a quarter of a century old. He had to know he could find out how it was done on the internet. Hell, he had probably looked it up himself—but it wasn't enough. He wanted to see it firsthand.

He wanted to own it.

"What is it you expect us to do, exactly?" Dad demanded.

"You're the magician," Higgins said. "Use your contacts. Find out where he keeps the stuff. Then acquire it."

Dad composed himself, brushed a finger across his mustache. "We are not thieves," he said. "And we are not traitors to our profession. Ellie, Ripley, let's go." He turned and strode toward the door.

Ripley stood to follow, but I stayed in my seat. Dad turned back to glare at me, his eyes boring a hole in my skull. Rule number two: *Never tell them how it's done.* I wanted to argue with Dad, to tell him that the rules didn't matter when our livelihood—our *lives*—were on the line. But I knew he wouldn't budge.

"*Now*, Ellie." He turned and stormed out.

Ripley stalled, glancing from Higgins to me.

"Damn," Higgins said. "The old man's ferocious."

"You're an asshole, Higgins," I said.

His face flickered, and I saw a brief flash of the angry, isolated teenager he must have been. For a moment, I felt sorry for him.

Then I took a deep breath and focused on the problem at hand. Or rather, the opportunity.

"If we get it," I said, "you'll let us borrow the props? For free?"

Higgins put out his hand, and I stepped forward to shake it.

CHAPTER 20

I EXPECTED TO FIND DAD pacing the driveway with clenched fists; instead, he was leaning against the Hyundai, shoulders slumped, massaging his temples.

"Are you okay, Mr. Dante?" Ripley asked.

"It's just a headache." He looked at me, gestured at the house. "What was that about?"

"I thought maybe Higgins would respond to pleading," I lied. "It didn't work."

Dad shook his head in disgust or defeat, I couldn't tell.

I hadn't wanted to lie—not again—but right now, Dad was too angry to be persuaded. I was going to have to solve the problem myself. Then, once I'd gotten us the props, he'd have little choice but to go along.

Ripley pulled onto Lake Mead Boulevard, and the three of us rode in silence for five minutes that felt like an hour. My head buzzed, my mind spinning this way and that like the dial on a safe as I frantically tried to find the right combination. My meds wouldn't kick in for another three or four days, and in the meantime, I knew I couldn't maintain this pace. I was headed for a crash—but for the moment, I couldn't bring myself to worry about it.

As we approached Downtown, Dad turned to Ripley. "Turn left on Main."

I looked at Dad. "Are we going to see Dr. Shah?"

He shook his head.

"We don't have the funds. We need a place to stay, and we need a way back to Fort Wayne. I need to find work, any work, and soon. Turn left," he said to Ripley. "We're going to the Four Jacks."

"What's at the Four Jacks?" Ripley asked.

"Maybe nothing," he said, and stared out the window.

When we arrived, Dad told us to go get something inexpensive to eat, and we'd all meet back at the car in an hour. Then he headed into the casino, and Ripley and I wandered off into Downtown Las Vegas.

This old part of Vegas was shabby but charming. Instead of blinding LED marquees, the casino signage comprised thousands upon thousands of old-school tungsten light bulbs blinking on and off in sequence, chasing one another around the edges of the signs. We found a walk-up window selling ninety-nine-cent hot dogs; I bought four and we sat down on the curb to inhale them. When I had finished scarfing down my first, I checked my phone. I had missed a call and a text from Liam.

> It's not what you think. I care about you. Please at least text me back and let me know you're okay.

A hot ball swelled in my throat, and before I could put the phone down, Ripley had read the message.

"Whoa," he said. "What don't I know?"

Reluctantly, I told him about my pathetic late-night text to Liam and the phone call from his girlfriend. I left out the part about how I had melted down afterward, and I wasn't sure why. Ripley was my best friend; I'd told him things I'd never told anyone else in the world. And yet, since he had shown up in person, things had been weird. It was almost like getting to know an entirely new person, and despite our bonding and brainstorming session, I didn't trust this new Ripley as much as I had trusted his avatar.

"So that's it?" he said, leaning back on his hands. "You're just never going to talk to him again?"

I drew back; I'd been afraid he wouldn't understand about Liam and me.

"What would I say? He had a girlfriend, and he cheated on her with me. Which makes me an asshole, too."

Ripley looked sheepish. "Look, I don't know anything about relationships and whatever. I just think maybe you don't have all the facts, and ghosting him isn't going to solve anything." He must have felt the heat of my glare, because he added, "But ignore me. As established, I don't know anything."

"No, you don't," I said.

For a while, neither of us spoke. Ripley finished the last bit of his hot dog before breaking the silence.

"Are you really thinking of going after Devereaux's stuff behind your dad's back?"

I nodded.

Ripley raised his eyebrows. "He lost his shit when he found out you'd said yes to Flynn & Kellar. How do you think he's going to react to *this*?"

I glanced up at the vintage mint-green facade of Banyan's Casino. This was the personification of classic Las Vegas—but despite the glow of a thousand lights, the place's romance was diminished. Vegas was like that in the light of day; you could see the cracks in the concrete, the peeling paint. But in just a few hours, an undeniable excitement would permeate the whole city and everyone in it. You just had to wait for the sun to go down.

"You should have seen Dad's face this morning when I told him my new idea for the Truck Drop. I haven't seen him smile like that since before Mom died." I swallowed hard. "We have nothing, Ripley. No home, no transportation. No way to make a living."

The sound of coins dumping into a bucket erupted from the casino behind us. Someone had just hit the jackpot. I stood up and dusted off my hands.

"This is our last shot."

That evening, we stopped at a supermarket for staples—we had descended once more into the world of Jif and Wonder bread. When we got back to the motel, Dad lay down and proceeded to cough until his face went red. I got him a glass of water from the sink.

"Are you coming down with something?" I asked.

"It's just Vegas," he said, rubbing at his temples. "All the damn dust. I'll get used to it again. I just need to rest for a bit." He swallowed our last three Advil, lay back, and closed his eyes.

Dad had said nothing about his meeting at the Four Jacks except that he had an appointment the next day with the director of entertainment. That was good; even if it didn't lead to a gig, at least the meeting would keep him occupied while I did what I had to do. Whatever that was.

When I was sure he was asleep, I grabbed my laptop and gestured for Ripley to follow me out. We found two dilapidated lounge chairs and pulled them up next to the pool. While I fired up my computer, Ripley got us Cokes from the vending machine. I chugged half of mine in a single go; the bubbles felt good on my throat.

"Is your dad going to be okay?" Ripley asked, taking a sip from his own can.

"Traveling is getting harder on him. I used to have to remind myself that he's sixty-four. But lately, he seems even older." I stared blankly at the laptop. "He always said Mom kept him 'youthful.' She was twenty years younger than him. Did I ever tell you that?"

Ripley shook his head.

"Sometimes it grosses me out when I think about it. But they loved each other, you know?"

Ripley looked away. "Love doesn't solve everything. I mean, my parents love each other and look what it does to them."

"At least your mom is alive."

"I wish she wasn't."

"That's easy for you to say," I snapped.

Ripley seemed to shrink. "I didn't mean . . ."

I turned to stare at the spidery light dancing at the bottom of the pool. "She died when I was six. I remember so little about her."

After a long pause, Ripley said, "I bet she was nice, though."

I bristled; why did he have to make this about him?

"She could be kind of a nightmare, actually," I said. "She used scream at me. I wouldn't put my shoes on fast enough, and she'd come over and rip them out of my hands and yank them on and tie them herself, so tight my feet would go numb." I blinked; mostly I remembered good things about my mom—but this thing about the shoes was true, and it had popped up seemingly out of nowhere.

Ripley said nothing, just listened, and I could tell he understood what I meant. My irritation ebbed.

"But she could be gentle, too. I never knew which Mom I was going to get. Sometimes when I couldn't sleep, she'd hiss at me to lie quiet and still in bed. Other times, she would stroke my hair and sing me that song—you know that song, 'Count Your Blessings'?"

Ripley shook his head. I ran a hand through my hair, and I could almost smell the smoke from her cigarette, feel the calluses on her palms as she held my face in her hands.

"Do you think you got it from her?" Ripley picked a thread off his jeans. "I mean, it's genetic, right?"

"Oh, I definitely got it from her. That's why I . . ." I dropped my hand into my lap. "Don't think I'm crazy when I say this, okay?"

"I never would," Ripley said.

I let out a heavy breath. "In a way, part of me is glad I ran out of meds." I closed my eyes. "I've had a couple of moments in the last few weeks where I . . . I don't know. I just feel like I understand her better now. The way she was sometimes. Is that stupid?"

"It's not stupid," he said. "But you're back on them, right?"

I nodded. I didn't want to explain how it took time for them to build up in the system.

"When I'm on meds, I'm more level. My edges don't feel as sharp. But it's like—is that the real me? Or is that just the pills?" I scraped my teeth against my bottom lip. "I want to be healthy. But sometimes I just want to ride the storm and I don't care what happens."

On the other side of the motel, I heard glass breaking. A car horn blared in the street.

A coldness sank into my chest. It was a vague and distant sensation—but still, I knew it was a warning. A dark cloud on the horizon.

Ripley said, "I've never heard you talk this much. Like, ever."

"It's a manic thing," I said. "Easy to hide online. Harder on the phone. Impossible in person."

"I dig it. It's like you ate an extrovert and then burped her up."

I laughed. "You're insane."

"Takes one to know one."

I leaned in and wrapped my arms around him. The laptop pressed uncomfortably into my ribs.

"Thank you," I said. "Thank you for coming. And everything."

The hug lasted just long enough to be awkward, and then I broke it off, adjusted the laptop on my thighs, and woke up the screen.

"First things first," I said, typing in my password. "I have to figure out where Devereaux keeps his flying rig."

"You mean you already know how he does the trick?"

"I have a theory. The props will tell me everything I need to know."

"Any ideas where to look?" Ripley sat back in his chair, took another chug of his Coke.

"No good ones." I Googled Daniel Devereaux, clicked on the first hit, and started to read. "Jesus! He's grossed over four *billion* dollars. He's the highest-paid solo entertainer in history."

"No way," Ripley said, leaning over to look at the screen. "Wait. You're on Wiki-fucking-pedia? Give me that." He put down his can and seized the laptop. He opened a new browser tab, and then, using only the thumb and forefinger of each hand, he began to peck at the keyboard at an irrational speed. He typed faster than I could talk. He typed faster than I could *think*. Before I knew it, he was deep into a website called LotZilla.

"What is that?" I asked.

Ripley kept clicking and typing, ignoring me, until finally he said, "He owns a home in Vegas worth eighteen million dollars."

"Devereaux?"

Ripley nodded. "It's less than three miles from Higgins's, up in the foothills. I bet that's why Higgins bought there. He's obsessed with the guy."

"Do you think he stores his props there?"

"Good question."

Ripley brought up Google Maps and turned on the satellite view. He typed in the address he'd found on LotZilla and zoomed in on the property. A giant, modern, glass-walled home stood on an isolated lot. The house was made up of three long wings pointing out from a cathedral-like central structure.

"Looks like a Scientology compound," Ripley said.

"Are there any outbuildings? Sheds? Hangars like Higgins's?"

Ripley scrolled and zoomed around the property. "There's a detached four-car garage."

"That could be it."

"Hang on."

He launched a new program, one I didn't recognize and didn't know I had installed; green letters glowed against a black background. It looked like something from an old spy movie.

"What the hell is that?" I asked, leaning in.

"It's called a command prompt. Don't distract me."

He typed in a line of code, hit Enter, and got a screen

full of gobbledegook in return. He read the string of symbols, then clicked back to Google Maps.

"Hmm," he said. "He probably uses it for cars."

"How can you tell?"

"Because he owns five vehicles registered in Nevada, all to this address. It's possible he parks them somewhere else, but why would he?"

I wanted to ask about a hundred questions, not the least of which was how he got Devereaux's car registration information, but there were more important things at hand.

I chewed my lip. "You're probably right. That garage doesn't look tall enough for rehearsing the really big stuff. He's got to have a warehouse or something. Can you do a search for that?"

Ripley clicked back to LotZilla. After five minutes, he sighed in frustration and sat back in the chair.

"If Devereaux owns other property in Nevada, it's under some kind of corporate entity. An LLC or something." He rubbed his eyes. "Oh. We could go to the hall of records and poke around." He surfed to the county website. "Buuut they're closed till Monday."

"We can't wait that long." I was starting to feel edgy, the sides of my vision twitching as if distorted by waves of heat. Hypomania had its upsides—it was almost certainly responsible for the all-night session that produced my Truck Drop breakthrough—but it could turn bad quickly. Excitement could morph into anxiety. Enthusiasm into anger. I could feel the tide rising, and I wasn't sure I could stay above water long enough for the drugs to kick in.

Ripley played with the tab on his Coke can. "What was your plan? You know, before I took over your laptop and started hacking?"

"Magic is a small world," I said. "I was just going to Google around, see if I could make a connection through one of Dad's old friends in the business. Go from there."

"Six degrees of Daniel Devereaux," Ripley said.

"Pretty much."

"Where do we start?"

Ripley handed back the laptop. I set my fingers on the keyboard, stared at the screen, and tried to think.

Devereaux was an institution in Las Vegas. Over the years, he'd employed dozens of magicians, consultants, and assistants; it was highly likely that Dad had worked with some of them. I hoped to find this kind of connection and use it to gain some bit of insider knowledge that might help me. But now that I'd said it out loud to Ripley, it seemed like the weakest plan ever. The half-baked invention of a manic mind.

It was exhausting, not knowing which thoughts were real and which were figments of my defective brain. I tugged at my hair, chugged the rest of my Coke, and forced myself to concentrate.

My first thought was Rico. He would know someone, I was sure. The problem was that Rico knew how desperate we were. He knew we resorted to stealing diesel from time to time, and he knew I had picked pockets. If I asked him about Devereaux directly, he'd know something was up. He might even feel obligated to tip off Devereaux's people. I couldn't risk it.

Ripley decided we needed more caffeine and snacks, so he wandered off in search of a 7-Eleven while I kept working. I scrolled through my contacts, then my Facebook friends, noting names of people who might help. But everyone on the list had the same downside as Rico: they might help, or they might give us away.

Ripley returned with a bag of powdered donuts and a two-liter of Mountain Dew. We ate and tried to brainstorm but came up with nothing. When Ripley started yawning in the middle of words, I told him to go up to the room and sleep.

"Go to bed," I said. "I'll text you if I find something." But he insisted on staying with me—so he wrapped himself in his hoodie, reclined the lounge chair, and fell asleep.

My mind was still crackling, now with anxiety instead of optimism. Four days left, and I was no closer to having the props. I started Googling aimlessly, looking for anything that might help.

It was almost five a.m. when I found what I was looking for.

The blog was a blinking, pastel nightmare called The-Magic-Ring.com, a hideous relic of the early World Wide Web. The article's date stamp read November 2, 2002, two years after Devereaux's debut at the Tangiers. A photo showed a blond woman in her twenties with a downturned mouth and choppy, shoulder-length layers. The headline read:

FORMER DEVEREAUX EMPLOYEE
CLAIMS CREDIT FOR HIS ACT

The production manager on his show at the time, a woman by the name of Renée Turner, had contacted The-Magic-Ring.com to complain about Devereaux after he fired her. Turner told the writer she had been let go because she "knew too much" about Devereaux's best-guarded secrets—including his flying illusion.

My heart rate raced as I scrolled deeper into the article.

Turner claimed it had been *her* ideas that had made the flying illusion possible, and that Devereaux could never have conceived or performed that part of his act if it weren't for her. She also claimed that, when Devereaux landed his multimillion-dollar contract with the Tangiers, she asked for a raise but was denied. Then, when he renewed the contract, he denied her again.

> "I lost it, I admit it," Turner said in a phone interview last Thursday. "I said some things I shouldn't have, things I didn't mean. But Devereaux took them seriously and fired me on the spot. I'd worked for him for almost ten years, but he had me escorted out of the building like a criminal. After I cooled down, I tried to apologize, but he wouldn't take my calls. Then he blacklisted me. I'll never work in magic again."

Turner went on, making more cryptic statements about what she knew and veiled threats about what she could do to Devereaux's career if she told. The writer of the story—I couldn't in good conscience call him a reporter—claimed that Turner's comments hadn't been corroborated because "no one from Devereaux's organization could be reached for comment."

I searched for other articles on the subject, anything that might verify Turner's claims, but I found nothing. Literally *nothing.* It seemed impossible that a scandal involving the highest-paid solo performer in history wouldn't yield more results—until I remembered that it had happened in 2002, years before Twitter or Facebook even existed. On top of that, the major magic publications—*MAGIC*, *Genii*, *The Linking Ring*—hadn't been online back then. If the story had burned out quickly, it might not have made it to the mainstream media; after all, this was magic, not Major League Baseball. It was possible that the Turner/Devereaux story *had* been a big scandal in the magic world but had left almost no residue on the internet.

But none of that mattered. What did matter was that Turner seemed to believe what she'd said. And she might still hold a grudge. I looked over at Ripley. He was completely unconscious. Probably, I should've let him sleep. But my brain was on fire, lit by a rapid series of tiny explosions, neurons going off like superheated kernels in a pan of Jiffy Pop. Images flashed and ideas raced, inflating that foil spiral into a dome.

"Ripley," I whispered. He didn't stir. I put a hand on his arm and shook him. "Ripley!"

He sat bolt upright. "What is it? What happened?"

"I found something."

CHAPTER 21

RIPLEY SIPPED LUKEWARM MOUNTAIN DEW, trying to wake up. I filled him in on Renée Turner and her beef with Devereaux.

"So, after sixteen years of banishment from the Wizarding World or whatever, you think she's still in Vegas?"

"I don't know."

"And if she is, what makes you think she can help?"

"I don't know," I said, irritated. We finally had a lead, and now Ripley was giving me the third degree.

"All right," he said, sensing my frustration. "Give me that."

He took the laptop and started pecking away at it; apparently, his fingers were more awake than the rest of him.

Two minutes later he said, "Elias Dante Jr., you are the luckiest person I know."

"Why? What is it?"

"She's still here. And I've got her address."

Dad's alarm went off at six a.m., and before I could crawl into bed and pretend to be asleep, he was sitting up, rubbing the back of his neck.

"What an awful pillow," he said, and then saw me at the desk. "You didn't sleep."

I considered lying, but I could tell by the look on his face that he wouldn't buy it.

"No," I admitted.

Dad looked grim. "Do you think you're starting a cycle?"

"Might just be the meds kicking in. Hard to say." It wasn't hard to say; I was exhibiting every symptom in the books.

"You should sleep."

"I don't think I could if I tried."

Dad sighed through his nose like he always did when he was exasperated. "Well, at least try to rest. Watch some free motel cable. And stick with this one." He jabbed a thumb at Ripley, who rolled over and yawned. Dad stood, moved toward the bathroom, and took out his razor.

"Why are you awake early?" I asked.

"I have my meeting with Alan at the Four Jacks. But first I'm going to get the paper and go through the want ads. It's time I found a plan B."

He forced a smile, but he looked as if he were preparing to serve a life sentence. As he closed the bathroom door behind him, I tried to imagine how he would feel onstage, playing to a row of senior citizens at the Four Jacks, or to empty bar stools at the Tack & Saddle. Or working retail again, wearing a blue vest and scanning items to a constant chorus of beeps and chimes. I didn't think it could get worse than birthday parties and backyard weddings—but he did. He found the idea of a "day job" demoralizing. I wondered how he would adjust once we finally settled down, or whether he would adjust at all. He seemed more put together when he came out of the bathroom, his face shaved and his hair combed. As he pulled on his suit jacket, he looked at me. "Stay in the motel," he said. "You've got food here, and I don't want you wandering off into the city."

I nodded, but I couldn't meet his eye.

Thirty minutes later, Ripley and I got into Heather's Hyundai and headed east on Tropicana toward Renée Turner's apartment.

Ripley glanced at me from the driver's seat. "How long have you been up?" he asked.

"Forty-eight hours? I'm not sure."

"And you're not tired?"

"I feel like I could sprint from one end of the Strip to the other."

"I guess I didn't realize it was that intense." He sounded concerned.

I shrugged. "Hypomania. It's the gift that keeps on giving. Until it doesn't."

"Do you think it'll last until the show?"

"I don't need it to. Once we've got the props, Dad will take it from there."

We pulled into a McDonald's adjacent to Turner's complex, and Ripley killed the engine.

"Okay, what's the plan?"

I looked at the apartments: foil in the windows, laundry hanging from the balconies. It made me nostalgic for the luxury of the Cedarwood Mobile Estates.

"I'm going to pretend to be a journalist. See if she'll open up about the Devereaux thing."

"Will that work?"

"You got any other ideas?"

Ripley smirked. "I'm glad you asked."

A shriveled succulent stood on Turner's small porch, a lipstick-stained cigarette butt jutting up from the potting soil. I took a deep breath and knocked twice on her door. No answer. It was only 8:17 a.m.; she was probably still asleep. I was considering going back to the car to wait until a more reasonable hour when I heard footsteps approaching.

"Who is it?" The voice coming through the door was low and gravelly, but I was pretty sure it was a woman's.

"My name is Purcilla Ripley. I'm a contributor to *MAGIC Magazine*." It wasn't a complete lie; they'd printed an essay I wrote when I was in eighth grade. "Could we talk for a minute?"

The door opened a crack, and the woman who peered over the chain at me was definitely Renée Turner. The shoulder-length layers from the blog photo had been replaced by a gray-flecked bun, but the downturned mouth was the same.

"What do you want?"

I hesitated. If I mentioned Devereaux too soon, she might get gun-shy and slam the door. On the other hand, I'd have to bring him up sooner or later.

"I don't think you ever got a chance to tell your side of the story," I said.

Turner frowned.

"Your interview should have made the *Review-Journal* at least. It wasn't fair."

"What are you talking about?" she said, but I sensed recognition in her voice.

"I'm talking about how Daniel Devereaux ruined your career."

Turner blinked, then closed the door. For a moment, I thought I'd blown my chance. Then I heard the scrape of the chain being drawn back, and the door reopened.

"That was a hundred years ago," she said, still suspicious. "Why ask about it now?"

"Rumor has it he's retiring soon." I hoped she couldn't tell I was making it up on the spot. "Maybe there's a story here."

She hesitated. I could feel my pulse surge in my wrists and neck.

"All right, then," she said, and stood aside to let me in.

Turner's apartment smelled like Pine-Sol and cigarettes and would have fit right in with some of the trailers back at Cedarwood: battered carpet, scarred linoleum, broken venetian blinds. I saw an ancient desktop computer in the corner of the front room, and then I spotted what Ripley had told me to look for: her Wi-Fi router.

"How'd you find me?" Turner asked.

"Google."

"Everything's on the goddamned internet now. Coffee?" She reached for a carafe on the counter.

"That would be great," I said, though my nerves were already twitching. I accepted a steaming mug and we sat down at her kitchen table. She took out a pack of Virginia Slims and lit one with a pink disposable lighter.

"How long have you lived in Las Vegas?" I thought a warm-up question was in order, but Turner got right to the point.

"Did you really come here to talk about Devereaux?"

"Yes."

She frowned and tapped her cigarette over an old Sam's Town ashtray. "You want to trash him on his way out?"

"I just want the truth." I shrugged. "I was hoping you could tell me what happened."

Turner laughed. "You read the thing. You already know."

"He fired you because you knew too much."

She took a drag, stood up, and extracted a bottle of Jim Beam from her pantry.

"That '92 special was huge. It made him." She poured a shot into her coffee cup, took a sip, and closed her eyes.

It was working; she was talking. "Do you mind if I take notes?"

"Knock yourself out."

She came back to the table, and I fired up my laptop. I was in a tender situation. I had to revive her anger at Devereaux so she'd spill some of his secrets—namely, where he kept his props—but if I pushed her too far, she might get offended and shut down completely. I started with an easy question.

"In the article, you said the flying illusion was Devereaux's idea, but that you came up with the method?"

She gave me a knowing shrug.

"How could he afford to let you go? Wasn't he afraid you'd talk?"

She laughed, a bitter bark accompanied by a rush of smoke. "Sweetheart, he has enough lawyers to fill T-Mobile Arena. If I'd said two words about it, he'd have sued the skirt off my ass."

I nodded, but I detected some playacting on her part. If he was so sue-happy, why hadn't he gone after the blog that published her interview? I needed to rile her up more.

"Do you have any proof that it was your idea? Notes, sketches, emails? Anything?"

Turner set her cigarette in the tray and leaned toward me. Her mouth was a thin line.

"You don't know what it was like being a woman in magic back then." She sat back and absently wiped a smear of lipstick off her mug with a thumb. "We were all glorified Vanna Whites. Look pretty in spandex and smile at the big magician. He thought I was lucky to have a job, let alone a job working for the greatest illusionist who ever lived."

"Devereaux actually said that?"

"What does it matter who said it? It was true. I was a girl in tights, and he was the best in the world."

I watched her pick up her cigarette again. I wasn't sure she was telling the truth, but her emotions seemed genuine.

"That would have pissed me off."

She made a dismissive gesture. "It was a long time ago."

"So he blacklisted you from magic. What do you do now?"

"Real estate," she said, deflating. "And I waitress a couple of nights a week at Boulder Station. The market's been pretty dry since the crisis."

I'd read about the crash of '08 in my online econ class—but that had been over a decade ago. Renée Turner was living in the past.

She took another sip of spiked coffee. "You want to see something?"

She got up and walked to a bookshelf in her living room, reaching out once to steady herself on a ratty armchair along the way; I guessed this wasn't her first cup. She returned with a photo album and flipped through it until she found what she was looking for.

"This was taken at his production office. Spring of 1990, maybe '91." She laughed. "You can tell the date by my perm."

There she was in a faded snapshot, her hand on Devereaux's shoulder. She looked to be in her midtwenties.

My computer had finished booting up, so I tapped out a few random keystrokes to make a show of taking notes, then clicked on the Wi-Fi icon as Ripley had instructed.

"His production office," I said. "That's the place in Summerlin?"

She frowned. "No, that's his house. The production office was downtown."

On-screen, the list of local Wi-Fi networks was still populating.

"It was Downtown, but it's not anymore?"

"Nope. He sold it."

I had her talking about his property now; I was getting closer, but I needed to tread lightly. Forcing my voice into a disinterested monotone, I asked, "What about that warehouse?"

"The one on Twain?"

"Right," I said, trying to sound casual.

"He sold that, too." She stubbed out her cigarette and lit another. "Bought a new one just off the Strip, right after the market took a dive. Good timing."

I tried to conceal my excitement. "Why would he need a warehouse, anyway?"

Turner looked at me like I was an idiot. "He does the biggest illusions in the world. Where do you think he workshops them?"

"Right," I said. "That makes sense."

"Plus he has to store all that equipment. The guy's a hoarder. Never throws anything away."

Never throws anything away. His flying rig had to be in that warehouse.

"You don't happen to have the address?" I tried to sound casual, but my voice quavered.

Her eyebrows drew tighter. "You'd have to call his PR people."

I'd pressed too hard. She was clamming up.

Turner looked down at the old photo and ran a finger

over its plastic sleeve, apparently lost in memories.

I took the opportunity to glance at my laptop. It had detected seven Wi-Fi networks—but, per Ripley's instructions, I only cared about the one with the strongest signal. It was called D-LINK, and there was a little padlock icon next to the name—it was password protected. Ripley would have to take it from here.

I looked up to check on Turner. She was still staring at the old photo, her cigarette burning forgotten in the ashtray. I shut my laptop and stood.

"I think I've got what I need," I said, giving her my best smile.

She licked her lips, glancing at my laptop bag. "You gonna print all that?"

"Would that be all right?"

She hesitated. "Maybe . . . maybe run it by me first?" She gave me a guilty smile.

"Of course."

Her shoulders relaxed.

I made for the door, then turned back. "Can I ask you one more thing?"

"Shoot."

"Were you really going to expose Devereaux's method?"

"No," she said, shaking her head. "And anyway, it doesn't really matter how it's done. It matters who's doing it."

Her eyes drifted back to the photo album, and I left the apartment.

CHAPTER 22

AS I WAS ON MY way down Turner's apartment steps, Liam called.

My stomach clenched as I stared at his name on the screen. Just when I had managed to push away my spiraling thoughts, he had to call and start up the whirlwind again.

Was it possible he was telling the truth—that I had somehow misunderstood the whole situation? I didn't think so. That girl on the phone had been genuinely pissed. Liam was probably calling in an attempt to relieve his guilt. Either way, I couldn't afford to let him distract me right now. I declined the call and kept walking.

I was about to exit the complex when my phone dinged with a new voice mail. My thumb hovered over the Delete button. Did I really want this drama right now? Was I really this weak?

Apparently, the answer to both questions was yes. I clicked Play.

"Ellie, it's Liam. Please don't delete this." He sighed. "I'm an idiot, okay? I owe you an apology. And I can explain everything." A long pause. "I just need you to call me back."

I stood frozen for a moment with the phone still pressed to my ear. I was so sick of this whole business. I should block his number. I should smash my screen again until I couldn't read it anymore. I should call him back and tell him I missed him.

Instead, I deleted the message and walked back to the car.

Ripley was on me the minute I walked into McDonald's.

"Did you get it? The SSID?"

"I think so," I said, opening my laptop and bringing up the screenshot. "Is it . . . D-LINK?"

He blinked. "You've got to be kidding."

Before I could ask what he meant, he seized my laptop and started typing.

"Her router is older than me!" He snorted. "And she's using WEP."

"Could you say that in English?"

Ripley ignored me, hammering on the keyboard as if I weren't even there. I tried to follow his moves on-screen, but all I saw was a vomit of numbers and symbols.

"Yup!" he exclaimed, gesturing at an incomprehensible line of code. "She's still using the default password. Some people deserve to be hacked."

"Can you just tell me what's—"

"Chicken-fried Jesus, she's got LogMeIn client installed!" He resumed typing.

Finally, I grabbed his wrist, harder than I meant to. He looked at up me, shocked.

"Could you please stop and tell me what the fuck you're doing?"

Ripley frowned. "Okay, wow. First, let go of my arm."

I did, and he rubbed his wrist. "What the hell, Ellie?"

I took a slow breath in through my nose. "I'm sorry," I said, only half meaning it. This new Ripley was a bit of a know-it-all. "I just need you to slow down, please. I don't speak computer."

"Okay," he said, shaking out his wrist. "Next time, just *ask*."

I *had* asked, but I bit my tongue.

"Here." Ripley double-clicked an unfamiliar icon, and the screen on my laptop changed. It looked vintage now, like it was running an old version of Windows.

"This is her screen," he said, pointing. "I'm controlling her PC by remote."

"How?"

He twisted the ring on his middle finger. "She did the internet equivalent of leaving her keys in the car and the windows down."

Ripley started scrolling through Turner's browser history. "Recipes, online banking . . . huh."

"Huh what?"

"She's gone to LotZilla like a thousand times."

"Isn't that the site you were using to look for Devereaux's house?"

He nodded. "It lets you search property values. She was looking at houses on the west side."

"She said she was in real estate."

"That would explain it." He scrolled. "She's got an eBay problem, too. And, wow. Craigslist personals?" Ripley turned to me. "Will your people stop at nothing to obtain sex? You realize it literally warps your mind."

"Wait," I said, pointing at the screen. "Scroll back to the LotZilla stuff."

"What am I looking for?"

"A warehouse somewhere near the Strip."

He scrolled up, shook his head. "These are all condos and townhomes. . . . Wait." He clicked on a link, and a new browser window popped up. A satellite map of Las Vegas appeared with a red dot just east of the Strip.

"Can you zoom in?"

The red dot marked a large warehouse located behind a restaurant on Hinson Street, a few blocks west of I-15.

My head was buzzing. "Does it say who owns it?"

He clicked and scrolled. "Flying Man Holdings, LLC."

My heart stopped. "That's it."

Ripley and I pulled up across from the address he'd found on LotZilla. The building facing the street wasn't a restaurant as the website had indicated—it was a strip club. Blacked-out windows, faded red awning, blinking marquee that read *The Strip—High Steaks, Hot Girls.*

"That's profoundly gross," Ripley said.

"Pull into the lot in back."

"Ellie, we don't have time to satisfy your perverse cravings."

"Can you not make stupid jokes right now?"

Ripley put his hands up like he was surrendering, then pulled into a spot at the far end. While he opened my laptop, I looked around to see if anyone had noticed two teenagers parking at a strip club. A girl in a long coat was vaping and texting near the back door, but she didn't look up. There was no one else in sight.

I turned my attention to the warehouse. It was signless, beige, and roughly the size of a cineplex; if Devereaux wanted a low-key place to workshop illusions and store props, this was perfect.

"Got anything?"

Ripley grunted. "If you want to know what kind of emails the manager of a strip-club-slash-steakhouse gets, I could tell you in about five minutes. But the Flying Man network is password protected."

"Can you hack it or not?"

He turned to look at me. "Did I do something to offend you?"

I clenched my jaw. I couldn't lose my temper right now; I needed Ripley's help.

"There's just a lot riding on this. Can you do it?"

"Probably," he said, with a condescending *what's wrong with you?* expression. "But it'll take me a while."

"How long is 'a while'?"

"I don't know, Ellie. Twenty minutes? An hour?"

I wanted to snap back at him, but I held it in. "I'm going to look around."

Ripley started to speak as I got out of the car, something about cameras, but I slammed the door before he could finish.

I paused for a moment outside the car. I should open the door and apologize—I was getting more irritable by the minute—but I couldn't bring myself to do it. It was like being stuck in the RV again with the power steering locked: I could see where I was going, but I couldn't change course. Without looking back, I headed toward the warehouse.

As I walked around to the back, I saw what Ripley had been talking about: there were security cameras mounted on the building. I pulled up the hood on my sweatshirt to obscure my face and counted six cameras in all: one on each corner, one overlooking the loading dock, and one above the only pedestrian entrance, a single door on the side farthest from the strip club.

There were two cars parked next to the loading dock—a vintage BMW and a red Mazda hatchback. That meant someone was inside, possibly watching me on a screen right at that moment. My pulse roared, and I savored the surge of fresh adrenaline; it would help me stay sharp.

I kept my head down and approached the pedestrian entrance. The door looked heavy and solid. Instead of a traditional lock, there was a keypad above the knob. My heart rate spiked; this couldn't be picked like a regular lock. And in combination with the cameras, it suggested that the security around this building was tight. This was going to be harder than I'd thought. I pulled out my phone and snapped a picture of the lock.

As I got back into the car, Ripley looked up.

"What did you find?"

I showed him the picture. "What do you think? Can you hack it?"

"No," he said. "Out of my league. But maybe I can get the pass code."

"How?"

He rubbed his eyes. "Most people's door locks aren't connected to Wi-Fi. That would be incredibly stupid. But if someone keeps a record of the pass code on a computer—one that's currently turned on and connected to the network—I might be able to find it."

My pulse quickened. "Great! Do it!"

"There's a risk."

"What risk? Can't you just hack in from here?"

"I could," Ripley said, his voice rising. "But I'd have to reset their router."

I sucked in a breath. He was being such a goddamn know-it-all. "I get it, you're a computer genius and I'm not. Could you please explain this in English? I don't have time to Google every word you say."

Ripley gaped at me, shook his head, and then answered in a defeated tone.

"If I restart their router, their IT guy will know immediately that they've been hacked."

"Does that even matter? I mean, what can they do?"

"Well, for one thing, they could change all their passwords."

I bit my lip. "Including the pass code to the front door."

Ripley nodded.

I glanced out the window at the looming beige warehouse. We were so close.

"Do it," I said.

"All right," Ripley replied, and started typing.

After five minutes, he seemed no closer to "cracking the network," and I was starting to get nervous about the security guy at the strip club. He had come out twice to glance around the lot, and both times his eyes had lingered on our car. I told Ripley we should move to the McDonald's next door, but he said the warehouse's Wi-Fi signal wouldn't reach that far.

"Will you please stop tapping your foot?" I said. Ripley didn't respond.

Ten minutes later, I was about to call the whole thing off when Ripley finally declared, "I'm in!"

I leaned over to watch the screen as he entered yet another incomprehensible command.

"What are you doing?"

"Unleashing a bot that will scour the network for strings of characters that look like passwords."

"So we just wait?"

"There are only two PCs connected. It shouldn't take very— Ha!"

"You found it?"

Ripley shot me a glare. "Will you please. Back. Off." He turned back to the screen and clicked on a folder. "People are so stupid." He gestured at the screen in disgust. "This guy Doug—Devereaux's stage manager or whatever—has a 'friend' in his contact file, first name *Top*, last name *Secret*. The Notes field is a list of everything a hacker could want. CCVs on his credit cards. Social security numbers. His wife's mother's maiden name . . . Jesus, his passport number is in here—who does that?"

"What about passwords?"

He scrolled, frowned. "Shit. No. He uses password management software."

"The guy writes down his credit card numbers but uses a program to hide his passwords?"

Ripley rolled his eyes as if explaining to a four-year-old why the sky is blue. I wanted to throttle him.

"It's not for security. It's because he's lazy. He doesn't want to have to remember them."

He scrolled, clicked. "Wait a minute." He pointed to a block of text that read:

Facebook = Janey middle + last 4 ssn
First NV Bank = Janey middle + Doug Jr. bday

"They're hints," he said. "Not the passwords themselves. But if we know his wife's middle name—"

"You don't have to mansplain hints to me. Is there one that says 'door code'?"

He shot me a hurt look, then scrolled down. The text read:

Front Door: Daniel's magic hero

"Boom!" Ripley said. "The pass code is the name of Devereaux's favorite magician." He looked at me expectantly.

I closed my eyes and knocked my head against the headrest.

"What, you don't know it?" Ripley's voice rang with disbelief. "I thought you knew everything about—"

"It's not that," I snapped. "Devereaux names the same influences in every interview."

"Well, who are they?"

I ticked them off on my fingers. "Fred Astaire. Frank Sinatra. Alfred Hitchcock."

"Those aren't magicians," Ripley said.

"No shit!"

He sank into the driver's seat. "So you don't know."

I shook my head, let out a long sigh. "But I know someone who might."

Ripley's eyes lit up. "Call them!"

"I can't."

"Why not?"

I looked over at him. "Because it's my father."

Ripley leaned his forehead against the steering wheel. I stared out the window toward the back of the strip club.

The momentary silence was interrupted by the chirp of my phone. I recognized the number from the motel—it was Dad.

What if something had happened? What if it was his heart?

My whole body tensed as I answered the call. "Dad? Are you okay?"

"Elias Dante Jr.," he said. "Where in God's name are you?"

I sagged with relief; he wasn't sick, just worried. "On my way back," I said, trying to sound contrite.

Dad spoke again, his voice like gravel and ash. "I thought I made it clear you were not to leave the motel."

I clenched my jaw and squeezed my eyes shut. I needed to stay in control.

"Did you hear me, young lady? Because this time, there will be consequences."

Anger heated my face, and my self-control evaporated. "Like what, Dad?" I asked, gripping the phone hard. "Are you going to ground me? Are you going to send me to my room? Because first I'd have to actually *have a room*!"

Before he could reply, I ended the call and brought my palm down on the dashboard.

"Jesus, Ellie! This isn't even my car!"

I clenched my fists. "We have to get back."

"Okay," Ripley replied. "But can you calm down enough to drive? I need to do some research."

We switched seats and got on the road.

I seethed behind the wheel. Here I was trying to save Dad's ass, and he was treating me like a child. Meanwhile, I could feel Ripley's eyes on me, judging me every time I braked or changed lanes. As I crossed Las Vegas Boulevard, a middle-aged hipster in a minivan cut me off.

"Watch where you're going!" I yelled, pounding the horn of Heather's Hyundai.

"Ellie," Ripley said. "You've got to calm down. You're going to kill us both."

I said nothing and kept my eyes on the road.

"Here's the deal with the lock," Ripley said, reading from his phone. "According to the manufacturer's website, you have to enter a five-digit alphanumeric code. You get three tries. Then it locks you out and alerts security."

"So how do we hack it?" I felt Ripley's exasperated stare, but I didn't look at him.

"We don't, Ellie. Not without special hardware."

"Where can we get that?"

"Hell if I know," he said. "I'm not a career criminal."

I gripped the wheel and stared straight ahead. We were fucked.

"What's plan B?" Ripley asked, his voice high and calm, as if everything was going to be just fine. "Are you going to ask your dad?"

"Great idea," I said, my voice dripping with sarcasm. "I'll just ask him straight out. 'Gee, Dad, who is Devereaux's secret magician crush?' And then he'll ask why. And when I don't answer, he'll know *exactly* what we're up to. Because unlike you, he is not a fucking idiot!"

Ripley threw up his hands. "What did I do to piss you off, Ellie? Why are you being like this?"

"This isn't some fucking scavenger hunt, Ripley. It's my life!" I was boiling over now.

"I'm just trying to help you solve the problem! We have to do something!"

"We?" I turned to glare at him, and the words poured out of me like hot bile. I knew they were awful, but I was powerless to stop. "*You* don't have to do anything. *I* have to do it."

"That's not fair," Ripley said, his voice rising. "I drove all the way out here to help—"

"Bullshit." My face was on fire. "You drove *all the way out here* to run away. You couldn't handle Mommy and Daddy fighting, so you left your four-bedroom, air-conditioned house and abandoned your little brother to run away to the desert. You're so noble, Ripley. So fucking noble."

Ripley opened his mouth, then shut it.

The rest of the ride was silent except for the sound of my furious breathing. I felt a tiny twinge of guilt, but it was buried under my rage. This was nothing but a joyride to him; he didn't care how it turned out. All he'd done since we'd arrived in Vegas was play on my computer and waste my time.

When we pulled up at the motel, I stole a glance at Ripley. His jaw was tight, his eyes downcast. I knew I should say something, but the blood pumping through my temples was deafening, and it was all I could do to suppress the urge to slap his face.

I looked away, feeling my chest growing heavier. This was my fault. As hard as I'd tried to hide my crazy, I hadn't even lasted two days. I had driven Liam away, and now I'd alienated the only real friend I had.

I wished he had never come to Phoenix. I wished we had never met in real life.

Without looking at me, Ripley held out my phone. I wanted to say I'm sorry, to say this was just how I was sometimes, to say this wasn't really me. Only it was.

I took the phone, got out of the car, and left him in the passenger seat with the motor still running.

CHAPTER 23

DAD STOOD UP THE INSTANT I walked through the door.

"Where were you?" His tone was equal parts rage and relief.

"I'm fine, Dad, thanks for asking. Ripley and I just went for a drive." My face was still hot.

"You didn't call; you didn't leave a note. I thought something had happened to you."

"I'm not a baby. I can go for coffee without getting mugged."

"You can't just walk out like that. You need to tell me where you're going."

My hands trembled as I tried to steady my voice.

"I've lived in a box with you my whole life, Dad. I'm not a pet. I need air. I need space. I need you off my back."

"We can talk about that. But let me be clear." He took a slow breath through his nose. "You are not to go out again without my express permission. I'm still the adult here, and you are still just sixteen years old."

"Okay, *you're* the adult?" I clenched both fists. "I get us money. I do the shopping. I book the gigs—I find the goddamn props! What do you do? You say no to everything and get in the way. You treat me like an employee. I don't work for you, Dad, okay? I'm not your fucking assistant. I'm not *Mom*!"

On the last word, my voice broke, and Dad's face went white. He put a hand to his mouth and sat down hard on the bed.

"Oh God." I rushed to him. "Are you okay? Is it your heart?"

My own heart had seized up.

Dad gasped, shook his head. "I'm okay. I just—I lost my breath for a second."

I covered my face in my hands and slid down the side of the bed to the floor. My shoulders hitched. My breath caught.

Dad was next to me in a heartbeat, putting his arm around me.

"It's all right," he said. "Shh. You've been without medication too long, Ellie. It hasn't had time to build up in your system yet. That's what this is. That's *all* this is."

"It's not," I said between gasps. "I fuck everything up. The RV. Your career. My friends."

"What are you talking about?"

"I *am* like her, Dad!" Now I was shrieking, hysterical. "And I'm going to end up like she did! I know it!"

He shook me by the shoulders. "Don't you *ever* say that!"

His eyes welled up. He let go of me and slumped back

against the bed. The two of us sat there for a long, quiet moment.

Finally, he spoke. "Did I ever tell you I waited tables in college?"

I cocked my head. "You did?"

"I was miserable. But I got free meals and went home with cash in my pocket." He scrubbed a finger across his mustache. "Today, I came full circle. I applied at the Denny's on Las Vegas Boulevard."

I stared at him.

"And at Guitar Center, and at a pawnshop on Charleston."

Unable to form words, I could only shake my head.

"I used to think that taking a day job meant giving up on my dreams. Betraying my true calling. Throwing away everything I'd worked so hard for." He swallowed hard. "But the truth is, I've been lucky all these years to make a living doing something I love. Many talented people never get that chance." His eyes grew dull. "In any case, my time seems to have come to an end." He smiled, but it was empty.

"Dad, why are you talking like this? What happened?"

As his focus dropped to the carpet, the empty smile collapsed.

"Alan turned me away at the Four Jacks. He said my reputation was . . ." He pressed the heels of his hands against his eyes. "I begged him, Ellie. I told him how we've been living. How I've made you live. He . . ."

The words seemed to dry up. I reached out and took his hand. It was heavy, and the palm was leathery from years of handling coins and cards. It was a magician's hand.

Dad let out a bitter laugh; it sounded nothing like him.

"He offered to put me in touch with the producer of a reality show. He said our life would make good television."

My mouth fell open. "Are you kidding?"

"No."

"What did you say?"

He raised his eyebrows. "I almost punched him in the face. I walked out instead."

"You should have punched him."

Dad shrugged. "It's not too late. We could go back."

I smiled. He returned it and leaned back against the rickety bed frame.

"We have to do this, Dad. We have to go after Devereaux's rig. It's our only shot."

He closed his eyes, set his jaw. "What if we're caught?"

"Then we go to prison, and they feed us and give us meds."

He shook his head. "*I* go to prison. You end up in foster care."

"In which case, again, we both get food and meds."

"Ellie, you need to take this seriously."

"I *am* taking this seriously. I've got a week's worth of pills left, and you're next." Dad's face darkened. "We have no money, no transportation, nowhere to sleep. An old man ready to have a heart attack and a teenager on the verge of a breakdown. We are the worst candidates for homelessness I've ever heard of.

"I've thought about this, Dad. I've thought about it until my head feels like it's going to pop. This is our only play. We have nothing left to lose."

His eyes drifted out of focus, as if he were staring into the distance at something I couldn't see.

"What if it goes wrong?" he whispered. "What if the truck drops, and I . . ."

Oh God. He wasn't worried about the grift; he was worried about the show.

"Then you get paid five thousand dollars for humiliation you've already felt." I took his hand again. "But if it goes right . . ."

For a moment, I thought he was going to cry, but when he spoke again, his voice was strong and clear.

"Then we give it all back."

"Give what back?"

"All of it. The props. The money we've stolen." He looked at me. "You've kept track?"

I nodded. "Every cent."

He stood, crossed to the window, opened the drapes. I got up and joined him.

He was staring north, away from the Strip, toward old Vegas. I could just see the top of the California Hotel & Casino and the sparkling Golden Nugget sign. It was like a postcard.

"My father was an insurance-company actuary," he said. "He assessed risk for a living."

I watched him intently; my grandfather had died before I was born, and Dad talked about him even less often than he talked about my mother.

"The first time I ever flew in an airplane, he said, 'Don't be nervous. You're two thousand times more likely to die on the way home from the airport.' Needless to say, I nearly got sick in the taxi."

I laughed. He smiled.

"Later that year, I told him that when I grew up, I was going to be a magician. I'll never forget what he said. He got an expression on his face like he'd eaten a bad prune. 'The odds are too high,' he said. 'You'll never make it.'"

Dad's face tightened, and suddenly I could see the ten-year-old he had been.

"That summer he put me to work at his company, filing. 'A proper job,' he called it. I hated him. I hated myself."

He turned to me, his eyes shining, his mouth drawn downward.

"I never wanted that life for you, Ellie. Rules. Numbers. Closed doors. I wanted you to be free. To be whatever you wanted. And then, when you asked me to teach you magic . . ." His eyebrows drew together and he shook his head, struggling to speak through the emotion. "You had so much talent, right from the start. And all I could think was that *you* could do it. You could achieve what I failed to. I would make sure of it." He turned away to face the window. "But now I realize I've done just what my father did. I've pushed you into a life you hate. I'm just like he was."

"You're not," I said. "You're nothing like him." Dad looked at me, his face tight with hope and regret. "I don't hate magic, Dad. I love it. The feeling of being onstage. It's like flying." He blinked rapidly, and I put a hand on his arm. "But the crash afterward . . . It's brutal. It takes me days to recover, but the next morning we're on the road again. I have no base. No routines." I swallowed. "The ups and downs are just—"

He turned toward me suddenly, put his hands on my shoulders. His eyes flashed with hope. "But that's normal, Ellie! All performers experience that. The highs and the lows, that's just part—"

"You're not listening!" Dad flinched. "It's not normal. Not for me. My highs and lows are not like yours. They're vicious. Unbearable. I don't bounce from happy to sad; I go from invincible to suicidal, then back again. And again. I can't live like that anymore."

He looked away, his face growing paler by the moment.

"I know you wanted a different life for me, a performer's life. But I can't do it. I'm sorry."

Dad let out a long breath, closed his eyes. "I'm the one who should be sorry." He looked at me, his eyes wet and fierce. "I've been selfish. You take such good care of me—but I'm supposed to be the one taking care of you." He took me in his arms then, and I hugged him tight. Tighter than I had since I was a little girl.

When I let go, he turned and placed his hand against the window. Silhouetted like that against the Vegas skyline, he looked like something from an old cover of *Time* magazine.

"All right, then," he said, turning to face me. "We've got work to do."

When I got outside, I scanned the parking lot below, but Heather's Hyundai was nowhere in sight.

Ripley was gone.

I pulled out my phone and tapped his contact. It went to voice mail. I called again; same result. A cold fist pushed against my breastbone, and for a moment I thought I might be sick. The things I had said to him. The way I had treated him, after he'd driven across three states to rescue me. I paced the concrete walkway, squinting against the hot red light of the afternoon sun.

It was times like this when I hated my illness, hated myself—and where was the line between the two? *Was* there a line? Even when the gray had loosened its grip, even when I was riding high, I did and said terrible things to the people I loved. I'd brought Dad to tears, and I'd driven Ripley away. If that's who I was off meds, wasn't that the "real" me? Didn't that make the medicated, "functional" version of me nothing more than a chemical marionette? Did the illness disfigure my personality—or did the medication build me a false one? I didn't know which Ellie was real. I just knew I didn't like her.

I looked down at my phone and typed out a text to Ripley:

I'm sick. I'm sorry. Please come back.

I clicked Send and stared at the screen for I don't know how long, dreading what I had to do next and trying to gather the courage to do it anyway. Then I opened voice chat, scrolled to the contact I needed, and tapped the Call button.

It rang three times. Four. I was about to hang up when his face appeared on the screen.

Liam had cut his hair since I last saw him, and it was now buzzed almost to the skin, making his ears look larger and giving him a goofier, friendlier look. I didn't want to, but I liked it.

"Ellie?" he said, leaning toward his camera as if he didn't

believe what his screen was showing him.

The sound of my name on his lips seemed to cut through my anger. I tried to steady my voice.

"Yeah, it's me."

"I'm so glad you called. I— How are you?"

"It's complicated," I replied.

Behind Liam, I saw a Bob Marley poster tacked to the wall and a thick stack of textbooks on top of a minifridge. Was he in someone else's dorm room? Was it hers?

"Am I bothering you?" I asked, hating the simpering tone in my voice.

"Not all at, no. How . . . Is your dad all right? How's his heart?"

"He's fine," I said, gripping the wrought-iron railing. Small talk was agony.

"I'm glad," he said. "Where are you calling from?"

Liam stood up and moved across the room. In the background I saw a Yankees cap hanging from a closet doorknob and a PlayStation on a dusty TV stand. That seemed more like him.

"I'm in Las Vegas," I said.

"Las Vegas, Nevada?"

"No, the one in Maine."

His face split into a grin, activating his dimple. "Are you always such a smartass?"

I took in a sharp breath. "I really can't flirt with you now."

His smile evaporated. "No, I get it. I owe you an apology and an explanation."

"Just the apology," I said. "I'm a smart girl. I figured out the rest."

"It's not what you think," he said. "I'm not a cheater. Kaylee and I were broken up when I met you."

Kaylee. I wanted to tear her hair out. I searched the background for evidence of her: a purse on the bed, a sweater on the back of a chair. I found nothing.

"It's none of my business," I said.

"It *is* your business. I don't want you to think I was jerking you around."

"Then you probably should have told me about 'Kaylee' first, huh?"

What was I doing? I needed a favor from him—a big one. Yet here I was, antagonizing him. I had to get a grip.

Liam ran a hand over his buzzed head, and the habit was so familiar, it felt like I'd known him for years.

"You're right," he said. "I should have told you."

"Why didn't you?"

"Because you wouldn't have gone out with me."

"But you don't know that. You don't know me." The words came out as if someone else were speaking them. "We could have just hooked up. It's not a big deal."

"I'm not like that," Liam said. "And I don't think you are, either."

"Well, I *am*. I'm not some fragile freak."

Liam looked like he was swallowing a giant pill. He cleared his throat.

"It's obvious you didn't call to forgive me. Do you need something? Is there anything I can do?"

His utter decency made me want to crawl through the phone and wring his neck.

"I need a truck." I just blurted it out. Liam didn't reply. "Your dad's company has a hub in Vegas. I looked it up."

He let out a long sigh and turned away from the camera for a moment, thinking. Probably he was wondering what kind of crazy bitch he'd gotten himself involved with.

He turned to face me again. "What do you need it for?"

"I'd rather not say."

He leaned back in his chair, blew out a breath. "You want me to get you one of my dad's trucks, but you won't tell me why?"

I bit my lip. This was going all wrong—I'd meant to be forgiving, charming, persuasive. I'd meant to get him wrapped around my finger. Instead, I was the woman scorned and he was the put-upon rich kid.

Liam reached across the desk, maybe for a notepad. "Where will you be going?"

I cocked my head. Was that a yes?

"Los Angeles."

"Will you be transporting anything illegal?" he asked.

My shoulders tensed, but I managed to keep my expression neutral. "Like what?"

"Drugs. Weapons. People. I don't know."

I shook my head. "Nothing like that." He hadn't specifically mentioned stolen property; it was a weak excuse, but I clung to it.

Liam's eyes narrowed, but he didn't press the issue. "I suppose you need a driver, too? Preferably a deaf mute with persistent amnesia?"

I put a hand over my mouth to stifle a manic giggle. Holy shit. Was he was going to do it?

"Yes."

He shook his head like a man about to do something crazy, and then said, "Okay."

"Okay?" I let out a short squeal. "You'll do it? You'll actually do it?"

I pinched my thigh to make myself stop. If I didn't shut up, I was going to talk him out of it.

Liam nodded. "I know the night manager there. I was the ring bearer at his wedding. When do you need it?"

"Tonight," I said, knowing it was impossible.

"Jesus." He glanced at his expensive watch. "Okay. I'm . . . I'll call you back in an hour."

I closed my eyes. "Thank you."

"You're welcome. And Ellie? For what it's worth, Kaylee and I are done. Permanently."

"Stop saying her name."

"Okay."

I took a deep breath. "Say mine again."

"Okay. Ellie."

Before I said anything else stupid, I disconnected the call. I sat there for a minute, hip bones pressed against the hard railing. Liam was sticking out his neck for me, and I didn't know why. Maybe he felt guilty. Or maybe he just wanted a story to tell someday when he was stuck at the country club, hiding from his pretty, boring wife while he drank scotch and bullshitted with the other potbellied executives. Maybe Liam was every bit as trapped as I was—just in a much nicer cage.

But I didn't have time to sit around feeling sorry for him, or for myself. I had another call to make, and then I needed to get ready.

Higgins answered on the first ring. "Is it on?" he said by way of greeting.

"It's on," I replied.

"Yes!" He sounded like a teenage boy who had just completed a mission in Call of Duty. "When?"

"Tonight."

"Great. I'm coming."

I hesitated. "That . . . might not be the best idea."

"I've waited a long time for this," Higgins said. "I'm going to make sure you don't chicken out or fuck it up."

"You don't want to get involved, Higgins. What if the cops come?"

Higgins snort-laughed. "You couldn't count the zeros on the checks I've written to the LVMPD Foundation. They won't touch me."

I squeezed my eyes shut. "Dad won't go for it."

"I'll make it easy: I'm coming or the deal's off."

My hand tightened around the railing. Dad wasn't going to like this. Hell, *I* didn't like it. But what choice did we have?

"Okay," I said. "I'll text you the address."

CHAPTER 24

IT WAS TEN THIRTY P.M. when our taxi pulled in to the truck stop. Half a dozen semis stood parked at the pumps, but none of them bore the Miller Logistics logo I'd seen online. I was about to call Liam and ask him where our driver was when my phone rang.

"Hey," the low voice on the other end replied. "Look up. Pump number four."

I did. A tall man with long red hair raised a hand. He was standing next to an unmarked semi. I glanced at Dad, and we walked toward the truck.

"Rodney," the driver said, extending a hand. "I hear we're picking up some cargo?"

"That's correct," Dad replied.

"Hop in; we've got to do something first."

In contrast to the sleeper rig we'd ridden to Phoenix, this cab was spotless and smelled like pine. Rodney pulled out of the truck stop, and we rumbled down a frontage road for a quarter mile before pulling over.

"I'll just be a sec," Rodney said. He grabbed a power drill from the center console and hopped out of the cab.

Dad let out a long breath.

"You okay?" I asked.

He ran a finger across his mustache, nodded. I could tell he was having second thoughts. Part of me wanted to draw them out. But the other part knew we needed to shut up and execute the plan.

I texted Liam:

Me: We're in the truck.

Liam: Everything OK?

Me: No.

Liam: What's up?

Me: This guy is definitely not mute.

Liam: LOL ☺ Good luck.

I frowned at my phone. Were we on *LOL* terms already? I had made a joke, but still.

Before I could overthink it, Rodney climbed back into the cab holding two license plates, which he slipped into the center console along with his drill. He didn't make eye contact, and I didn't ask questions. We rode in silence, the rumble of the truck's diesel engine reminding me painfully of our RV and the trailer full of props we had abandoned. I wondered if they were still rusting in the Arizona desert, or if someone had already towed them away.

Rodney eased the truck onto Industrial Road. We passed

an auto-parts store, a machine shop, and a porn mart, its blackened windows reflecting the lights of the Strip half a mile east. Finally, I spotted High Steaks.

I leaned forward and pointed. "Pull in there."

Rodney flipped on his blinker. "Hunker down. I'll tell you when we're clear."

Dad and I leaned toward the center of the bench seat, hiding ourselves from view. A moment later, the truck stopped and Rodney rolled down his window.

"You going to the club?" a voice hollered over the idling diesel.

"Yeah, thought I'd get out of the rig for a bit, see some girls."

"Cool, man. Park in the alley. You can pull around the back of that warehouse when you're ready to leave."

"Thanks, brother," Rodney said. The truck rolled forward for a few seconds; then Rodney cut the engine and spoke to us without turning around.

"I'm going to go into the club, order a beer, and chill. Wait five minutes before you get out of the truck. Then do what you need to do, and text me when you're ready to load up. I'll meet you in back."

Before I could ask questions, Rodney hopped out of the cab and closed the door.

Dad and I stayed hidden for a few minutes, then sat up and looked around. The parking attendant was distracted, smoking a cigarette and flirting with one of the dancers.

"Come on," I said, and the two of us climbed out the passenger side, keeping the truck between us and the club.

I turned the corner and stifled a scream.

I was face-to-face with a man in a ski mask standing by the warehouse door.

"Shit!" I scrambled backward, knocking into Dad.

"It's me!" the man said, then pulled up his ski mask.

It was Higgins, and he was grinning like a horror-movie clown.

"Jesus," I said. "You scared the crap out of me."

Higgins chuckled.

"Take that ridiculous thing off," Dad said.

Higgins's grin turned into a pout. "Why?"

"Because if we're caught, we can't exactly claim to be lost if one of us looks like a damn bank robber," Dad said.

Higgins shrugged and peeled off the mask.

I glanced around. The same two cars were still parked in the lot: the hatchback and the Beemer.

"Whose cars, do you think?" Higgins asked.

"Employees of the club, perhaps?"

"Maybe," I said. "They were here this morning."

Higgins gestured at the door. "Is that how we're getting in?"

The three of us moved toward it. I squatted in front of the lock, and Dad put a hand on my shoulder.

"Ready to work your magic?" he asked.

I nodded. "Ready as I'll ever be."

"It's a combo lock," Higgins whispered. "How are you going to pick that?"

I glared at him. "If you insist on being here, please keep your mouth shut."

He looked hurt, but he kept quiet. I turned back to the keypad.

Dad and I had spent the afternoon brainstorming

Devereaux's likely heroes. We debated until we had narrowed it down to three—because, according to Ripley's research, we had only three tries to get it right. I reached for the keypad, one finger outstretched—then withdrew my hand. What if Ripley was wrong? What if I punched in the incorrect code and the alarm started squealing straightaway? Probably, the thought should've petrified me; instead, I found myself savoring the first trickle of adrenaline.

The name at the top of our list belonged to one of the first TV magicians ever. In a 2008 interview in *Genii*, Devereaux had called him an inspiration. It was the only time he had ever publicly mentioned a magician as an influence. He was a solid choice, but I had my doubts—because the man had called himself Dante the Magician. He hadn't just been Devereaux's hero, he'd been my father's, too. So much that Dad had changed our family name to honor him. It seemed like too much of a coincidence. What were the odds that our last name was Devereaux's password?

But this was no time for second-guessing; we'd discussed every name on the list for hours, making our decisions in the calm of the motel room precisely so we wouldn't have to choose in the stress of the moment. Dante was the only magician Devereaux had ever called out in print. I had to trust our choice, no matter how unlikely it seemed.

I typed:

3-2-6-8-3 (D-A-N-T-E)

I heard no click, no sound of a bolt being thrown—and, after a moment, a red LED above the keypad blinked once.

Shit.

"What the hell?" Higgins said.

Dad laid a hand on my shoulder. "It's all right," he whispered. "We've got two more chances."

I swallowed hard and looked back at the keypad.

According to the archivist at the Magic Castle, Devereaux had once owned a vintage poster from a 1922 performance by the Great Blackstone. Blackstone was the most famous illusionist of the early twentieth century, best known for his take on the classic levitation illusion—the same effect that Devereaux paid homage to in his flying routine. Because of this, Blackstone had been our second choice. It had the right resonance; plus, the first five letters of his last name formed a coherent word.

I took a deep breath, let it out slowly, and typed:

2-5-2-2-5 (B-L-A-C-K)

The red LED blinked twice, then went dark.

"Fuck!"

Dad let out a hiss of breath through his teeth.

Higgins leaned in. "I thought you said you knew the code?"

I turned to curse at Higgins, but Dad intervened.

"No one asked you to come," he said.

Higgins took a few steps backward and folded his arms.

Dad turned to me. "It's got to be him," he said. "It's got to be Houdini."

Houdini was, inarguably, the most famous magician in history. Like Devereaux, he was known for performing public exhibitions of magic in front of huge audiences; his 1904 handcuff escape in London had strong parallels with Devereaux's vanishing of the Arc de Triomphe. Plus, like Devereaux's, his mother had been a Jewish immigrant.

The problem was, *Houdini* had seven letters, not five—and on top of that, it wasn't even his real name. Weisz, the name on his birth certificate, fit the bill—but the spelling had later been changed to Weiss, which also had five letters. We had gone round and round, finally deciding on *W-E-I-S-Z* because it was the most authentic.

Now, though, it felt like we'd made it too complicated. Like there was something stupid and obvious we had overlooked. But we'd agonized over it for hours, and this was the best answer we had come up with. I had to trust it.

I closed my eyes. Took two deep breaths. Reached out my hand—

And froze.

Dad whispered, "What is it?"

"What was Dante's real name?" I said. "His birth name."

Dad frowned. "It was Jansen. Harry August Jansen." His eyes drifted slightly out of focus.

"Harry," I said. "Harry Jansen, Harry Blackstone, Harry Houdini."

Dad looked at me, his expression blank. "How did we miss that?"

"What do you think? It's stupid, right?"

His shook his head. "Do it."

I blew out a breath, licked my lips, and typed:

4-2-7-7-9 (H-A-R-R-Y)

The green LED went solid, and the door clicked open.

Breath rushed out of me in a gust, and I slumped against the wall. Higgins pumped a fist in triumph.

Dad smiled. "Showtime."

CHAPTER 25

IT WAS PITCH-BLACK INSIDE, SO I turned on my phone's flashlight. We were standing at the base of a long, enclosed ramp with no lamp or light switch in sight. The place was eerily quiet; it reminded me of haunted houses back in Fort Wayne where you paid ten bucks to be chased through a strobe-lit labyrinth.

Higgins whispered, "What now?"

"Now we find the storage area."

"And what are we looking for, exactly?" There was a sparkle in Higgins's eye, as if he thought I was about to reveal some part of Devereaux's secret to him.

"A big road case, probably," I said, enjoying watching Higgins's smile turn into a scowl. "It'll probably have *DEVEREAUX* stenciled on it. And, if we're lucky, *FLYING*, or something to that effect."

I shone my phone light around to confirm there was only one way forward. "Looks like we stick together for now. Come on."

I took the lead, walking as softly as I could. The ramp turned out to be a switchback, and the pathway took two sharp U-turns before coming to a T intersection. One way continued upward, and the other broke off right and sloped down.

"We'll cover more ground faster if we split up," I said. "Higgins, do you have a light?" He held up his phone and turned on the flash. "Okay. You two stick together." Dad started to protest, but I cut him off; there was no time to argue. "If you find something, text me." I gestured to the descending ramp. "I'll take this one."

As I made my way downward, I heard their footfalls above and hoped no one else was listening. Higgins was big and far from stealthy; if there was attention to be drawn, he would draw it. As I moved forward, I felt a slight breeze, and then the passageway opened up. I stopped and shone my light around again.

I was in a very wide room, at least fifty feet high and twice as long, the ceiling getting lower as it stretched away from the outer wall of the building. It looked like I was underneath a set of bleachers, or maybe the terraced house of a theater. I saw no boxes or road cases, just a nest of snake-like cables running to electrical panels mounted on the walls. There was nothing to find down here. I turned and headed back up the ramp, hoping to catch up with Dad and Higgins. After a minute or so, a haze of indirect light came into view, and I switched off my phone.

A pair of voices drifted toward me, but they didn't belong to Dad or Higgins. They reverberated as if the people speaking were standing on the floor of a large auditorium. I paused at the mouth of the passage, listening. Someone was giving instructions. Someone else was laughing.

As quietly as I could, I stepped out of the tunnel. There were Dad and Higgins, standing six feet away with their backs to me. I approached.

We were looking down from the back of a huge black-box theater. Plywood tiers packed with rows of folding chairs stepped down toward a broad stage that rose ten feet off the warehouse's concrete floor. Above, a battery of lights clung to a truss, but the stage was illuminated only by a single spotlight, which cut through a billowing blanket of stage fog.

As the fog thinned, a figure resolved: a man in black lying faceup center stage. I took a few steps forward and squinted down at him.

It was Daniel Devereaux.

I held my breath. Dad's hand gripped my shoulder like a claw. Devereaux was here? Now?

For a moment, he lay still as a corpse. Then, slowly, he began to levitate, rising off the stage as if supported by an invisible platform. The same way he had risen off the stage in the video Higgins had shown us yesterday. I remembered the banner I had seen plastered over the windows of the Tangiers Hotel & Casino as I drove north on Las Vegas Boulevard:

DANIEL DEVEREAUX: SKY'S THE LIMIT
COMING THIS CHRISTMAS

Oh my God. He was going to fly again.

For a moment, I lost myself, fascinated by the sight of one of my magical heroes floating in midair; then I snapped back to reality and remembered why I was here. I scoured the stage with my magician's eye, searching for a clue that might give away Devereaux's method. But even though the smoke had cleared and the spotlight was bright, I saw no harness, no ropes, no wires.

Without warning, Devereaux turned a cartwheel and shot into the air. I put a hand over my mouth. He pivoted, put a fist forward like Superman, and dove toward the stage. At the last moment, he pulled up, soaring toward the wings, only to turn again.

It was nothing like the video; there were no words to describe it. I was six again, and I believed in magic.

I glanced over my shoulder and saw Higgins, his face slack with awe.

"I don't believe it," he said. "Is that . . ."

"Just watch," I whispered.

And we did. For how long, I don't know; we were entranced, all three of us. What we were seeing was beyond belief.

"Who the hell are you?"

I jumped at the sound of the voice and wheeled around. A tall security guard stood at the entrance to the ramp, wielding an eight-cell Maglite in one hand and a walkie-talkie in the other.

I glanced at Dad, then at Higgins. Both looked shell-shocked.

"I'm a huge fan," I began, trying to sound as young and

sycophantic as I could. "I've always wanted to meet Mr. Devereaux, and I thought—"

"Save it," the rent-a-cop said, and pushed the talk button on his radio. "I need the SM at back of house. Right now." Then he lowered the walkie-talkie and gestured toward us with the flashlight. "You all just hang out right where you are." He clipped the radio back on his belt, folded his arms, and settled in to watch us like we were a gang of teenage vandals.

The waiting was interminable. We couldn't make a plan because the guard stood six feet away. And there was no place to run because the rent-a-cop blocked our only exit. Dad and I exchanged nervous looks. Higgins was pale, and I began to wonder if what he'd had said about the LVMPD Foundation was a lie.

Finally, I heard footsteps coming up the ramp. Dad shot a deadly look at Higgins, then glared at me to make it clear that *he* would do the talking.

A man in a purple button-up came out of the tunnel, and when he stepped into the light, I had to bite my lip to stop myself from gasping.

It was Rico. When he saw me, his eyes went wide. He looked at my dad, then at Higgins, frowning as if contemplating a hard math problem—and then his face split in a Lando Calrissian grin.

"I didn't think you were going to make it!" he said, striding forward and clapping me on the shoulder so hard, it hurt. He turned to the security guard. "It's all right, Chris. They're with me."

Rico crammed the three of us into his tiny production office and shut the door behind him.

"What the hell are you doing here?"

I started to answer, but Rico held up a hand to silence me. Then he leaned forward, put his palms on the desktop, and looked from Dad to me and finally to Higgins. Realization swept over his face like the beam of a spotlight.

"Holy shit," he said, blinking rapidly. "You were going to— Holy shit."

He stood, paced behind the desk, ran a hand over his shaved head.

"Let me explain," I began, my voice pleading, but he cut me off again.

"Tell me I'm wrong. Please tell me you did not come here to steal what he couldn't buy." He pointed at Higgins.

"I didn't know you were working for Devereaux," I said. "You wouldn't tell me, remember?"

"That's not the point," Rico said. "You can't just— Ugh." He dropped into the chair and stared at the desk.

"I didn't know what else to do, Rico. We're—"

"I can't even talk to you right now." He looked at Higgins. "And you. You arrogant ass. This is why no one in magic wants to talk to you. You don't care about the craft; you don't care about the performers. You just want to collect things."

"That's not true," Higgins said, sounding like a scolded teenager.

Rico folded his arms. "I should call the cops. I really should."

I looked at Dad, hoping he would step in to negotiate—but his jaw seemed wired shut.

I couldn't believe this was happening, couldn't believe we'd been caught. After everything we'd done, after how far we'd come—it couldn't be over. I had to do something. I had to get Rico back on my side.

"Please don't," I said, forcing my voice to break, and finding it was easier than I'd expected. "Our RV is totaled. We're broke." My eyes grew hot; I wasn't faking it anymore. "We didn't have any other choice."

Rico pinched the bridge of his nose. "Look. I'm sorry you're in a bad place. I really am. But what do you expect me to do?"

I tried to take a deep breath, but that lead X-ray vest was compressing my chest again. I needed to act quickly—I could already feel the rush of adrenaline slowing to a trickle. The wheels in my mind were grinding down, finally succumbing to friction. But if I could just hold on a little longer, delay the downslide for another hour—I might be able to keep us out of jail. There was still a vague tingle of mania in the back of my mind. I grabbed onto it like a life preserver.

"There's a way."

Rico leaned forward. "I'm listening."

"Pretend to give us a tour of the facility. We touch nothing. We say nothing. We're not magicians; we're just your friends from back home, visiting Las Vegas on vacation, and you decided to give us the VIP experience." I was improvising, riding on pure instinct, flying with no visible means of support. I didn't know what I would say next, and I didn't know how we were going to get our hands on the flying rig. I only knew I had to keep Rico from calling the cops.

He scowled. I was losing him.

"At the end of the tour you escort us out, and we never come back."

He tilted his head back to stare at the ceiling, and the fist in my guts tightened its grip. If he agreed, we'd stay out of jail—but how would we get the rig?

Rico sighed, shook his head, looked at Higgins. "Keep your face down. I don't want you recognized." He turned to Dad. "I'm doing this because you meant a lot to my father." Then to me. "Don't make me regret it."

Rico stood. We followed him out of the office, down a long hallway, and through a wide steel door.

Devereaux's warehouse was cavernous. Fluorescent bars cast a greenish pall over a forest of misshapen lumps—big props, I assumed, covered by black shrouds. Against one wall, I spotted an enormous rack of road cases; it would have taken a forklift to reach the ones on the highest shelves. My heart sank; even if we gained unhindered access to this room for an hour, we might not find what we were looking for.

Still, my heart beat faster as if aroused by the lengthening odds; I supposed this was what kept gambling addicts at the table even when they were losing big.

Rico made a grand gesture as if to say, *Feast your eyes—this is all you get.* Higgins stared around like he had just landed in Willy Wonka's chocolate factory. He took three steps toward the nearest covered contraption, but Rico grabbed his arm.

"Don't even think about it," he said.

We moved through the warehouse quickly, slaloming among the giant cloaked props. At the end of a long black corridor, a twenty-something guy wearing a headset stood guarding a steel door. He glanced nervously at our group.

"Hey, Dougie," Rico said. "I'm going to take these VIPs into the wings for a quick look."

Dougie. This was the guy whose incompetence had provided us with the clue to the door code. I physically turned to point this out to Ripley—then remembered that he hadn't come with us. A ball of heat seemed to form in my chest.

"Um," Dougie said. "This is a closed rehearsal."

"I know, dude. It's not a problem."

Dougie looked dubious but nodded, and Rico clapped him on the arm. Then we followed him through the door.

The stage was a vast black deck a hundred feet from wing to wing and almost as deep. Devereaux was nowhere in sight; he must have finished his run-through while we were still on our tour. Rico looked relieved.

"Do you mind?" Dad said to Rico, gesturing toward the stage.

Rico glanced over his shoulder, then nodded reluctantly.

Dad stepped onto the stage and the lights spilled over him, blanching his skin and making the silk threads in his dark jacket shimmer. His face lit up and his eyes sparkled a deep blue. Despite our predicament, he was completely at ease, as if there was nowhere else he belonged. He strode to the apron and spread his arms wide as if to receive a standing ovation. He looked so natural onstage. For him, the real world required performance; only on the planks, under the lights, could he be his authentic self. He turned to me and reached out his hand, inviting me to join him. I shook my head; I needed to keep a level head right now. I couldn't afford to lose my grip on the moment, no matter how good it might feel.

Higgins, meanwhile, was staring at the rigging overhead. No doubt he was looking for wires. Rico smirked, confident that any visible secrets would be inscrutable to him.

"My goodness," a voice said. "It's the Uncanny Dante."

The voice was calm and low and seemed to issue from every direction at once; it was coming through the sound system. I looked around to see who was speaking, and then Daniel Devereaux stepped out from between the long drapes on the far side of the stage. My father turned, too, and at the sight of Devereaux, his whole body stiffened as if a thousand volts had just shot up his spine. Devereaux walked toward Dad. My face went numb. Was this really happening? I turned to Rico, who moved forward and tugged Higgins back into the wings.

"I saw you perform once," Devereaux said, his voice no longer amplified by the sound system. "Years ago, at the Castle. Your Sub Trunk was flawless."

My dad looked flabbergasted. "I'm . . . I admire your work very much."

"Thanks," Devereaux said. "That means a great deal coming from you." I noticed Devereaux didn't shake his hand. I wondered if he was a germophobe, or if he just didn't want to risk injury from a fan's overenthusiastic grip.

Devereaux's eyes drifted to the wings, and when they found me, my stomach dropped out.

"Rico," he said. "Introduce me to your friends."

I heard Rico mutter a curse under his breath, but he covered it with a smile.

"This is Dante's daughter, Ellie."

Devereaux strode toward me, stopped, and looked down at me as if I were a mildly interesting zoo exhibit.

"Hi," I said.

"It's a pleasure." Devereaux turned to Higgins. He squinted, seemed to recognize him, and his face took on a calm but exasperated expression. "Hello, Jif," he said, sounding like a mother greeting her teenager's delinquent friend. "How are you?"

Higgins looked like a cat about to be hit by a car. "Hi. Um, good."

"Dougie," Devereaux called. The guy with the headset appeared from the wings. "Grab me three blank nondisclosure forms from the office, would you?"

Dougie scuttled off to oblige.

Devereaux put his hands on his hips, shot Rico a look I couldn't interpret, then glanced back at us as if unsure what to do next. Finally, he turned to Higgins.

"You deserve some credit, Jif."

"What?" Higgins said.

"You've helped a lot of a performers retire with more than they would have otherwise. You probably don't get thanked very often."

Higgins's eyes went wide. "Never, actually."

"Well, that's because you're a giant pain in the ass."

Higgins looked confused. Dad stifled a laugh. Now it was Rico who looked like the cat in the road.

Devereaux folded his arms. "I'm not selling, Jif. Never, ever, ever."

Higgins's jaw tightened, but he nodded. Thirty minutes ago, he had looked a kid on Christmas Eve; now he resembled an addict midintervention. He gave me a sort of *oh, well* look, and his message was clear: we had failed. I clenched my fists.

Devereaux turned to Dad. "I'm surprised at you, Mr. Dante. Breaking in here like this. I would expect more consideration from a fellow magician."

Dad opened his mouth, but I jumped in before he could speak.

"It's not his fault," I blurted, taking a step forward. "It was my idea."

"Right." Devereaux squinted at me. "You're the girl in the hoodie. Where's your friend?"

His words brought back the hot weight in my chest; he must have seen Ripley and me in the security footage. Ripley should have been here with me to see this—even though we were about to lose everything, he should have been here. He'd earned it, but I'd driven him away.

When I didn't answer, Devereaux turned his attention to Rico, who looked mildly horrified by the whole scenario. "Since they're your friends, I'm not going to press charges. They'll sign NDAs, and you'll escort them out." He turned back to us. "It was a pleasure to meet you both. Circumstances notwithstanding." Then he turned and strode toward the exit.

I watched him walking away, heard the click of his heels on the stage like the tick of a timer counting down. We'd been caught. We'd failed. This had been our last chance, and it was walking away with Daniel Devereaux.

He was reaching for the stage door when I heard myself call out.

"Wait!"

To my surprise, he stopped and turned back.

"Wait, Mr. Devereaux. Please."

Maybe it was the desperation in my voice, or maybe he'd only been testing—but he walked back toward us.

"What is it, Ms. Dante?"

"I need your help." I looked back at my dad. "*We* need your help."

"What kind of help?"

I tried to swallow, but my mouth was suddenly a desert.

"We need you to show Higgins your method for the flying illusion."

Devereaux smirked, but it faded rapidly. "You're serious?"

I nodded.

"Why in the world would I show *him* the secret to my best-known illusion?"

"Actually," Higgins broke in, "the whole Arc de Triomphe thing is probably— Ow!"

Rico had stomped on Higgins's foot.

Devereaux turned back to me. "Jif is obsessed. He's been trying to get his hands on my rig for years. But what's in it for you?"

I exchanged a glance with Dad; what did we have to lose?

"We're broke," I said. Devereaux didn't react. "Dad's

been invited to perform on *Flynn & Kellar's Live Magic Retrospective.* It's his only shot at a comeback. But Higgins has our props. He wants five grand, and we don't have it."

Devereaux frowned. "So he what—said he'd hand them over if you could sneak him in here and persuade me to show him my method?"

"Yes," I said, a little too quickly; this was far better than having him think we'd come to steal his rig.

Devereaux laughed. "And I thought I'd seen everything." He sighed, tugged at the cuff of one sleeve, and turned to Dad. "I need a new bit. Something to fill the time while my crew clears the stage after my car production. Something simple I can do in the audience. What have you got?"

Dad raised his eyebrows. "You're serious?"

Devereaux shrugged. "I don't like anything my team has come up with yet. Show me something new. If I like it, maybe we can do a swap."

Dad's eyes sparkled. "A close-up bit? Sleight of hand, something that'll print on the big screen?"

Devereaux pointed a finger at him. "Exactly."

Dad thought for a moment, then smiled. "Ellie's got just the thing."

Devereaux leveled his gaze at me, and my guts turned to ice.

"Show me."

CHAPTER 26

MY HANDS WERE SHAKING AS I set up backstage. There was no Wild Turkey on hand, but Dougie had some Jack Daniel's stashed in his office. I wasn't used to working with a square bottle, so I practiced half a dozen times. I almost dropped it twice.

"Breathe," Dad said.

"I *am* breathing," I snapped, though, in fact, I'd been holding my breath the whole time. I set the bottle and the shot glass on the desk and put my face in my hands.

"I'm going to screw this up just like I did in Mishawaka."

"No, you're not." Dad squeezed my shoulder. "This is where you shine."

"You don't understand. I've been . . ." *Up* is what I meant to say, but the word hovered just past the edge of my mind, unwilling to step forward and present itself. It happened sometimes, when I started down the slope. Words got lost.

"I know it's hard," Dad said. He put his hand under my chin. "This thing you tow around with you—it drags you through wreckage, I know it does. But it also gives you an eagle's-eye view. A perspective most of us never achieve."

I couldn't look at him. "You make it sound romantic."

Dad shook his head. "It is what it is. But, Ellie, you already have the design. The method. The moves. It doesn't matter that it all came to you during a bright time. You have it now. No amount of darkness can erase that."

Just then, Rico poked his head into the wings. "You ready?"

I met Devereaux in the aisle above the fifth row. He nodded and folded his arms. "Show me what you've got, kid."

I produced a deck of cards from my pocket.

"Just an ordinary deck of playing cards," I said, extracting them from the box and fanning them out. "Fifty-two plus two jokers. Three, if you count my father."

Devereaux rolled his eyes at my lame attempt at vaudevillian humor. I swallowed and went on.

"Please take the deck and examine the cards. Make sure there are no spots, no marks, no clipped corners."

As he took the deck and began to thumb through it, I felt an icy trickle down my back. I couldn't tell if it was sweat or twitchy nerves. Devereaux handed it back, and I squared up the cards before holding them out again.

"Choose a card, any card you prefer, and pull it from the deck. Good." I pocketed the rest of the deck. "Without letting me see it, show your card to the audience."

With a condescending smirk, Devereaux played along, displaying the card to Higgins, Rico, and my dad.

"Now, keeping the face of the card toward you—I don't want to see it—place it here between my thumb and forefinger." He did so, frowning slightly as if he wasn't sure where this was going. Good; I had him intrigued. Once the card was between my fingers, I snapped, and the card burst into flame.

Devereaux didn't react. I had to remind myself that he literally knew all the tricks.

I closed my hands like a clamshell around the ashes to extinguish the flame—and when I drew them apart again, a shot glass was perched upside down on the palm of my right hand.

Devereaux gave a slight nod; he'd expected this move, or something like it, but he seemed satisfied by my performance so far. It was a compliment from the greatest illusionist alive, and my head began to buzz. I made fists with my toes—I needed to stay grounded. Devereaux nodded as if to say, *Go on.*

I reached into the pocket of the oversized blazer I'd borrowed from Rico and extracted a red silk handkerchief. Carefully, I draped it over the hand holding the shot glass—then, with my thumb and forefinger, I pinched the top of the silk and whipped it off, revealing a three-quarters-full bottle of Jack Daniel's now sitting on my palm, with the inverted shot glass resting on top.

A broad smile broke across Devereaux's face, and he uncrossed his arms and stuffed his hands into his pockets as if he couldn't wait to see what happened next.

Now my heart was pounding. The edges of everything seemed to sharpen. My face split into a wide, stupid grin, and I took a small bow.

Then I asked him to hold the glass—and I poured him a shot.

"Bottoms up," I said.

He took the shot, shook his head slightly to ward off the bite of the whiskey, then held the glass out to me. The look on his face seemed to say, *Was that it?*

I pointed to the glass. "Look closer."

He frowned and looked down into the shot glass. Etched in the bottom was the image of his card: the nine of hearts. After a moment, his frown turned into a wide smile. "Well, I'll be damned," he said, holding the glass up for an imaginary camera. "That's my card!"

Devereaux gave me a small round of applause. Blood pumped like rapids through my ears. My limbs tingled. I glanced at Dad, who was grinning broadly. Rico was applauding, too, but with both eyes on Devereaux, wary of what he might do next.

"That was cool," Devereaux said. He glanced at Rico. "Think we can make something out of that?"

Rico's eyes widened for a moment, but then he recovered. "Yeah. Yes. Totally."

Devereaux nodded, eyes distant, contemplative. The room was suddenly quiet. I could hear the hum of the rooftop AC units forty feet above my head. Finally, Devereaux turned to face Higgins.

"I'm going to show you something," he said.

Higgins squirmed in his seat.

"I'm going to show you, and then you're going to leave my people alone. Dougie?"

The stage manager hurried down the aisle and handed out forms and pens to Higgins, Dad, and me. When we'd signed them and passed them back, Devereaux gestured to Rico.

Rico stood up and gestured for Higgins to follow. To my surprise, he led him backstage.

Devereaux took a seat next to Dad in the sixth row and motioned for me to join them. He looked over at me, smiled.

"This'll be fun."

The trick worked like this: I didn't know. What I had seen Devereaux do tonight defied every method I could think of. And even though Higgins was strapped or hooked or clipped into whatever it was, I don't think he knew, either. What I did know was that I was sitting between the Uncanny Dante and Daniel Motherfucking Devereaux when Jif Higgins rose ten feet into the air, squealing like a twelve-year-old at a Shawn Mendes concert. As the sweeping orchestral soundtrack blared through the speakers, Higgins soared around the stage like an awkward neophyte superhero, cackling and whooping with unironic glee.

Devereaux watched him, his eyes shining with boyish delight. He caught me staring, but I couldn't look away.

He leaned toward me and said, "That bottle production was elegant. You ought to be performing."

I could still feel my pulse pounding in my neck. I shook

my head. And then I said something—I don't know why I said it—something I'd only admitted to three people in the world.

I looked at Daniel Devereaux and said, "I can't handle the pressure. I'm bipolar."

Devereaux cocked his head, then reached out his hand. Confused, I shook it, and he said, "Welcome to the club."

I felt my mouth drop open. "The club? You mean . . ."

"I prefer to say I *have* bipolar. It's a diagnosis. Not an identity."

I couldn't seem to close my mouth.

"Don't let it stop you," he said. Then he sat back and watched Higgins fly.

"DID YOU SEE THAT?" Higgins said, literally jumping up and down. "I was fucking FLYING!"

The four of us—Higgins, Dad, Rico, and I—were standing in the parking lot behind the warehouse.

"Dude," Rico said to Higgins, "will you please shut up?" He looked at Dad. "Please shut him up."

"Yes, of course," Dad said. "Ellie, we'll meet you at the truck." Dad took Higgins by the elbow, who let himself be led away, still flapping his hands like a spastic bat.

When they had rounded the corner, Rico turned to glare at me. "You could have gotten me fired."

"I know," I said.

"I might still get fired."

"You think he's that pissed?"

Rico let out an exasperated breath. "The truth is, he's

been trying to get Higgins off his back for years. This might have done it."

"You don't think Higgins will talk?"

Rico laughed. "Daniel may seem like a pussycat, but his lawyers are brutal." His smile faded. "Your close-up has gotten really good. Forget assistant stuff—you should be onstage."

Inside, I was beaming, but I shook my head. "I'm not cut out for it."

He shrugged. "Well, I think you're crazy."

"You're not wrong."

Rico gave me a quizzical smile. "In any case, I think you persuaded Higgins. What's next?"

"We go to LA," I said. "It's up to Dad now."

Before the words were even out of my mouth, I felt myself slowing down, as if someone had shot me with a tranquilizer dart. The high of performing was draining away, and the weight of what we had to do next settled on me like that lead X-ray vest. I could no longer feel my pulse throbbing in my throat. My nerves had ceased to buzz. The world began to dim as if I were seeing it through a tinted window.

No, no, *no.* It was happening too fast. I needed another day. I needed another week.

Rico glanced over his shoulder. "I'd better get back in there."

"Yeah."

"Take care of yourself, okay?"

"I will," I said.

But I wasn't sure I could.

By the time I got to the truck, Rodney was behind the wheel. I climbed in next to Dad.

"Change of plans?" Rodney said.

"Yeah," I replied, my voice once again reverting to that flat, robotic tone. "Can you drop us off on Fremont? We're staying at the Uptowner."

"The hell you are," Higgins said.

I raised my eyebrows.

"I have like nine bedrooms."

Higgins rode shotgun, gushing the whole way about how amazing Devereaux was, and how he had been flying, *really* flying. I stared out the window, turning away from the lights of Vegas and the false hope they transmitted. Now that the grift was over, I felt empty. Numb. I knew we'd gotten a better outcome than we could have hoped for, but still I felt only a vague sense of indifference. The hardest part was still ahead, and there were so many ways we could fail. I should have been worried, maybe even desperate—but that way was blocked.

People think depression is the same as sadness, a blue gauze that descends to tint the world a shade darker. But in truth, it's like a snowfall of ash, obscuring the color and the taste of everything.

Rodney pulled his rig up to the gates, and Higgins leaned forward.

"You got a card?" he asked.

Rodney frowned. "I'm a truck driver, man. We don't have cards."

"Oh." Higgins rifled through his pockets, pulled out a crinkled receipt, and jotted something on the back. "That's my cell. Be here tomorrow at . . ." He looked at my dad. "Nine? Jesus, that's early. Okay, be here at nine. And bring some guys. I'm not loading that shit."

Rodney said, "Not loading what shit?"

Higgins smiled. "I have an old Chevy pickup and a big Plexiglas tank that need to get to LA fast."

CHAPTER 27

ELLA, ELLA, EH, EH, EH . . .

I awoke with the song playing on a loop in my mind. My head hurt, a dull, insomniac ache, despite the fact that I'd slept hard. For a moment, I wondered why I couldn't feel the thrum of the RV's diesel engine beneath me—and then I remembered where I was and what had happened last night. The headache and the song and the disorientation—they were all symptoms of a postshow crash. Or, in this case, a post*grift* crash.

Shielding my eyes against the harsh desert sunlight blasting in through the window, I got up, stretched, and stepped into the cavernous shower. I let the scalding water pound down on me for as long as I could stand it, then dried off and dressed.

I found Dad in Higgins's kitchen, sipping coffee and writing in his journal. He looked up as I walked in.

"Good morning!" he said. His cheer hurt my head.

"Morning."

I poured myself a cup while Dad launched into a soliloquy about the flaw of the original Truck Drop, and how this new version was going to blow the original away. I tried to look commiserating—but he saw through it.

"You're coming down," he said.

"The meds will kick in soon."

Dad reached for my hand. "You've done so much, Ellie. I'll take it from here. And when we get that check, we'll get you a refill."

"On yours, too, okay?"

"Pharmaceuticals all around!"

He threw up his hands as if tossing confetti or pills into the air. I couldn't help smiling.

"There she is," he said.

A few minutes later, Dad and Higgins went out to clear a path to the old Chevy so Rodney's crew could get to it. I stayed in the kitchen, sipping coffee I couldn't taste, tracing the ring of steam it left on the countertop. I should have felt excited about the performance to come; it would be by far the most important of our lives. And while part of me insisted that my apathy was just my sickness rearing its head, another part knew for a fact that it wasn't. That I deserved to be unhappy because of the people I'd damaged along the way. I'd used Liam, I'd nearly gotten Rico fired, and I'd said the worst possible things to Ripley. I pulled out my phone and stared at its cracked display. Ripley had never responded to my text. I unlocked the screen and typed out a new message.

I don't blame you for ghosting me, and I don't deserve your forgiveness. I'm sorry for what I said to you in Las Vegas. It wasn't true. You didn't desert anyone. You spend so much time taking care of everyone else—Jude, your dad, me—that you just needed to take care of yourself for once. They're lucky to have you, Ripley. And so was I. You made me feel like I wasn't alone. Like I wasn't crazy. You saved my life, and for that, I'll always be grateful. I love you.

I clicked Send and pocketed my phone.

Once everything was loaded into the semi, Rodney went inside to raid the fridge for a Pepsi, leaving Dad and me standing awkwardly at the gate with Higgins.

"Well," Higgins said, squinting at the southern horizon, "you guys better get out of here before traffic starts to suck."

"Thank you, Jif," Dad said. "For everything."

Higgins flapped a hand. "Don't get mushy. I'll see you guys in a couple of days."

I raised my eyebrows. "You're coming to LA?"

Higgins laughed. "After all this, you think I'd miss it?"

Rodney emerged from the house with an armful of soda cans, and we crawled into the cab. He fired up the engine—its diesel rumble was comforting—and drove through the gate. In the side-view mirror, I watched Higgins disappear as we turned onto Lake Mead Boulevard and drove out of sight.

Traffic on the 15 did suck, and it took us ninety minutes just to reach Primm. I spent the time on my laptop going over the schedule. We were supposed to load in at three p.m., and if Waze was right, we were barely going to make it. Our tech run-through was tonight, full dress was tomorrow, and the show went live Wednesday night—just over forty-eight hours away. The last eight days had passed at a crawl, but now I was free-falling, gaining speed, the ground rushing up to meet me.

An hour after we crossed the California state line, I heard the ding of a new text message and began frantically searching the back seat for my phone. It was Ripley. It had to be. He had finally responded.

Only he hadn't. The message was from Liam.

Liam: Everything work out ok?
Me: Yes.

I paused with my thumb over the Send arrow. Then, somewhat reluctantly, I added:

Me: Thank you.
Liam: I have a confession.
Me: Okay.

The little dots bounced, then stopped. Bounced, then stopped.

If heaven and hell exist, then purgatory is filled with those little dots.

Liam: I did the truck thing so you would forgive me.

The ghost of a smile turned up the corner of my mouth, then evaporated.

Me: I have a confession too

Liam: What?

I blew out a breath. I often felt like words erupted from my mouth without my consent; now it was happening with my thumbs.

Me: I asked you to do the truck thing because I knew you wanted forgiveness.

Me: Do you think I'm manipulative?

Liam: Maybe. But I probably deserve it.

Liam: Do you forgive me?

I typed a few words, then deleted them. Let him suffer the bouncing dots for a minute, see how he liked it.

Me: I want to.

I waited for two solid minutes, but he didn't reply. Maybe someone had called him. Maybe his phone had died.

Maybe he'd written me off.

Suddenly, I wished I hadn't sent that last message. The first time I'd made myself vulnerable to him, I had been more or less stable. If he took advantage of me while I was on my way down, I wasn't sure I could recover.

Traffic came to a dead halt just south of Baker, and I

started to worry that we were going to miss the rehearsal. I thought of calling Grace to tell her we'd been delayed—but I was terrified that she would tell Flynn and he would drop us from the show. It was an irrational fear, but reason didn't have much sway when I was on the downslope.

By the time we made a pit stop in Barstow, we were two hours behind schedule, and I had bitten my nails to the quick. Dad took forever in the bathroom at the Taco Bell; I was about to ask Rodney to check on him when he finally emerged, looking seasick.

"Everything all right?" I asked.

"Not sure breakfast agreed with me," he said, grimacing.

Two hours later, when we finally merged onto the westbound 210 freeway, I took a deep breath and called Grace.

"Grace Wu, how can I help you?" She said it rapidly and with no inflection. In the background, I heard clanking metal and loud voices.

"Hi, Grace. It's Ellie Dante."

"Where are you?"

The tension in her voice was contagious, and I felt my shoulders tighten.

"We hit a snag with our equipment," I said. "We're an hour away."

"You're going to be late for load-in."

I closed my eyes. I couldn't overreact. I had to stay calm.

"Head straight to the Dolby," she said. "We'll make it work."

As we shot past the 57 freeway, I saw a billboard for Park Hills Hyundai and realized I was passing within a few miles of Ripley's house. I took a photo of the sign and texted it to him—maybe my proximity would move him. Then I shoved my phone back into my bag and stared out the window.

It was five p.m. when we finally arrived. We were two hours late, so Rodney let us out while he backed the truck up to the loading dock. My bottom lip was raw from nervous chewing, my legs and neck stiff from seven hours on the road. Dad looked even older than usual, his skin ashen, his hair rumpled; he insisted he just needed to splash some water on his face. While he went off in search of a restroom, I went into the theater to find Grace.

Backstage areas are usually disappointing: Instead of red carpet, the floor is scarred concrete. Where you'd expect chandeliers, the ceiling is decorated with tangled wires and ugly ducts. There are no glamorous celebrities in tuxes and gowns, just crusty stage crew in black Dickies. I had seen it all. At least, I thought I had—but backstage at the Dolby was different. The walls were black and sleek and covered with flat-screen monitors showing every angle of the stage. The managers had lecterns on wheels, and the stagehands drove Segways. Even their clipboards were iPads. And I did, in fact, see celebrities. Cynthia Sixx walked right past me, her tower of curly hair even taller than it looked on TV. I saw Tommy Takai come out of a dressing room wearing a baseball cap and a silver-sequined blazer. He nodded at me as he walked by.

Suddenly, it hit me: I was here. I had arrived. Magic didn't get bigger than this. Last week we'd played for fifty people at a bar. In two days, we would play for *millions*. I had to shake myself back to reality. We were late, and I needed to check in.

When I spotted Grace, I knew immediately that it was her: dark hair, late twenties, Starbucks in one hand, iPad in the other, talking rapidly into her headset. As I approached, she held up the index finger on her Starbucks hand in a *hold on* gesture.

"I need it here tonight," she said into the headset. "Make it thirty minutes." The call apparently ended, because she let out a frustrated sigh and turned to me. "Can I help you?"

"I'm Ellie Dante," I said.

"Oh my goodness! It's great to meet you." She made a helpless gesture with her full hands. "When does your gear arrive?"

"It's here," I said. "We came in the same truck."

"That sounds awful." She turned her focus to her tablet. "I'll get a crew down here to unload it. Hold this for me?" She handed me her coffee and swiped at her iPad. "We've got you at the Magic Castle Hotel. Go check in, drop your bags, be back here in an hour." Her phone rang. She answered it, grabbed her coffee, and rushed off. I turned to head back to the truck, then paused midstep.

I was standing under the giant roll-up door that looked out onto the Dolby Theatre stage. It was wide and black and big enough to park a 747 on, but that wasn't what stole my breath.

Beyond the proscenium gaped a cavernous auditorium. I found myself pulled center stage, where I stared out at three thousand red velvet seats starting in the orchestra and rising three balconies high to a domed ceiling. The hair on my arms stood up, and I felt blood surge through my veins, warm and fast. I visualized a packed house, a hot spotlight, the glimmer of sequins on my costume. The hush of the audience, the rush of adrenaline—and then a forklift beeped behind me, and the fantasy popped like a soap bubble. I felt an almost physical sensation of whiplash as I came back to reality.

It was this coming down, this caustic deceleration, that made it impossible for me to continue performing. It was too much for me; it was just too much.

Feeling heavier than I had before, I turned and fled the stage.

At the hotel, Dad urged me to eat something, but I wasn't interested in food. I watched him fix his tie in the mirror. He looked pasty and exhausted.

"I'm fine," he said, reacting to my look. "Just a little woozy from being cramped up in the cab of that rig." He smoothed out his lapels.

"It's just tech, Dad. You don't have to dress up."

He cocked an eyebrow. "You think there won't be cameras? This is Flynn & Kellar we're talking about."

He was right. I frowned at my jeans and T-shirt, then grabbed my bag and pulled out my little black dress. I hadn't washed it since before Phoenix, but it would have to do. I set up the hotel's ironing board but paused before turning on the iron. Suddenly, dread flooded my chest.

"What is it?" Dad crossed the room and put his hand on my shoulder.

"Nothing," I said, switching on the iron and straightening my dress on the board.

"There's no space for secrets, Ellie," he said. "Not now."

I stared at the damask-patterned carpet. "What if we're not ready? We've had no rehearsal. What if—"

He stroked my hair with one of his big hands. "I was doing escapes twenty years before you were born. And you're even readier than I am."

I looked at his face. He radiated confidence. I wished I could feel it.

The theater was only two blocks from our hotel, but they sent a car anyway—a limo. After spending the last year riding around in a torn-up RV and the back seats of big rigs, it felt strange and luxurious to slide around on a leather seat.

Grace met us at the stage door and ushered us into the wings, where a tall man in a black turtleneck greeted us.

"Frankie Clemente," he said, shaking Dad's hand. "I'm the stage manager. Big fan."

"You're too kind," Dad said.

"Your equipment is onstage. This isn't a dress rehearsal; we'll be stopping and starting. We want to run through all the big tech moments to make sure everything's working."

Dad nodded, and Clemente turned to me.

"You must be Ellie. Would you like to watch your dad from the wings?"

That's when I became aware of the cameraman standing six feet away. His lens was pointed at us.

"Actually," Dad said, putting a hand on my shoulder, "she's in the act."

The cameraman smiled and took a step closer to capture the warm, fuzzy father-daughter moment. It would probably make for good television, but it made me feel sick.

The tank had been placed center stage, and a hose roughly the diameter of a telephone pole was filling it with water at an alarming rate. Downstage stood the 1947 Cape Maroon Chevrolet pickup, stage lights gleaming on the polished hood like little suns. While Dad went over the suspension setup with Clemente, I gravitated toward the prop lever.

It was like something out of a steampunk novel: a tarnished bronze-painted shaft jutting up from a pair of brass sprockets the size of hubcaps. I grasped the handle—and even though I knew it was a prop, part of me expected to feel cold, smooth metal against my skin. Instead, my palm rustled against the hollow fiberglass bulb, finding a jagged seam where the mold had come together. I pulled the lever—but instead of hearing the satisfying metallic click that would project through the PA tomorrow night, I heard only a clumsy, plastic scrape. This was how magic felt when I was low: like a cheap lie, like a toy sword with no edge. My disappointment was ludicrous and vivid.

I practiced with the handle a few times, willing my muscles to simulate the resistance of real gears so it would play for the audience. It was a joyless effort; I was going through the motions but feeling no excitement, no anticipation. Feeling not much of anything, really.

When the truck was hooked up to the suspension rig, Dad called me over. He handed me a hank of cotton rope and held up his wrists. Ignoring the hovering cameraman,

I bound Dad's hands with a clunky, amateurish knot; unless Dad picked a sailor from the audience by mistake, that's what he'd be facing on show night. I yanked hard on the ends of the rope—Dad would insist his volunteer do the same.

"Oof," he said, laughing. "You're cutting off my circulation, Cora."

At the sound of my mother's name, my hands seized up. It was as if my chest had been plunged into icy water; I felt heaviness seeping into my body like an injection of mercury.

The last time Dad had rehearsed this illusion, it had been my mother binding his wrists.

Without being willed to, my hands went back to work, tying his ankles. When I had finished, Dad tested his bonds and smiled.

"Perfect," he said. If he had noticed his flub or my reaction, he didn't show it.

I opened the door to the old Chevy and helped him climb in. Once he was settled behind the wheel, I closed the door and stepped back.

Clemente looked up at the catwalk. "Go!"

With a jolt, the truck lurched into the air.

"Easy, there," Dad called out to Clemente.

"My bad," shouted one of the stagehands on the catwalk. The truck paused in its ascent, techs muttered over the walkie-talkies, and then Dad was lowered back down.

"Let's try that again," Clemente said.

The stagehand activated the winch. This time, the truck rose gracefully off the stage. I imagined the spotlight shooting down from the back of the house, painting Dad's face white, illuminating a cone of stage fog in its path. When the Chevy reached its apex, the crane arm, hidden from the audience by the proscenium, moved the body of the truck until it was suspended over the now-full tank.

"All right," Clemente called, crossing downstage. "You ready for the drop?"

Dad stuck his arm out the window and gave Clemente the *okay* sign.

Out of habit or showmanship—I wasn't sure which—I pulled the lever.

The truck dropped.

It hit the surface with a tremendous splash, sending water over the sides of the tank. Clemente shouted to an underling that they would need mops and a pump waiting in the wings—but all my attention was on Dad. Water was gushing into the cab, and I held my breath as he began to work at the ropes that held his wrists.

The water rose to his chest, then over his head. Now he started to thrash, twisting this way and that inside the truck. I felt my pulse spike—but the next moment, he stopped thrashing and thrust his hands out the window. He was free of his bonds. He'd made it look like a struggle—and even though I knew exactly how he'd shrugged off the rope, I had been caught up in the lie, just like the audience would be tomorrow night. Dad kicked out through the window and swam to the top of the tank.

It took another half hour to get the winch speed just right for the new finale—but once that was done, Dad crossed downstage, still wet but smiling. The crew applauded.

"That was perfect," I said, crossing the planks to join him.

"Thanks to you," he replied, putting a hand on my shoulder.

I tried to look affected by the compliment—it's how I should have felt. Honored. Inspired. Instead, I felt flat and slightly ill, as if I'd just swallowed a mouthful of paper. I hoped Dad was too caught up in the moment to see through my act.

"I'll get you a towel," I said. As I walked offstage to retrieve one, Clemente started talking with Dad.

There were no towels waiting in the wings, so I headed toward the dressing rooms. A stack of white towels sat on a plastic cart in the hallway; I grabbed one and jogged back to the stage.

As I reentered the wings, I heard Clemente call, "That's it for Dante! He's back for a full rehearsal at seven p.m. tomorrow!" His voice echoed in the rafters.

Dad exchanged a few more words with him, then shook his hand and began to walk toward me. He smiled, spreading his arms wide in triumph—but then his smile faltered.

He paused midstep, put a hand to his chest, and collapsed onto the stage.

CHAPTER 28

EVERYTHING HAPPENED AT ONCE.

I stood paralyzed as Clemente rushed forward and dropped to his knees. He yelled at one of the stagehands, who pulled out his cell phone and made a call. Then he bent over my father and started doing chest compressions. He looked at me—and his eye contact shocked me back into motion.

I remembered seeing a red defibrillator box on the way in. I bolted through the stage door, yanked the AED from its mount, and rushed back to where my father lay.

Clemente took the defibrillator from my hands. As soon as he opened the box and pushed the red button, an automated voice began to give instructions, but I didn't wait.

"Let me do it!" I said. Clemente stared at me. I grabbed both sides of Dad's dress shirt and yanked. Buttons flew like popcorn. I pulled up his undershirt and rolled him onto his side. His skin was shockingly pale.

"It's okay," I told him. "You're going to be okay."

Ignoring the quaver in my voice, I took the first adhesive paddle from Clemente and applied it next to Dad's left shoulder blade, then rolled him on his back again. I placed the second paddle on his chest, over his heart. The automated voice confirmed that the electrodes had been applied correctly, then directed us to stand clear.

I bit down on my fist.

The machine beeped three times and then emitted a loud buzz, and Dad's muscles tensed. His eyes went wide, staring—and then he gasped for breath.

The strength left my body in a rush, and I sat down hard. I didn't hear the sirens or feel the footsteps of the paramedics as they crossed the stage, but all at once they were shunting me aside, lifting Dad onto a gurney, calling out his heart rate and blood pressure into their radios. I followed them to the loading dock, and one of them walked up to me.

"You're his daughter?"

I could only nod.

"You did the right thing."

The other paramedic shouted, and he answered before turning back to me.

"We're taking him to Hollywood Presbyterian."

"Okay," I said as he climbed into the back of the ambulance and closed the doors. It peeled out from the loading dock, lights flashing, siren blaring. I staggered, and two hands reached out to steady me. They were Grace's.

"Is there someone I can call?"

Forty minutes later, a faded red Prius pulled into the alley. At first I thought it was a crew member coming back from dinner, but then a familiar-looking boy got out. He was tall with broad shoulders and wore a Yankees cap, and I rushed forward and fell into his arms. They were strong, and he held me as if we'd never fought, as if he hadn't cheated and I hadn't used him.

"It's all right," Liam said. "It's going to be okay."

There were so many things I wanted to say: *thank you*; *fuck you*; *I'm scared*. But the words locked up in my throat, so I just pushed away and climbed into the Prius's passenger seat. Liam got in, glanced briefly at me, then handed me his phone.

"The address is already in there. Just tell me where to turn."

He fumbled with the oddly placed gearshift, then backed out of the alley onto Orchid Avenue. He stepped on the gas, and the Prius hummed toward Hollywood Boulevard.

Other than "go straight" and "turn here," I said very little. In return, he didn't ask how I was holding up, or offer a further apology. He just drove, and I was grateful. After a few blocks, it hit me that the car smelled like perfume. I looked down and spotted a handful of hair ties cinched around the gearshift. Liam saw my face and said, "It's not . . . This is my buddy's girlfriend's car."

My shoulders relaxed. Jealousy was a pretty ridiculous emotion given the circumstances.

When we got to the ER, Liam came with me to the desk and stood close as the receptionist calmly told me that yes, my father was here, but no, she didn't have any further information, and no, I couldn't see him right now. She told me to take a seat, and that somebody would call my name when there was more to tell.

Liam guided me to a worn vinyl chair and sat down next to me. When I didn't do or say anything, he grabbed my small hand with his larger one.

"Thanks for coming," I said.

"Of course," he replied, shifting in his seat. "So, your dad. Is he . . . ?"

"He was conscious when the ambulance came."

"That's good."

"Yeah." I picked at a hole in the chair's upholstery. A glance at the clock told me that only four minutes had passed since we'd checked with the nurse.

Liam shifted in his chair. "I want to talk about something, but I don't want you to feel obligated if you're not up to it."

"Okay," I said, dreading another chain of apologies or excuses, but grateful at the prospect of something else to think about.

Liam seemed to get more uncomfortable. "It's just . . . You're the first girl who's ever called me and asked for an eighteen-wheeler on short notice."

I laughed out loud. So loud and for so long that the other people in the ER waiting room must have thought I needed the psych ward. Little did they know.

When I had calmed down and wiped the tears from my eyes, I told Liam what had happened—from the call from Flynn Bissette to my wrecking the RV. It was strange; even after all the drama between us, I still felt like I could trust Liam. Talking to him was easy, but not effortless like it was with Ripley. Like it *had been*, I reminded myself. On impulse I checked my phone, but Ripley still hadn't replied. I thought about calling him to tell him what had happened to Dad but decided against it. He might see it as manipulative, me exploiting yet another crisis to make up for my awful behavior. And maybe he would be right.

Before I had time to consider it any further, a voice called my name.

"Elias Dante Jr.?"

I jumped out of my seat. "Yes?"

The man standing in the doorway wore a white lab coat—so he was a doctor, not a nurse. I strode across the waiting room to him.

"I'm Dr. Saroyan, your dad's cardiologist."

"Is he all right?"

"He's stable," he said, which wasn't an answer. "Why don't you come on back."

I turned to Liam.

"I'll be right here," he said.

Dr. Saroyan led me down the hall into a small office.

"We're not going to his room?" I asked.

"Not right now. Please take a seat."

Reluctantly, I did.

"I understand you operated the defibrillator."

"Yeah, I did. Look, tell me what's going on with my dad."

Dr. Saroyan sat and folded his hands on the desk. "Your father had a heart attack."

I'd figured out that much on my own, but the news tightened my chest all the same.

"He needs to undergo a procedure."

I couldn't seem to catch my breath. "Are you putting in another stent?"

"I'm afraid it's more serious this time," Saroyan said. "Your father needs emergency bypass surgery. They're prepping him now."

"How risky is the surgery?"

"It would be riskier not to do it."

I pressed my hands against my numb face. This wasn't supposed to happen. I was only sixteen, and I'd already lost Mom. I couldn't lose him, too.

Dr. Saroyan shifted in his seat. "Our cardiac surgeon, Dr. Houts, performs these procedures every week. His success rate is far above the mean."

I bit my lip. "We don't have . . . There's no insurance."

Dr. Saroyan glanced at the door, then leaned toward me. "Patients can't be turned away for lifesaving treatments. You can work it out later."

"How long will it take?"

"With no complications, three to four hours."

I gripped the arms of the chair. "What should I do?"

"Stay close. The front desk has your cell. You'll get a text message when we have news."

I nodded.

"Have your friend take you down to the commissary on the first floor." He gave me a weak smile. "Stay away from the tuna salad."

Liam and I ate Froot Loops from single-serving boxes and drank Starbucks coffee from paper cups. I asked him to distract me, so he started telling me about his senior trip to New York. About what it was like to crunch the snow in Central Park and drink whiskey in a speakeasy behind a Laundromat. I tried to nod and smile in all the right places, but the adrenaline from the emergency was waning, leaving me even more exhausted than I'd been before. Liam saw me crashing and insisted that I take a nap. So after two hours with no updates from the doctor, we returned to his buddy's girlfriend's Prius, tilted the seats back, and tried to sleep. Despite the maelstrom of thoughts twisting my neurons, I felt my eyes droop. Sleep came more easily in the gray—maybe because it was so much more pleasant than being awake.

Then my phone chirped, and my eyes shot open: it was a text from the front desk. I scrambled out of the car and ran for the hospital door.

CHAPTER 29

THIS TIME IT WAS DR. HOUTS who met me at the receptionist's desk. When he smiled, I let out a gasp of relief and had to wipe my eyes.

"Is he okay?" I said, trying to catch my breath.

Liam caught up and took my hand.

"The procedure went smoothly," Dr. Houts said. "Your dad is recovering in the ICU."

"When can I see him?"

He glanced at an expensive watch. It was past midnight. "Go home and get some sleep. Come back around six a.m. He should be awake by then."

Liam insisted on staying with me, crashing out on the other bed. I was grateful; I didn't want to be alone.

I awoke to Liam's hand on my shoulder. Orange light poured in through the gauzy hotel curtains, and it took me a moment to remember where I was. I felt drugged. There was a cold burning in my head, and my thoughts were slow.

"What time is it?" I asked. My mouth tasted like old tires.

"Seven fifteen."

I sat up. "I was supposed to be there at six!"

"You needed the sleep," Liam said. "The hospital sent you a text. Your dad just woke up, and he's asking for you."

"Shit. Okay, let's go."

I pulled my hair into a ponytail and brushed my teeth while Liam made us hotel room coffee to go. We were at the hospital by seven forty-five.

Only family members were allowed in the ICU, so I left Liam in the waiting room and followed the signs down a long second-floor corridor until I reached Dad's room. Someone had written *DANTE, ELIAS* on a whiteboard next to the door. Somehow, seeing his name on that whiteboard made everything more real. I dug my nails into my palms and walked into the room.

Dad lay in bed with his eyes closed. Tubes ran into his nostrils. An IV bag dripped clear liquid into the back of one veiny hand. The sight of all this, the smell of menthol, and the sound of beeping and hissing machines made me feel sick. I never wanted to set foot in a hospital again; how had I ever thought I wanted to be a nurse?

I crossed to Dad and put my hand on the cold bed rail. His eyes opened, and he covered my hand with his. His skin was almost as pale as the sheet, and the lines on his face seemed deeper in the harsh green light.

"Daddy," I said. It came out a whisper.

He rubbed his paper-dry fingers across my hand. I leaned

over and pressed my cheek against his knuckles.

"How do you feel?"

"I'm all right."

"You scared the shit out of me."

"Rule number three," he said, smiling. "Always keep them guessing."

A sound came out of me, half sob and half laugh. "I'm glad you're still here."

"Thanks to you."

"Clemente did the CPR. He would have done the rest if I'd let him."

"That's not what I meant." He gripped my hand. "When your mom—when she left us . . . Without you, I would have been dead a long time ago."

I felt a hot tide rising behind my eyes.

"Knowing how she suffered . . . I should have seen it. In her, and in you. I should have taken better care of you both."

I wanted to throw my arms around him, hug him, but he was too fragile. So instead I clutched his arm and squeezed.

"I miss her," I said.

"I do, too." His voice was soft and thin.

"I'm sorry." I took a deep breath and let it rattle out of me slowly. "We got so close."

He frowned. "What are you talking about?"

"The show. Your comeback." I glanced at the sheet stretched over his chest, imagining the inflamed incision beneath. The reality of it struck me like a pipe to the head: They had cut him open. They'd cut straight to his heart. I couldn't think about it anymore or I'd fall apart.

He started to move, as if he intended to prop himself up on his elbows.

"Dad, stop." Gently, I pushed him back down. "You'll rip your stitches."

He grunted in protest but complied. "They use staples now."

"You just had a goddamned heart attack. You're not sitting up until a doctor says it's okay."

"That's some way to speak to your father." He made a tutting noise. Sometimes his sense of humor was infuriating. Dad licked his lips, glanced at the bedside table. "Could I have some water?"

I shook my head. "You're not allowed to eat or drink anything for the next twenty-four hours. IV nutrients only. But the nurse said I could get you get some ice chips."

When I returned from the nurses' station, he sucked greedily at the ice, then sank back into the pillow. I pulled up a chair and sat down so that our heads were on the same level.

"Better?"

"Much."

He closed his eyes, and I thought he might fall asleep—but then he spoke, and his voice was stronger and clearer than it had been a moment before.

"You were right, Ellie. I'm too old, and you need stability." He opened his eyes. "My performing days are over. Sunny's Roadhouse was my swan song, and my proudest moment. Because of you."

He squeezed my hand, and my heart ached. Dad had

always pursued his dream, no matter how many times it danced out of his grasp. Sitting there next to him as hospital monitors beeped and hummed, I realized that it was the chase that drove him. If it had been money or fame he was after, he would have given up years ago.

"Once I've recovered, we'll settle down for good. We may have to couch-surf for a while, but we'll land on our feet. We always do." He smiled, but the expression was manufactured. Plastered on over a thick layer of disappointment. I wanted to share his hope—but even if we did find jobs and a couch to sleep on, we'd have medical bills weighing us down for years. There would be no money for an apartment of our own, no money for college. And with the RV gone and our props destroyed, we couldn't even make a living doing magic anymore. We were so much worse off than we had been—and he had to know it.

"Don't worry," I said. I sounded ridiculous, a teenager telling her sixty-four-year-old father not to worry as he lay in bed recovering from open-heart surgery. But what else was there to say? "I'll find a way to pay the bills. Rico said I could get work as an assistant."

"Did he now?" Dad muttered, and then his eyes drifted shut. Our brief conversation had exhausted whatever energy he'd managed to summon, and now he really had fallen asleep.

I watched him for a few minutes, taking comfort each time his chest rose and fell—but I also felt dread sinking into my bones like a deep winter chill. We had hit bottom, and I knew Dad couldn't save us. It was up to me.

I knew what I had to do, and it scared me to death.

Always keep them guessing, Dad had taught me. It had been my favorite of the four rules. *Keep them guessing* meant I could always deliver a surprise, delighting people with the unexpected, with the unforeseen. But now I had to gather my strength in pursuit of a different rule of magic. The last and most important rule of all:

The show must go on.

Liam was waiting for me in the lobby and stood up as I approached.

"How is he?"

Liam had dark circles under his eyes and a two-day beard. For the first time, I wondered what he had sacrificed to be here. At the very least, he'd borrowed a car and lost a night of sleep. He'd probably missed classes, too.

"He's fine," I said. I meant it to sound reassuring, but it came out flat, almost bored. At Liam's confused look, I said, "Sorry. I'm just wiped out."

"I can tell. You're down, huh?"

I opened my mouth to give a sarcastic response, but I swallowed it instead. He had noticed. And it was no small feat to tell the difference between the shock of witnessing my dad's heart attack and the onset of a depressive episode.

"Yeah," I admitted. "I am."

We headed out to the parking lot and got into the Prius, but Liam didn't start the engine.

"Listen, Ellie, I know there's a lot going on right now. And you don't owe me anything—not even the chance to explain. But please let me tell you what happened. Then you can decide whether you want to date me or murder me in my sleep."

I turned away, stared out the window at the vintage *Wendy's* sign across the street. I didn't want to talk about this right now—I was afraid more disappointment might crush me. But I *did* owe Liam something. For the truck, and for the rescue.

"Okay."

"Thank you." He gripped the steering wheel. "I met Kaylee at orientation. We went on three dates, and then—"

"I don't want details," I said. "Just skip to the part about why you lied."

Liam took off his cap and ran a hand through his hair.

"We went on three dates—that's it. But she thought it was something more. So I had to make a big deal out of it and 'break up' with her. That was two weeks ago, before I came home for Becca's wedding."

"Right before you asked me out."

"Yeah."

"That doesn't explain why you ghosted me. Or why *she* picked up your phone when I texted you in the middle of the night."

Liam stared out the windshield for moment. "Can I explain the second part first?"

"Fine."

"I was pledging a fraternity—Pi Kappa Alpha, the one my father insisted I join. Anyway, I was at this rush party, and Kay—she was there. I was doing a stupid drinking game, and I left my jacket hanging over a chair. She must have taken my phone, seen your text, and called you. I was pretty drunk. I didn't realize what happened until I looked at my call history the next morning."

I couldn't look at him. "Why do these stories always involve 'I was drunk'?"

"I'm not proud of it, and I'm not making an excuse."

"Okay, fine. But why didn't you answer my calls or texts for two days after our second 'date'? You know, the one where you basically asked me to be your girlfriend?"

Liam let out a long breath and tilted his head back. I had the feeling I wouldn't like what he was about to say.

"I just . . . got cold feet."

"About what, exactly?" I glared at him. If he was about to wreck me, I wasn't going to make it easy.

"About the bipolar thing."

I gaped at him. I had never used that word; he must have figured it out on his own.

I closed my eyes and pressed the heels of my hands against them. I expected to feel something. A stabbing pain in my heart, a rush of breath, a flood of tears. But I just felt empty.

"You were so different that night at Sunny's," he said. "So much more, I don't know, aggressive? I just got freaked out."

"Stop," I said. "Stop talking." I couldn't stand to hear him say how different I was when I was up. How he would have wanted to be with me, if only I weren't so fucked up.

"You can hate me," Liam said, "but I'm going to be honest. It's who I am."

"Except when you're scared?"

"I panicked, okay? I Googled, and I read the worst, and I panicked. I never meant to—"

"What was 'the worst'?"

He frowned. "What do you mean?"

"What was the worst symptom you read about? Which part did you not want to deal with?"

Liam's mouth opened slightly, but I cut him off before he could answer.

"Was it the depression that freaked you out? Listlessness, bad hygiene, lack of interest in sex? Suicidal thoughts? Because I've had all those. I've had all those *this week*." I savored the look of shock on his face. "Or was it the hypomania? You thought I was aggressive the other night? You haven't seen shit. I've broken promises. Stolen things. Made out with strangers. Driven away my best friend." His eyes had softened, but I didn't feel like letting up. "But those are only the extremes. Mostly, I'm just impossible to be around. One minute you'll think I'm pissed off, and the next you'll hate that I'm being so needy. You'll never know what's going through my head, and when you ask, I won't tell you. I'll be up and down and frantic and sedate and you'll never know whether it's you or me or the drugs or just my fucking disease. So if you've got cold feet now, I suggest you get as far away from me as you can, as fast as you can."

And then the words dried up like someone had shut off the faucet. I folded my arms and stared out the window.

Liam was quiet for a long time, and as the seconds dragged on, I was afraid that I'd succeeded in scaring him off.

I was afraid that any moment now, he was going to tell me to get out of the car. That he was going to drive away and I would never see him again. Actually, I was sure that's what was going to happen—so I beat him to the punch. I opened the car door and had one foot on the pavement before I felt his hand on my arm.

"I read all that," he said. "I read it all, okay? And I thought about it." He sucked in a breath. "But . . . I just like you."

I got back in the car, but I couldn't face him. "Why?"

Liam reached across me and closed the car door. "Because you understand things about me that I barely understand myself. And the way you look at the world . . . You see things I've never noticed my whole life. So, yeah. I like you. All the versions of you. Sad, sarcastic Ellie from the wedding. Inappropriately horny Ellie from the railroad tie. I even like pissed-off, depressed, in-crisis Ellie from the hospital parking lot. I like them all. I like *you*." He paused, took a shuddering breath. "I don't pretend to know how to deal with all your stuff. I don't think anyone does. But I'm willing to try. So bring it on. Show me the dark shit. I'm right here."

Heat swelled behind my eyes, and I was only slightly disgusted to feel a tear streak down my cheek. I sniffled. Liam made no move to comfort me, to touch me in any way. He was so goddamned decent, I did want to murder him. Finally, I looked up. His eyes were blue and wide and seemed to be dreading whatever I was going to say.

"You practiced that speech, didn't you?"

Relief showed in every feature on his face. "A little."

"You're so fucking honest."

"You'll hate it, eventually, if you let me stick around."

I ran both hands through my hair, tugged. "I already do."

Liam smiled.

"Take me back to the hotel," I said.

"Yes, ma'am," he said, and started the car.

CHAPTER 30

AS WE DROVE BACK TO the hotel, the relief I felt from making peace with Liam faded, replaced by a vicious loop of thoughts about what I had to do next. When we pulled into the lot, I wasn't ready to be on my own again, so I swallowed my pride and asked him to stay with me for a while. We got hot chocolate from the lobby and sat on wicker chairs in the courtyard, looking up at the Hollywood Hills, now green from an autumn rainstorm that had beaten us to California.

I took a sip and stared into the distance. "Dad's too sick to perform, so I'm going on in his place."

Liam set down his cup. "Are you serious?"

I nodded. "His surgery's going to cost like forty grand, and we don't have insurance. So I don't have much choice."

"Ellie, that's—"

"I know. But first I have to persuade Flynn to let me do it."

"You think he will?"

"I don't know." I picked at the rim of my cup. "But I have a plan."

"This is big."

"It's *huge*. And I should be terrified. But instead I'm numb."

Liam picked up his cup again, then set it back down. "But you know the routine, right?"

"Backward and forward. I've been thinking about it nonstop for ten days."

"And you get paid something, even if you fail?"

"Thanks for the vote of confidence."

"That's not what I—"

I smirked, and he rolled his eyes.

"I just mean you've got nothing to lose. There's no downside."

I stared at the clumps of undissolved chocolate powder at the bottom of my cup. "With me, there's always a downside."

"Oh." There was recognition in his voice, and I believed that he really did get it. I felt a swell of gratitude.

"Do you remember I told you how my mom died?"

He nodded.

"She did it right after what happened on TV."

Liam let out a long breath.

"Dad failed big, and it triggered a cycle, and she never recovered." My throat tightened. "What if that happens to me? What if I fuck up like he did? What if I get it *wrong?*"

I expected Liam to comfort me. To encourage me. To spout platitudes.

Instead, he said, "I don't think that's what you're scared of. Not really."

"How would you know?"

"Because I know you," he said. Something in his voice told me he believed it. My anger cooled a little.

"What am I really scared of?"

He hesitated, as if calculating the cost of what he was about to say.

"I think you're afraid of having the best moment of your life, and then facing the comedown. I think you're scared of what happens if you get it *right*."

I sat there with my jaw tight as a piano wire, glaring at the stupid burbling fountain in the courtyard and hating Liam for being right. After what probably felt like forever to Liam, I turned and looked him right in his stupid perfect blue eyes.

"I'm not going to apologize for putting you through emotional whiplash. The same way I wouldn't expect someone in a wheelchair to apologize for wrecking the carpet. I am what I am. I'm better on meds, but I am what I am."

Liam met my gaze and said, "Okay."

"Okay? You think 'okay' covers this?"

He shrugged. "I am what I am, too. And I didn't have time to practice this part."

Liam had to return the car he'd borrowed, and I had a dress rehearsal to prepare for. He promised he'd be watching tomorrow night. I wanted to ask him to come to the theater, to stay with me backstage—but he had already done enough.

As we said goodbye in the lobby, he didn't try to kiss me or anything. I wasn't sure how I felt about that.

I arrived at the Dolby just after twelve noon and surprised Grace at the stage door. She threw her arms around me, her headset digging into my shoulder. Finally, she pushed away, holding me at arm's length. "How's your dad? Is he okay?"

"He will be."

"I know your equipment is on loan," she said, swiping at her iPad, "and you're going to need it back. We've got two more acts to rehearse, and then we can get a crew to load—"

"Actually," I interrupted her, "I was hoping to speak with Flynn. Mr. Bissette, I mean."

Grace looked up. "About what?"

I took a breath, trying to relieve the pressure building in my chest. It would be a huge risk for Flynn & Kellar to allow a total unknown with no TV experience to take up three minutes of their live national airtime. But I had to persuade them. I tried to harness my inner grifter. The suburban pick-pocket, the diesel-pump distracter. Hot tears began to trickle out of the corners of my eyes; maybe I was better at this than I thought.

"I just need to speak to him." My voice cracked in all the right places, and I could tell by the surrender on her face that it had worked. The thing was, the tears were real, and now that they'd started, it was hard to choke them back. This time when Grace hugged me, I leaned into it.

I heard his laugh before I saw him. Grace and I were striding toward the back of the house when a delighted baritone chuckle drifted in from the lobby. It was like a baby's laugh, but slowed down by two hundred percent. There was nothing cynical about it; he was just completely tickled by something.

I steeled myself, then pushed confidently through the double doors—and walked straight into Flynn Bissette.

"Whoa!" he cried out in surprise.

I rebounded off his large frame, but he reached out and caught me before I could fall on my ass.

"Are you all right?" he asked, setting me upright.

"Yeah, I'm fine, I'm good." I brushed hair out of my face, tugged down the hem of my dress.

"You were flying like a bat out of hell. Where were you going?"

Flynn was even taller than he seemed on TV; I barely went up to his chest.

"Actually, I was coming to see you."

He squinted down at me, and then recognition sparked in his eyes. "Ellie Dante." He stretched out a big hand, and I shook it. "How's your dad?"

"I mean, considering they cut his chest open and stapled it back together, not bad?"

Flynn laughed, that baritone chuckle again. "You're all right, kid. He's lucky to have you. Is the prognosis good?"

I'd heard that Flynn was friendly and "normal" in person, but I hadn't really believed it.

"He's going to be okay."

"Glad to hear it." He pushed his circular eyeglasses up on his considerable nose. "I'm sorry it didn't work out for him to appear on the show. But don't worry. More opportunities will come. They always do."

I opened my mouth to reply. To say that there wouldn't be any more opportunities, not for us. To tell him this was it. That it was now or never.

Flynn gave me a compassionate smile—he was probably used to people turning speechless in his presence—and then he started to move past me down the aisle. Grace followed.

"Wait!" I yelled. My voice echoed in the auditorium, sounding equal parts desperate and confident. Perfect.

Flynn stopped, glanced down at his watch, then up at me. "What's up?"

I looked out at the stage. Flynn raised his eyebrows impatiently, then started to turn away.

"I want to do it." I spat out the words.

Flynn frowned. "You want to do what?"

"The Truck Drop," I said, my voice tremulous. "I want you to let me take his place on the show."

Flynn pressed his lips together and scrubbed a finger across them as if stalling for time. As if calculating how to let down an emotionally distressed teenage girl without causing a scene.

Finally, he asked, "Why?"

I hadn't expected the question, and I scrambled to answer it. "Because we need this show, Mr. Bissette. We—"

"No," Flynn said, cutting me off. "Not why do you *want* to. Why should I let you?"

I blinked. He'd caught me off guard again.

He took a step toward me. "I know you're in a tough

spot. But this is a multimillion-dollar production. I don't know you, and I don't know your magic."

"You know the Truck Drop."

"That's not yours," he said, wagging a finger. "You may have tweaked it, added a twist. But it doesn't belong to you; it belongs to your father. He earned his place on this show. Whereas I've never seen you do anything, let alone something that impressed me. And don't take this wrong way, but I'm hard to impress."

The room seemed to tilt, and I had to grab one of the seats to keep myself upright. I took a deep breath and looked him straight in the eye.

It was now or never.

"Reach into your back pocket," I said.

Flynn frowned.

"Go ahead."

Slowly, with suspicion darkening his features, Flynn reached into his back pocket. When he withdrew his hand, he was holding a playing card. A blue Rider Back. He glanced up at me, bewildered.

"Turn it over," I said.

He did—and stared at it for a long moment. Then his face started to change, his mouth widening into a grin. He shook his head and laughed, not a chuckle, but a basso profundo guffaw.

"Son of a bitch," he said, and held the card up so Grace could see it:

It was the nine of hearts—and on its face, written in his own unmistakable hand, were three words:

FAIL BIG.—Flynn

He looked at me, started to speak, shook his head again. Then he turned to Grace.

"I guess you're going to have to reprint those production schedules."

CHAPTER 31

THE RUSH OF FOOLING FLYNN evaporated like water off a hot pan. I knew I hadn't really persuaded him with my parlor trick. He must've already wanted to let me do the show; all I'd done was give him an excuse. Plus he probably figured that if I reprised my father's failure, it would make for spectacular television.

I decided to walk back to the hotel, hoping two blocks of trudging up a steep hill would revive me; instead, every step was heavier than the last. Autumn was nowhere in evidence; today, Hollywood was hot and smoggy. The sky might have been a clear, deep blue, but all I saw were constellations of old gum stains and cigarette butts on the concrete. I was gearing up for the biggest moment of my life, but there was a giant hole in the middle of my chest. A Ripley-shaped hole. Liam had found the courage to be straight with me; maybe I needed to do the same with Ripley.

I stopped at a McDonald's, got a Diet Coke, and logged into the free Wi-Fi. I thought about sending him another text—but since he'd ignored my first one, I decided an email would be better. That way he could read it when he was ready. I opened a new message and began to type.

Dear Ripley,

I've been thinking about you a lot, and about what I said to you back in Las Vegas. I won't apologize for being an emotional wreck. That part isn't my fault. But I can take responsibility for how I treated you. I hurt you, and then I played the sick card to excuse it. For that, I'm sorry.

Being my friend must feel lonely and exhausting. I'm always having some kind of crisis, and you have to come to the rescue. I can't remember the last time we had a conversation that was all about you. I read this BuzzFeed article once about cutting toxic people out of your life, and I know I've been one of those toxic people to you. I don't blame you for cutting me out, and I don't expect you to reply.

The problem is, I'm about to do the biggest thing I've ever done in my life, and I can't feel complete without telling you. For reasons I won't go into, my dad can't do the Truck Drop tomorrow. So I'm doing it instead.

I'm so scared, Ripley. I'm scared of failing, but I'm also scared of what happens if I succeed. I'm scared of getting so high that the fall will kill me.

I wish you were here to talk me through it, to dismiss all my nonsense and tell me how things really are. But I know I haven't earned it.

Anyway. I hope you and Jude and Heather and your dad are okay.

I miss you.

Love,
Ellie

I reread it twice; it seemed sappy and not enough, but it was all I could think to write. I clicked Send, and suddenly my whole body felt like a giant sandbag. Despite the near-fatal dose of caffeine pumping through my bloodstream, I was exhausted.

I went back to the hotel, set two alarms, and crashed.

Five hours later, I was backstage at the Dolby Theatre, glaring at myself in the dressing-room mirror, lit by a frame of old-school tungsten light bulbs. I had awoken in the hotel feeling more exhausted than before, and it had taken every bit of resolve I possessed to get out of bed and splash cold water on my face.

Now I raked my fingers through my hair, which hung down on all sides like a cowl, frizzled and wavy from lack of conditioner. My eyes were dull and ringed with red. I looked strung out. Fried. Spent. The costume designer hadn't finished my outfit yet, so for rehearsal I'd borrowed a black bodysuit. It was a size too small and suffocating. I felt faint and confined, like a Jane Austen character, bound by corsets and the legacies of old men.

A thousand dark thoughts flipped through my mind like frames of film through a broken projector, but the one that stuck the longest was that this was all Dad's fault. He hadn't taken care of himself, and now I had to clean up his mess, just like I always did. He had convinced me to take time off school, coerced me into performing, sabotaged my chance at a normal life. Some part of me knew these thoughts were twisted, that they were just my sickness talking—but I couldn't stop myself from believing them. Despite all my plans, all my protests, I was doing exactly what Dad had wanted me to do all along.

What about what *I* wanted?

I imagined stepping out onto the Dolby Theatre stage. The click of my heels on the planks. The hush of the vast auditorium. But the exhilaration I'd felt before was gone as if it had never been there in the first place. Instead, there was only a gaping gray void. What did I want? I wanted *out.* I wanted to lie down on the cool concrete floor, close my eyes, and never wake up.

"Ms. Dante?" It was Grace calling from the hallway outside. I opened the door.

Her expression changed instantly from impatience to concern. "Are you all right?"

I vowed to slap the next person who asked me that.

She led me down a long concrete hallway, and I paused

for a moment in the wings. The tank loomed center stage, ten feet tall and three-quarters full of crystal-clear water. If I stood on the bottom, I could stretch my arms straight up and not touch the surface. My chest tightened in anticipation.

Clemente called out, "Ellie, we're ready for you."

A stagehand bound my wrists, but I paid no attention. A buzz had started up in the back of my head. This was going to go wrong. I was going to fail. Just like my father.

Ella, ella, eh, eh, eh.

I hardly noticed the loop starting up again as I climbed into the driver's seat. The door closed, Clemente spoke into his radio, and the truck lurched into the air.

"Goddamn it," Clemente yelled up at the catwalk. "When are you going to get this right?"

"We had it weighted for the father," the tech called down. "Won't happen again."

Clemente approached, leaned in the window. "Are you all right?"

"Yes," I said, hearing my own voice as if from a distance.

Clemente gave the signal, and this time, the truck rose smoothly off the stage.

I had craved the sensation of suspension—that empty-stomach roller-coaster feeling. I'd made a tacit wish that the thrill of it would lance the gray like a blister and drain the darkness from my sick mind. But it didn't happen.

The rehearsal went as last-minute rehearsals always do: lots of starts and stops, shouting and adjustments, leaving me with a lingering sense that everything could still go wrong. Afterward, Grace had a car take me to Hollywood Presbyterian, but

Dad was asleep when I arrived. The nurse told me his vitals were good and his recovery was on track. I sat next to his bed for an hour, hoping he would wake. I wanted to tell him what I was going to do. I wanted his praise, his encouragement—but more than that, I wanted his advice.

When he didn't wake up, I wrote him a note and left.

I ordered a room-service cheeseburger mostly out of duty, then picked at it until the fries went cold. When I realized I'd been watching the same looping video-on-demand previews for forty minutes, I flipped off the TV, put my tray in the hall, and took a long, hot shower. Then I crossed to Dad's bag and searched through it.

I wanted to look at his journal one more time, to study every detail of the Truck Drop diagram. I wanted to burn it into my mind so that during the performance I could see it objectively, as if I were watching from the front row. The journal must have been buried deep in the bag; when I pulled out his old corduroy sport coat to look underneath, I heard a rattle. I reached into the pocket—he'd left his pills behind. But it was no problem; they would give him everything he needed at the hospital. I set the bottle aside, started to go back to the bag, then paused.

I looked at the bottle more closely. The pills inside were white, but they were the wrong shape. I seized it, twisted off the lid, and poured a pill into my palm. It wasn't round and flat like his heart medicine; it was oblong and rounded. I stared at it for a moment—and then I touched it to my tongue.

The clear, cold taste of spearmint flooded my mouth. He hadn't bought his medication after all; he'd filled his bottle with breath mints to trick me, and then he'd spent all his money on mine instead.

I sank onto the bed, staring stupidly at the amber plastic bottle filled with worthless mints. I was angry at him for lying, and I felt guilty for his sacrifice. I didn't deserve it; I was a burden, a dead weight dragging us both down.

Time condensed and stretched in the darkness—and then, at some point, blackness overtook me.

I'm sitting in the truck, wrists and ankles bound. A red stage light glares in the rearview mirror. I hear the click of the prop lever echoing in the auditorium. I hold my breath.

The truck drops, and the seat falls out from under me.

My head hits the roof and then the truck strikes the water with a great slap, driving me down into the springs of the old bench seat. I hear water sloshing over the sides of the tank. I feel the rush of cold as it begins to pour in through the open windows.

I rotate my wrists, trying to create enough slack to free my hands—but the bindings only cinch tighter. Fighting off panic, I struggle against the ropes—but the more I pull, the tighter my bonds become. The water rises to my knees. I bend forward to free my ankles, but my head hits the steering wheel, honking the horn. It comes out burbled, like a crying baby half submerged in a bathtub.

Laughter sweeps through the audience; people are looking at me now, and they are enjoying watching me drown.

The water is up to my chest.

I throw my body against the door but manage only to bruise my ribs. My cage. My bodysuit is too tight, like a corset. I'm going to pass out. The water is at my neck. My chin. My bottom lip.

My head goes under.

I look out into the audience. Through the thick wall of the tank, my vision distorts, darkens. The seats are empty again, all but one in the front row, which is occupied by a very old man. I look closer and see that it's my father.

It's my father, and he's dead.

I choked and sputtered and sat up in bed.

Desperate to get free from the twisted sheet, I thrashed and slipped off the bed, landing hard on the floor. There was something in my mouth; I clawed at it, pulling away a lock of hair that had found its way in like a hungry spider.

Dad's dead face stared up at me from the front row.

My shoulders shook as I began to cry in big, heavy gasps. I stuffed a fist into my mouth, but the sobs only seemed to gain momentum.

I would fail, and he would die homeless and alone.

My knees burned against the cold tile as I crawled to the bathroom, still wailing. All my life I had suffered the weakness of my parents. His inability to provide. Her unwillingness to survive.

I would fail like him.

I would die like her.

Finding the cold porcelain edge of the tub, I mashed the rubber plug into the drain and opened the tap. Steam filled the room, obscuring the mirror like a cataract. I stripped off my clothes and stepped into the scalding water. The heat took me, obliterating my thoughts, overwhelming my nerves until it felt like needles, then like ice.

I shut off the tap and lay down in the water, crying out as fresh nerve endings succumbed to the heat. I put my ears under the surface and listened as the world turned amniotic. My heart beating, slower, slower. My breath like a diver's.

I could step out and steal a blade from the razor on the sink.

I could retrieve the hair dryer from the wardrobe. The cord would be long enough.

Or I could just submerge my head, gulp water into my lungs, and surrender.

All at once, I sat up and scrambled out of the tub. My feet slipped on the wet tile and I fell in a heap on my clothes. The cold air shocked me back to myself, and the thoughts that had bitten into my mind fell out like so many rotten teeth.

I got to my feet, pulled the plug, and watched the water drain away. Then I turned on the shower, closed my eyes, and let the cold water wash over me. I felt hollow. Exhausted.

But I was alive.

I didn't understand why I'd suddenly had the impulse to survive. Maybe it was the medication finally kicking in. Maybe it was Dad's recovery, or the promise of a show. Maybe it was down to the random firing of one particular neuron. I would never know.

When my skin finally stopped steaming, I shut off the tap and pulled on the hotel robe. I stood in the bathroom for a moment, covered in goose bumps and shivering, trying to decide what to do next. Finally, with a terrible effort, I reached into the tub and yanked the rubber stopper off its chain. I crossed to the sink and picked up the disposable razor. I opened the wardrobe and retrieved the hair dryer. Then I crossed to the sliding glass door, opened it, and hurled everything over the railing and out onto Franklin Avenue.

I went back inside and found my phone. The first call went to voice mail, so I dialed again. This time, he picked up on the second ring.

"Ellie?"

The sound of Ripley's voice jolted me back to life like a defibrillator, and before I could speak, I began to cry again, heavy, chest-heaving sobs.

"Hey," Ripley said. "What's going on?"

It took me a while to calm down enough to talk, but once I did, the words spilled out of me like water from a shattered tank. I told Ripley about my dad's heart attack. About my dream.

And then I told him what I had almost done.

The silence was long and protracted—or at least that's how it seemed. Time was distorted in the gray.

"Are you safe now?" Ripley asked. I had been afraid that when he spoke, he would sound distant or disgusted, but he didn't.

Then I glanced at the sheets on the bed, at the clothing pole in the closet. I hadn't suicide-proofed the room—not really—but the impulse was gone, even if the thoughts weren't.

"I think so." I swallowed. "Ripley, can you come here? Now?"

He cleared his throat. "I can't, Ellie. I'm sorry."

"Oh." His refusal stung, and I withdrew like a flower closing up at dusk. "That's okay. I mean, I'll be fine."

"Don't be an idiot," Ripley said. "We're going to video-chat for the next three hundred hours with no pee breaks. I just don't have a car because my dad is working and Heather moved to Portland to find a boyfriend with a beard."

Relief forced a sound out of me; it was less like a laugh and more like a screech.

Ripley made me get up and raid the hotel vending machines; I returned to my room with a Pepsi and a package of Hostess Donettes. Once we were on video chat, I took one look at Ripley and almost burst into tears again. It felt like years since we'd broken up in Las Vegas.

"Thank you for rescuing me. Again."

"Turns out rescuing people is one of my vices," he said.

"What do you mean?"

"My Alateen sponsor has informed me that I am an 'enabler.' It's kind of like being a Hufflepuff, only nobler. I'm embracing it. It's already in my Insta bio."

I made a snuffling laugh.

Ripley cracked open a soda. "So I guess you got the props?"

I nodded.

"You will now tell me the whole story. Begin."

I filled him in on everything that had happened: breaking into the warehouse, running into Rico, performing for Devereaux. Watching Higgins fly around cackling like a kindergartener in a jet pack.

"Wish I hadn't missed that," he said. Then he pressed his lips together; he was holding something back.

I looked down at my pruny hands. "Ripley, I'm so, so sorry. I—"

"I'm not going to lie. What you said hurt me. Really badly." His face seemed to set like drying concrete. "I deleted your text without reading it. When I got your email, though . . . I called my sponsor. She agreed I should write you off."

I shut my eyes. "It's what I deserve."

"I don't know about that," Ripley said. "You were sick and off meds, and none of that is your fault. Like, if you had one of those brain tumors that make you violent, could I blame you for hitting me? It would be like blaming someone with a cold for sneezing. I mean, it's more complicated than that, but not really, you know?"

My chest seemed to unfreeze. "I think so," I said.

"Plus," Ripley continued, and his voice was oddly light, "it doesn't feel like a good punishment, cutting you off. Then I lose a friend, too. I think, instead, I'd prefer you to feel extremely guilty for a very, very long time. I would find that quite satisfying."

I smiled, and he smiled, and I wanted to reach through the screen and put my head on his shoulder. I would never take him for granted again.

"Now," he said, "let's have a conversation that's all about me." He pointed both thumbs at his chest and grinned like an idiot.

"Agreed." I laughed. "So, then how are you?"

Ripley's grin dissolved. "Kind of a mess."

"Why?"

"I just—I shouldn't have have left Jude."

I felt a stab of guilt—he had left his brother behind for me, and I had even shamed him for it. God, I could be a monster.

Ripley sensed my distress. "No, Ellie—look, I'm glad I

came and helped and everything. But while I was gone, my mother moved back in."

"Oh, no."

"Yeah. She brought meth, and she got my dad high *that night.* He fell off the wagon big-time, and they went on a bender. By the time I got home, Jude was holed up in his room, living off Pringles and peanut butter."

I put a hand over my mouth. "Ripley, I'm so sorry."

He gave a half-hearted nod. "Sometimes I wonder if Jude would be better off in foster care. But then I think I'm selfish for even thinking that. Because maybe I'm not worried about his best interests. Maybe I just want to get away. Escape. Go to college."

I tried to think of something to say that might pull him out of his misery. I was no good at comfort; I was usually the one being comforted.

"Where would you go? If money wasn't an issue. If you had your pick."

"MIT." He said it like he was pronouncing the name of someone who had just died. "La Sorbonne. University of Fucking Jupiter. It doesn't matter; I'm not going anywhere. I'll be stuck on the shitty side of Park Hills until I die."

We sat in silence for a few seconds, and then Ripley shook his head like a wet dog.

"So, that's self-pity. Huh. I can see the appeal."

I laughed. Ripley downed the rest of his soda and crushed the can in his hand, making a mad wrestler face.

"Where do you get all that energy?"

"Meth. Just kidding. Good genes? HA!" He cracked another soda. "Okay, we haven't talked about you in like seven minutes. I'm starting get uncomfortable. Can I ask you something?"

"Only if it's superficial."

He made a game-show-buzzer sound. "*Errrnt!* Not happening."

"Fine." I rolled my eyes, and then Ripley's expression turned serious.

"Are you going to tell your dad?"

"Tell him what?"

He raised his eyebrows. "About your . . . suicide attempt."

"No," I said, all humor draining from my body. "No way."

"Okay. I get it." He took a deep breath before continuing. "Is it because of your mom?"

I broke eye contact.

"You never talk about it."

"I don't want to."

"Yeah, but maybe you should. If not with me, with someone. Keeping that kind of thing inside . . . can break you. I've seen it."

Reluctantly, I nodded. Ripley's family had self-destructed, and as a result, he hated secrets. He tried to respect my boundaries, but I knew it was hard for him when I held things back. He knew my mom had died by suicide—I'd told him ages ago—but I'd never told him *how.* I had never told anyone; I hadn't wanted to say it out loud.

But maybe Ripley was right. Maybe keeping it inside was breaking me. Before I could form the words in my mind, I felt them creeping up my throat like hot bile.

"She drowned herself in the bathtub," I said. "Dad and I

were in the other room. Ten feet away."

"Oh, Jesus, Ellie."

A drop of water fell from my hair to land on my thigh, cold and slick.

"I've been so angry at her for so long," I said. "I thought she chose death over us. Over me. But now, I don't think she chose at all. I think she was just unlucky. Her sickness won."

Ripley replied, his voice strong and clear. "And you can't afford to underestimate yours anymore."

I bit my lip. "No. I can't."

"Thank you for telling me."

I couldn't speak, so I just nodded.

Ripley sat up and cleared his throat dramatically. "Now, on to more important business: my VIP tickets for this show you're in. I'm going to need a limo, too, considering my current transportation situation."

I laughed, he laughed, and then we fell into a perfectly comfortable silence. He sipped his soda. I scarfed a donut.

"Can you stay on with me for a while? Until I fall asleep?"

"It is my duty as a Huffnabler."

I plugged in my phone, put it on speaker, and laid my head against the pillow.

CHAPTER 32

I STOOD ON THE BALCONY, sipping coffee and breathing in the morning air. On the street below, I could see shards of black plastic and the twisted white cord of the hotel's hair dryer, the only evidence of how close I had come.

I texted Ripley: *Thank you.*

I wasn't due at the theater until two, so I decided to get dressed and go check on my dad. I called Grace, and she sent a car to pick me up.

Dad was sitting up in bed when I walked in. He was still wired and tubed all to hell, but looking significantly less pale.

"There she is." He muted the TV and brightened as I pulled up a chair.

"Since you can't eat solid food yet, I brought you a raw organic smoothie. It has kale."

"Such decadence!"

I sat down and looked him over. "How are you feeling?"

"My chest still hurts, but I have a button to manage the pain. And I got a sponge bath."

"Dad. Ew." I pulled the wrapper off the straw and set the smoothie on his tray. As I did, he frowned, probably noticing the purple bags under my red eyes.

"What's the matter?" he asked. "Are you all right?"

I had planned to break the news slowly, but it clearly wasn't go to happen that way. I decided to head him off before he could ask any more uncomfortable questions about my state of mind.

"There's something I need to tell you."

If he looked concerned before, now he seemed panicked. "What is it, Ellie? What's wrong?"

I licked my lips. "I went to see Flynn yesterday, and—"

"Yes?"

"Will you let me finish?" He looked scolded, but he nodded. "He's going to let me do the Truck Drop."

Dad frowned and tilted his head. "He what?"

"I'm doing the show, Dad. Tonight. In your place."

I watched as his confusion melted into disbelief. "You . . . you are?"

"I am."

His mouth opened and closed. "But I thought you didn't want to perform anymore. I thought you were worried about—"

"I *am* worried," I said. "But it's just one show. And I have you and Ripley and Liam to catch me if I fall."

Slowly, a wide, bright smile broke across his face.

"Oh, Ellie. This is *wonderful*!"

He opened his arms, and I leaned in and let him hug me harder than he probably should have.

"I'm so . . . ," he began, but his voice gave out.

"I know," I said. And he hugged me tighter.

Dr. Saroyan chose that moment to walk in.

"Good morning," he said, striding up to the bed and tapping his tablet as we broke off our hug. "Your father has been performing for the nurses."

"Flirting, you mean."

"Now, now," Dad said. "I'm respectful."

I rolled my eyes.

"So, Doc," Dad went on, "are you going to let me out of this place, or do I need to stage an escape?"

Dr. Saroyan gave him a half-amused smile. "I need to run a few more tests, but if they come back the way I want them to, you'll be out by tomorrow afternoon. Friday at the latest."

Which meant he'd miss the show. Dad tried to hide his disappointment, but I could tell his smile was forced. I had inherited it from him.

"Any way you can speed that up?"

Dr. Saroyan looked up from his tablet. "Mr. Dante, a second heart attack at your age is serious business. I'm not releasing you until I know we're out of the woods."

Dad's face fell. "It's just . . ." He looked at me, and the light came back into his eyes. "Did you know my daughter is going to be on live national television this very evening?"

Dr. Saroyan turned to me. "Is that right?"

Dad beamed. "On *Flynn & Kellar's Live Magic Retrospective*."

When Dr. Saroyan didn't immediately respond, Dad's smile faded. "Which is why I need to be out of here by, oh, say, five thirty."

Dr. Saroyan shook his head. "That's not going to happen, Mr. Dante. However"—he tapped on the tablet—"if you behave, I can arrange for you to watch it on the big screen in the doctors' lounge. What would you say to that?"

Dad sighed. "It'll have to do." He looked at me again, and his disappointment seemed to melt away.

Dr. Saroyan checked Dad's monitors, listened to his heart, and left. When the door had closed behind him, Dad reached over the bed rail and took my hand. His grip was stronger than it had been yesterday.

"You are going to be amazing, Ellie. You'll do it better than I could have."

I knew my heart should've swelled when he said that, that I should have felt love and confidence—but that way was blocked. I returned his smile anyway and hoped he was too excited to notice the cracks.

"Now," Dad said, rubbing his hand together. "Have you practiced getting tied? You've really got to tense up to create that gap, or—"

"Dad. I'm freaked out enough as it is. Please don't coach me right now."

He opened his mouth to do just that, then shut it and nodded. "Of course. You don't need it; you'll be amazing."

He contained himself for about ninety seconds before launching into a tirade of advice.

I smiled and let him.

Anything can trigger a cycle: a close call on the highway, a text from the wrong person, the adrenaline rush of a performance. There's no logic to it; good news can prompt a downswing, and stress is just as likely to set off a hypomanic episode. Sometimes the effects are fatal; someone jumps out of a window, thinking they can fly. Other times they're spectacular, like a standing ovation.

Sometimes the timing is catastrophic. And sometimes it's perfect.

I sat down and faced the mirror. The sequins of my green bodysuit sparkled, reminding me of Tinker Bell in flight, but from the neck up, I looked like hell. I plucked a brush from my toolbox and started applying concealer to the matched set of purple luggage under my eyes. An image popped into my mind of actual snakeskin suitcases clinging to my lower lids. A goofy smile played across my face, and I let out a giggle. By the time I was putting final touches on my eyebrows, the giggles had escalated. I tilted my head back and blinked rapidly, trying to prevent my mascara from running; I hadn't been able to afford the waterproof kind for months. Then I remembered that an hour from now I would be literally submerged in water, rendering all this careful preening totally worthless. This struck me as hilarious, and I began to cackle outright.

In two minutes, the curtain was going up on the show of my life, and I was ascending rapidly into full-blown hypomania.

I paced the dressing room, taking deep breaths; if I didn't

get a grip, I would be out of control by the time I hit the stage. But if I could keep the energy bottled up, I could use it in my performance. Eventually, I was able to bring the laughter back down to a giggle.

I had some time to kill—I was performing in the second-to-last slot—so I turned on the TV in the corner of my dressing room and hopped up on the makeup counter to watch. On-screen, a housewife in a pastel cardigan frolicked in a field of dandelions while a soothing voice detailed the horrific side effects of whatever medication was being advertised. The image faded to black, and the next shot looked down from high above a packed auditorium.

"*Live from the Dolby Theatre in Hollywood, California—it's* Flynn & Kellar's Live Magic Retrospective*!*" The audience applauded, and the announcer started naming off acts, some of them old burnouts like my dad, others more contemporary. *"Featuring performances by . . . Chris Gongora! Cynthia Sixx! Dane Madigan!"* The crowd applauded for each name. *"Tommy Takai! And introducing Elias Dante Jr.!"*

At the sound of my name, a flight of butterflies did a collective somersault in my stomach. I remembered that night in Mishawaka, lying inside the trunk, listening to Dad's footsteps on the plywood stage. The sound of the latch popping. The smell of spilled whiskey and cheap cigarettes. The bright lights blinding me as the lid swung open. The cheers of fifty drunken Hoosiers as I rose up with my arms raised in a V.

The dressing room around me seemed to brighten and resolve, as if my vision had been buffering but was finally going high-def.

Tommy Takai opened the show, producing no fewer than fifty doves as the *William Tell* overture pounded through the TV speakers. The audience seemed unimpressed, but I loved it—the guy was flawless. Next, Cynthia Sixx trotted out her old 1980s pyro schtick. I knew she had been a trailblazer for women in magic, but her act looked like something from a Def Leppard video, and I could barely stand to watch. Dane Madigan, on the other hand, was hilarious and brilliant—and when he pulled his volunteer's iPhone out of a glass bowl of lime Jell-O, I laughed out loud. It was the best take on Card to Fruit I'd ever seen.

I couldn't watch Chris Gongora. I'd seen him once, back when Rico was consulting for him, and he was just too good. If I watched his act, I would be intimidated and lose my nerve. The moment his opening music started, I turned off the TV and went out into the corridor to pace.

I stopped in my tracks as the door closed behind me, the hiss of the pneumatic hinge like a loud whisper in the concrete hall. Kellar stood six feet away, talking on a tiny, antiquated flip phone. He looked up when I came through the door, and I realized it was the first time I'd ever heard his voice. Silence was Kellar's trademark; the man hadn't said a word in public for almost forty years. I turned to walk back into my dressing room—but then I heard the flip phone snap shut.

"Ms. Dante," he said.

I turned. "Hi."

"I'm Kellar." He approached and stuck out his hand.

I shook it. "I know. My dad took me to see you when I was ten."

He squinted. "Did we do the Bullet Catch?"

"Yeah," I said, remembering. "Everyone was quiet before Flynn pulled the trigger, but I totally shrieked. You shot me this look from the stage, and the whole audience cracked up."

"That was *you*?"

I laughed—as if he would remember something like that six years later. "Yeah, that was me."

Kellar smiled, put his hands in his pockets, and rocked back on his heels. There was something childlike about him. "Listen, I heard about your father, and I just wanted say I think it's very brave what you're doing."

"Or crazy," I said.

He shrugged. "You say *tomato*."

"Thanks for letting me do it."

He waved away my comment as if allowing the unknown daughter of a washed-up magician to perform on live TV was no big deal.

"You know," he said, "I was watching the night your dad did the first Truck Drop."

"You were?"

He nodded. "Broke my heart. But, you know, the road to fame is paved with the corpses of magicians far better than Flynn and me." He shrugged. "You've got to find a way to live, onstage and off."

"Yeah."

He rocked on his heels again. "I'm stalling," he said. "I can't watch Gongora. He's too good."

"Right?"

He laughed.

Just then, a voice called from the end of the corridor.

"Ms. Dante? You're up."

In my midsection, those butterflies flapped up a hurricane.

"Don't suck," Kellar said.

I smiled. "I'll try not to."

I took a deep breath, turned, and walked down the corridor toward the stage.

When I met him in the wings, Clemente frowned and barked into his headset.

"Makeup, I need somebody stage left, stat." Then, to me: "You're sweating. No, don't touch—let the pros handle it."

Sometimes during an upswing, I perspired uncontrollably. It was murder on makeup.

While a girl in a black apron powdered me down like a donut, the wardrobe assistant arrived to aggressively check and double-check all the snaps and closures on my outfit.

There was a burst of orange light from the stage—Gongora's finale—and then an explosion of cheers and applause. As he passed me on his way offstage, he smiled and wished me luck. I don't remember how I responded. I was already in the zone.

Ella, ella, eh, eh, eh . . .

The next two minutes lasted an hour as the network cut to commercial, and then Flynn Bissette took the stage to a crush of applause. He motioned for the audience to be quiet.

"More than any magician on this stage tonight, our next performer deserves your respect and attention, and I'll tell you why. A decade ago, the Uncanny Dante took a big risk on live television. But instead of succeeding and cementing his legacy, he failed—and ruined his career." Flynn crossed downstage. "We magicians love to forget performers like Dante. We love to forget, because each of us knows we're only one mistake away from ending up just like him."

I was riveted—and I could tell by the silence in the auditorium that the audience was, too.

"I offered Dante a chance at redemption. I invited him to come here tonight and re-create the illusion that failed so spectacularly ten years ago. Unfortunately, he's not here with us tonight. Two days ago, he suffered a severe heart attack, right here on this stage." An *ohh* reverberated through the auditorium. "But I spoke to him on the phone this morning, and there's something he wanted me to tell you."

My breath caught in my throat. Flynn had talked to my dad?

"Dante told me that, at first, he didn't want to come on our show. That he hadn't even received my invitation until a few days ago. His daughter—who manages his career, helps design his act, and assists him onstage—accepted the invitation on his behalf, but didn't tell him. She tricked him into coming to Hollywood. Dante's daughter knew he needed a second chance, but she also knew he would refuse the opportunity when it came."

I could feel each bead of sweat as it evaporated off my rapidly warming scalp.

"When Dante had his heart attack, Kellar and I set about rescheduling the show to work around his absence—not an easy task in the eleventh hour. But then a young woman showed up and saved our asses." Laughter in the audience. "Tonight, it is my privilege to present our youngest performer. But before she takes the stage, let's watch the performance that, a decade ago, almost ended her father's career."

As Flynn walked offstage, the lights went out, and a giant projection screen descended from the rafters.

Clemente leaned forward and whispered in my ear. "Places," he said.

Shielded by the huge screen, I walked onto the stage.

CHAPTER 33

I WATCHED MY FATHER'S FAILURE play out on a cineplex-sized projection screen. And though I was hidden from their view, I felt three thousand pairs of eyes on me, watching me watch him. I was out of my body, head buzzing, nerves crackling. I took in every sound, every image dancing on-screen—but I remembered only flashes:

Craig Rogan standing before the red curtain on his talk-show soundstage.

The massive tank. The creak of steel cables.

Then my breath rushed out of me as I watched my mother enter the frame. She was beautiful—dark hair hanging down her back as she crossed the stage with a grace I didn't inherit. She smiled, and there was no sign of turmoil in her deep brown eyes. No hint of the darkness to come. For the first time, I wondered whether she was manic when it happened, or whether she was in the gray.

The click as she pulled the lever.

The splash as the truck hit the water.

Dad, thrashing beneath the surface, wrestling with the ropes that held him. The thump as he kicked desperately against the door of the truck.

A gasp from the audience—both on-screen and in the theater—as he ceased struggling and floated, suspended, like a dead goldfish.

Stagehands rushing the tank. Throwing the emergency release. Water gushing from the dump hatches, flowing over the apron and into the audience.

Screams as the crowd rushed for the exits.

Men rolling my father onto his side as he coughed and sputtered. His suit soaked and dripping.

The stage going black.

The projected image faded, and for a moment I was in total darkness. Overhead, I heard the hum of the motor drawing the screen up into the rafters.

Then—sudden as a flash of lightning—a spotlight struck out from the back of the auditorium, bathing my body in hot white light.

I closed my eyes and pictured the stage as if I were watching from the back of the house. In the bright oval cast by the spotlight, my shadow stretched out behind me, long and crisp and dark.

It was showtime.

Tepid applause rises from the orchestra section, swelling into an ovation as it rolls toward the balcony. The girl bows.

Lights come on upstage, revealing a massive Plexiglas tank.

Stagehands approach and lean a shining aluminum ladder against the wall of the tank. The girl climbs to the top, reaches in, and flings a handful of water over the side. Droplets sparkle in the spotlight, then hit the stage like rain.

The house lights go up. The girl selects a volunteer from the fifth row, a middle-aged woman who will look suitably reliable to the skeptical crowd. The woman mounts the steps and circles the tank, inspecting it. When she seems satisfied that no trickery is in play, she returns to her seat.

The girl selects a second volunteer, a firefighter type with bulging arms and a movie-star smile. She offers him not the traditional hank of cotton rope, but two zip ties, the kind used by law enforcement. The man fastens one tie around her wrists, pulling it tight with a decisive zip. When he binds her ankles, she flinches. The man returns to his seat.

Now the music starts; not the dramatic swell of Richard Strauss, but a subharmonic boom like a distant explosion. The slow tick of a heavy hi-hat. A hypnotic bass-guitar riff, a tinkling of piano keys, and an urgent, smoky voice, singing about falling.

This is not her father's score. This is not her father's trick.

The girl turns her back to the audience, raising her bound hands high into the air. The spotlight drifts upward toward the proscenium—and slowly, the truck descends from the rafters. First to appear are the whitewall tires, then the running board, then the shining chrome grille. Bright white lights illuminate the gleaming maroon body of the 1947 Chevrolet pickup as it finally touches down on the stage.

The girl—the magician—senses the people in the front row leaning forward in their seats.

It happens fast now: a stagehand helps her into the driver's seat, closes the door, retreats toward the prop lever. A backbeat kicks in under the bass riff, and the truck jerks into the air, rising slowly on its steel cable. When it reaches the top, the truck swings upstage and settles, rocking gently, suspended over the tank.

The music dropped out, and the sudden silence drew me back into awareness. I'd been distracted, out of my body, elsewhere. But now I was no longer watching the show like the audience, I was performing it.

I sat high above the stage, hands bound tight and gripping the steering wheel of the old truck. All I could hear was the creaking of the cable and the faint hum of the stage monitors. The hum was in my head, too, numb and electric on my scalp. Beneath, my neurons fired off in a spastic frenzy. I felt raw. My eyes stung. My breath was shallow.

The truck gave a sudden lurch, and the audience gasped, but this was part of the show, a device to ratchet up the tension. I put my bound hands out the window to show that I was okay. The spotlight was hot as the August sun on my face. There was a low creak of stressed metal as the truck swayed slightly on its tether. For a moment, there was only quiet and light, and then—

My body jolted upward as if yanked by an invisible hand. The top of my head struck the ceiling of the old Chevy, stars popped in my vision, and then I was driven down into the seat as the chassis struck the surface.

Immediately, water began to gush through the open windows of the truck. It was shockingly cold on my ankles, and for a moment, I was completely entranced by the sensation—icy, slippery, hypnotic. Then, through the Plexiglas, I saw stagehands approaching, padlocks in hand. I watched the massive lid descend from the rafters and settle into place. *Click, click, click, click.* I was locked in.

The water rose to my knees, and my pulse spiked. I needed to move fast. I turned my wrists inward and began to work my hands out of the zip ties.

Thousands in the auditorium and millions at home watch as the old Chevrolet truck sinks below the surface—with the girl inside it. As she struggles to free herself from her bonds, the water level rises to her chest, then to her shoulders.

I finally slipped my hands free of the zip ties—but it had taken too long, and the water was already up to my chin. I was going to have to hold my breath longer than planned. Fighting off panic, I huffed in half a dozen short gasps of air, saturating my lungs with oxygen. Then, more frightened than I'd ever been in my life, I plunged beneath the surface.

Now the magician is completely submerged. As the seconds pass, her struggle becomes more frantic. She's thrashing now, desperate. In the front row, a woman screams; this is the same scenario she witnessed on the video only moments ago. But this time, it's the girl who is drowning.

I twisted and pivoted, but the zip tie around my ankles was cinched too tightly. Fear took hold. I began to thrash and kick, but I couldn't get free.

That's when I sensed more than saw the stagehands approaching, waiting for me to signal the abort. Their presence seemed to exorcise my panic. I shook my head vehemently at them—no, don't pull the levers. Let me finish this.

My chest was growing tight, my head thick. I needed air now. I would have to escape with my feet still bound.

I began to work my way out through the truck's open window. As I wriggled my torso free of the truck, I kicked out with my legs—but something yanked me back.

I gasped in surprise, sucking in a lungful of water. A cough shook me, and my abdominal muscles convulsed. I pulled again with my caught leg, but it held fast.

The magician has been underwater for a full minute now; she can't seem to escape the submerged truck. In the auditorium, the audience is visibly uncomfortable. A man on the aisle gets up and leaves the theater. Another follows.

A dark oval swelled in the center of my vision. Muted music thumped outside the tank; underwater, it sounded like distant bombs. My skin went icy hot—

And I was back in the hotel bathtub. The water was scalding. The water was freezing. My lungs burned, my head throbbed, my muscles ached. I was tired. So tired. I wanted to be still, to rest.

I blinked, and through the water, I saw a blurry black form approaching, his image refracted and disfigured by the tanks and the water. He was coming to pull the plug, to drain the tanks, to stop the show.

I had failed. I had gone under. It was over.

Ella, ella, eh, eh, eh . . .

The song erupted in my mind, jarring me back to awareness. I shook my head, waving my arms at the approaching stagehand—*Give me ten more seconds.*

I bent in half, moving my head back in through the window, and immediately saw the problem: the zip tie around my ankles had caught on the Chevy's window crank. As quickly as I could, I pushed my feet back into the cab, dislodged the tie, and bolted out the window.

Just as the girl finally escapes the truck, a white Kabuki cloth descends, obscuring tank, girl, and truck from the audience's view. The stage lights flicker. The music cuts out. Three thousand people hold their breath.

Then blinding white light floods the stage, the Kabuki cloth drops—

And the truck is gone.

The audience erupts into applause—but then the applause falters, devolving into gasps as the crowd realizes:

The girl is still in the tank.

She's free of her bonds but trapped by the padlocked lid. The girl turns toward the audience, waving her hands, her wide, bulging eyes magnified by the water.

Suddenly, lights flash onstage, blinding and bright as a bolt of lightning.

And then they fade—

And the girl is suddenly outside the tank, kneeling, coughing, soaking wet. Slowly, she stands and raises her arms in a triumphant V.

The applause is deafening as a waterfall.

CHAPTER 34

AS SOON AS THE CURTAIN hit the stage, I staggered backward on my bound legs and landed flat on my ass. Two medics appeared and muscled me into the wings. I couldn't stop coughing—and smiling—as they shone a light into my eyes, listened to my lungs, took my vitals.

I had done it.

"She's all right," said one of the medics, draping his stethoscope over his neck. Then, to me, "You got lucky, miss."

From the other side of the curtain, I could still hear the applause. Holy shit, I had done it.

"That was incredibly reckless," said a familiar baritone.

As a stagehand clipped the zip tie off my ankles, I looked up to see Flynn Bissette's six-foot-six frame looming over me.

"I know," I said, trying hard to wipe the smile off my face. "I picked the wrong guy to tie me up. And I lost control in the tank."

Flynn raised his eyebrows. "That's incredibly self-aware," he said. "Doesn't make it any less stupid."

I bit my lip to keep from laughing.

"I almost pulled the plug on you. But apparently, I'm just as reckless." He looked at me for a long moment. "Nice job, Ms. Dante."

Clemente motioned to Flynn, and he turned and strode onto the stage.

As soon as I opened the dressing-room door, I heard an earsplitting shriek.

"YOU WERE FUCKING AMAZING!!!"

There stood Ripley, his red hair swept back neatly from his forehead. He was wearing what I could only describe as a leisure tuxedo: the lapels were wide black satin, and the coat had tails down to the backs of his knees. He was a John Hughes character. He was an original.

He was my best friend.

I pulled him into a tight hug, and he clamped his arms around me.

"Holy. Crap. Ellie," he said, pushing away to look me in the eye. "That was incredible!"

"I can't even right now. Tell me in three days, when I need it."

"Noted," he said, and mimed locking his lips and dropping the key into his shiny breast pocket. I loved that about Ripley; even when he didn't understand my boundaries, he respected them.

"You look handsome as fuck," I said.

"All I did was put on a suit. You, on the other hand, look like the survivor of a horror movie."

I laughed. I'm pretty sure there was snot involved.

Ripley grabbed a handful of Kleenex from the counter and thrust them at me. "There's somebody I want you to meet," he said, looking suddenly sheepish.

"Right now?"

"Yeah, right now." He opened the dressing-room door and motioned to somebody outside.

A scrawny teenager entered, almost as tall as Ripley but skinny as a rail. He wore black jeans and a button-up still creased from the store, and his dark brown bangs hung over acne-riddled skin. He shot me a wary glance.

Ripley said, "Ellie, Jude. Jude, Ellie."

Jude gave me a cool nod, but I stepped forward and hugged him. "I've heard so much about you," I said.

He stiffened in my embrace, so I stepped back.

"Your show was sick," he said, brushing aside his bangs. "But you should've had fire."

"That's a good idea," I said. "Maybe next time."

The three of us stood there for a long, uncomfortable moment, and then Ripley said, "You should call your dad."

I made my way to the loading dock. My hair was still wet, and it was chilly out here, but I didn't care. I pulled my hood over my head and took out my phone.

Dad answered on the first ring. "You did it! You did it!"

I heard cheering and applause in the background; it sounded like at least a dozen people.

"Who's with you?" I asked.

"The whole damn cardiac unit!" he said, and there was more cheering on his end. "Nurses, specialists . . . You should have seen Dr. Saroyan. He actually chest-bumped one of the surgeons."

"No way," I said, laughing.

"Oh, Ellie," Dad said. "You were marvelous. Just *marvelous*."

"I almost drowned myself." I sat down on the concrete dock, letting my feet dangle over the edge.

"We had contingencies in place. You were never going to drown."

The background noise faded; I imagined nurses and doctors filtering out of the room, going back to work.

"You know," he said, "your mother would be very proud of you."

I opened my mouth to say something, but the words got lodged in my already swollen throat. I felt my tear ducts start to dilate. I bit my lip, tilted my head back, and blinked rapidly. My makeup was already wrecked from the whole nearly drowning thing, but old habits died hard.

"Ellie?"

"I'm here." The words sounded choked, but I was back in control.

"I want to thank you."

"Dad, please don't."

"You hush and let your father speak."

I did.

"I want to thank you for taking care of me. For fighting for me." He paused. "You are better than the best daughter I could have imagined. You are *magic*."

I covered my face with my hand. My shoulders shook. I felt as if, after years of climbing, I had finally reached the summit, only to realize that from here all roads led down. That in order to arrive at the next peak I would have to descend again into the shadow of the valley. The thought of going back down left me exhausted. My brain crackled. The power lines weren't down yet, but it would only take one storm.

But I *was* on that summit now. And maybe I could stay here for a little while longer. Rest. Soak up the sun. Recharge my batteries before I headed back down the mountain.

"Dad?" I said.

"Yes, sweetheart?"

"I want to do it again."

I could almost hear him smile. "There she is."

After cleaning up my face and changing into a fresh black dress I'd borrowed from Grace, I dragged Ripley and Jude into a limo, and we rode to the Magic Castle with Dane Madigan and Chris Gongora. While Jude and Ripley obsessed over the curved TV and the built-in bar, I talked shop with Dane and Chris. Both of them offered generous compliments about my performance; I nodded and smiled and tried to be gracious, but my brain and stomach were both doing cartwheels. I wouldn't be sleeping tonight.

Maybe not the next night, either.

My phone buzzed.

Liam: Wow. Just Wow.

Me: You watched?!

Liam: No, there was a Notre Dame game on. I'll catch it on YouTube later.

Me: You are the actual worst ever!!

Liam: Seriously though. I had no idea you could do that.

Me: There are a lot of things you have no idea I can do.

Liam: . . . Are you flirting with me right now?

I let him enjoy the bouncing dots for a long time before I sent my reply.

The limo pulled into the driveway in front of the Castle, and a valet opened the door. Chris got out first and offered me his hand. I took it and we emerged into a blinding fusillade of camera flashes. I posed and smiled and tried to surrender to the surreal.

Chris leaned toward me and said, "You'll be trending before you make it to the bar."

I laughed. And then, through the dozen floating green rectangles popping across my vision, I spotted a familiar silhouette. He was tall, broad shouldered, and uncommonly handsome in a black suit and tie—Liam. I lost whatever cool I had and ran toward him.

"I thought you were at school! What are you doing here?"

He leaned in and kissed my cheek, setting my whole face on fire.

"You look incredible," he said, holding both my hands in his. I could barely breathe—but this time, I found the sensation rather pleasant. My eyes were locked on his blue ones, but I could sense Ripley and Jude hovering behind me.

Liam released me. "You're Ripley, right?" he said. "Ellie won't shut up about you."

"I know the feeling," Ripley said.

The two of them stared at each other for a moment, and

I wondered if their silence was part of some primordial masculine bonding ritual.

They were interrupted by Jude, who pulled out an earbud and asked, "Do you think they're going to check my ID?"

I smiled at him. "Not tonight."

Liam took my arm, and Ripley and Jude flanked us as we walked through the front doors.

Nostalgia hit me like a cold Pacific wave. The musty smell, the dim lighting—it was like a scene from my childhood projected in Technicolor on all five of my senses. The foyer of the Magic Castle was precisely as I remembered it from a decade before: red velvet wallpaper embossed with a damask pattern; oversized fireplace complete with carved-wood mantel and golden peacock screen; and, finally, wall-to-wall shelves of dusty books with improbable titles.

Ripley whispered, "How do we get in?"

"Stop worrying. They're not going to check our IDs."

"No, I mean, literally, how do we get in? There's no door."

The evening's host, who looked like a maître d'–slash–secret service agent, stepped forward to greet us.

"Welcome to the Magic Castle," he said. Then, turning to Ripley, "Kindly step up to the owl and say the magic words."

Ripley goggled as if the guy had just cursed at him in Portuguese. I pointed to a tarnished brass owl perched on one of the bookshelves. "Say, 'Open sesame.'"

"You're kidding, right?"

"Not even a little."

"Open sesame?" he said. The owl's jeweled eyes glowed red, and the bookshelf slid to one side, revealing a hidden passage. After all this time, it still gave me goose bumps.

"Is this happening?" Ripley said, eyes wide. "Wait, am I dead right now?"

Liam gave a genuine belly laugh, and it lit me up inside. For some reason, it was crucial to me that these two guys liked each other.

Liam and I followed Ripley and Jude through the secret door. The décor of the bar hadn't changed, either: the elaborately carved banister, the navy carpet with its gold floral pattern, the dark red walls. But most of all, the art. Vintage posters featuring Thurston, Blackstone, Houdini, Silvan, Doug Henning, and countless others dating back a century. Etched portraits of ladies in petticoats and men with handlebar mustaches. The place smelled like gin and cinnamon and cigar smoke. I never wanted to leave.

As we approached the bar, I spotted Jif Higgins leaning against the long mahogany slab. He wore a loud cobalt-blue suit and nursed a glass of something orange with a celery stalk poking out of it. When he saw me, he raised his glass.

"That was epic," he said as the four of us approached. "Everyone thought you were going to drown. People were freaking out."

I had an impulse to tell him how close I had come, but I suppressed it.

Rule number three: *Always keep them guessing.*

"Good to see you, Ripley," Higgins said as the two exchanged an awkward handshake.

I made the rest of the introductions.

"Nice suit," I said to Higgins.

He glanced down as if he didn't remember what he was wearing. "It is, isn't? I bought it forty minutes ago so I could meet this joint's draconian dress code." He struck a pose.

I laughed, but it came out a cackle. I wondered if anyone else heard the mania in it.

Liam ordered four Sprites with lime while Ripley and Higgins compared notes on my performance. I pretended not to eavesdrop. Jude gaped around at the room for a minute, then popped his earbud back in and retreated into his phone.

When our drinks finally came, I turned to Higgins. "Want a tour?"

"I really do," he said, glancing at his Apple Watch, "but I have a plane to catch."

"LAX?" Liam asked.

Higgins frowned. "No. My jet is waiting at Burbank."

Ripley laughed, then realized Higgins wasn't joking and took a gulp of his Sprite.

"Hey, Higgins," I said, moving a little closer to put my hand on the arm of his new suit. "Thank you."

He gave a dismissive wave. "That stuff was collecting dust anyway." He looked genuinely uncomfortable; I wondered why he was so allergic to gratitude. "Plus, like you said, it's going to be worth *way* more now."

I smiled. "I hope so."

He stared into his unfinished drink. "And, uh, thank you, too. For the whole . . ." He mimed flying around like Peter Pan. "That was awesome."

"It was a thing to behold," I agreed.

He took another sip of his drink, then set it on the bar with a clink of finality.

"Well. Next time you're in Vegas, look me up." He gave me an awkward smile. "I have a lot of free time." Then he nodded, turned, and headed for the exit.

Ripley watched me watching him leave. "That guy is a unicorn."

When we had finished our drinks, I gave Liam, Ripley, and Jude a VIP tour. I introduced them to Irma the invisible pianist, who knew every request—even the Drake song Jude called out. Then I took them downstairs to the museum to walk through the aisles of dusty props and costumes, some of them over a hundred and fifty years old. Ripley and Jude stopped to examine an antique Zoltar machine, giving Liam and me a chance to be on our own. It was nice to have a moment alone with him in a quiet place. We didn't say anything, just walked together, fingers intertwined.

Liam paused in front a large framed poster. It was a sepia-toned illustration of a grim-looking African American man wearing a tuxedo and sitting on a globe. The caption read: *Black Herman, The World's Greatest Magician. Secrets of Magic, Mystery, and Legerdemain.* The date on the bottom right corner read: *Printed in 1938.*

Liam pointed at the caption. "What's legerdemain?" he asked.

"Close-up magic," I said. "Coins, cards, stuff like that. But I've always liked the literal translation: lightness of hand."

We caught Georges-Robert's mentalism and fork bending in the Parlour of Prestidigitation, Yuji Yamamoto's classic silk production in the Palace of Mystery, and then headed to the Close-Up Gallery to watch Johnny Ace Palmer, the best close-up magician alive, perform his famous version of Cups and Balls to a standing ovation. I still don't know where he hides those live baby chicks.

The night was next to perfect; the only thing missing was Dad. Throughout the evening, I took dozens of pictures so he could relive the night with me the next day, adding his quips and comments and memories. It would almost be like he'd been there.

Just before midnight, I excused myself to use the restroom. I put a damp paper towel on the back of my neck and looked in the mirror. My eyes were bright, my skin was clear, and my smile looked genuine. I felt invincible.

Then I noticed the subtle red rings around my eyes; they were my tell. The one reliable indicator that this burst of joy I felt was nothing more than a neurological fireworks display—and that soon enough it would end, leaving behind only trails of smoke.

But I smiled anyway, wide and bright, as if none of that were true. As if those thoughts were just the dark fantasies of a self-indulgent girl. I would suffer soon enough; tonight, I would celebrate.

I was halfway back to the table when I heard another familiar voice call my name; apparently, it was my night for familiar voices.

"I told Devereaux he should have hired you before you got famous."

"Rico!" I turned and pretty much ran into him.

"Whoa. Hey," he said, laughing as he returned my awkward hug.

"Did you see it?" I asked.

"I saw you thrashing around like a wounded sea lion, if that's what you mean."

I swatted his arm. "You saw it!"

He smiled. "Front row. Daniel insisted that I come." His smile faded, and he put his hands on my shoulders. "That was, hands down, the coolest escape I've ever seen live."

"Really?"

He paused. "Well, the coolest one that didn't involve lava or the Space Shuttle."

"I'll take that." I grinned. "Oh, hey, do you know if Devereaux watched? Probably not, right? I mean, he's still prepping his new show. He was probably—"

"Actually," Rico said, running a hand nervously over his bald head, "he watched it on TV. He thought you were good."

"No way!"

"Yeah," he said. Then, sheepishly, he pulled a folded document from his jacket pocket and handed it to me.

"What's this?" I said, unfolding it.

Rico grimaced. "That's a restraining order. You can't go within one hundred yards of Daniel, his warehouse, or the Tangiers."

"Are you serious?"

He nodded. "Higgins is getting one, too. And your dad. Between you and me, I think you got off pretty easy."

I looked down at the paper. "Do you still have your job?"

"I do."

"Then this doesn't bother me," I said, and stuffed it into my purse.

Rico let out a relieved breath, then jutted his chin in the direction of my table. "Who's the dude?"

I glanced over my shoulder at Liam, who raised a hand.

"He's my boyfriend," I said, and found that I liked the way the word felt on my lips.

"Oh, yeah?"

"Yeah. And you're too old to be jealous."

"I'm not old. I mean, I'm not jealous."

I introduced Rico to the gang, and to my surprise, he and Ripley hit it off. It turned out they shared a penchant for 1970s fashion and indie rock bands. While the four of us talked, Rico pulled out a gold dollar coin and started fidgeting with it. I think he was trying to show off in front of Liam, but he was clumsy as hell with sleight of hand; the guy could tell you how to vanish a skyscraper, but he couldn't do close-up to save his life. I snatched up his coin and showed off my French Drop, appearing to make the coin change hands, then producing it from the bottom of his glass, Ripley's ear, Liam's inner coat pocket. A couple of tourists wandered over, and Rico lent me a deck of cards. I started doing card magic, and after a few minutes, a small crowd had gathered. I'd seen it happen at the Castle when my dad was the one behind the table; he was a master of small-crowd patter, and his card magic was solid. Tonight, mine was flawless.

I started doing more complex tricks, forcing cards, faking mistakes, working the crowd. Then a very tall man appeared at the back of the congregation. It was Flynn.

"Excuse me," he said, and the crowd parted for him.

Somebody said, "Holy shit, is that Flynn Bissette?"

Kellar was with him, hands stuffed into his pockets. Again, something about his posture reminded me of a little boy. When they got to the table, Flynn looked around at the crowd, drawing their attention like a lamp attracting moths.

"Young lady, we have some business to settle." He sounded serious.

"We do?"

"We do indeed. Kellar?"

Kellar held up his right hand to show that it was empty, then reached into my purse. When he pulled it out again, he was holding an oversized playing card—the nine of hearts. I smiled at him, and he smiled back. Then he reached into his jacket pocket, produced a butane cooking torch far too big to have fit in there, and lit it. He held it to the corner of the nine of hearts until it burst into flame. The onlookers *ooh*ed. And then, suddenly, he wasn't holding a burning playing card anymore but an envelope, charred around the edges and smoking slightly. Without a word, he smiled and handed it to me.

"Open it," Flynn said.

I looked at him, at Kellar, and then at Ripley, who nodded. I slid a finger under the flap and pulled out the contents. It was a check.

"Jesus Chr— I mean, I thought it was supposed to be . . ." I leaned in and whispered, "Fifteen thousand! But this says . . ." I read it again, still not believing:

Pay to the Order of Elias Dante Jr.
Twenty-Five Thousand Dollars

"The fifteen figure was for your dad. But we didn't get him. We got a talented up-and-comer, and for her"—he tapped the check—"that's a fair price."

For the second time that night, I felt a wide, sloppy grin cross my face. The crowd around us, most of whom had no idea what this was all about, began to applaud. Flynn pulled a Sharpie from his inner pocket.

"Hold out your hand," he said.

I did, and he scrawled ten digits on my palm.

"That's my personal cell-phone number. Give me a call if you come back to Vegas. I have some stalls you can muck out." Then he turned and walked away.

Kellar watched me for a moment, then leaned toward me and said, "You didn't suck." He dropped me a wink and disappeared into the press.

The appearance of two bona fide celebrities had outshone my impromptu performance, and the crowd quickly dispersed. I stared down at the check, shaking my head.

"That was classy as shit," Rico said.

I nodded.

"And it's way more than you're worth."

I swatted him again.

Liam knocked back the last of his Sprite and said, "How are you going to spend all that?"

I thought for a moment. "I'm going to buy some drugs."

EPILOGUE

Eight Months Later

THE SUN WAS JUST BEGINNING to set when I grabbed my water bottle and stepped out onto the tiny balcony of our new Las Vegas apartment. A wall of August heat hit me like the blast from a giant hair dryer, and I reached back to put up my hair, only to remember that I'd cut it short a week earlier—not out of some cliché need for emotional resurrection or anything like that. Vegas was just fucking *hot.*

When we moved back, Dad had vetoed my trailer-park idea, and we ended up in a two-bedroom on the third floor about six miles east of the Strip, not far from where I'd interviewed Renée Turner half a lifetime ago. I had absolutely hated it—until I stepped out onto the balcony. From up here, I could see the whole Strip, from Luxor to Stratosphere. Sometimes I would wake up in the middle of the night, missing the rumble of the big diesel engine beneath me. But then I would come out here to look at the lights, and it felt like home.

A hot wind kicked up, so I poured the contents of my water bottle into the shriveled cactus on my balcony and went back inside to stand in front of the AC vent with my eyes closed and my head titled back.

Dad knocked on my bedroom door—I had an actual door!—and poked his head in.

"Are you heading out?" I asked. "I thought curtain wasn't until eight o'clock."

"Indeed," he said, glancing at his old, but newly functional, gold watch. We'd paid the pawnbroker before we even started making a dent in Dad's hospital bills; I had insisted. "But I want to run through Sub Trunk a few times before the show. My new assistant lacks your sense of timing."

After the *Live Retrospective*, Dad got several job offers, including a headliner slot at the Four Jacks. But Dr. Houts insisted that he couldn't go back to work full-time, so he had to decline. Then one night, Jif Higgins invited us over for dinner and offered Dad a show at his hotel, the Maxim, and said he could make his own schedule. He was thrilled—so now he worked three nights a week in a 250-seat theater. I had never seen him happier.

I, on the other hand, had been completely inundated with offers. I got calls from half a dozen casinos on the Strip, three in Atlantic City, and a touring company in Asia.

I turned them all down.

Dad was right; performing was in my blood. But I was scared of putting all my eggs in that basket. What if, even on meds, I couldn't deal? I needed something stable to fall back on. I wanted to get my diploma, and then I had my sights set on UNLV's theater design and technology program. That way, if performing didn't work out, I could give Rico a run for his money in the consulting business.

So I enrolled at Nevada Virtual Academy, and then I called the number Flynn Bissette had scrawled on my palm in Sharpie. He offered me a job on their development team, designing new tricks for their Vegas residency, but there was a condition: I had to open for Flynn & Kellar, performing close-up magic at the Havana six nights a week.

I almost turned him down, too.

Bipolar II warps my self-image and distorts my judgment. For a long time, I was ashamed of what I perceived as a weakness. Sometimes I still am. Sometimes, when I'm down, I still think about holding myself underwater.

Our apartment has a shower, but no bathtub.

I told Flynn what I was dealing with, but he wouldn't take no for an answer. He sweetened the deal by adding full medical insurance for me and my dad, including mental-health care. It was an offer I couldn't refuse.

Dad cleared his throat, reached down, and adjusted the cuff of his sleeve. "Want a ride to work?" he asked. He had bought a used green Hyundai with some of our TV money. It was the same model as Heather's.

"I'm off today," I said. "Liam's driving up. He'll be here in a few minutes."

Liam had finally told his father that he didn't want to play in the major leagues—and his dad had surprised him by supporting his decision. So he changed his major to business, and planned to work for Miller Logistics when he graduated. He had his eye on their hub in Las Vegas.

Dad ran a finger across his mustache. "He's a good boy. Just don't get too attached, Ellie. You don't know where he'll end up."

I rolled my eyes. "You're going be late for work." I moved forward and kissed him on the cheek. "Don't suck," I said.

"It's a promise." He winked and headed out.

I grabbed my new phone off the desk and texted Ripley.

Me: It's SOOO HOTTT HEEEERE

Ripley: I'm at school. Please stop obstructing my education.

Me: Turn your phone off during class then.

Ripley: Can't. I'm recording this lecture on the history of screen printing. Did you know it dates back to the Song Dynasty in China?

Me: Zzz

Ripley: You're a dick. Talk later?

Me: Can't. I have a HOTTT date.

Ripley: Have fun. I'll call you after Alateen. [Inebriated unicorn Bitmoji]

Me: Is it really healthy taking that Alateen stuff so lightly?

Ripley: Ugh. You're so smug since you started therapy again.

I laughed and set down the phone. Ripley and I had been "crisis buddies"—his term—for so long that it felt weird to have normal conversations. Not that my life was perfect—my psychiatrist and I were still dialing in the right dosage. And anyway, it wasn't a thing that would ever go away completely. There was no cure, only treatments. Drugs. Therapy. Meditation. Forever and ever, amen.

Ripley still had drama, too: Heather was out of their lives, which was hard, but their mom had left again, which he counted as a win. His dad was back in Narcotics Anonymous, and even though Jude had upgraded to cannabis, at least he was going to meetings. Ripley had plans to come visit for Labor Day. And if worse came to worst and he couldn't make the drive, we'd both go to our local McDonald's and video-chat over Sausage McGriddles. It was becoming a weekend tradition.

Liam would be here soon, but instead of getting ready I pulled my old wooden box out of its drawer. I opened the lid and stared at the only thing left inside: an Arizona driver's license with the number *23* written on the back in Sharpie. The small portrait showed a bespectacled guy with a thick brown beard. The text said he was Michael Boslaugh, and that he lived at 17 Primrose Drive in Scottsdale, Arizona—roughly two hundred miles from where Dad and I left our broken trailer. We hadn't gone back for it; somehow, it represented our old life, a life we never wanted to revisit.

I flipped Michael Boslaugh's license through my fingers like a playing card, wondering why I hadn't returned it; I only owed him twenty-three bucks.

I grabbed my phone and searched until I found his Instagram. It was mostly pictures of him at concerts or cuddling his French bulldog, but the latest one showed him with his arms around a petite brunette girl with a long curtain of dark brown hair. It seemed that since our encounter at the mall, Beard Boy had gotten himself a girlfriend. I felt a pang of jealousy; it was stupid, but there it was.

I wondered how differently things would've turned out if I had given his wallet back. Would he have turned me in? Would he have helped me? Would it be Michael driving to Las Vegas to see me instead of Liam?

I did that a lot now that I wasn't preoccupied with trying to survive—thinking about all the what-ifs. Thinking about my life as just one possible route through a system of crisscrossing streets and highways. At any time, I might choose a different path, make a U-turn, pull off at the next exit. Michael Boslaugh might have been a road to a different life—but instead, he'd been a detour. And now that way was blocked.

I glanced at the stack of envelopes on my desk, thinking I should stuff twenty-three bucks and his driver's license into one of them and drop it in the mail. Instead, I replaced the license and put the wooden box back in the drawer.

I felt a momentary heaviness, a muscle memory of the lead vest that seemed to settle on my chest when things got bad. I walked to the bathroom and opened the medicine cabinet. There on the top shelf sat a little orange bottle with my name on the label. I picked it up and rattled the pills inside. It was disorienting to think that two hundred milligrams of something could so drastically alter my experience of life, my personality, my *self.* That my humanity came down to one missing chemical compound thanks to a string of bad code copied from my mother's defective genes. But then I would remind myself that it only took one burned wire to run an RV off the road. An RV was not a wire, and I was not my sickness.

I replaced the bottle and closed the mirrored cabinet. I was caught by surprise again at the sight of my chin-length hair in the mirror. But the real difference in my reflection was my eyes; they were bright and clear and showed no sign of those red rings. I put on some makeup, and then Liam rang the doorbell.

He held my hand as we tore west on Tropicana with the top down, my hair flying as we drove into the twilight. Behind us, away from the surreal glow of the Strip, a three-quarter moon hung in the sky. Above it, Jupiter shone, a yellow pinprick above the velvety teeth of the mountains, which stretched out in every direction as if guarding the horizon against our escape.

As we drove toward them, I thought about how any place ringed by mountains was, by definition, a valley—and that I had moved to one, more or less permanently. But mountains were also a promise of something beyond, somewhere to climb, peaks to break up the low-lying landscape. Maybe just the knowledge that those heights existed, that they could be reached, was enough.

Liam glanced at me and shouted above the sound of wind rushing past. "What's so funny?"

I hadn't realized I'd been laughing.

"Me," I said. He smiled quizzically. Cue the dimple.

A big rig pulled in front of us, with Idaho plates and girls on the mud flaps. Liam made a face and waved away invisible fumes, but I inhaled the comforting, familiar scent of diesel and laughed again. I remembered worrying that I would miss the highs if I went back on meds. But the way I felt now was better—light, but grounded. Up, but without the frenetic buzz that threatened to overwhelm my nervous system. I stood on a peak with a view, but there was a railing here, and I had less fear of falling.

When we were coming up on Las Vegas Boulevard, Liam said, "Which way do I turn?"

"Go straight."

"Where are you taking me, anyway?"

I pointed toward the darkening sky. "To meet my mom."

I reached over and turned on the radio, twisting the old-fashioned dial through the stations in search of something upbeat. A familiar drum loop caught my attention, and I let go of the dial and shifted in my seat, unsticking my thighs from the hot upholstery. A synth patch came in, and then the voice of Jay-Z introduced "Little Miss Sunshine." It was Rihanna, singing "Umbrella," and I realized I hadn't even thought of the song in weeks.

AUTHOR'S NOTE

This book is not autobiographical. And yet, as with all works of fiction, there are pieces of the author in it. My father is a magician, and he did teach me a thing or two around my tenth birthday, before I was seduced by the guitar in his den and the typewriter on my mother's desk. The Magic Castle, too, is real, and I spent many memorable Sunday mornings at the old mansion in Hollywood, watching performances by the brightest minds in magic.

I never lived in a trailer park, but I've had good times in Fort Wayne—and in my rock-band days, I toured the country twice in an RV quite like the one Ellie and her father inhabit. That was probably the seed of this book: my desire to share what it's like to be a traveling performer. How glorious and how isolating it is. How romantic and how brutal.

I did not intend to write a book about mental health.

When I sat down at the keyboard, I was hoping to get lost in an adventure, a road trip, a teenage fantasy set in the real world. But writing is a kind of magic, too, and it has a way of extracting what is important to its writer and exposing it on the page without his consent.

I have bipolar II disorder, and sometimes it disfigures my experience of life. It can make fine food taste like ashes and reduce the most breathtaking sunset to a gray smear. It can make my amazing life seem starkly not worth living. There are highs, too, and sometimes they're spectacular: every song that comes on the radio is perfect. I'm funny and fast and everything seems to fit. But mostly, the ups are as hard as the downs. I'm angry and sleepless, I make bad decisions, and my mind races. (I never got "Umbrella" stuck in my head, but "Wrecking Ball" was on a loop for two years, and that's enough to test anyone's sanity.) Bipolar II can make it hard to work and hard to love, which can make it hard to live.

I take my illness seriously. I'm in therapy and on meds. I try to meditate and exercise every day, limit my intake of caffeine and alcohol, and track how much I sleep. It can be exhausting, all the stuff I have to do just to be able to function. It's hard not to compare my output with that of healthier people, but I try to be compassionate with myself. I've shared my experience with my family and friends, so they know what to look for when I get too high or too low.

I want to be perfectly clear about one thing: treating my bipolar II disorder has in no way limited my creativity. On the contrary, when I'm taking care of myself, my work is clearer, more powerful, and more satisfying.

Bipolar isn't something we're going to eliminate, like smallpox, or try to eradicate, like cancer. For all we know, it may serve an adaptive function. It has long been linked with creativity in the arts and sciences; maybe the cycles of mania and depression are just by-products of a neurology necessary to advance our species. As medical science evolves, perhaps we'll learn more. In the meantime, I can't stress this enough:

Life with bipolar is life worth living.

To learn more about bipolar I and II disorders and the differences between them, please refer to the resources page at the back of this book.

If you or someone you know is suffering, please get help. The resources on the following page are among the many amazing organizations working to improve the lives of people suffering from mental illness. Please also note that while all efforts have been made to ensure the accuracy of the information as of the date this book was published, it is for informational purposes only. It is not intended to be complete or exhaustive, or a substitute for the advice of a qualified expert or mental-health professional.

RESOURCES

Information about Bipolar I and II disorders

WebMD—Types of Bipolar Disorder
www.webmd.com/bipolar-disorder/guide/bipolar-disorder-forms

Verywell Mind—An Overview of Bipolar Disorder
www.verywellmind.com/bipolar-disorder-overview-378810

National Suicide Prevention Lifeline

www.suicidepreventionlifeline.org
1-800-273-8255
The Lifeline provides 24/7 free and confidential support for people in distress, prevention and crisis resources for you or your loved ones, and best practices for professionals.

Crisis Text Line

www.crisistextline.org

Crisis Text Line offers free, 24/7 support via text message for those in crisis. Serving the US, Canada, and the UK. Visit the website for more information.

The National Alliance on Mental Illness (NAMI)

www.nami.org/bipolar

NAMI is the nation's largest grassroots mental health organization dedicated to building better lives for the millions of Americans affected by mental illness.

International Association for Suicide Prevention

The IASP is dedicated to preventing suicidal behavior, alleviating its effects, and providing a forum for academics, mental health professionals, crisis workers, volunteers, and suicide survivors. Find a crisis center in your country at: www.iasp.info/resources/Crisis_Centres

The Mighty

www.themighty.com

The Mighty is a digital health community created to empower and connect people facing health challenges and disabilities.

The Affordable Care Act

We live in uncertain times when it comes to health care, and mental health care in particular. While, in the story, Ellie and her dad have few options, you may have more than you think. Visit www.healthcare.gov for more information.

ACKNOWLEDGMENTS

THANK YOU:

To Rachel Ekstrom Courage, for her brilliant counsel, flawless navigation, and unwavering friendship. Huzzah! To Kristin Rens, for her patience, perseverance, and commitment to making my second novel the best it could be.

To Alessandra Balzer, Donna Bray, Kelsey Murphy, Caitlin Johnson, Sarah Kaufman, Janet Robbins Rosenberg, Renée Cafiero, Heather Doss, Victor Hendrickson, and everyone at B+B/HarperCollins for their hard work.

To the booksellers and librarians who have made space for my words on their shelves.

To Enrico de le Vega, Dori Belmont, Ezra Deering, Don Houts, MD, Todd Harmonson, Chris Gongora, Adrian Preda, MD, Marley Teter, Ema Barnes, and Johnny Ace Palmer for lending authenticity to Ellie's world. Though the people and events in this novel are fictional, I was inspired by several real magicians while writing it—but in keeping with rule number two, I'll never tell. To David Neil Black and Corey Manske for surviving the Hobbit Bridge, defeating the Wall of Death, and clearing the water from the fuel lines so we didn't die at that northern Illinois truck stop.

To Roger, Priscilla, and Riki Garvin, Dan Zarzana, Tara Sonin, Lissa Price, Derek Rogers, Brian Perry, Scott Sanford, and Curtis Andersen for holding me up; I couldn't do this without you. To Anna Shinoda, John Corey Whaley, Marisa Reichardt, Jasmine Warga, Romina Garber, Brandy Colbert, Stacey Lee, Joshua Butler, Adam Epstein, Brittany Cavallaro, Farrah Penn, and all the amazing writers I've met for letting me eat lunch at the cool kids' table.

To my children for making me a better man.

To my wife, Ami, who deserves far more than to have her name printed on the first and last pages of this book.

And to you, dear reader, for letting me keep my dream job. I'll see you at work tomorrow.